THE LIES THAT BIND

THE LIES
THAT BIND

Edward DeAngelo

WILLIAM MORROW
75 YEARS OF PUBLISHING
An Imprint of HarperCollins*Publishers*

HarperCollins books may be purchased for educational, business, or sales promotional use. For information please write: Special Markets Department, HarperCollins Publishers Inc., 10 East 53rd Street, New York, NY 10022.

FIRST EDITION

Designed by Oksana Kushnir

Printed on acid-free paper

Library of Congress Cataloging-in-Publication Data has been applied for.

ISBN 0-688-17493-0

01 02 03 04 05 QW 10 9 8 7 6 5 4 3 2 1

For Miriam

Acknowledgments

I received encouragement and advice from several readers, and, largely as a result of their generosity, this book is not still buried in the back of a desk drawer. I wish to thank them all: Tracey Garvie-Kipnis, Paul Warner, Sonja DeWitt, Deahn Leblang, Amy Baron-Evans, Lee Johnson, Tim Stein, Amy Berkovitz, Rebecca Sacks, Karin Hauck, and Elizabeth and Neal McNamara. Special thanks to Randy Blume, a natural editor, who patiently endured several drafts, improving each one with careful (and unrelenting) criticism and judicious praise. Thanks also to Dr. Carlo Buonomo, Dr. Jean Kelly, Tina Schneider, and Laura Shragowitz for advice on questions medical, legal, and technical; I, of course, am solely responsible for any inaccuracies. My agent, Ruth Kagle, amazed me with her enthusiasm and sensitivity. My editor, Claire Wachtel, helped me immeasurably by asking all the right questions. I am grateful to all of them.

THE LIES THAT BIND

1

I had never planned to take the blood test until the moment I decided to do it. In fact, I had probably decided a dozen times beforehand not to do it. But, despite all my efforts to stop thinking about it, in the last few months before I did it, there was never a time when the idea wasn't lurking somewhere in the back of my mind, like a burglar waiting for the moment when my good sense had temporarily left home with the windows unlocked. It was never a plan; it was more like a feeling that I had each morning. The alarm would go off and I'd wake up to the sound of the public radio voices droning on about the latest, even more boring political sex scandal. I'd pull myself out of bed, feeling pretty cheerful—as cheerful as you can be when you're middle-aged, and starting to put on some extra weight and too busy at work and divorced and always late for everything.

And then by the time I got to the bathroom, I would remember. I'd be examining my face in the mirror or groping for my razor or just standing there getting ready to open my eyes, and I'd get the feeling. It wasn't sadness. It was more like dread, but a helpless dread. I would stand at the sink and look into the mirror and say, "This isn't my son's face. He's not mine."

I can't say when I had my first suspicions. It may have been from before Sam was even born, thirteen and a half years ago. Every once in a while in the midst of all the excitement and anticipation of the pregnancy, I would look up and catch my then-wife, Joan, staring at me, both hands resting lightly on her stomach, with this odd look, as if she was about to say something, and it would flash through my mind that she was going to tell me not to bother with becoming a father; this was all a hoax.

Of course, once Sam was born, all seven and a half wrinkled pounds of him, the idea that he wasn't mine never occurred to me. Every time I walked out with the stroller, some old lady would stop and say something like, "He has your coloring" or "I can see your smile." Even then, in the first few weeks, when I was still brimming over with the grandiose belief that this new life could never have taken shape without me, I knew that a baby's looks change every day and that, to be honest, he resembled a science fiction character more than either Joan or me. But still it was reassurance; I believed that someday I would see a grown Sam smile, and it would be my smile.

And then one day my mother, Joan, and I were all watching Sam sleep in his crib. My mother was looking down at his face, crinkled up in a particular way that seemed to me the only way a baby could look, and she sighed and said to me, "You never looked a bit like that when you were a baby. I can't believe he's yours."

It wasn't a bad thing to say. I couldn't believe he was mine either. The fact that he was my son was a mystery I accepted on faith, like the mystery that each morning, when I peeked into his crib before hustling off to work, he was still breathing, still pink and warm and clutching his stuffed elephant upside down in his fist.

Maybe it was nothing more substantial than that. Maybe it was just all the times during those first few years of Sam's life when we should have been a perfect family, but Joan was holding back. Maybe it was the way she seemed to withdraw from me after Sam's birth, the way she checked so far out of the marriage that when she finally asked for a divorce five years later, it was an anticlimax. It was just a hundred little things she did or said that didn't make any sense, but that always made me wonder.

I watched Sam grow and loved him more than anything else, loved him even more fiercely and devotedly after Joan and I were divorced because he was all the family I had left. He kept changing every day, and I kept waiting to see myself in him. And that didn't happen.

It's not like there weren't a million things about him to love and delight over. It's just that not very many of them seemed to come from me. He was a nice-looking kid—small, skinny, and dark, with big brown eyes and a mop of curly hair that my mother always said was wasted on a boy. And I'm tall and fair, with green eyes and a thick thatch of sandy hair that I had always hoped I'd pass on. People would look at the half dozen pictures of him that I had placed around my office and I could almost see them hesitate a moment before they asked, "Your son?"

And at times it seemed as if he and I would have had more interests in common than we did if we had been matched at random. I'm a senior executive in a high-tech corporation; for most of my career I've crunched numbers and, now that I'm the boss, I review numbers that other people crunch for me. Sam struggled with long division and got a look of panic when I tried to convert some daily situation into a little pre-algebra word problem. I'm tone deaf and never listen to anything on the radio but the news. Even as an infant, Sam lit up when he heard music, and by the time he was thirteen, he was teaching himself guitar and harmonica, and actually struggling to make time for piano practice.

But even so, I didn't believe it was true. I might lie awake at three in the morning, absolutely certain about it, but when the morning came, I could shake it off as if it had been a nightmare. And then, when Sam was a little over thirteen, he had appendicitis. Joan called me at home and told me to rush to the hospital. We waited through the surgery and when he was back in the room recovering, his mother went off to get something to eat. I wandered in the hall and noticed Sam's chart hanging outside the door of his room. It was nothing more than curiosity that made me pick it up and glance at it. And then my eye caught the place where his blood type was written down. It was B. I've given blood every year since I was in college, and

I know that I'm an A. And I remember, when Joan and I were dating, we gave blood together once, and realized we were the same type; it was the kind of thing that you think is cute when you're just starting to go out. I heard Joan walking up the hallway of the hospital, and I shut Sam's folder quickly, stuffing it back in its place, without ever saying a thing to her.

For the next couple of days, I was nearly exploding with the need to talk, but couldn't think of who I could talk to. My parents were both dead by then—not that I'd have had the courage to say something like that to them anyway. I have no brothers or sisters. I couldn't reveal this mess of doubt and shame to my friends, men I knew from work or school with whom I shared lots of activities and interests and very few confidences. From time to time, in the years after the divorce, there had been women in my life, but nothing that worked for long or went very deep; besides, this was not exactly a topic you'd bring up on a date.

The only person I could really have talked about it with was Joan. We had been divorced for eight years by then. We were polite and friendly; we shared custody of Sam and we bent over backward to help each other raise him. But I couldn't imagine talking to her about this. If I was wrong, she would never forgive me for suspecting it. And if I was right, I wasn't sure that I could even stand to hear her say it.

So in the end I did what you're supposed to do when you have a problem that no one in your life can help you with: I went to an expert. Our family doctor, Jim Atkinson, is an old friend of mine from college. We had lived in the same fraternity house and, whenever I went in for my annual checkup, we spent an extra minute or two trading updates about the dwindling number of old friends that we still kept in touch with. He wasn't a close friend, which maybe made it easier for me to call and ask if I could see him.

I sat in his office, across from him at his messy desk, and told him about my suspicions. Jim had been a good-looking guy in college, tall, fair-haired, athletic, and amiable. I have to say that, as we both started on the long decline of middle age, he was picking up more speed than I. His blond hair had thinned to the point where the word "balding" would have been a compliment, and his tall frame was showing the familiar signs of a comfortable, sedentary life. But he was still an amiable guy with a toothy smile that started to fade as he listened to me spill out my problem. When I finished talking, he simply shook his head. He wasn't answering me; he was telling me to stop. He smiled a little in a way that was meant to be fatherly and came off as pitying. "You know, most parents of teenagers wonder where their children came from. It's natural."

"It's not that," I said. "He's not a bad kid. He's a great kid. But I don't believe he's mine."

"But you don't have any real reasons to believe this."

I told him about how I had checked Sam's folder, about our blood types. He listened, his high, unlined brow starting to furrow as he took in what I was telling him. When I finished, he looked nervously around his desk as if he could find something to say lying among his papers. Finally, he mumbled, "You shouldn't be looking at other people's medical records."

"Oh come on."

He sighed. "You know, it's not at all unusual for a child to have a different blood type than one of his parents."

"But both parents? Is that possible?"

He shook his head. "Not in this way. But you might have misremembered Joan's blood type. I mean, most people don't know their spouse's type—"

"I told you I do know. I remember."

He shook his head again and started to stand up, trying to end the conversation. But I leaned closer to him and whatever was in my face must have made him stop and settle back in his seat. He waited for me to speak and after a moment, I said, "Listen. This thing is driving me crazy. I have to know for sure. Isn't there some kind of test you can do?"

He wrinkled up his lips in a face that let me know he didn't want to impart this information. "I'm not recommending this," he said finally. "In fact, I'm recommending strongly against it. But there are labs that perform DNA testing on blood samples. Medically speaking, it's a straightforward process. You just need to get the blood drawn from yourself and the child."

I thought for a moment of Sam's skinny arm stretched out, his brown eyes clenching shut as he made a fist. I recalled when he'd gotten a vaccination as a baby, how the needle would prick him and his eyes would bulge open, not with pain, but with betrayal, and Joan or I would wind up nearly crying more than he did. Sitting in the doctor's office, I shut my eyes and started saying to myself, over and over, I don't need to know this. I can live without knowing.

But then a week or two later, at three in the morning, I found myself in front of my computer, dashing through the Internet to find the web pages of paternity testing services. They were all written in that soothing, slightly mournful tone that you find in ads for assisted-living complexes or funeral services. "There are times when you need to know," they condoled. "This is a service for the whole family." They had numbers like 800-YOUR-DNA and they offered home-testing kits. "Who's the father?" one of them asked. "You should know."

———

I decided to put it all out of my mind. Maybe I had misremembered Joan's blood type. Or maybe it didn't matter. For the next couple of months, everything went on as it always had. I picked Sam up for our weekends together, and dropped him off at the end, and everything was as it always had been, except for the nagging, sick feeling in my stomach.

And so, that Saturday morning in late May when I was rushing off to pick up Sam for our weekend together, I wasn't thinking about any of this. Instead, as I hurried about looking for my car keys that were never in the same place two days running and wondering if I should use my spare two minutes to make some coffee or fry an egg, I was thinking about nothing but getting out the door. Joan and I alternated weekends with Sam, and I got a night a week as well. On this day, I was running late and I didn't want to face Joan standing on the porch of her house, with her coat on and her arms folded.

Joan and Sam still lived in the house we had bought when he was born. It was a big house, on a shady street, in a suburban town with great schools, about ten miles west of Boston. Because of our shared custody arrangement, I had never moved more than two miles away in the years since the divorce. But I knew that my attachment to the house was more than geographic. This had been my dream house and, on that Saturday when I pulled up in front of it, admiring its dignified, symmetric white facade, the row of columns on the porch, the long expanse of lawn rolling up to the front door, I felt for a moment as if I was returning to the only home where I ever wanted to live.

"You're late," Joan said mildly when I walked into the kitchen. But I was only a few minutes late and she seemed unconcerned. Sam had let me into the house and then gone upstairs to mess up his hair and scruff up his clothing so it wouldn't look as if he was doing anything special by going out with me. So I wound up sitting in the kitchen, drinking coffee while Joan finished cleaning up after breakfast.

When I first met Joan seventeen years ago, I thought she was the most beautiful woman I had ever seen, aside from on a movie screen or magazine page. While we were dating, I sometimes sought objective confirmation of this from my friends, who would smile at me indulgently and ask me if I had broken my arm when I fell so hard. But, even now, despite the years of marriage and divorce, a part of me still believed it to be true. Of course, she no longer looked like a twenty-six-year-old art student—the spiky haircut was gone; her blue eyes were no longer rimmed in black; she had replaced the red lipstick with pale pink. She looked more like a mom; her blond hair was long and curly now, and even I could see that the blonde was streaked with just the slightest bit of silver. But her eyes were still so pale blue that, when she looked at me, I felt as if I were floating up to the sky.

She called my name and I came to with a start. "Pete, what are you planning to do with him this weekend?" she was asking me.

I had no plans, but I didn't want to admit it, so I mentioned some dinosaur show at the exposition center; the *Globe* had made it sound interesting.

"You know, he's over thirteen," she said. "I think he's outgrown dinosaurs."

I shrugged. A part of me always rebelled at the thought that she knew Sam better than I did. From her point of view, this was perfectly natural; she was the mother, after all. But somehow I thought that the force of my love for him could overpower maternal instinct or whatever it was that gave her the edge. After all, I thought, he was just as much my son as hers. And then I remembered and my stomach clenched.

"He outgrows things pretty quickly, don't you think?" I asked, watching her as she moved slowly around her clean, well-organized kitchen, touching each object lightly just to check that it was in its place.

"No more so than any other kid, I suppose," she said absently. "It's an age when they're trying things out."

"I wasn't like that at his age."

"How would you know? You can't really remember what you were like then. Not accurately."

"I do remember," I insisted. "When I was thirteen, I was into baseball and that's all I was into and that's all I was ever into. He doesn't seem to care much about baseball."

"In his school, soccer's more important," she said knowingly.

"But he doesn't do that either."

"Maybe he doesn't like doing it. You know, he's not a jock." She smiled. "He's an artist like his mother."

"Do you think he's like me at all?" I asked.

She had just placed a pan on one of the top shelves and, when I asked my question, she stopped, her long, graceful arms stretched up in the air, her profile tilted back and her eyes toward the ceiling. She didn't move for a moment. I could almost feel her calculating her response. She seemed to take a breath and then slowly relaxed and turned toward me. "Of course he is, Pete. He's bright like you are."

"Not in the same ways."

She tried to smile. "He loves you."

"And I love him." I didn't take my eyes off her.

"So isn't that enough?" she asked.

I was about to speak when we heard a noise behind us. Sam was standing there. He was dragging a sweatshirt on the floor behind him.

"You have to wear the sweatshirt," his mother said. She moved toward him quickly, escaping my gaze. But Sam stepped out of her way and planted himself between us. He was looking at us through glasses that were already too thick. He always complained that it was unfair he had to wear them when neither of his parents did. They slid a little down his nose; he had a nervous habit of pushing at the bridge and, sometimes when I told him to stop, I could see for a while afterward that he was trying to move them up by some other method, scrunching his face in ways that would make me want to scream and laugh and cry all at once.

"You guys fighting?" he asked in a voice that sounded almost hopeful.

"Discussing," I said.

He rolled his eyes. "She tell you about the doctor yet?"

I looked at her. "Is something wrong?"

She was relieved to be talking about what was on her agenda, not mine. She ran her hands quickly down the front of her tailored slacks to smooth them out, and said, "He's not been feeling well. He's had this headache and is feverish."

I turned to him and lifted one of my eyebrows. This was my way of needling him; he wanted to be able to do it, and couldn't, no matter how doggedly he tried. "You dying on us, Sam?"

He shook his head. He tended toward little ailments that I thought were largely ploys to manipulate some coddling from his mother, who was only too eager to please. And she thought they were the result of some lack of proper maintenance on my part. This apparently was how we had divided responsibility for health care in the divorce agreement.

"You know," she continued, "he's been feeling a little off since that camping trip you took him on two weeks ago." It had not been the best-advised trip, I had to admit. Ever since Sam was able to walk, I had been on a campaign to make him an outdoors person. We had

been on countless hikes during which he spent most of the time
stopping to look for a pebble in his shoe. Stargazing gave him a neck-
ache, and even the mention of a nature preserve made him start to
scratch. But he was a good kid and he wanted to cooperate. When I
had mentioned this campground in a state forest west of Boston,
where I remembered camping as a Boy Scout, he agreed. The trip
started out well; he smiled generously at me when we spotted a wood
duck and for a moment betrayed interest when we saw a fish jump
out of a pond. Then it rained all night as we huddled miserably under
our tent, smelling the musty, moldy air and listening to the blackbirds
complain.

"I'm worried that he has Lyme disease," Joan said.

I rolled my eyes. "He got a cold. At most. You have to have a rash
or something for it to be Lyme disease."

"I did have that red stuff on my arm, Dad," Sam said helpfully.

"That was from you scratching mosquito bites too much. Lyme
disease comes from ticks."

"And you can get tick bites when you're outdoors," Joan said
reproachfully. "And he wasn't wearing long-sleeved shirts like I
wanted. I looked it up in Dr. Spock, Peter, and if Lyme disease isn't
treated, it can lead to arthritis. Do you want him to get arthritis?"

"You still read Dr. Spock?" I asked. But I knew I was defeated. I
sighed, then looked at Sam sideways. He winked.

When we got in my car, he pulled a paperback book out of the
pocket of pants that were way too big and hung down off his waist.

"You really can read in the car?" I asked.

He shrugged.

"It would make me sick."

He shrugged again. "I'm not you."

I felt my hand shake as I tried to get the keys into the ignition.

"Where are we going?" he asked. The appointment at Dr. Atkinson's office that Joan had already made was not until three-thirty. It
was barely eleven.

"Where do you want to go?" I asked.

"Where do *you* want to go?"

And so it went every weekend we spent together. Sometimes it worked perfectly. We could go to the mall or the car wash or downtown and every stop would be an adventure; we'd try out the equipment in a sports store or nonchalantly stroll through a hotel lobby, or play table hockey with a sugar packet at McDonald's, and it would be perfect. And then there would be times when I was just dragging him around and there was no place he wanted to go and all I could think of to do was shake him and say, "Listen, my father never spent a weekend taking me places during my entire life. And if he had, I wouldn't have dared tell him I was bored."

But then, my father stayed married to my mother until he died. And Sam knew that. And he wouldn't have dared say it to me—not out of fear, but out of shame, shame that his parents' marriage had failed and that we could both feel so bad about it.

So, on that day, instead of arguing, we went to the shopping mall. As we headed out the door, Joan had tossed out a suggestion that we pick him up a pair of dress shoes—another blow, because shopping was one of those things that Sam loved and I hated. So we trailed around the mall, him wanting to buy everything but the shoes, me wanting to get out into the fresh air. At least we both enjoyed complaining.

"Why don't you buy some shoes now?" he said when his purchase was finally completed.

"I don't need any."

"Sure you do. You can't keep on going around in those."

I looked down at my Top-Siders; they were worn, maybe worn through in a few places. But I put them on every Saturday morning, April through October, and it was always one of the happiest moments of my week.

"These are fine," I said.

"Oh yeah, very fashion forward." He sighed in exasperation; he was obviously thinking, What am I going to do with this parent? Then he grabbed a pair of brown-and-white wing tips that were about five sizes too big. "These would look good on you."

"They look like something you'd wear if you were in vaudeville."

"What?"

I put my hand on the back of his head and pulled him toward me; his face smothered in my softening side, we walked out of the store.

"Let's eat," I suggested as we reached the mall's food court.

"No red meat."

So we spent half an hour negotiating our way through the food court's various greasy options and ended up as always, with him listlessly picking apart some purported Chinese food and me tearing into a Big Mac.

"That's why you're always sick," I said through my mouthful of red meat. "You don't eat right."

He picked up one of my fries by the tip and examined it as if it were a clue at a murder scene. "You expect me to take that remark seriously?" he asked.

"You know, I'm supposed to be the good influence here," I said. "This present arrangement is not natural."

He nodded seriously. "It *is* hard to believe that you're the dad."

I put down my food and stopped moving. The food court was a clamor of crying children and loud teenagers and irritable shoppers, all competing with this jangly Muzak on the the mall's loudspeaker. And I didn't hear a thing. My face was hot and I felt a pounding in my ears.

"Hey, Dad, are you okay?"

"Why did you say that?" I asked.

He squinted at me, confused. "Say what? You mean about you not being the dad?" He laughed nervously. "Listen, I didn't mean anything. It was a joke."

He stood up to go and, without thinking, I grabbed his arm. For a moment, we faced each other across the grease-stained paper plates and crumpled napkins. He looked scared—scared that he had hurt my feelings, scared of my strange response. He hadn't meant anything. He had only been making a joke. I let go of his arm and when I looked down, I saw red marks where I had gripped him. Our hands were lying next to each other on the table, palms down, his small and pale with a few freckles, mine large and tanned with a sprinkling of fair hair. "We have to go," I said.

When we walked into Jim Atkinson's office, he greeted me with the usual small talk about college buddies and sports. I could see Sam shifting around in his seat impatiently, rolling his eyes with embarrassment while Jim and I reminisced. After a few moments, Jim finally turned to Sam with an overly hearty manner and started asking him how he felt.

Sam mumbled a bit about his symptoms, trying to avoid both my eyes and Jim's. He liked it when some ailment won his mother's attention, but suddenly this was a little more than he had bargained for. He hadn't really felt *that* feverish, he recalled now. Maybe it was just a small fever, like a degree or two.

"So you got tick bites on this camping trip?" Jim asked earnestly.

Sam shifted in his seat and I suppressed a smile. "Maybe they were mosquitos," Sam said. "I couldn't tell."

"But you say there was a rash?"

Sam looked at me for help. I shrugged. I didn't think he had Lyme disease but I could picture Joan standing over my shoulder, Dr. Spock in hand, pointing to the section on crippling arthritis. "Maybe there was a rash," I said, trying not to sound as if I was actually worried. "You should check for Lyme disease. Just to be sure."

Jim nodded and closed the file. He told Sam to go into the examining room and wait for the medical assistant. As I heard the door close, I asked, a little nervous despite myself, "If it is Lyme disease, can you treat it?"

"We've had some success with antibiotics. But honestly, Pete, I'd be amazed if it was anything but a cold."

I sighed. "That's what I thought. But how can you be sure?"

"We do a blood test."

"A blood test?"

For a moment, everything felt very clear and still. I closed my eyes. I could hear Jim moving about behind his desk, scratching out some form for the medical assistant before heading to the examining room. "You *have* to do a blood test?" I heard myself ask, my voice calm and sure.

"It's perfectly routine. Sam's a big boy, it won't hurt him."

"As long as you were drawing blood though, you could draw some extra. That wouldn't hurt him, would it?"

Jim put down his pen and looked across the desk at me. "I know what you're thinking and forget about it."

"Why? You said yourself it's a simple test. There's no legal reason why you can't do it."

"Because it would be wrong. It isn't fair to Joan."

"If the test shows that I'm the father, she'd never have to know. And I'll feel better and it will all be over."

"And what if that's not what it shows?"

"Then why would we be worrying about being fair to Joan?"

"All right. Forget about Joan. What about Sam? What about you?"

It was as if some part of me, the part that knew better, just got up from my chair and walked to the other side of the room to watch what was about to happen. I didn't want to do this, but I didn't want to stop myself either. I knew I would never be in this position again, where it was so easy to take the test and finally learn the truth, and I knew that I could never stop myself from wanting to learn that truth. Looking back, I can say it was just about the biggest decision I ever made in my life. Even then, sitting in the doctor's stuffy office, I knew that I was about to throw a rock into a stream that might never stop rippling. But, in fact, I never had a choice.

"You know what, Jim? I have to know. I can't go on like this, with it always in the back of my mind. You think that's not going to affect Sam and me? Let's do the test. If it turns out that I'm his father, then we'll just think I was crazy and we'll never talk about it again. And if it doesn't, I have to deal with it."

"But I don't have to be the one to help you."

I leaned back in my chair. "You know I can get the test done elsewhere if I'm bound to do it. I can go to some doctor-in-the-box clinic and they'll take the blood for me."

Jim ran his hand impatiently over where his hair used to be. He was starting to get angry with me, but seeing that only made me more determined. He paused a minute to gather his thoughts before speaking. "Peter, I am certain you shouldn't do this test. It's only going to make you unhappy."

"So you already know what the result's going to be?" I asked.

He threw up his hands in exasperation. "Of course I don't know. But if what you told me about the blood types is true—and I have no way of knowing—then I can guess what you might find out. And I don't see why you need to know."

"Jim. Listen to me." He turned around reluctantly and tried to face me. He wanted to be an authority figure, and that's hard to do with someone who could remember you playing drinking games at the age of twenty. I got him to settle down and then I leaned forward. "Tell me honestly. If it were you, if you really thought one of your kids wasn't yours, are you saying it wouldn't matter to you?"

Instinctively, despite himself, his eyes darted over to the pair of children's photos on the corner of his desk. He had a boy about Sam's age, and a girl a few years younger. He reached out and touched the boy's picture. The resemblance between him and his son was so strong that nobody could miss it. And that was something that made him happy every time he looked at the kid. He was trying to imagine it a different way, and he couldn't. "It shouldn't matter," he said finally, his voice quiet and not very strong.

"But it would. Right? It would matter to you."

Almost imperceptibly, he nodded his head. I waited for a moment, watching him think. He looked away from the pictures, back to the open file on his desk. He started talking, more to himself than to me. "You have the right to have the blood drawn, I suppose. He's your kid." He stopped when he said that, and made a little face. "And you're right. If you don't do it here, you could get it done somewhere else." He looked up at me, his eyes sad. "I shouldn't do this. I know I shouldn't."

I didn't say anything. I knew he was going to do it. In that moment, I almost backed out, almost said forget it. But I knew I had already gone too far to turn back.

I stayed in the office while he headed into the examining room. As he opened the door, I could hear the medical assistant chatting to Sam, reassuring him that this wouldn't hurt a bit. I could imagine him rolling his eyes the minute she walked out the door.

When it was my turn, Jim was grim-faced as he waited for the medical assistant to get the vial ready. She made small talk as I rolled up my sleeve. I looked down at the tender patch of skin just inside my elbow where she dabbed the alcohol-soaked gauze. "This won't hurt," she said. I watched as the needle extended and then nestled, like a child under the covers, into my veins.

2

I met Joan at a time in my life when I wasn't thinking much about romance. It had been seventeen years before. I was twenty-five years old, in business school, about two months short of graduation. I was living like a cross-country runner trying only to keep breathing until he gets to the finish line. And for me that finish line was making a hit in business, finding the right company and the right product and scoring big. I had been an athlete through high school and college, until I twisted my knee on a basketball court when I was twenty. Now, business was my new game.

I didn't care that much about the money. Instead, success was about making something happen, about selling a product that made a difference. And so, even though most of my classmates at Harvard Business School were heading for large financial institutions or management consultant firms, I had lined up a job in marketing at one of the little high-tech companies that were popping up all around Boston at the time, putting out software and information systems that most people couldn't understand. The company that hired me was developing a new accounting software designed for retailers. It was a time for thinking big; when I met with the company's founders, a couple of men not much older than I, we talked about how we could change the way America did business. I signed on without a second's hesitation. I wanted to be part of something little that got large.

Once I lined up the job, I figured that all I had to do was make it through the last few weeks of school before I could start my life. When I thought about my future, I was thinking about work; if I fantasized, it was only about stock options. Of course, I had always assumed I would get married and have children someday, but only because everybody else did. My parents had a happy marriage and I knew that if anyone ever asked them, they would have said that having a kid was the best thing they did with their lives. But my parents were steady people who didn't expect much; their dreams were exceeded the day my father made supervisor at the factory where he spent his working life and they got to buy a little split-level in a subdivision north of Boston. I would look at them in their retirement, my father fastidiously tending his garden, my mother cleaning and re-cleaning a house that never got too dirty anyway, and I would think that marriage was a wonderful thing for someone who had already done everything else.

Of course I had dated in high school and college. But they were never the kind of relationships that seemed likely to last longer than the next semester. And by the time I got to business school, I barely found time even for that. In those days, Harvard Business School was a place where the last thing people did before they went to bed was plug in their pocket calculators to recharge. It did not put you in the mood for love.

So my expectation that Saturday night in April, when I set out for a party at the apartment of a classmate of mine, was simply to have three beers and graze on enough food to make up for the fact that I hadn't bothered to feed myself all day. I was standing in a corner at the party, talking to another guy in my class whom I spent too much time talking to during the week anyway. As we talked, I looked restlessly over the crowded living room that was stuffed with shabby student furniture, expensive stereo equipment, and the usual assortment of grad students, all dressed in jeans, wearing unbecoming eyeglasses, and talking about themselves. And then, tucked uncomfortably at one end of a couch, talking to no one and looking as if she was there because she had lost a bet, was Joan.

Like I said, I thought she was the most beautiful woman I had ever seen in real life. And if she had wanted to stand out, she couldn't have picked a better setting than that party. She was dressed differently than everyone else, all in black, with a short skirt and dark stockings. She was wearing a sleeveless top that dipped down in the front; the tops of her breasts were tanned. She had crossed her legs and one foot was dangling, the shoe hanging off from her toes. She was smoking, which, even in those days, was something you were barely permitted to do in public. She was tall, with a long neck, and had a way of sitting—calm, straight, and very still—that made the beat-up paisley couch look as if it could be a throne. Her eyes were fixed on some point across the room; then, she caught me watching her. She tilted her head just slightly, so she could see me better, then turned her attention back to the cigarette that she was languidly smoking.

I moved so quickly toward her that my shoulder banged the head of the guy I was talking to. My only idea was to say something to her before I had time to choke; when I got to her side, I blurted out exactly what was on my mind: "What are you doing here?"

She must have liked that because we wound up talking. She wasn't at the party because she had lost a bet, although she liked that too when I said it. She had wound up there because she had a cousin in business school and her parents, who lived in Florida, were pressuring her to spend time with him. I suppose they had hopes that she would meet someone "promising" at the party, and of course she had set out to thwart them by hating everyone.

But something I said changed her mind. I suppose it flattered her that I saw her as different, because she was someone, I realized later, who wanted to be different and wasn't quite sure she was pulling it off. She was a suburban kid, from a well-off family, who wanted to be a struggling artist. She had gone to Rhode Island School of Design, and, after graduation, moved to Boston to take art classes and paint. She shared a loft with another painter and a sculptor. They wanted to dedicate themselves to art, but instead spent a lot of their time wondering how to hustle up the rent money without having to call their parents for help. She talked about this opening and that performance, but by the end of the evening, I got a clue that she was actually lonely and just a little scared. And I think she must have seen the same thing in me because she let me drive her home, and when I pulled up outside the dark featureless building where she lived, she told me to come in without even waiting for me to ask. We pushed open the door to her apartment and tripped over the piles of books and clothes, the half-finished canvases, rushing to the bedroom through the sexy, sweet-smelling squalor that made my heart race from thinking about what was ahead.

I had always been the kind of guy who wasn't very imaginative in his choice of women. In high school, when I was a jock, I dated cheerleaders. In college, when I was a frat boy, I dated women from sororities. My longest relationship had been ten months, when I was nineteen, with the younger sister of one of my frat brothers. She broke it off because she wanted someone less well-adjusted; "You're a nice fellow," she said as she gathered up the few toiletries she had left lying around my bathroom, "but I'm looking for someone who actually needs something from me."

All that changed when I met Joan. I loved her because she wasn't at all like me, or like anyone else I knew. She may have had doubts about herself, but I believed completely and uncritically that she was an artist. I traipsed after her from gallery to gallery, trusting her judgment about what was "genuine" and what was "posing," without even caring what those words actually meant. When I was with her, I forgot about the job I had just started and all its pressures; I actually enjoyed the fact that she understood nothing about my business and I would laughingly resist when she tried to learn more. I had needed to get a life, and she was the life I wanted. Finally, I had found a woman whom I needed something from.

And more than anything else, I wanted her to need something from me. She was leery at first, afraid that I might be overpowering her with dates and gifts and calls. But we had fun together. I was always coming up with some new place to go or some new sport to try. I think it was a relief for her to stop having to be jaded like all her other art friends. Despite herself, she liked rafting or snowshoeing or holing up for a weekend in some Vermont getaway. And she liked that it made me so happy to do these things with her.

And I made her feel safe. I talked about us living together in an apartment that had room for her studio, where she could paint to her heart's content without ever worrying about the rent, and even though she brushed me off at first, I could see that she was listening. In the end, the sheer force of my devotion carried her away. I don't know now if she ever really loved me, but she loved being loved by me. Looking back, I have to say it wasn't the worst beginning for a marriage, but if I hadn't been so lovestruck, I might have had second thoughts.

The first couple of years we were married were fine. I was working harder than I wanted, but doing well at it. She worked at odd jobs here and there, receptionist in a gallery, administrative assistant at some public art program, never making very much money or feeling very certain about what she was doing. We lived in an apartment on the Boston harbor, with a beautiful view and a characterless, white-walled interior, and we went out just about every night that I wasn't working. But she wasn't happy. Her painting wasn't going well. She thought she was losing her "edge." She felt as if she was drifting and didn't know what to do about it.

She was the one who first talked about having a kid. It wasn't a very firm plan on her part, just a hope that a baby would be the thing to help "snap her out of it," whatever "it" was. At the time I was so worried that "it" was me, I would have done anything to make her happy; I said yes to the idea of a kid without ever envisioning a real kid who might someday share our characterless white-walled space with us.

We didn't do much to advance the project, except conveniently forget to use birth control from time to time. A few months passed and I wasn't even thinking about it when, one evening, we sat down to our usual dinner of overpriced and oversalted takeout from the gourmet food store down the street, and Joan started crying. She was pregnant, she said between sobs. "And, Peter, I'm sorry," she said, "but I really have to have this child. I can't bear the thought of an abortion."

It was one of those things she would occasionally say over the next few years that made no sense at the time, statements that I disregarded or misunderstood but never really forgot. Of course we wouldn't have an abortion, I said. This was great news. She looked at me through her tears while I jumped up and walked around the table, babbling about a million ideas and plans. Every once in a while I would stop talking and look at her, waiting for that movie moment when she ran into my arms, but she was still at the table, looking down at her untouched food, biting on her lower lip so hard it made me flinch.

We were about halfway through the pregnancy when it dawned on me that our apartment was the wrong place to raise a kid. We lived in a young professionals ghetto; within walking distance were five different stores that sold squid ink pasta and not one of them carried rice cereal. I wanted to move to the suburbs.

Things at work were going according to my plan; our company had launched a software program that was selling beyond our expectations. I was feeling flush. I started sounding out friends and colleagues about the best suburbs. I would come home and tell Joan everything I found out, assuming she would agree. But she seemed listless in the face of my enthusiasm.

"Don't you want what's best for little Jake or Marisa?" I would ask mournfully.

She nodded in that preoccupied, abstracted way she had assumed since the first days of morning sickness. "This is all happening too quickly," she protested feebly.

I thought the problem was that our different backgrounds made us feel differently about this move. I had grown up in a small house in a low-priced subdivision in a not very fancy town just outside the city limit; to me, moving to a suburb with big house lots and town pools and modern schools was about declaring victory and claiming the prize. For Joan, the child of a successful lawyer, who had grown up in Lake Forest, outside Chicago, it was about becoming her mother.

So we continued to debate the pros and cons. I kept pushing the idea of moving, and she never said no. In fact, she usually said yes, just not right now. She pleaded exhaustion when I pulled out real estate ads. She had a headache on weekends when there were open houses to visit. And so, nine months into the pregnancy, I was still calling up Realtors at my desk, over lunch, trying to track down a lead on the perfect home.

"Well," I heard the Realtor's cigarette-raspy voice drawl, "there *is* this one place that's about to go on the market."

"Tell me about it."

"You wouldn't be interested. Besides, I have this other couple that's coming from Dallas this weekend and they have to buy right away and . . ."

She was good; she made me beg. And with each detail—good schools, short walk to the train station and the town center, space that could be a studio for Joan, a large lot big enough for the jungle gyms and swing sets and basketball hoops I was already constructing in my mind for my soon-to-arrive child—I was more sold. I wanted to see it that night, before anyone else.

I pleaded with Joan to come with me. She agreed wearily, but when I pulled up to the curb outside the house with the FOR SALE sign, she wouldn't get out of the car. "I can't bear looking at a house," she said.

"But I think this is the one."

She made a sound like a snort. "You thought I was the one."

I reached over and shook her knee. "And I was right about that, wasn't I?"

Looking out the car window, her back to me, she shook her head just slightly. I pulled my hand away and we sat, me grinding my teeth, my hands clasped in front of me as if I was trying to keep them warm.

We heard a tapping at the window and saw the Realtor bending over next to us. "Come in, come in," she mouthed.

I looked over at Joan. "Please do this for me."

"No."

I got out of the car and walked over to the Realtor. "My wife isn't feeling too well," I started explaining before I was completely out of the car. The Realtor looked at Joan, her brow creased suspiciously; this was not the first time Joan had sicked out and, even for a very pregnant woman, there were limits.

I rubbed my hands on the legs of my pants. "She's really not feeling well. I shouldn't have taken her out tonight. But we were both so excited." I looked at the house longingly.

It was a beautiful old house that stood on a slight rise behind a wide front lawn that swept up from a stone fence. It had a large, square porch buttressed by three columns, dentate molding under the eaves and above the windows, and a gabled, slate roof that rested like a hat on top of the house's high brow. An elm presided magisterially over the lawn; the stone walkway was lined with mounds of impatiens and phlox. I listened as the Realtor fumbled through her big bunch of keys, muttering, "Now is this the one?" The door opened and I stepped into the big foyer and fell in love.

The Realtor could see it as soon as she turned around. She was about to launch into an explanation of the layout and caught herself. She knew she just had to wait a few moments and then start reeling me in.

I walked through the rooms, already seeing my family in them. We were huddled together in the living room, the three of us, Joan, me, and little whoever, nestled under a big blanket in front of a fire roaring in the marble-mantled fireplace. We were sitting in the dining room under the brass chandelier, passing plates and all talking at once. I saw us grabbing breakfasts at the granite-topped kitchen counter, worried that the school bus was about to arrive and we were still in pajamas. "This would make a nice office," the Realtor said about the boxy, 1970s addition in back, but I already saw the floor littered with trucks and race cars, the oversize couch in the middle of the room where I would lie, sprawled, next to little whoever, who was quickly becoming a boy, watching the game, him listening while I explained each play, our legs just touching, my arm around his shoulder.

The Realtor had to remind me to check the basement. When I got back upstairs, she had already gotten out the paperwork for an offer. "I'm telling you, this couple is arriving from Dallas tomorrow and this is the first house I am taking them to," she said, not even bothering to pretend I was still shopping.

"Let me talk to my wife."

She sighed and nodded.

When I walked back to the car and got inside, Joan was pulling at her rings nervously. She gave me a little smile and then turned away. "So is this the one?" she asked, with something in her voice that could have been bitterness.

"Joan, what's with you? If you don't want to buy a house, just say so."

She shook her head as if she was trying to get rid of an insect hovering near her. "Oh, Pete, I'm so tired. I just can't go on with this."

"With the house?"

"With everything." She waved her hands at her bulging stomach. "With this."

These moods of hers had been going on for nearly nine months. I thought, probably because it was the safest thing to think, that Joan's behavior was a by-product of hormonal imbalance and we would all be better off if I just pushed us forward despite her. "Joan," I said firmly, "if we lose this house, we won't find another one like it."

"Oh, Pete," she said irritably. "America is full of these houses. There's one on every quarter acre of land between here and Seattle."

"I'm not talking about America. I'm talking about our lives."

She shook her head, still looking down at her hands. I opened the car door and jumped out. I stood on the sidewalk, gazing up and down the street that I wanted to come home to each night, the newspaper under my arm, waiting to hear voices call "Daddy" from the other side of the front door. I went inside and saw the Realtor sitting at the table checking her watch.

"Listen, my wife's still not feeling well, but she's very excited," I said.

The Realtor began gathering her papers up into her bag. "You know, Mr. Morrison, maybe you two just aren't ready."

I let out a little laugh. "Not ready? We're due in three weeks."

I sat down in the chair, an angular leather contraption that didn't belong in my living room, and shook my head dejectedly. "What am I doing wrong?" I asked the big house filled with a stranger's furniture.

The front door opened. Joan awkwardly stepped in. The Realtor started talking about the school district without missing a beat. I trailed behind them as they toured the house, watching worriedly as Joan struggled up the stairs, my ears burning a little as the Realtor enthused over the master bedroom that had its very own fireplace— "Just perfect," she said with a sidelong glance at Joan. The Realtor started converting the prissy guest bedroom into a nursery; I imagined hanging the three black-and-white mobiles we had already gotten from Joan's overenthusiastic mother, who was in her retirement condo in Florida counting the days until she became a grandmother. I walked into the kitchen and pictured the alphabet refrigerator magnets spelling out whoever's yet-to-be-decided name. I urged them into the big, airy room in the converted attic that we were already calling Joan's studio. "You can't get this kind of space in the city," the Realtor kept saying.

Joan didn't speak. She kept her coat on the whole time, clutching it around her although it was too small to close over her stomach. She hadn't said a word when the tour ended and we headed back to the table where the paperwork still waited for us.

"Where's the bathroom?" she asked.

"Which one?" The Realtor started reviewing the lineup: powder room, guest bath, full master bath with Jacuzzi.

"I'll go upstairs," Joan said brusquely, moving as quickly as her swollen feet could take her.

When we heard the door upstairs shut, I turned to the Realtor and started talking numbers. She made a disapproving face. "Mr. Morrison, aren't you jumping the gun a little bit?"

"No, I know her. I can tell she's ready."

"She does not look like a woman who's ready."

"Hey, I'm her husband. I know my own wife."

The Realtor looked at me pityingly. A door opened upstairs and Joan called my name.

"One minute, okay, honey. Listen, have the owners gotten any offers yet?"

"Pete, come upstairs now please."

I was busy crunching numbers in my head. The Realtor had pulled out her calculator. Joan called my name one more time. "Okay," I said to the Realtor. "I'll be back in a minute."

When I got upstairs, Joan was standing, her coat still on, in the middle of the bathroom. I stood there, waiting for her to say something. She looked down at the floor. There was a little pool of water. It took me a moment to realize what had happened.

I was down the stairs shouting, so fast I almost forgot about Joan. Halfway down, I turned back and tried to get her. She was still frozen in the bathroom. "I'm not ready," she said.

"You are ready. We're both ready. Let's go."

"You're ready?" the Realtor asked happily, her paperwork in hand as she met us at the foot of the stairs. It took her a minute to figure it out too, as she stood there, watching me flail about and Joan move stiffly down the stairs like a woman who was afraid she was about to break.

We were blocked in the driveway by the Realtor's car. As she fumbled through her endless supply of keys, she kept saying, "I'm sorry," and shooting worried looks at Joan. "I'm really sorry."

We got in the car and started pulling out when we realized that we didn't know the way to the hospital from this house. I waved down the Realtor, who had already started driving off. She jumped out of her car, I jumped out of mine, and we began frantically arguing about directions in the middle of the road while Joan sat in the car, her hands folded in her lap, her lips quivering.

"Okay, I'll follow you to the highway," I shouted at the Realtor as we headed to our cars. I got inside and a minute later jumped out again, waving her down one more time. She jumped out too and I shouted, "Listen, don't show this place to that couple from Dallas. Promise?"

She threw up her hands and started to turn away.

"I mean it. Promise?"

"I promise. For God's sake, let's get going."

Once I got on the highway, I kept pressing on the gas and Joan kept telling me to slow down. "It'll be okay, it'll be okay," she was murmuring to herself. I could hear her try to do the breathing they had taught us in Lamaze class; not speaking, I started counting with her. One, two, three, hold.

"I can't do this," she said.

"Do you remember the exit number?"

"Pete, did you hear me? I can't do this."

"Don't start."

She began to cry.

I looked at her, genuinely amazed. "Aren't you happy?"

She shook her head. "No. Of course I'm not happy." She gulped. "I'm too terrified to be happy."

"It'll be fine. Women do this every day. In the old days they did it at home. Or in the fields."

"What if it doesn't love me?"

I sighed in exasperation. "Oh, Joan, it has no choice. It's programmed to love you. He. He or she. It's guaranteed."

"What if we don't love it?"

I smiled. "I don't think you have to worry. I already love it. It's mine."

"And that's why you love it?"

"That's the basic idea."

She took a deep breath. I was staring up at the signs on the highway trying to find my exit, and when I finally turned to her, she was looking at me with the saddest expression I had ever seen. I almost stomped on the brakes.

"Joan, what is wrong?"

"Oh, Pete, I just want this baby so much. And I want everything to be good for it. And you'd be such a great father."

I nodded, not sure what I was supposed to say.

She thought for a second. "Just promise me everything will be okay. Promise me we'll be good parents. And that you'll always love it."

I knew I should try to be sympathetic; I thought this was one of those moments that they lecture fathers-to-be about in pregnancy classes. But I didn't understand what she was feeling, and I needed to check the directions, and the car behind me was honking because I had slowed down to about ten miles an hour. Trying to sound as solemn and sincere as I could, I said, "I promise."

She nodded, then leaned back in the seat. "Good," she said tearfully. "That's all I want."

I saw the sign for the exit up ahead. Within minutes, we were on the street, within sight of the hospital. My heart had stopped racing, my neck was starting to unclench. I looked at Joan to smile and let her know everything was okay.

She had stopped crying and was lying back in her seat with her eyes closed. After a moment, she opened them and looked at me with a weak smile.

"Now will you promise me one thing?" I asked.

She was too exhausted even to think. "What?" she said.

"Promise I can buy that house."

First she shook her head, then she nodded it. "Whatever you want."

The obstetrics nurses in their blue jumpsuits all said it was the easiest first baby they had ever seen. "You sure you people haven't been practicing?" one of them joked just seconds before the head started to appear.

I held the baby first because Joan was still clinging to the sides of the bed as if she were about to be washed off it by a wave. I brought him over to her like he was a gift I was giving her. "Look what we did," I said goofily, and when she took him from me, she never lifted her eyes from his slimy, compressed face. For a moment, just for a moment, our heads were all three pressed together, and together we breathed his first lungful of air.

3
___

I called Jim Atkinson's office each day to see if the results had come in from the lab. Each day the receptionist crisply told me they had not. Then, one day, she simply said that the doctor wanted to see me in person.

Late that afternoon, we sat in his office; the windows were shut and it smelled like the inside of an old book. My eyes wandered over the walls, examining the plaques and photographs of him accepting awards, as he started out with the usual pleasantries.

I could see how much he hated this. He looked down at the file on his desk as if we both didn't know what was already there. He looked up for a moment and smiled. "The Lyme disease test came back negative."

I nodded and waited, my face blank. He didn't say anything, and after a moment, I asked, "I'm not his father, am I?"

Jim shook his head. The moment he did, we both looked away from each other and he started talking nervously about genetics. He was hiding behind his professional manner, and he almost seemed to be lecturing me. These tests compare the DNA in a child's blood with that in the "putative" father's, as he put it. They were extremely reliable, much more reliable than the blood tests that had been used for years earlier to test paternity. The chances of unrelated people having the same DNA were thirty billion to one; you could determine paternity with over 99 percent certainty.

He sighed a little as he said that of course the tests weren't only useful to identify the father; they could also be used to exclude someone. It was not possible for a child to obtain all its genetic characteristics from only one parent. Therefore, you would have to find certain matches between the child and the "putative" father.

I knew what he was saying before he finished his sentence. None of my characteristics had been found in Sam's blood. I heard him say, "You were excluded."

We sat silently for a minute. Jim rubbed his palm on the surface of his desk.

"Are you certain?" I asked. "Do you need to test Joan too?" I could hear my voice croak.

He shook his head. "Given the results, I don't think it's necessary. Unless some other man was being tested at the same time in order to evaluate him—"

He stopped speaking when I started to cry and waited patiently, the tips of his fingers dancing lightly on the desktop, his eyes looking at some spot in the back of his office where there was nothing to be seen that would shame us both. I kept shaking my head and starting to speak so that it would be over, and each time, my voice broke again.

When I was done, he leaned forward. "I can recommend someone for you to talk to. Maybe your whole family could talk to someone."

"What family?"

"Does Sam understand what is going on?"

"No."

"You've spoken to Joan?"

"No."

He leaned back. "I can't do much more for you. You've had a shock, but you're healthy. You can always call my office if you're having trouble sleeping in the next few days." He pressed his hands on his legs and stood up. "I'm sorry, Pete. Although I suppose it's better to know."

————————

It was raining lightly as I drove home. The streetlights were coming on, although it wasn't really dark yet. I was driving slowly, following two teenagers on bicycles, a boy and a girl, who swerved and darted in some odd courtship dance in the travel lane. I pounded my horn, making the girl stop and the boy swing around to give me the finger so fast that his bike skidded and he had to jump off.

I didn't even take off my coat when I stepped inside my home. I sank down into a chair and, after a while, it occurred to me that I should have a drink. I pulled out a bottle of Scotch I had been nursing since a colleague had given it to me for Christmas a year before, and when I tilted it, I realized that in all that time I had barely made a dent in it. The first taste made me flinch and I set the glass down on the end table beside my chair.

The doctor was right, I told myself; it's better to know. And then the next second I tried to figure out if it could possibly not be true, if there was something I could do to put me back into the state of not knowing.

I closed my eyes and saw Sam's face. I pictured him sitting here with me, and wondered how the next time we saw each other would be different than the hundreds of times before.

It doesn't matter if he's your son or not, I told myself determinedly. You still love him. I got up from my chair and stalked into the kitchen, then stopped. Of course it matters, I realized. If it didn't, maternity hospitals wouldn't put ID bracelets on newborns. I still love him, I thought. But it's still different. And what I couldn't understand, what I couldn't imagine, was what that difference would be.

I was up all night. At various points, I was raging at Joan as I finally began to realize what she had done, what she had hidden from me for years. I tried to figure out who the real father was, trying to re-create our life as it had been in the months before she told me she was pregnant, trying to remember every single man who was in it. I went back over a million incidents in our marriage, in the years that we raised Sam, a million inexplicable things that were now painfully clear.

But then these fevers of anger would break and I'd be left, exhausted and empty and still picturing Sam, still wondering what I was if I wasn't his father, who he was if he wasn't my son. I looked back on all those times that he and I had been out of sync, unable to figure each other out. Before I had felt frustration, now simply grief. I thought of the Christmas when he was five, the last one before the divorce, when I spent hours in the sports store picking the perfect baseball bat to lay under the tree. And then, on Christmas morning, he unwrapped it, held it in his hands upside down, then right side up, and then put it aside to draw with the set of Magic Markers his mother had gotten the night before at a twenty-four-hour store.

"Draw me a picture," I had said.

"Of what?" He looked up, eager to please.

"Of a baseball player."

A few minutes later, he handed me a picture of what looked like a house with smoke coming out and three stick figures, their heads higher than the roof, standing on the green squiggles of lawn—a mom, a dad, and a kid.

I thought of the time when he was three and I took him down to the train tracks to watch the engines, but he chased the pigeons instead. When I tried to teach him long division, he had asked me how you could blow square balloons. When I took him to Concord to see the Old North Bridge and started telling him about the heroic Minutemen with their blazing muskets, he wanted to know how come butterflies had thin wings.

"Do you think he's angry with me?" I would ask Joan after one of our unsuccessful weekends when I had dragged him from activity to activity, watching him become more and more bored.

"Why would he be angry with you?"

"Because of the divorce. Maybe he blames me."

She shrugged. "Maybe it's just not about you."

I would nod my head and resolve to do better, to be less egotistical and controlling. But now I finally figured out what she had been saying. She had been telling me the exact truth—it wasn't about me.

But in all those years there had never been a time that I didn't want to see him. There was never a week when I didn't think that the happiest moment of my life was the minute he opened the door and stood there all ready to go out, looking up expectantly, undeterred by the failures and false starts of the weeks that had passed.

In the early hours of the morning, I wondered if he could still be mine even if he really wasn't. Slumped in my chair, the bottle of Scotch half empty, I started grasping at memories of the times when everything between us had been just perfect. When we took the amusement park ride that turned you upside down half a mile above the ground, and we had both screamed the whole time and then, the minute we got off, still shaking at the knees, we got right back in line again. When we drove races down speedway tracks, screaming and careening into each other with earthquake-provoking collisions, as we sat in stationary cars in the video arcade. How could we have had those good times, if I hadn't been his father? And then I remembered: "Maybe it's just not about you."

I stood in front of my refrigerator, swaying from the alcohol, dizzy with hunger. I had put one of his paintings on the door, one he had given me months after he got the Magic Marker set that disappointing Christmas morning. It was a picture of a baseball stadium, just like the one I had taken him to that summer, the first summer he and I were living apart. He had drawn a row of round, featureless heads in the stands, a player with a bat that was bigger than he was, and a red-white-and-blue smear that was the flag Sam had kept trying to find at the ballpark while we sang the national anthem. There were the two of us in the Red Sox caps that I had bought and that he had worn religiously for months afterward, even when his became too small and sat perched on the crown of his head. He had given me the picture, looking very serious, and asked, "Is this what you wanted?"

4

The first thing I saw when Joan opened the door was a trace of a smile around her lips. "Have you been sleeping in your clothes?" she asked.

"Of course not," I answered, my voice hoarse from the barely digested liquor of the night before. I looked down at the crumpled suit pants that I had worn to the doctor's office. "I just haven't been to the dry cleaners."

"And why do you smell like a distillery?"

"Could you let me in please?"

I had called in sick at work and driven to Joan's house first thing that morning, acting as if it were an impulse although I had thought of nothing else since I saw the sun rise from my living room window. I still hadn't figured out what I would say or how I would act. I didn't even know anymore what I felt. I had stopped being angry, stopped wanting to scream or accuse. I think, by then, I was mainly just confused and scared; I knew I wouldn't believe it until I heard Joan say it herself, and, if she denied it, I might even believe her because I wanted to so badly.

She opened the door wider, letting me come in. "Sam's not here," she said.

I stood looking around the living room. Everything was perfectly neat. She had redecorated twice since the divorce; each time, the room looked crisper, richer, and less like home.

"This isn't your regular day to see Sam, is it?" Joan asked, looking confused.

"I didn't come to see Sam."

"Actually, he's off from school today. It's some kind of teachers' conference. But he went over to a friend's house. He should be back soon if you want to wait."

I wandered into the dining room, my jacket still on, my hands dug into my pockets. I looked at the papers and books strewn on the table and then across the room at Joan, who had followed me into the big, airy room.

"You taking a course or something?" I asked.

She nodded.

"I was thinking of getting a master's degree in occupational therapy." She shrugged with an awkward shyness that she often displayed when discussing her ideas about working. "So I could do art and actually make some money at it."

Joan's painting had been moderately successful on a local scale; she'd had shows in a few galleries in town and on two or three occasions had actually sold a canvas for a sum that barely repaid her for that year's expenses. But still, for several years now, she had talked about giving up painting to do something that paid. And for years I had argued against it, urging her to keep at it so she could stay at home, always available for Sam.

She had started gathering up the papers on the table and arranging them in orderly piles. "Peter, Sam is getting older. He doesn't need me as much. Do you want to keep supporting me forever?"

"You know that doesn't bother me."

"Well, it bothers me. And I don't have that much time to study, so if you don't have anything . . ."

She stopped straightening the papers and walked back to the front hallway, as if she was about to escort me to the door. I followed her, and stood there mutely, my tall frame planted in the middle of the foyer. "I came here to talk to you," I said.

"You couldn't call first? And why aren't you at work?"

"I got the results of the blood test."

She made a little face. "So it wasn't Lyme disease. I figured. Sam told me the doctor said it was probably a cold." She waited a second, but I didn't move or say anything. She was standing with her back to the stairs up to the second floor. In a patient, talking-to-a-child voice, she said, "I'm sorry I made you go to the doctor when it wasn't necessary. I was worried about his fever—"

"That's not what I'm talking about. I got another blood test at the same time."

She stood still a second, staring at me. "What are you saying, Pete?"

"You know—" I felt my voice start to shake. I looked around for something to throw, but there was nothing, just the two of us face-to-face in the entryway to the home where we had briefly lived our family life. I forced out the words. "I got a paternity test. I'm not his father."

She didn't say anything. For a moment, she didn't even move. I saw her mind working behind her impassive, perfectly made-up face, and then I saw it stop. Slowly, she lowered herself until she was sitting on the bottom step. She leaned forward, grasping her knees in front of her, and started rocking back and forth, her face blank.

I backed away from where she sat. I knew I had to keep distance between us. I wanted to pull her apart so I could find out what was inside. I felt myself weaken and I leaned back with a thud on the wall opposite her. I looked over my shoulder; the wall was covered with autumn leaves that she had lacquered and framed the first fall after I moved out.

Then she slowly stood up. I waited a moment for her to speak, but she kept looking at me, her face unreadable. In frustration, I said, "Are you going to give me an explanation?"

"What do you want me to say?"

"What do I want you to—?" I stopped and caught my breath. "First, you can tell me if it's true."

"You're the one telling me. What did the blood test say?"

"It said I wasn't the father. I was 'excluded.' That's the word."

"Well then." She was standing on the bottom step now, leaning against the stairway wall. Her face was in shadows. Her voice was perfectly flat. It was like getting the error message on the computer; no matter how hard you struck the keys, the message was the same and told you nothing. She didn't say anything for a few moments, then asked, "Are you sure about this blood test, Pete? Can they tell for certain?"

"I got the results from Dr. Atkinson. You can call his office."

She nodded. "All right. I'll do that."

"Is that all you have to say?"

She shrugged. "I've had a shock. I have to think."

"*You've* had a shock?" I was incredulous. "What about me? Are you thinking of me at all?"

"No. You've done that already." She paused, and when I started to speak, she broke in. "Come on, Pete, don't play games with me. Tell me what you know. You must know something. Why else would you have gotten the blood test?"

"Know what? What is there to know?"

"All right, forget it. I'm going to call Dr. Atkinson and see what he thinks."

"This isn't something he can cure, Joan. And you can't just stand there and act like this is some new idea that you need to turn around in your mind for a while. I mean, for God's sake, what were you thinking about for thirteen years? Every time you saw me with Sam, what the hell were you thinking about— What the hell am I supposed to say to him?"

"Have you said anything to him?" Her voice sounded panicked.

"To him? No, of course not. What would I say to him? That his mother—"

"Don't." She held up her hand and I stopped in mid-sentence. Then I heard the sound of Sam's key in the door behind us.

"Hey, Dad."

I turned around and watched as Sam walked in the door. He stood there in front of me, in his T-shirt and baggy pants, with his baseball cap askew. I looked at Joan, who was now motionless, halfway up the stairs, her eyes fixed on Sam; then I looked back at the boy. "Hey, Sam."

"You here for the day?" he asked eagerly.

"No, I just had to drop something off for your mom. Some papers or something."

He shrugged. "You staying awhile? I have this new program to show you. It's like a game thing."

"The one with the haunted spaceship?" My voice sounded tired.

"*Hello*. That was, like, ten minutes ago. No, this one is really cool. Let me show you."

He was past me and on the stairs before I could speak. He got to where his mother was still standing, blocking the way; then he turned around to look at me.

"What's with you guys?" he asked.

His mother shook her head and stepped aside, pressing her back against the stairway wall, as if she could edge out of this scene altogether. She stood between the two of us and looked at neither.

"Can Dad stay for a while to see this program?" he asked her.

"If he wants," she answered quietly. She lifted her head slightly and turned in my direction. My vision was blurring from tears; I could feel a rock in my stomach. "Why don't you stay awhile?" she asked.

"Joan, we have to finish talking."

She moved suddenly, darting past me on her way down the stairs and toward the front hall. I reached out to grab her arm as she passed me, but she was too quick. "Hey, Mom," Sam called out, "what's with you?"

"I have to go to the store," she said over her shoulder as she grabbed a sweater from the rack by the front door. "Pete, stay with him until I come back."

We heard the door slam. I looked back up the stairs.

"What is with you two?" Sam asked.

"Nothing. Just—something about something."

"Well, that's very helpful. Come on, Dad; could you stop acting like the night of the living dead already?"

In a race with me, the zombie would have won. I followed Sam up the stairs and into his bedroom. He was having one of his preteen adrenaline rushes, bouncing off the mattress of his bed, kicking sneakers and flinging clothes in every direction, swinging around on the desk chair; then the computer booted up and the burst of light on the screen froze him in place. "Wait until you see this," he said, enraptured. "It is so cool."

I stood over him, listening to the tapping of his fingers on the mouse. The computer had been my greatest triumph as a father. Sam had been indifferent when I insisted on giving him one for his seventh birthday. Joan, who equated computers with air rifles and underground comic books, offered no support. But I set it up and, every chance I got, I tried for a few minutes to get him to pay attention while I taught him some new trick. We had a few false starts—some scary program with little letters that stood on their heads and danced the merengue when they were supposed to spell; a virtual reality construction program that would freeze the screen just as the menacing-looking forklift was about to plow us down. Desperate, I begged the salesmen at the software store, skinny guys with bad skin or unflattering sideburns, to recommend programs that a kid might actually like; I'd buy them and try unsuccessfully to interest Sam, while his mother stood at the bottom of the stairs yelling up words of discouragement.

Finally, one of the salesmen, the one who was shapeless and soft-voiced and had the worst skin of all, someone you just knew had had an unhappy childhood, handed me a program that colored. "He already has coloring books," I complained. "What's this going to do—teach him to stay in the lines?" But I succumbed and took it to Sam's house that Saturday. I loaded it on the computer and it played some tinny little jingle. Listlessly, Sam pushed the mouse over to a streak of color; then he didn't move away for two hours. From then on, it was a smooth run down the slope; six years later, there wasn't a thing on a computer Sam couldn't do. "So you turned our son from a flake into a nerd," Joan conceded. It felt like a twenty-one-gun salute.

Now I stood there, in the middle of his messy, boy-smelling room, and watched Sam bound from icon to icon. "There's like these aliens, and they have this kingdom, but it's like in the Dark Ages or something. And you have to build these fortifications. Wait. This is so cool. Look, this is the parapet. Do you know what that means? And there's these things of boiling oil. Look what happens when I turn them over." I heard a scalded alien scream. "That is so extreme." He started scaling a tower, collecting an armory of head-bashing implements on the way. "So later you want to go driving, Dad?"

"Whatever you want."

"Can we go someplace really deserted?"

"Sure, Sam. Whatever."

"Can I drive?"

"Sure."

He swung around in the chair, almost kicking me in the knees with his outstretched legs. "You mean it?"

"Mean what, Sam?" I said, coming down from my perch of sorrow and distraction.

He sighed in frustration. "Can I drive?"

"Today?"

"Yeah, today. You know, we go up where there's no cars and you can show me how to drive."

"Sam, you're only thirteen."

"Farm kids can drive when they're thirteen."

"No, Sam."

He took a moment to think, putting his finger up to his lips as if he was about to tell me to shush. I had always loved this gesture because it came from nowhere; it was like another little mystery of Sam's individuality. Now I saw it and my heart sank.

He had a plan. "You know? About baseball tryouts next month?"

I nodded. This was a familiar struggle between us. Our town had a youth league that played over the summer. He had been cut from the team last year and was scared to face it again; I was urging him to try one more time, turning it into an object lesson on perseverance. "If I try out," he asked, "can I drive?"

"You're too young to drive, Sam."

"How about if I make the team?"

"You're not old enough."

"I only have two years until I get my learner's permit."

"Three years."

"No way. Two years and a little bit."

"Ten months."

"So I can drive then?"

I looked over his head out the window. The plum tree, which I had planted the year he was born, was just starting to put out buds. I remembered carrying him out, all bundled in the baby clothes we kept him buried in to protect him from drafts until the pediatrician told us we were suffocating him; I held him while his head lolled back and forth and dribble ran down his cheek and told him he could have a race with the tree to see who got taller quicker. The tree, so far, was winning.

"Won't that be cool when I can drive you places?" Sam was saying. "Maybe we could go on a trip together?" He swung around to the computer and started pounding the keys again. A dragon caught a spiked mace between the nostrils and roared in pain. "Don't you think that'll be excellent, Dad?"

"Excellent, Sam."

"And maybe I can buy your car when you want to get a new one?"

"Maybe."

"And I'll be a good driver, just like you." He grabbed a steering wheel in the air, reached up to adjust his rearview mirror, frowning at it just as I always did, getting it angled just right; then he pulled an invisible pair of sunglasses from his jacket pocket and slowly slipped them over his ears. "What a beautiful day for a drive," he intoned in my voice. "Now buckle up. And don't stick your hand out the window." He turned the key in the ignition. "Do I have it all right?" He swung around in the chair. "Hey, what's wrong?"

I could hear him jump up from his chair and run after me as I headed through the hall, down the stairs, into the dining room. He caught up to me next to the French doors that looked out on the deck that I had had built during our first summer in the house, riding the workmen to make the railing just perfect for fear that Sam, who was barely starting to crawl, would fall through and impale himself on our hydrangeas below. "Dad, are you crying?"

I shook my head, pressing my face against the window, feeling cold glass against my moist skin. He was tugging my arm. I turned around and looked down. I dropped to my knees in front of him and pulled his face toward me, staring into his eyes.

I had finished kidding myself. His eyes had turned brown years ago; there was never a chance they would be green. He might well be short despite all the times I promised him he would shoot up in his teens like I had. His hands might always be too small to palm a basketball.

There should have been a million things for me to say to this boy and instead my mind went blank. He was peering into my face, trying to figure me out so he could do what I wanted him to do. I closed my eyes so I couldn't see him watching me.

"Sam, listen, about the tryouts next month—"

He flinched. "Dad, I told you. I'm going to try out again. I promised."

"No, forget about it. I don't want you to do it if you don't want to."

He bristled. "You think I'm going to flub it again. I told you I've been practicing."

I forced my jaw to stiffen. "That's not it. I don't want you to do anything you don't want to. You don't have to try to be me."

"Why not? You think I'm not good enough?"

My mouth dropped open. "No, Sam, that's not it." I tried to speak and nothing came out. Clumsily, I reached out and pulled him toward me. I felt him struggle in my arms.

"Let me go," he protested. "What's got into you? I told you I would try out for the stupid team. I can do it."

"That's not what I meant."

"You know, I can do things myself too."

"You can do lots of things, Sam. You're a talented person. You can draw and you can color—"

"*Color?* For God's sake, Dad, do you think I'm a little kid—" He yanked himself out of my arms and backed away from me, his hand up to ward me off. "You know, I won the free-throw contest in school last month." His voice started getting higher; he could hear it about to crack and his face flushed. "My science project got the best grade this quarter. I—" He started to cry. I was kneeling there in front of him, speechless and paralyzed, watching him cry because he thought I thought he should be more like me, when I knew that he couldn't be, and shouldn't even try. But I didn't have the words to tell him that; I didn't even know the truth of it myself. I wanted to let him off the hook and he thought I was tossing him back in the lake. I kept shaking my head, my mouth open, as he struggled with his tears and running nose and gasping breath.

"Sam—" I said, reaching out my hand.

"Leave me alone," he shouted.

We heard the key in the lock and turned as Joan walked in. She stood frozen in the doorway, looking at Sam with tears streaking his face, and me, on my knees in the middle of the dining room, my face drained and frozen. "What are you doing?" she demanded.

Sam shook his head. "Dad's getting on me about that baseball thing again. He thinks I'm not going to make the team. He thinks—"

"Pete, what did you say to him?" Her voice was as cold as I had ever heard it. For a long time now, she had wanted nothing from me for herself; all she had asked for was what I could give Sam. And now she was starting to wonder whether I could give even that.

She marched into the room and held Sam to her, cradling his head against her body. "What are you saying to my son?"

I shook my head. I couldn't get out words. She had left her son alone with a stranger and now she was taking him back.

"Sam, tell her I didn't say anything."

"It's okay, Mom," he said, his voice muffled in her clothing. "Don't get mad at him."

She was past being angry. "Pete, maybe you better go."

"Mom, I don't mind—"

"Pete, please leave us."

This had once been my house, my wife, my son. Now there wasn't a single thing left I could insist on keeping. Unable to speak for fear I'd bellow as loud as the dying dragon on the computer screen, I walked to the door Joan had left open and headed out into the dewy spring morning.

5

The Field and Meadow Health Club provides neither. It is located on the ground floor of a three-story building that seems to be constructed entirely of opaque glass, in the middle of a suburban office park. The exercise equipment is lined up against the windows, so people peddling, running, or skiing nowhere can look out at the highway sweep over the horizon. The TVs that hang from the ceiling make no noise; the evening newscasters mouth about disasters while aerobics music pumps out from another direction. The only steady sound is the whirring of gears and the slapping of feet on the treadmill.

For about three years, this has been the one place where I might happen to run into my best friend, Dave. Usually we'll see each other in the locker room, and will talk awkwardly while holding skimpy towels in front of our chests, keeping our eyes planted on each other's faces, which in a way feels even more embarrassing than if we inadvertently let them drift off. We promise to make plans to get together and don't. We try to be competitive about our workouts, but don't have enough time. If we're clothed, we'll shake hands warmly and for a moment, I'll think that he really is a great guy and that I should get together with him and his wife, Marcia, if I only had a house to invite them to and a wife, who would be in it with me.

I met Dave over fifteen years ago in my first job out of business school. We had offices next to each other. For a while we eyed each other edgily. I was the one with the fancy graduate degree. He had spent years as a salesman for a big manufacturing outfit, pounding doors to peddle office equipment. But we had one thing in common: We had each taken a leap to join this start-up company. And together we were supposed to wind up with a plan for marketing the new software that we hoped would make us rich. We were both young, ambitious, with a sense that we had to hurry up and take our best shot.

It was like a marriage, actually. In fact, during those first years, I spent more time with Dave than I did with Joan. We'd start work early in the morning and, more evenings than not, I'd be calling Joan to say I was staying late. As we got closer to the launch date, the hours were endless. I designed the presentations for potential customers, big, thick-headed corporations that had to be convinced they needed our product. Dave harangued our sales force and our production people. We spent hours in tiny, windowless offices, stretched out between a phone and a computer screen, barricaded behind piles of paper and empty pizza boxes. We got used to seeing each other late at night, bleary-eyed, unshaven, and scruffy, talking in that late-night stream of consciousness when you have to let your guard down because you're just too exhausted to keep it up. Our friendship was the kind you make with the kid you knew from summer camp or your college roommate—sprung from a seed planted so deep that, even when you don't tend it for years, it still keeps growing.

Our product was successfully launched during our third year together. This was three months before Joan announced she was pregnant. It was a time when I came to believe, sincerely, that nothing in my life could go wrong.

The next year our company went public. Dave and I cashed in the stock options that we used to joke about papering our walls with;

suddenly, we were two guys who had made a whole lot of money before we turned thirty and we had each other to thank for it.

In the years since, our work paths had diverged. When our business got acquired a few years later by a bigger company, Dave took his golden handshake and went off grumbling about bureaucratic managers. He had gotten addicted to the excitement of start-ups and since then, he'd joined several ventures, never as successful as the first. But I had stayed on, making friends with the new managers, and then becoming one of them myself. I realized from time to time that I had become one of the bureaucrats that Dave grumbled about. In all the years since, in the increasingly impersonal world where I did business, I had never even had a spark of friendship like the one I had with Dave. And I suppose it had been the same way for him.

Not that we were great at the hand-holding stuff. He had been good through my divorce with Joan in a back-patting, buck-up kind of way; for a while he had stood me drinks after work and would stay with me as long as I needed, even though we both knew that his wife, Marcia, was at home with two screaming toddlers, watching the clock and toting up grievances. And I tried to reciprocate, listening sympathetically as he grumbled about each of his new business ventures, making helpful but cautious suggestions about each new scheme to make a killing.

I had never confided my doubts about Sam to Dave before the blood test. I would think of him and his two daughters, the way, despite all his gruffness and cynicism, he would still get delighted as he bored me with stories of their latest accomplishments, and I just couldn't bear it. But after I got the news of the blood test and went to Joan's place, I needed to talk and there was no one else to call.

I told him only that I wanted to get together and he suggested we meet at the health club. He was waiting by the front desk, trying to talk to the twenty-something staff person behind the desk. She was dressed in a bright green leotard, with a pile of long blond hair pulled up and somehow balanced on top of her head. She flashed me a big smile when I handed her my membership card. "Have a great workout," she exhaled as she gave me a towel.

Before we could enter the locker room, I pulled Dave by the shoulder. "Listen, let's not go in there just yet. Do you have a minute?"

Instinctively, he looked at his watch to check on his supply of minutes. Then, remembering that he had set aside an entire lunch hour to work out with me, he shook himself and looked up. "You don't want to get changed?"

"I just want to talk for a minute."

We looked around the health club lobby. People in gym clothes stood around drinking water from big, bright containers with flexible plastic straws. The aerobics music was making our legs jiggle. The female attendant smiled and asked us if she could help us find something.

"Come on," I said, pulling Dave's shoulder.

"You can't take the towels outside," the attendant called out from behind the desk. I grabbed Dave's towel, balled it up with mine, and tossed them to her. They missed and fell on the floor. Two of the people in gym clothes looked up from their containers of water and stared at me.

When I got outside, with Dave following me, he looked at me accusingly. I had made him look ridiculous in front of people before whom he wanted to look only successful. "What is with you?"

"Let's go for a drive," I said.

He was horrified. "Drive where? What's there to drive to?" He waved his arm at the expanse of suburban Boston. Looking around, we could see only three gas stations and an entrance to a mall.

"Maybe we could have lunch," I suggested feebly.

"You know I don't eat. Besides, everything will be crowded and smoky. And then we have to work out *after* work."

"Look, I want to talk about something."

He seemed to freeze. He thought I was going to tell him I had cancer. I was afraid for a moment he would put his hand on my arm. "Tell me."

Now I was horrified. "I can't just talk to you while we're standing out in the middle of everything," I said. "Let's go back inside."

"No, they'll think we're crazy. Listen, I have an idea; let's just get in my car."

There was a pile of magazines, reports, files, and one of his kids' dolls on the passenger seat; I had to throw them in the back. I couldn't help noticing the motivational tapes stacked up on the console. I pictured Dave enclosed in this pine-smelling, leather-and-velour capsule, bobbing down the river of life on a current of self-esteem.

"There, that's not so bad," he said as he settled in behind the steering wheel. "You want some radio?"

"No, for God's sake, just let me talk."

"Okay, okay, talk."

And then I had nothing to say. I started fumbling with the buttons on the car radio; I pressed the wrong one and some excited, self-assured man blasted into sound, telling us that we had only to envision a plan to make it come true. Dave shut him off.

"How can you listen to that stuff?" I asked.

"Do you have something you want to say to me?"

I took a deep breath. "It's about me and Joan."

"You're getting back together again?" I shot him a look of annoyance. But he seemed so happy. "You know, Marcia was just saying recently that she wouldn't be surprised if you two—"

"Dave, listen to me. We're not getting back together again. It's about Sam."

"Oh." He settled back. Dave's two daughters were eight and twelve. Between them, they participated in every form of sport and activity known to yuppie children. Their family life was so full of soccer and jazz dancing and advanced placement geography that none of them had had a moment of silence in years. I know that he looked on me with pity.

"Are you two feuding about how to raise him? Is it religion? Marcia and I have been worrying about that lately. She's getting more interested in being Jewish, but she's not observant—"

"It's not religion. It's not anything to do with Sam."

"You just said—"

"No, it's about Joan. About when we were married." I took a deep breath. "You know how I always wondered what was wrong with our marriage?"

He shrugged. "I thought you knew what was wrong. She was miserable."

"I meant, why she was miserable."

"Well, *that* was pretty obvious."

"Not to me it wasn't." I took a deep breath again, then stopped. "What do you mean it was pretty obvious? How would you know what was going on?"

"I don't, really. Just what you told me. And what I could see. Listen, Pete, are we going somewhere with this?"

"I just found something out. About Joan." I took another breath. "There was someone else."

I could barely force myself to turn around and look at him. And when I did, he was shaking his head and looking as if I had just spilled some dip on a new tie. "Pete, you got to put that stuff behind you now. You knew something was wrong with the marriage at the time, didn't you? It's not surprising that there was someone else. I guess it must be a shock to find out now. Who told you?"

"Told me? No one told me. I figured it out. I just had a feeling."

"You just had a feeling, now? How long has it been—eight years since you were divorced?"

"No, no, this happened longer ago than that. Before Sam was born."

Dave rolled his eyes, then forced himself to be patient. "All right, who was it?"

"I have no idea."

"Wait a second. I don't get it. You just had an idea but you don't know who—"

My voice started racing. "I keep trying, but I can't figure it out. I mean, she wasn't working then. She spent most of her time painting. She didn't even leave the apartment much, from what I could tell. It could be the fucking mailman for all I know."

"You don't have to figure it out, Pete. You should just let it go. What good is it going to do you now?"

"I want to know. I mean, for Sam's sake."

"Is she seeing this guy now?"

"No, I told you, it was years ago. But I still have to know. What if he was—" I shook my head. "You know, a mental defective."

"Well, that would fit Joan's pattern."

But I was too busy talking to myself to listen to him. "I mean, what if this guy, whoever he is, was sickly. Some kind of hereditary thing. I mean, I'd want to know that."

"Why, are you thinking of breeding him?"

I stopped and looked at Dave. My mouth opened, then shut. It took him maybe a full minute to figure out what was going on. Then another full minute to go back and work it all through, starting with why I had called him up in a panic on a weekday morning insisting that we meet that day, ending up with how bad what he had just said was, given what I was trying to tell him. A couple of minutes is a long time and I could actually see his mind work. I was there way before him and waiting when his face finally registered horror and really deep pity.

"You're not sure of this," he said, making it a statement of fact.

"We had a blood test."

"You're kidding."

"No. At the doctor's office. Easy as getting a flu shot."

He shook his head, confused. I took a deep breath and told him the story—my doubts, all the odd things Joan had said over the years, the day I sneaked a look at Sam's medical folder, and then the moment when I realized I had to take the test. I stopped, exhausted, and looked at him, waiting for him to say something. I think I expected him to be angry with me for taking the test, or maybe to absolve me. But instead, he shook his head and let out a low whistle. Then he said, "That fucking bitch."

"Who?"

He looked at me as if I was crazy. "Joan. I can't believe she led you on for all those years."

Hearing him accuse her made me, perversely, want to defend her. There wasn't anything he could say about her that I hadn't already thought. And yet, for some reason, some residue of love, I suppose, I didn't want to believe she had been as bad as she must have been. "Maybe she wasn't sure. I mean, he could have been my kid."

He shook his head. "How could she have thought that? Come on."

"I don't know. We *were* married. It could still have been my kid, even if she was seeing someone else at the same time."

"If? She obviously was seeing someone else. How else could this have happened?"

"It could have been only one time."

He leaned back too. It was as if we had just run a race and were at the finish line, panting and dazed. "You know, I always thought he didn't look much like you."

"You're kidding? You never said that."

"You called a lawyer yet?"

"What for?"

Again he looked at me as if I was crazy. "You've been paying child support all these years, haven't you? You're not going to keep on paying, are you?"

You know, I would have prided myself on the fact that I always saw the financial angle first. But this hadn't occurred to me.

"That's nuts, Dave. What would she live on if I stopped paying support?"

"She should have thought about that back then, when she was doing the ugly with the mailman."

"She didn't have to think of it then. We were still married."

"Well, you're not now. And you should get back that house too. No way the judge would have given her that house if she had run off with that mailman instead of just seeing him a little on the side."

"But where would Sam live?"

He hadn't thought about that. Was it just that the brain can accommodate only so many thoughts at once? Or was it the fact that we were sitting in a parked car, looking out through the windshield at a road that never moved, and a horizon that never got any closer?

Now he did put a hand on me. And, although it came as a shock, I let him leave it there, right on my leg. The warmth of his palm felt good; it was something I had earned, like a stiff drink after a hard day's work.

"You know, Pete. You got a lot to sort out. You should really talk to someone."

"The doctor gave me the name of someone."

"A lawyer?"

"No, a shrink."

"Well, sure, if you want to, maybe you should. Maybe it would be a good idea." He removed his hand. Maybe thinking I'd see a shrink got him thinking that I might take his hand and hold it. "But you should be seeing a lawyer as well."

"Enough with the lawyer. You're obsessed."

"Listen, buddy of mine, I'm telling you. You should see a lawyer and you should do it soon, because I can guarantee you, if you don't, she will."

"Why would you say that?"

"Because I know how people work. And she's sitting there, depending on you for her entire livelihood and well-being, and she must be thinking that one of these days you're going to wonder why, exactly, that is still the case. She's going to start thinking about what she can do about that. And if you're not happy now, you may be even less happy then."

I shook my head. "I have nothing to worry about. She can't take anything more from me than she already has."

But there, it turned out, I was wrong.

6

One day, when Sam was four, I came home from work and found the house in order, Sam in bed, and dinner on the table. I sat down and looked at Joan, who wasn't eating. She stared at her plate and said that she wanted us to split up.

Later, when I told Dave or some other friend that this announcement had come as a total surprise, they would look at me knowingly and say, "But you must have seen it coming." The truth was, though, I hadn't. I knew she wasn't happy. Since Sam had been born, she was always distant, almost wary. But I attributed that to the distraction of raising a kid. She loved being a mother, maybe loved it too much. She worried over everything—whether he was healthy, whether he was growing, when he would crawl and walk and talk, whether he was listening to the right music or looking at the right mobiles. I had gotten assigned the role of the calm parent, nodding patiently and suggesting solutions without really believing that there were problems. "This is all just a phase," I kept assuring her through the bouts of colic, teething, and nightmares. For me, that was reassurance enough. But Joan never seemed to break out of her cage of worry and abstraction.

And of course my work kept Joan and me apart. I fought that, fought to get home each night as early as possible. But it was a struggle. By that point, my company had been acquired and was now a division of a larger company. Executives from the parent company's headquarters were always flying in and swaggering around, talking about how they wanted to "grow" our business. It was a time when there were a million new, barely understood ideas—CD ROM, the Internet—and we were all scrambling to figure out which way to grow. I was a vice president for marketing and was responsible for doing a lot of that. I had to fight to make time for my family, and the time I had, I devoted to Sam. I'd walk in the door and he'd toddle recklessly across the room, falling into my legs. While he and I were rolling on the rug screaming, Joan would just slip away to do the things she wanted to do whenever she had a free moment. What those things were—reading, painting, talking on the phone to friends—I scarcely knew and, absorbed in Sam, I probably forgot to ask.

And, I have to confess, I didn't want to know if something was wrong. I kept thinking of my stable, solid parents, my father banging away at his workbench, my mother whistling in the kitchen. Suddenly their uneventful marriage no longer seemed like some boring fate to be avoided, but instead, an ideal that I feared I might never achieve. My father had died the year before Sam was born and, in some odd way, it had seemed as if he was handing off the ball. Now I was in charge of making everything smooth and sure and solid. But I wasn't handy around the house, I didn't have a workbench, and I worried that if there was even the slightest imperfection in my home, I wouldn't know how to fix it.

I tried my best. I was making plenty of money at the time, so I spent it. I put an addition on the house—a master-bedroom suite with a sybaritic bathroom, a playroom that could have accommodated a small video arcade. I planned elaborate family vacations by the ocean or in the mountains. I urged Joan to spend some money on herself, buy herself whatever she wanted. She would look up dreamily and ask, "What do I want?" Then, before I could answer, she would look away.

Mostly, though, I did the one thing that I knew would make us all happy. I devoted myself to Sam. The only times I ever saw her smile were when she was watching him and me together, him riding on my back across the living room or us dueling with his plastic swords. The only times she and I really spoke were when we talked about him, when I pointed out his latest amazing accomplishments. With Sam, at least, everything *was* perfect. After a testy babyhood, he had turned into a delightful toddler who would romp around the house joyously. He loved other kids and adjusted well to preschool. He and I adored each other. I was content and I kept waiting for Joan to start enjoying our life together again. But it didn't happen.

When I would ask her what was wrong, she would wave her hand or shake her head, saying it was nothing. I realize now that she just couldn't bear looking at me and thinking about the possibility that Sam wasn't mine. The sight of me made her feel guilty and anxious, and so if I walked into the room, she wanted only to shut her eyes.

But at the time, I didn't understand any of that. Instead, I made excuses or ignored the problem. And after a while I just forgot what it was like to have a real marriage, where the two of you talk and are honest and help each other. So, the truth was, I was shocked that night when she finally told me she wanted to call it quits.

I tried to get an explanation. She gave me some line about having married too early and needing to figure out what she would be like if she lived on her own, things I just couldn't believe were true. I began to apologize for anything I thought I might have done wrong; I would work less, help out more, do anything.

She shook her head. "It's not you. You're a wonderful father. I almost didn't want to do this just because of that, so Sam could have you around all the time. But," she sighed, "I can't go on feeling like this, Pete, and we'll just have to find a way for Sam to have you with us being apart."

I wouldn't listen. I kept talking wildly, blaming myself, pleading with her to reconsider. She told me again it wasn't my fault and started crying; when I tried to comfort her, she got angry and started blaming me. I threw down my napkin in frustration and she walked out of the room. When I went upstairs, she was in bed, pretending to be asleep.

The next morning Joan took Sam to preschool and I headed to work just like normal. I was getting ready for some presentation I was supposed to give to the board of directors about our plans to upgrade our latest product. I spent all morning yelling at my staff for not having compiled the right data, for having put the Power Point presentation in the wrong order. By the time the phone rang, I had almost managed to forget about what Joan had said the night before. Then I heard her voice on the other end of the line.

"Do you want me to pack for you?" she asked. Years later, I realized that what I was hearing in her voice was fear—fear that I would explode, that I would argue, that I would make her back down. But that day, standing in my office, surrounded by a desk full of papers and a pile of charts that were falling all over the place, that thought never occurred to me.

"Why would I want you to pack for me?" I shouted.

"I figured if you would be leaving—"

"And where did you expect me to go? To some motel off the highway?"

"I figured you would be able to work that out—"

"Well, I can't. Not now."

"But you can't keep staying here. I mean, Pete, come on. You don't want to make it harder for us than it has to be—"

I hung up the phone, looked at my desk, and almost fell on the ground. I had to find a place to live. I started to run through options and, as Joan predicted, it wasn't hard to figure it out. There were suites where my company put up new hires and long-term visitors; they were furnished and convenient and completely suited for the anonymous half-life that I was about to start living. And then I realized Sam wouldn't be there when I got home at night. I grabbed my car keys and drove to the Timothy Mouse House preschool.

The girl who ran the place recognized me because I often dropped him off, but you could tell from the minute she saw me that she expected trouble. I could feel how big and loud my size-thirteen, shiny, polished wing tips sounded in this space where everybody else wore sneakers or socks and sat on pillows on the floor. She was about twenty-four and already turning a little gray. She met me at the entrance. In the distance, I could hear a woman's voice singing "Twinkle Twinkle Little Star."

"We need to be quiet," the young woman whispered. "We're about to have a nap."

"I have to take Sam out."

"Sam's mom didn't say anything about Sam leaving early when she dropped him off this morning." She had a quiet and even voice; each word was carefully chosen and then articulated. It took a long time to get through a sentence that way and I had to make myself breathe regularly as she went through the process.

"Maybe Joan forgot."

"We really ask our parents to let us know if there's going to be a change in the schedule—"

"It's something that just came up."

She was thinking about that one. "You said that Sam's mom forgot to mention it this morning. Now you're saying it just came up *since* this morning—"

"Excuse me," I said as I pushed past her and headed toward the singing.

I turned the corner and saw the room where the children were. There were about eight of them, almost all blond, most tinier than Sam, huddled together like a litter. A heavyset, white-haired woman sat in front of them holding up a book; some of the kids were staring at the book, others were starting to nod off. Sam was wandering around at the edge of the group. He rested against one of the little girls, almost putting his head on her shoulder; she let it stay there a second, then shrugged and moved him off. He seemed to sway a little, as if he couldn't really stand, then leaned against another little girl behind him. I stood there holding my breath, listening to the woman's thin voice carry the steady, metronomic rhythm.

The young woman started tugging at my arm. "You really shouldn't be here—"

I held up my hand and she stopped talking. The song continued, each verse sounding exactly like the last, like one of those rounds that never end, and the children were swaying back and forth to the steady tick-tock of the words. The young woman's hand came to rest on my arm, and we both seemed to move back and forth too, our eyes on the bright, impossibly perfect star twinkling on the page of the picture book.

Then Sam saw me and broke loose from the litter. He threw himself at my legs and screamed, "Body heat."

The children shuffled, rolling over sleepily to watch us. The woman with the book kept singing. And Sam was jumping up and down against me, saying, "Body heat. Body heat."

I looked at the young woman next to me. "That means he wants me to pick him up." I picked Sam up and held him, his soft, dangling arms now bunched up against my chest. He closed his eyes and pressed his head against mine. He was crooning "body heat" over and over.

I laughed nervously. "He got that from me, actually. When he gets in bed with us at night, my wife and me, I always say he's just looking for some body heat."

"He's really getting too old to be sleeping with you."

Sam had circled my head with his arms, swamping me with his warm body; when I turned to talk to the young woman, my nose bent against him and the soft, detergent-smelling cotton of his playsuit filled my mouth. "We don't let him do it every night. You know, just when he's cold."

"Setting boundaries is for the child's sake, not the parent's."

"We're leaving now. Have a good nap."

The song was over; the woman was holding the book, folded against her chest; still the children rocked back and forth as the silent sound of the words hung in the air

---

Sam wanted to go to the park. I wanted to take him across state lines and change our names. So instead we continued driving around and around in circles. I didn't have a car seat in this car, so I put him up front, strapped into the passenger seat. I worried that I would be stopped by a policeman and given whatever sanction they give to murderously negligent parents, but I realized that he was so little his head didn't show above the dashboard, and when I realized that, my heart nearly stopped with panic. I was afraid to get on the highway, so we kept going up and down the streets around Timothy Mouse House, in and out of subdivision roads that were bare and empty and named after flowers or women. Perfectly content, Sam sat beside me, oblivious to the danger he was in, his hands up in the air holding his imaginary steering wheel, singing to himself, "Watch me driving, watch me driving."

After a while, he asked, "Where's Mommy?"

I drew in a breath. "You know, Sam, there's something I need to talk with you about—"

"Mommy said she would take me to the park."

"Maybe she will soon."

"No. Today. After Timothy Mouse House." He actually said "Mouf Houf," probably because that was how he said it the first time he tried and we fell in love with it and always repeated it that way afterward, so he never got to hear it said right.

"Is that where Mommy takes you after Timothy Mouse House?"

"Yes. Every day."

"Sam, that can't be right— Oh my God." A teenager on a bicycle pulled in front of me; before my foot touched the brake, I could picture Sam's head going through the windshield and I jerked my hand out to stop him, landing it too hard on his tiny chest.

"Daddy, you hurt me."

I leaned my head out the window. "Listen, sonny, if you ride your bike through stop signs like that, you're going to get hurt."

"Eat shit," he answered.

Sam started snuffling. "Are you okay, Sam?" I asked, my voice sounding frantic.

"My stomach hurts."

"From school? What did they feed you?"

"No, from where you hit me."

"Hit you? You know I never hit you— Oh, before. That wasn't hitting. I was trying to stop you from getting hurt by that bad boy on the bicycle."

"Then why didn't you hit him?"

"But I didn't want to. That was the whole point."

"I think we should get Mommy."

"Why? What do you need Mommy for?"

"So she can look where you hit me and put something on it."

"Now, Sam, stop saying that I hit you. What would Mommy think?"

"Maybe she'd put the paper rubber on it."

"The what? No, Sam, that's vapor rub. It's only for colds. You don't have a cold, do you?"

"Daddy, why are you angry at me?"

"I'm not angry. Now, listen to me, Sam, I have to tell you something. You may not be able to understand it."

"I have to go to the bathroom."

"Sam, please listen to me."

He started twisting around in his seat and pulling at the belt. "I have to go to the bathroom."

"All right, all right. We'll look for a place. Let's try down here." I made a right turn and struck the side of the curb. "Oh, fuck, now look what you made me do."

"You said 'fuck.'"

"Sam, could you please give me a moment's peace? I think we have a flat."

I got out to look at it. There was a big, wide scuff mark on the side of the whitewall. I kicked it to see if it was losing air, but couldn't tell anything. Muttering under my breath words of self-pity and resentment, I went to my trunk and dug out my pressure gauge. As I bent down to use it, I slipped and landed with a thud in a patch of mud. Pulling myself up, I swiped the seat of my pants with my hand; my palm came up with streaks of mud on it. I kicked the side of the car, forgetting for a second that Sam was inside, and the next minute I heard him crying.

I opened the door and found Sam huddled in his seat, holding on to the seat belt, his head curled down almost on his lap. In a tiny voice, Sam whimpered, "Daddy, why are you so angry?"

Choked with injustice and impotence, I couldn't speak. My face dropped to my hands. I hit my forehead against the inside of my wedding ring. I yanked it off and started to fling it toward the sewer grate. Then I caught myself and saw Sam. I pulled him off his seat and held him to me. It took me a second to smell it.

"Damn, some dog must have crapped here. I wonder if it's on me."

Sam's crying got louder.

"Oh, don't cry, Sam. It's not the end of the world. I can get the suit cleaned."

Sam shook his head; his eyes were closed tight so I couldn't see him.

"Oh, Sammy, you're too big a boy to be doing that."

"I told you I had to go, Daddy."

"All right. All right. Just don't cry. It's okay. Here, take my handkerchief." It was starched bright white with my initials in the corner; it was bigger than Sam's face. "Let's get back in the car and we'll find a bathroom and wash up."

"I want to go home."

"No."

I tried to buckle him in, but he didn't want to sit down.

"Promise me we'll go home," he wailed.

"Just sit down," I said through gritted teeth, wrestling him into a sitting position.

We started driving and, in a minute, Sam started to protest. "Daddy, we're not going home."

"This is the way."

"It's not the way Mommy goes."

"You know, Mommy doesn't know everything."

"Why are you mad at Mommy?"

"I'm not, Sam."

"You're mad at me."

"I'm not mad at anybody," I shouted. "I'm really not."

I stopped outside a dairy restaurant. Sam resisted, but I pulled him off the seat, grabbed his hand, and dragged him inside. "My, you two look like you both need a bath," the waitress said.

"Where's the bathroom?" I demanded, not breaking my stride.

"We don't have a bath there," she said, alarmed.

"Lady—"

She pointed. I pulled Sam through the crowd of diners who turned to watch us, a muddy man with a face of rage and a cowering, smelly boy trailing behind. They probably thought I was going to drown him.

The bathroom was small and fetid. I locked us in. "Okay, now listen to me, we'll just go into the stall and take off your pants and clean you up—"

He shook his head and pulled his hand away from mine. Then he stepped in the stall by himself and shut the door.

"Sam, you can't do it yourself."

"Don't come in."

"Now come on, Sammy."

"I don't want you to see me."

"All right. But you call me if you need help."

I heard the sounds of zippers and clothing as I leaned against the door.

"Daddy."

"Yes."

"You won't leave me, will you?"

I sank down onto the floor. I felt my trouser seat soak with dirty water.

"Sammy, listen. I have to tell you something."

"I don't want you to."

"I have to, baby. I'm sorry."

So I told him that his mother and I were splitting up. He didn't say a thing as I talked, stopping in the middle of every sentence to keep my voice from breaking. We couldn't see each other; the stall door was between us. I rested my head against it, feeling the cold of the chipped-paint metal against my cheek. And inside, all I heard was the determined sound of clothing being pulled down, pulled off, and pulled back up.

"I'm ready, Daddy."

"Okay."

When he stepped out, he wouldn't take my hand. I watched as he went to the sink and stretched to reach the faucets. I stood behind him and turned on the water; he cupped his tiny hands and held them out. We both looked at ourselves in the mirror, me towering over him, his head barely at my belt, our four hands, palms up, in the center of the sink.

"Body heat," I said.

He turned around, patted me on the leg, and then walked outside, leaving me alone with my face in the mirror.

7

The Saturday after I talked to Joan about the blood test, I came to pick up Sam at the normal time to start our weekend. No one answered when I rang the bell. I rang a few times, then pounded on the door. I walked to the back and banged again; then I looked in through the windows. The downstairs was empty; the blinds were drawn.

Shaking my head, I got in my car and drove away. I had only gone about three blocks when I remembered the extra set of house keys hidden in the trunk of my car. They had been there from the days of our marriage, buried in the well of the trunk with the spare tire and the jack, in case I accidentally locked myself out. I knew I should have returned them after the divorce. I could say I forgot about them, but I have to admit that I had traded up my car several times since then, and each time I transferred the keys, each time thinking that I should throw them out, each time grabbing them shamefacedly at the car dealer's lot just as they were about to drive away my trade-in. "You know, if you leave your keys there and someone steals your car, they could break into your house," one salesman had warned.

I stopped the car by the side of the road and checked the back, almost hoping the keys had disappeared so I couldn't do what I wanted to. But my heart was already pounding and I wasn't thinking very hard about anything except getting inside the house and finding out where Sam was. The keys were there. I got back into the car and turned around.

I let myself in through the back door, to the kitchen. I moved quietly, even though, as far as I could tell, nobody was home. The breakfast dishes were drying in the drainboard. Hanging on the refrigerator was a notice from Sam's school about some parent-teacher meeting. The dining room table was clear; in the corner of the room, in a neat pile, I saw Joan's textbook and papers. Then I heard footsteps upstairs.

I could actually feel my muscles clench so I would be still. The footsteps stopped; they were in the bedroom, "our" bedroom. I began walking softly across the dining room, sidestepping the place right near the door where the floor creaked. At the foot of the stairs, I stopped and waited. A door opened; footsteps crossed the hall and headed down the steps. She saw me when she was halfway down.

Joan's hair was wet and hanging limply around her face. She was wearing a short bathrobe I didn't recognize; I could tell she had nothing on underneath. Even though it was tied around her waist, her first instinct was to grab the robe and pull it tighter about her.

"How did you get in here?"

"Where's Sam?" I insisted.

"Pete, how did you get in here? The doors were locked."

"You locked me out."

"Pete, I'm not kidding. You tell me how you got in here."

"You let me ring and ring and you didn't come down."

"Get out."

"Why wasn't Sam waiting for me today?"

She started speaking as if she had rehearsed a speech. As she talked, I saw that she was nervous and the realization made me angrier than anything she had done so far; she was killing me, and she was afraid that I would ask her to stop. "I need some time to think about this situation," she said in a too-calm, too-rational voice. "I don't want Sam to know and I can't trust you not to tell him. I can't figure out why you got this test. And I can't figure out what we should do about it. But I'm not going to let you say or do anything that's going to hurt my son . . ."

She was halfway through her speech when I stopped hearing the words. I just saw her mouth move, her eyes carefully studying me, as if I were an intersection she was about to drive through. When I spoke, I was amazed to hear my voice as low and even as it was. "Tell me where Sam is."

"I'm not going to, Pete. I've made a decision."

I took a step forward, my legs shaking beneath me. "Tell me where Sam is."

"Pete, get out of here or I'm calling the police."

There was no question that I was the faster one of us. She had barely taken three steps toward the phone before I caught her. She tried to get away from me, but I stepped in front of her and blocked the way. All I could think about was Sam. I wanted to be with her not a moment longer than it took me to find out where he was.

"Pete, I'm just trying to sort this out. We need some time."

"Where is he?"

"This isn't fair. It's not fair to him."

I grabbed her shoulder and pressed it against the wall. I didn't say anything; I had nothing to say; I just wanted to find out where Sam was and leave.

"I don't want you looking for him," she said. "You have no right—"

I pressed her shoulder harder. She tried to push me away but couldn't. Her face turned red with frustration.

"The Steiners'," she said. "He's at the Steiners'."

She was crying as I headed down the stairs. I never looked back at her.

———

The Steiners lived across the street, a few houses down. We could see each other's lawns from our own living rooms. They had had their first child, Bethany, three months after Sam was born, and we spent our children's early years trading equipment and advice and baby-sitters.

Sam was sitting by himself on the front step of their house. He had his baseball cap pulled down over his eyes and was tossing a softball from one hand to another without much force. I drove past and parked my car a few houses up, then headed back on foot, trying not to come close enough so that the Steiners could see me from inside. I made a funny noise, a "woo woo" sound; it was our signal. When he was little, we would go to the supermarket with Joan and stand in different aisles calling "woo woo" to each other until she screamed at me to stop egging him on.

At first, Sam didn't look up. He was dropping the ball to the ground, then picking it up and dropping it again. I called out again. Still not hearing me, he got up and headed back into the house. I shouted, "No!" Then he turned.

I put my finger to my mouth before he could say anything and waved for him to come over. He looked for a second at the Steiners' front door, but it was only a second. Then he was bounding toward me. I put my arm on his back as he got close to me and pushed him into the open passenger door. Then I jumped into my side and drove off.

"Hey," he said. "I have to tell Mrs. Steiner. I was waiting for Mr. Steiner and the kids to come back and we were all going to the library together."

"Boring."

He smiled. "Mrs. Steiner wanted Bethany and me to work on this school project together." He rolled his eyes. "She's such a stage mother."

"Don't worry about the Steiners. I'll take care of explaining to them later."

"Mom said you were sick."

"Is that what she said?"

"You weren't sick?"

"What else did she say?"

"Nothing. Why, what's wrong?"

"Did she say anything after the last time I was over?"

"No. Nothing really."

"What? What did she say?"

"Just, you know." He sort of chuckled, but nervously. "You know, that you were being your usual crazy self."

I actually smiled. "My *usual* crazy self?"

"Yeah, well, you know."

"No, I don't, as a matter of fact." I looked at him sideways. "So did you defend me?" He giggled. "Did you stick up for your pal?" He shook his head. I reached over and tickled his stomach.

"Hey, quit it."

"You stick up for your buddy?" I said again, tickling harder as I spoke.

"Quit it, Dad." He was curling over my hand.

I pushed his baseball cap over his eyes. "What do you expect from a crazy man? This is my *usual* crazy self."

He was laughing hard now. I put my arm around his shoulders and pulled him close to me. I could feel his skinny limbs against me, his face scrunched into my side. Then he remembered that he was thirteen and no longer permitted this kind of thing. He pulled away and organized himself in his seat. He even buckled the seat belt without being told.

"If you're not sick, what *is* wrong with you?" he asked.

I faced ahead into the traffic and clung tighter to the steering wheel. I thought about his question. I would never have told him the truth about what was wrong with me, even if I could put it in words. I imagined myself, as Joan had obviously imagined me, telling Sam that he wasn't my son. It was insane, crazier even than she could ever have imagined me being. But then, I thought, would we ever tell him? Or would we keep on lying to him for years, as Joan had lied to me?

I took a deep breath and said, very casually, "Nothing's wrong with me. What's up with you?"

He gave me his great, gap-toothed smile that I feared some orthodontist was going to destroy someday. "I have something to tell you."

A little bomb of panic detonated in my esophagus. "What? What?"

"Tryouts."

"They're next week."

The grin widened. "No, this week. I told you they were next week so you wouldn't be pressuring me."

I looked down at him, mystified. "What are you talking about?"

He leaned back in his seat and folded his hands over his stomach like a department store Santa who'd just made a kid's day. "I'm in," he tossed off, then reached casually for the radio.

"In?"

He nodded, his head bouncing up and down just a little too hard to be offhand. The next minute, I was pounding his back and he was screaming, "Dad, the steering wheel!" The car had started to swerve. I leaned back and grabbed the wheel. He leaned back too. He held his hands up in the air, holding the imaginary passenger-side steering wheel. "Signal before a lane change," he intoned. We both signaled. "Turn the wheel gently. Hand over hand." We moved into the fast lane. "Accelerate."

Awestruck, I said, "I can't believe you did this for me."

He rolled his eyes and waved his hand at me. "Not for you. For my fans."

I closed my eyes to hold this moment, to print it on my retinas so I could see it whenever I wanted, no matter what the future held.

"All right," I said. "Let's celebrate. Where do you want to go?"

"Not the library to do my science project."

"How about a movie? Some bloodcurdling nauseating slashing screaming horror show?"

"Kid stuff."

"Top of the Hancock tower? Canoe ride on the Charles?"

"Been there. Done that."

"There's a small airport around here. Maybe we could find a pilot to take us up."

"Hey, what's gotten into you?"

"I don't know. Let's do something special."

He shrugged.

"Fried clams and disgusting ice cream sundaes?" I said.

"Both?"

"Too crazy for you?"

He smiled and sank back in his seat.

We went to a clam shack up by the ocean, in Essex, a beach town north of Boston. We took the grease-saturated cardboard containers to the picnic tables out back, and sat looking out over a marsh. It smelled like salt air and rotten eggs. In the distance, you could see small motorboats navigating their way through the inlets that wend in and around the islands of tall grass. A pair of seagulls circled over us, then landed on the ground a couple of yards away, waiting patiently as we ate.

We were barely halfway through one order of clams before we both felt sick. Sam was dangling a clam over his open mouth as if he were a trained seal being fed.

"Watch out that seagull doesn't take it," I warned.

Sam stopped, then tossed the clam at the bird. There was a loud squawk and a flutter of wings as the two birds dived for the prize.

"Whoa, look at that one go." He tossed another one. There was another squawk, another struggle; then the same bird got it again. "Hey, no fair. That big one is hogging everything."

"That's how it goes," I said. "Wait until you get into business."

"Forget that. I'm not into that dog-eat-dog stuff. I'm going to be a TV sportscaster."

"Oh, well, I'm sure all the big TV stars are very nice people who are into sharing."

He smiled.

"You know that space between your teeth is getting smaller, Sam. You're looking downright handsome these days."

He stopped smiling and tossed his napkin at me. Then he crossed his arms on his chest and slumped down on the bench.

"Mom says I'm going to have to get braces one of these days," he said glumly.

"That okay by you?"

"Everybody gets them."

"You have to suffer to be beautiful."

"Not *beautiful*."

"Oh God, I forgot. Handsome. Rugged. Manly. Studly."

"Gross."

"You can't help yourself. You're my son. You're going to be good-looking."

"You think I look like you?"

And then I remembered.

"Hey, Dad, where are you going?"

I could hear his footsteps following me. He caught up to me and fell into step as we walked down the incline of grass to the water. We sat down, pretty close to each other.

"Dad, what's wrong?"

"Your mother's pretty. I bet you'll grow up looking like her."

"Fine."

I turned to him. "So don't worry about it. I know you're going to turn out great."

"All right already. It's not like we have to worry about it right this very instant."

"You're right." I picked up some stones and tossed them into the water. "You know how to do that?"

"Skip rocks? Come on, Dad, you show me that every time we get near water. It's like we go to a water fountain and you want to skip rocks."

"Okay, forget it. So I never told you anything useful."

He grabbed a rock from my hand and tossed it. It skimmed obligingly across the stagnant water.

"Not bad for a scrub," I said.

"Not bad for a fossil."

I pushed him, getting him down to the ground. We wrestled in the wet grass. I could feel him straining to push me off. When he was trying as hard as he could, the tendons in his neck sticking out with the effort, I rolled off and landed on my back.

"Whoa, boy, you been working out?"

"Get a life."

"Let me see those muscles."

"Leave me alone." But he let me grab his arm and tried feebly to flex his biceps.

"Hey, look at Popeye here."

"Who?"

"Forget it. I can't carry on a conversation with a kid."

"Who else would talk to you?"

"Uh-oh. Now you're done for." I grabbed him and tried to push him down again, but this time the angle was wrong and he was able to hold me back. We struggled, then stopped. I kept my arms around him, he let himself relax, and then I just pulled him to me and held him there.

"Dad, we have to go back."

"Not yet."

"Dad, come on, Mom's going to be worried."

"What about the sundaes?"

"I'd puke. Besides, we shouldn't have gone off without telling Mom."

"She won't mind." I couldn't let him out of my arms. We both lay there, the sun beating on our faces, the grass soaking our backs.

"Dad, you're not supposed to put me in the middle when you two fight."

"Where'd you get that? Dear Abby?"

"That shrink guy you made me go to after the divorce."

"That wimp? I told your mother we should just send you to a military academy instead."

I could feel his shoulders move as he laughed. "He was a wimp, wasn't he? Remember when he wanted me to draw all those pictures of my feelings?"

"And that sickie aquarium he had? Remember how the fish always kept dying?"

"It was hell."

"You didn't need to go. Your mother and I should have gone."

"I know. But I survived."

"You forgive us?"

"I'll get my revenge."

I kissed the top of his head; then we got up and headed for the car.

When we pulled up in front of the house, there was a police car parked outside. I stopped my car in the middle of the street. We both sat there, looking out at the house, the empty lawn, the shut door.

"Sam, listen, I have to tell you something."

"We better go in, Dad. They probably think I ran away."

"No, that's not what they think. Listen, Sam. I'm sorry. I've really screwed this up."

"No, you didn't, Dad."

The door of the house opened. Joan stepped outside and saw us in the car. She turned and started talking to someone inside.

"Listen, buddy, there isn't time now to explain. You better get out."

"Dad, don't be crazy. Come inside with me. I'll get my stuff and we can go over to your house just like normal."

"Not this week. Now, listen, Sammy, I'll talk to you. Okay. It may be a little bit of time, but I'll talk to you."

"What are you talking about?" His voice rose a pitch and cracked.

I leaned over to open his door and as I moved past him, I stopped and touched my fingertips to his cheek. "Just tell them we spent the day together like normal. You promise?"

He got out of the car and shut the door. Then he bent down and stuck his face through the window. "Mom's right. You're crazy."

I pushed his head out of the car so I could pull off. From the corner of my eye, I could see one of the policemen come out the front door, Joan behind him, talking. He looked no older than a college kid and when he saw me, his Adam's apple shifted nervously in his throat. He was opening his mouth and lifting his arm when I stepped on the gas and headed to the highway.

8

O h, well, you are in a mess of trouble."

Barry Bernstein, my new lawyer, nodded his head, trying to look grave although I could tell he was gratified. Barry was a short man with a lot of energy; as we talked, he moved constantly, twisting in his chair, grabbing at things, putting on and taking off a pair of dark-framed half-moon eyeglasses that he perched on the tip of his nose when he wanted to read. He had a big head that was bald except for a bushy fringe of black hair above his ears; his eyebrows arched and dipped expressively above a pair of dark eyes that drilled right into you. Dave had referred me to him; he had "done" a divorce for one of Dave's pals who had a high-volume cash business he didn't particularly want to share with his soon-to-be-ex and Barry had made it happen. Dave thought he'd be a good choice for me in my present "predicament."

Barry shuffled through the papers. "Your ex-wife says you broke into the house. Then you took the child without authorization."

"It was my regular weekend to spend with him."

Barry nodded. "Noted."

"And," I went on, "the doors to the house were unlocked."

"She told the police otherwise."

"She's a flake. She leaves the goddamn front door wide open half the time."

Barry stroked his chin reflectively. He probably wanted to grow a beard, but didn't have the courage.

"She states in her affidavit that you grabbed her and threw her against the wall and shook her until she nearly passed out."

"I threw her?" I asked incredulously. "That's ridiculous."

"All or some of it?" he asked mildly.

I caught myself. I wasn't proud of what had happened when I went to Joan's house, but I had been panicked at losing Sam and I knew I hadn't hurt Joan. Now, looking at the lies she had written in the affidavit, I realized that this war between us was escalating. I felt dizzy and scared, as if I was on an elevator that was dropping down a shaft and I didn't know how to get off. I took a deep breath and said to Barry, "I never saw her."

Barry lifted his eyebrows, then pulled a piece of paper from the pile lying in front of him. He handed it to me. I had seen it before. It had been delivered by a uniformed police officer the day after I took Sam from the Steiners'. The cop showed up on my doorstep that Sunday morning, while I was still in pajamas and slippers. He handed me the paper and started reciting a speech about what it meant. "This is a restraining order; you are forbidden to go within five hundred feet of the following named individuals." I started arguing. The cop was an old guy who had spent his life stopping cars, breaking up disturbances, and making people listen to things they didn't want to hear. I could have been talking to the wall. "The following named individuals: Joan Bessette Morrison. Samuel Peter Morrison. Violation of this order will lead to arrest and is punishable by up to two and a half years in the house of correction." When he was done, he started to swing back to his car. "You better get yourself a lawyer, pal," he said over his shoulder.

Now my lawyer was watching me look at the document again. It had a seal on the top and stamps on the bottom. Sam's name—typed crookedly on a blank in the form—was in the middle of the page.

"I've seen this before, Barry. What's your point?"

"The judge believed her. That's why he gave her this restraining order."

"I wasn't even there in court. I didn't get a chance to testify."

Barry nodded. "True. The proceeding was what we call ex parte."

I rolled my eyes. Don't use a dead language to talk about my life, I thought.

He caught my expression and nodded. He laid down the file, folded his hands, and looked right at me. He had a little smile on his face, as if he had seen me coming when I left home that morning.

"All right," he said. "You want plain English. This is it. She swore that you assaulted her. There isn't a judge in this state who wouldn't give a restraining order to a woman who made these accusations. And because she says it's an emergency, she gets a hearing without giving you advance notice. So that's done. Until the order is lifted, you can't go to the house or see the kid. All you get is the bills."

"So what are you going to do about it?"

"We can go into court and have a hearing. Then you both testify under oath."

I lifted my chin. "Fine. Let's do it."

"And if the judge believes her, those visitation rights you had are gone. And you still get the bills."

"And the alternative is—"

"We figure out what she's really after and work on her."

"You can't figure her out. She doesn't know what she wants herself."

He shrugged and picked up the file again. "Okay. I look at this and I can't tell what's really going on. You have what looks like an amicable divorce." He pulled out the papers I had brought to him today— the separation agreement, the financial arrangements. "And frankly, considering what you gave up in this settlement, I can't imagine why it wouldn't be amicable."

I had decided not to tell him about the blood test. I wasn't thinking clearly, but my instinct was to keep this information to myself. If I didn't, I thought that something would change in some legal way that I couldn't foresee and couldn't fix. And, although I sat up at night worrying about it, I was pretty sure Joan wouldn't tell anyone either. She was never someone to confide in others, and she had kept this particular lie to herself for a long time now. And she didn't want Sam to know either; she might have been more afraid of that than I. So I figured I would keep the blood test to myself and let my lawyer think this was just some typical postmarital flare-up. All I wanted was for him to get rid of the restraining order; I couldn't plan beyond that. From the minute the cop told me I couldn't see Sam, the only thing that mattered was to see him, and I was sure that, once I did, everything else would just work out.

Barry was looking at me to see my reaction. I didn't budge; I didn't change expression. After a minute, he started talking again. "For eight years since the divorce everything is going along smoothly. You pay generous support. You see the kid. We have no court involvement. Everyone is happy. Then she goes into family court and signs an affidavit of abuse and accuses you of trying to kill to her."

"She didn't press charges, did she?"

Barry wagged his head. "She called the cops. They investigated."

"But they didn't bring charges? That means they didn't believe her."

His smile got just a little wider.

"True enough." He pulled out a form with handwriting and started reading it. Then he lifted his eyes as if he had just remembered I was there. "The police report. I sent my paralegal down to the station to get a copy."

"And what does it say? Did they believe her?"

"They don't have a box to check for that." He went back to reading. "They say she had a red mark on her upper body near her shoulder."

"Did they say bruises?"

"They said a red mark."

"It was from the hot water. She had just gotten out of the shower."

His eyes leveled on me. "You never saw her. How do you know she got out of a shower?"

I paused for just an instant. "I lived with her for five years. That was her Saturday morning routine. She got Sam out, then took a long, hot shower and washed her hair. Never missed it once."

He shrugged. "Not bad," he said. Then his eyes went back to the report. He read it a little bit longer, then put it down. "She told the cops that you took the kid from the front of a neighbor's house without getting permission."

"I'm his father. Why should I ask the neighbors for permission?"

"That's the whole question, isn't it? Why would she want to suddenly out of nowhere take away your visitation rights?"

I shrugged. "She's crazy."

"There's all sorts of crazy in this world." He scratched his chin again, still checking to see if maybe a beard was there. "She been looking for more money?"

"She couldn't spend any more money than what I already give her."

He smiled. "My experience of money is otherwise."

I nodded. "Okay, maybe so, but she's wasn't asking for more money."

"Then what?"

I shook my head. I was looking over his shoulders at the wall behind his desk. There was a big poster with some object on it that could have been either a shell or a disembodied sexual organ; it was neither black and white nor in color. It was from some gallery in the Southwest that I'm sure Barry had never been to. Maybe it came as a package deal with the beige leather reclining chair on which he was seated. I started asking myself why this was the place that I deserved to wind up.

"Is there more in the report?" I asked. "Did Joan tell the cops that I said anything?"

"No, she didn't." He lifted his eyebrow quizzically. "What did you say?"

I smiled. "I wasn't there. Remember?"

He nodded his bald head, not saying a word.

"What did Sam say to the cops?" I asked.

Barry moved his glasses just a little lower on his nose and began to read. " 'The child states that his father came to the neighbor's house as usual to pick him up for their regular visitation. He denied the use of any coercion.' "

"Good boy."

"True?"

"Of course. Do you think I'd 'use coercion' on my own son?"

Barry gave me a pitying look. I moved forward in my seat and spoke in my scariest voice. "Listen, Mr. Bernstein, I don't care what your experience is, but I've never hurt my son and I wouldn't. I'd kill anyone who tried."

"Including your ex-wife?"

I sat back in my chair. "She wouldn't hurt him either."

"Then why is she asking a judge to keep you away from him?"

I looked down at the floor to the side of his desk. There was dust in the corners of the imitation Oriental rug.

"Listen, Pete." I moved my eyes back to his face. He was trying to look human. "Is Pete okay? Or do you prefer Peter?"

I shook my head. "Doesn't matter."

"Let's talk about what you want in all this."

"I have choices?"

His smile broadened. "Of course. There are always choices in life."

"I want Sam."

"Then you have to fight for him. Unless all she wants is more money. In which case you can either fight or pay. So that's a choice."

"And if it's something going on with her?"

"A father has some rights. She can't just take visitation away without a reason. She has to prove that you're a danger to the child. If she can't do that, then she loses."

"And if she wins?"

He shrugged.

"I lose Sam. That's what you're saying, right?"

Barry looked at the restraining order that was lying on the desk between us. He touched it with the tips of his fingers and slid it toward me. "As of this moment, you don't have him anyway."

I grabbed the paper and crumpled it, then tossed it to the corner of the room. Barry leaned back in his chair again and smiled. He was enjoying this. "Doesn't make a bit of difference that you did that," he said. He leaned back, patting his stomach as if he was checking to see if it was still round and full. "If you want, I can file a motion in court tomorrow for an emergency hearing to lift the order. I can suggest that your ex-wife is using this ex parte"—he paused and waited, smiling, to see if I said anything; I was silent—"procedure to get an advantage in a dispute over visitation rights or support. I think I could get a judge to listen. Depends on the judge, of course, but I think I could raise a doubt. At the least we can get an expedited hearing on lifting the order—maybe get supervised visitation in the meantime. If that's what you want."

He leaned forward. "But you have to figure out what it is that you want."

"You do that. Let me know how it goes." I stood up.

I waited for him to say something, but he sat there silently, half smiling. He watched me as I put on my coat. I paused for a moment, standing over him; we were waiting to see which one of us would reach out to shake hands first. He leaned back in his chair, cupped his chin with one hand, and swung his glasses lazily with the other. "You know, Pete, I get the distinct feeling that you're not telling me everything."

"I'm telling you I want Sam back. That's the only thing that matters."

He reflected for a moment. "Well, we'll see about that." Then, without getting up, he nodded good-bye and turned back to the papers on his desk.

9

The first thing that struck me the next morning in court was that Joan and I had each dressed for a part. And the funny thing was that it was the same part: a nice, sane, rational suburban person. I wore a boxy, American-made gray suit—a suit I hadn't worn since my first year out of business school when I didn't know better—and a tie with Ivy Leaguey shields on it. She had on a hair band, a sweater, and a string of pearls about which I remember her saying, "Now where am I ever going to wear these?" when she inherited them from her grandmother. In fact, we looked made for each other as we sat at opposite ends of the courtroom, perched on hard wooden benches, our hands folded tightly on our laps, our teeth set on edge.

Joan's lawyer was the woman she had used in our divorce. Marjorie was a nice woman, kind of mussed-looking, with a big mound of hair barely holding together on top of her head, that she was always touching or jabbing with her hand. She smiled at me when I came into the courtroom and asked how I was doing. Then I saw Barry at the other end of the room, motioning for me to walk over without saying anything to the enemy.

We all waited. The courtroom was long, divided in half widthwise by a thick wooden rail. In front of the rail was an empty bench for the judge; on the other side were the public benches, all of them crammed with people. Mostly there were young women, usually with children, either talking with the friends or mothers who accompanied them, or yelling at their kids to sit still. Some of the kids were crying. A three-year-old boy kept trying to climb over the back of the bench; he'd get one leg over and his mother would grab him by the collar and yank him down. There were a couple of young men, looking angry in warm-up jackets and blue jeans; every once in a while a guard would come by and tell one of them to take off his baseball cap. Next to me, an older woman was talking to her lawyer; the lawyer was trying to get her to fill out a form and the woman was crying. On the bench behind me, an old lady, dressed all in black, sat huddled with her three grandchildren, holding the baby on her lap and rocking back and forth, singing under her breath. We waited for an hour and a half before the judge came out.

The judge was a middle-aged woman with thinning hair that she obviously dyed. She rushed out, nodded at the crowd, then sat up behind her high bench, which was already covered with stacks of files. A woman clerk stood in front of the judge's bench and one by one called off names in a nasal voice.

"Morrison versus Morrison."

We were one of the first. I had to push past the older woman and her lawyer, still struggling over the half-completed form, and when I got off the bench, I almost collided with Joan in the aisle. I drew back, then held out my hand so she could go first. Her eyes narrowed and she started to say something, then caught herself and walked ahead.

The four of us—the lawyers, Joan, and me—lined up in front of the judge's bench. The bench was on a platform and, from where we stood, we could see only the judge's head and the top of her shoulders. I could feel my legs shaking and, stretching back my head for air, I looked up at the gold-leafed dome above us. The courthouse was 150 years old. Standing in this room, men had been sentenced to hang. I shut my eyes and listened as the judge shuffled through the papers.

"I'll hear you," she said, lifting her eyes slightly without raising her head, as if she was ready to listen but was still hoping it wouldn't be necessary.

Joan's lawyer, Marjorie, started to speak, but Barry cut her off instantly. "Your Honor, it's the father's motion. Mr. Morrison is seeking immediate relief from an order that Mrs. Morrison had entered ex parte based on a completely uncorroborated affidavit. This is a man who has supported his family—very generously, I might add, if Your Honor will look at the papers I provided. . . ." I saw the judge's eyes shift from Joan's affidavit to the columns of figures Barry had extracted from our divorce papers. She nodded slightly. "He's a family man, Your Honor, absolutely devoted. He's a senior vice president at the Shattuck Company. Very stable background. No history with the courts." The judge looked up from the papers, first at me, then at Joan, then back at me. I could feel myself sweating under my jacket. Barry had warned me not to say a word. I breathed in and out; I forced myself not to smile.

"The parties agreed to joint custody eight years ago. There's never been an incident, not a suggestion of anything untoward."

"Your Honor—" Marjorie tried to interrupt.

"You'll get your turn, Counselor," the judge said, not turning to Marjorie.

Barry went on. "In fact, Mrs. Morrison has left the child with the father for several week periods on any number of occasions, when it suited her."

"Those were scheduled vacations, Your Honor—"

The judge held up her hand toward Marjorie and continued speaking to Barry. "Counselor, what does your client have to say about the allegations in the affidavit?"

"He absolutely denies them. And he's ready to take the stand this moment and testify."

From the corner of my eye I saw Joan look at me, her mouth open. I kept my eyes straight forward, looking at the spot just behind the judge's shoulder. My heart pounded. I lifted my head up and faced the judge, trying to look like a man about to pledge allegiance to the flag.

The judge waved her hand at the crowd. "Mr. Bernstein, this courtroom is full. When you called the clerk to schedule this hearing, you didn't say that you wanted the court to take testimony—"

"But until we have a hearing, Your Honor, my client is cut off from the child, based on uncorroborated charges in an affidavit. And the claims are ridiculous. She states in the affidavit he kidnapped the child. But the child told the police that there was no force. It was their regular weekend together. The child wanted to see his father."

"The police investigated?"

Marjorie tried to speak. But Barry had the judge's attention and never let it go for a second. "Mrs. Morrison called the police and they investigated and no charges were brought. No one ever spoke to Mr. Morrison. The first he heard of it was when he got this temporary order. Now if we can't take testimony today, then I would request that the order be lifted and we schedule a hearing—"

The judge waved her hand and motioned to the clerk. "When's the next available date for a hearing?"

The clerk fumbled with her book. I shot another sidelong glance at Joan. She was staring straight ahead at the smoked-glass window behind the judge's bench; it was bleached white from the sun. Joan's cheeks were flushed; I could tell she was breathing fast.

"Three weeks. June 24."

"All right, Counselors, I'll see you then."

Marjorie started to move away, but Barry didn't budge. "Your Honor, this will be the first week in the child's life that he goes without seeing his father."

The judge looked up, then turned to Marjorie and Joan.

"Is that true, Counselor?"

Caught as she was leaving, Marjorie half-turned around. "Well, yes, Your Honor, but given the circumstances—"

"We can't know what impact this will have on the child," Barry interrupted. "The father and son are devoted to each other."

"Do you allege that the child was harmed in this incident, Mrs. Morrison?" the judge asked.

Joan stiffened. She was still looking at the window. She didn't turn to the judge. After a moment, she shook her head. "He wasn't harmed." She stopped and stole a glance in my direction. "Not physically."

"And is it true, as Mr. Bernstein says, that the child wants to keep seeing his father?"

Joan moved her head and looked straight at me. She didn't move a muscle in her face. The flush was gone from her cheeks; her breathing had quieted. She stood perfectly still. She shook her head up and down once, just slightly, not taking her eyes from me. Then she looked back at the window.

"Your Honor," Marjorie said, "my client—"

"Mrs. Morrison can't deny that the boy wants to see his father," Barry insisted. "What is the basis for keeping them apart?"

"All right, stop. I want an evaluation of the boy. You pick one of the psychologists from the court's list. Have it done by the hearing in three weeks."

"And if it's done sooner than that, can we get an earlier date to address the court?" Barry asked.

"If you can get it done," the judge said, shrugging.

"Your Honor—" Marjorie protested.

"Next case."

We walked out of the courtroom in single file, Joan leading the way, me last. I looked out over the crowd. The older woman was still whispering to her lawyer, still clutching a tissue. The men were all still slumped in their seats, their hands stuffed in their pockets. The baby had fallen asleep in her grandmother's lap and the old woman kept rocking, the other two children clinging to her arms.

———

The moment we got to the hall and the courtroom door closed behind us, Barry planted himself in front of Marjorie, pointing his finger in her face. "I already called the psychologist before court today to set up an appointment for tomorrow. Your client had better get the kid there or we'll be back in court the next day for an injunction."

Marjorie started to speak, but it came out in a sputter. Her eyes darted around, then landed on me; she looked sad, and, for a moment, I thought she was going to ask me to help her. I lifted my eyes to the ceiling.

"All right, Joan, let's get out of here," I heard Marjorie say. When I looked down, they were headed toward the elevator.

"Not bad, huh?" I heard Barry say. I turned around to look at him. He was stuffing the file into his beat-up leather briefcase.

"What?" I asked.

"What?" he repeated, laughing. "I said, 'Not bad for a day's work.' The psychologist sees the kid and Joan tomorrow morning. Then you go in at one P.M., we have the report done the next day, and we're back in court by the end of the week. You'll be all set for next Saturday's visit."

"You have this all lined up already?"

He shrugged as if he was really a modest fellow. Then he slapped me on my arm. "It's going to cost you, of course."

I looked down the hall. Joan and Marjorie were standing in front of the elevator with their backs to me. The elevator door opened and Marjorie put her hand gently at Joan's elbow, steering her forward. When they entered the elevator and turned around, I saw that Joan was crying.

I could hear Barry calling after me as I ran across the hall. The elevator door was starting to close and I stuck my arm out, hitting the edge of the door with a bang. The door creaked back open.

"Peter, what are you doing?" Marjorie asked.

I looked right at Joan. "Did you tell him?"

She was crying harder now. "Why did you start this?" she sobbed.

"Did you tell him?"

The doors started to shut again. I stuck my arm out, but, from behind me, Barry reached over and pulled it away. I started to shout and struggle as the doors shut in front of me. The last thing I heard before they pressed together was Joan's voice, no higher than a whisper, saying, "No." Then the pulleys began to whine as they lowered the elevator to the lobby.

When I stepped away, Barry was studying me, a little smile of amusement playing on his lips. I left him standing there as I headed down three flights of worn marble stairs to the street.

10

The psychologist's office was in the ground floor of a three-story Victorian on a busy street in Cambridge, about ten minutes' drive from the courthouse. Anxious and unable to concentrate, I left work far too soon for my appointment and got there half an hour early. A storm was threatening, and even though it was early afternoon, it had gotten dark. A piece of litter was blowing around the parking lot. I sat in my car, going over and over in my head all the possible contingencies, as if I was back in business school creating some elaborate decision tree.

If Joan had told the psychologist about the blood test, then I was sunk, as far as I could tell. What kind of psychologist would say it was in Sam's best interests to be with a father who wasn't a father and who had actually taken the blood test? But I didn't think Joan would tell. Because, if she did, could she be so sure that the psychologist would take the part of the mother who had, in some real way, created this whole situation years earlier? Plus, I tried to picture Joan, sitting there in her tailored clothes and her pearls, telling some court-appointed shrink that she had borne another man's child and foisted him off as mine for years. Plus, Sam would be right next to her; she would never say it in front of him.

So i figured the psychologist would be in the dark, and I certainly wasn't going to change that situation. I was going to be the earnest father, unable to understand why Joan had done this to me. I counted on Sam to say that he still wanted to see me. And I believed that, if he said so, if the psychologist agreed, if the judge ordered it, if everything went back to normal next Saturday when it was time for my visit, we would all somehow be okay. I was desperately clinging to the blind idea that this was something we could work out on our own as a family, ignoring the fact that we were not and had never been the family I once believed we were.

I finally walked into the psychologist's waiting room a minute before my appointment was supposed to start, checking myself nervously in a hallway mirror as I headed in. Everything was in place— my bushy hair was neat and combed, my tie was straight, my suit conservative and well-tailored, my shoes shined. I tested out a little smile to see if I could still do it, trying to ignore the bags under my eyes, the lines of worry at the corners of my mouth.

When the psychologist finally summoned me into her office, she introduced herself as Dr. Ellen Sprague and then sat down in a high-backed chair in the center of the room, a few feet from her neat, paper-free desk. She motioned for me to sit on an uncomfortably low couch across from her.

She was in her thirties, thin and birdlike, with brown hair that fell over her eyes when she moved quickly. She reviewed her papers for a few minutes as I sat fidgeting on the couch. Then she closed the file and looked up. She was perched on the edge of the chair, her small hands folded on her lap, her back straight. "You seem like a man in a hurry, Mr. Morrison," she began.

"I want to see my son again."

She nodded, then looked down at the thin file of papers on her lap. "These are serious allegations that your wife has made."

"But they're not true."

She shrugged, not looking at me. "That's for the judge to decide, of course. My job is to decide whether continued visitation would be in the child's best interests."

"What did Sam say?"

"I'd rather hear from you right now." She paused for a moment, maybe waiting for me to say something. But I sat there, the good student, trying hard not to explode with anxiety. Finally, she said, "All of this is very rushed, I must say."

I thanked her for being so accommodating. My voice shook when I told her how much this meant to me. I saw her back relax a little as she settled in her chair.

"You and your wife had joint custody after the divorce?" she asked.

"Yes. Joan agreed to give me whatever rights I wanted. I had every other weekend, and one day during the week as well."

"But she kept physical custody?"

"I have to travel sometimes for work, so it was easier for Sam to stay in our old house with Joan. But I always lived within a fifteen minutes' drive of their home. I was always available. I'd come over any night if Joan needed a break or to go somewhere. We split vacations. We split holidays. A couple of times, we even spent a holiday or Sam's birthday together because he wanted us to."

She tilted her head sideways, lifting an eyebrow. "The three of you?"

"We don't have any other family in Massachusetts. My parents are dead. Joan's are in Florida."

"Neither of you has any siblings?"

"I don't. Joan has a brother in Chicago, but they don't see each other much. It's really just the three of us." My voice caught.

"And up until this incident there's been no friction between you and Mrs. Morrison?"

"Not about Sam."

"Can you tell me what caused the divorce?" she asked.

I shook my head again. "It was Joan's idea."

She settled back in her chair and folded her hands on her lap. "It's often the woman who forces the issue. But that's not the cause. Was there much conflict in your marriage?"

"No," I said. "I don't know why she wanted a divorce." I shook my head in a bewildered way. But I did know. Since the blood test, for the first time, I finally understood. Joan had simply been unable to live with herself—or rather, to live with me. She hadn't wanted to tell me the truth and risk losing me as Sam's parent. But for better or worse, she couldn't lie well enough to endure the intimacy and scrutiny of marriage.

But I didn't want to talk about this with Dr. Sprague. She was still waiting for some explanation as to why we had broken up, and if I kept on shrugging my shoulders, she would write me off as an unen-lightened, unperceptive male. So I floundered wildly in my mind for some fight between Joan and me, and, without thinking very clearly, I blurted out, "I made us go to Disney World."

Caught off guard, Dr. Sprague laughed. "That doesn't seem like a very significant conflict."

"No, it was, really. It was the only time we actually fought that I remember. I wanted to go. I mean, I could hardly wait. It's all I thought about. I planned it myself; it was supposed to be a present for Sam's fourth birthday. But Joan was just dead set against it. She said Sam was too young. It was too hot. It was too expensive. She hated the lines. She hated the food. The hotel room was plastic. Sam wanted to buy every souvenir he saw and she hated that."

"Did you let him?"

I smiled guiltily. "We had the money."

"Did Mrs. Morrison ever say no to the trip?"

I remembered the night I brought home the promotional video that I had gotten Disney to send to my office. While Joan was in the kitchen fixing dinner, I popped it in the VCR to show Sam. He and I were sitting on the living room floor, just a foot or two from the TV, rocking back and forth while Mickey and Minnie appeared on the screen, waving and beckoning us to follow. When I looked up, Joan was standing in the doorway, looking down at us, her face set in stone. "I guess I didn't really give her a chance to say no."

Dr. Sprague wasn't very impressed. "I'm sure she could have objected if she wanted to. And why was this trip so significant for you?"

"Fun, I guess. Something I always wanted to do." For a brief moment, I just wanted to tell this woman the truth, at least the truth about this, and suddenly I knew it. "I was trying to cram everything in. It was like I knew somehow that our days as a family were numbered and I wanted one perfect memory."

"Why?" she asked.

The simple one-word question stumped me, as it usually did. What was the reason? Because every man wants his family to be perfect, I could answer. Because it's a basic human wish. I shut my eyes to think and saw the little tract house that my parents had bought when I was ten. I saw my mother painstakingly measure the living room windows for curtains that she stitched each night for weeks, after she had cleared up dinner. I saw my father on the lawn at dusk, endlessly watering the scruffy maple tree that the subdivision developers had plopped into the ground a week before they started showing model homes to eager buyers like us. I saw myself on the living room couch, staring fascinated at the tiny fireplace with the fake marble mantelpiece that had been one of the house's major selling points, but that my parents never used because they were afraid of having a real fire in the house. Then I remembered that moment when the realtor had opened the door on the much grander house that I had bought for my family, a house that you could actually call a castle; I remembered how I had pictured myself tending a fire in front of the elaborately carved 100-year-old mantelpiece. I opened my eyes and looked at Dr. Sprague, and when I spoke, my voice was scratchy. "I couldn't understand why everything shouldn't be perfect for us. We had all the pieces: great kid, beautiful home, good health, money in the bank. I really thought all I had to do was try hard enough. But by the time Sam was four, I could see it wasn't happening. By then, all I wanted was a moment. One moment."

She thought about my answer, not making a sound. I heard the

papers move on her lap. Then, in a businesslike voice, she asked, "Did
you seek counseling at the time of your divorce?"

"The lawyer made us go to one or two sessions, but no, not really."
The counselor had been a woman much like Dr. Sprague, I thought,
maybe just a few years older. We had sat in a room much like this. I
had pleaded and Joan had looked away. "But I don't think Joan's heart
was ever in it." I looked over at Dr. Sprague, who was watching me
intently, her eyes sympathetic. "I don't think she loved me."

"Ever?"

I shrugged. "Maybe not."

"And you loved her?"

"Yes. I had never loved anyone like I did when I met her."

"And by the time of the divorce, did you still love her?"

I thought for a second. "I loved us. The three of us." I looked over
at her. "That's not the same thing, is it?"

Her eyes seemed to drift off to the side, as if she was seeing something of her own in the empty space beside her. She shook her
head. When she looked back at me, I was still staring at her, waiting,
and she gave me a small, nervous smile. "No, it's not the same thing.
But it's something." Then she shook herself and looked back at her
file.

For the next hour, she questioned me about my relationship with
Sam, about where we went and how we spent our time, about how
I helped him with his homework, about the times I ferried him to
activities or went to his school for conferences. I got to talking
about the time he had signed up for Little League when he was in
first grade. He had done so badly his first day that he never wanted
to go back. I told him he could do what he wanted, but the next
Saturday when I picked him up, I had a mitt and a ball in the backseat and we wound up at the park and spent the day playing catch.
I knew he knew what I was doing, but he let me do it anyway. In a
couple of weeks, when he was ready to go back, his coach refused.
The coach was this guy with a nothing job at the gas company who
thought the "team" was the most important thing in the world and

Sam had blown his chance in life forever by missing practice. I talked myself blue in the face, flattering, cajoling, pleading, telling him Sam could never make it to productive adulthood without the coach's guidance at this critical time in his life. And then, in Sam's very first game, his third time at bat, he came up when the bases were loaded and he just struck out. One, two, three. Whiff. As he walked away from the plate, he looked for me in the stands; then he just shrugged and smiled. I started cheering and the other parents stared at me as if I was crazy.

I could hear my own voice getting quicker and louder as I told the story; when I looked over, Dr. Sprague was smiling at me. She caught herself again, and again she returned to business.

"Well," she said, when we were done, "that was helpful. I'll let your lawyer know what I'm going to recommend about visitation."

"Can you tell me what Sam said?" I asked anxiously.

She started to shake her head, then stopped. "I can't reveal very much. That would be inappropriate. But I—" She spoke slowly, choosing her words carefully. "Sam is a very intelligent, well-spoken boy. You must be very proud of him."

"He said he wants to keep seeing me."

She kept her mouth shut, but nodded her head gently.

"And Joan? What did she say?"

She shook her head imperceptibly. "Mr. Morrison, would you consider your wife to be a good mother?"

I didn't have to think for a moment. Whatever Joan was, she was a good mother. "Yes. Absolutely."

"Then why is she so dead set on keeping your son from you?"

"She said that?"

"Yes. They actually started fighting here in my office—" She caught herself. "I'm not inclined to disregard a mother's wishes, particularly when she feels as strongly as Mrs. Morrison. But I just felt that she wasn't telling me her reason." She looked up at me, puzzled, as if I could help. I met her with a blank stare. I had no desire to help her understand. I believed that her confusion was only going to help me. After a moment, she stood up and reached out her hand weakly;

her fingers barely pressed against my palm when we shook. "I'll be in touch with your lawyer shortly."

———

So I drove home and waited. I had some earnings reports to read, but I couldn't concentrate. I took a walk around my apartment complex, but when a neighbor approached me with a smile, I rushed in the other direction. By the end of the afternoon, I was back in my living room, rummaging through the boxes I had brought from the house after the divorce, until I found the pictures from Disney World. Joan had let me take them all. I sat on the couch, fingering through them, wondering if we looked happy.

In every one, Sam had something in his hand, a cone or a toy or a soda. He looked happy, I thought, but maybe he was just high on sugar. Joan had on her pose-for-the-photographer smile. I either had my mouth open or my head cut off. When I had first started on my fantasies about this trip, I had in mind that we'd wind up with a perfect photograph of the three of us somewhere in the Magic Kingdom, framed and sitting on my office desk for me to look at all through the day. None of these pictures was that. Then the phone rang.

It was Barry. He was jubilant. "I just got a call from the psychologist. I don't know what you said, Pete, but you really kicked butt."

I felt tired listening to him blare. "So the shrink recommended visitation?"

"She sided one hundred percent with the good guys. I have to say I was a little worried about this one—she's usually very pro-mother. But that ex-wife of yours just blew it from what I could tell. She got all agitated in the shrink's office when the kid said he wanted to see you, and cried, and said the kid didn't understand. What's going on with her, anyway?"

I didn't answer. After a moment, I asked instead, "So this is it? The judge will give us back visitation?"

"Ellen Sprague—the shrink—said she'd have the report in to the judge by the day after tomorrow. That's Thursday. I called the clerk and set up a hearing for Friday. It's smooth sailing from here on out."

I went to bed early that night. As I closed my eyes, I thought that maybe I had actually avoided the disaster that I had risked when I'd gotten the blood test. I lay in bed, keeping my breaths calm and regular, as I told myself that this would all be behind me, that I could wipe clean the slate. I didn't know it at the time, of course, but that same night, as I lay in bed, Joan was in her house across town, telling Sam about the blood test.

11

S uper Bowl Sunday the year that Sam was eight, five years before the blood test, was the perfect day to watch the game. It was cold and gray and bleak in a New England way that warned you to hide under a blanket with a bowl of popcorn and burn off your energy by yelling at the TV set.

Sam made a little whining noise when I mentioned the game. He never actually said no, just emitted enough of a sound to let me know that I'd be guilty of child stifling if I forced him to watch with me. Then he retreated into the fascinations of the handheld video game that he hunched over and pounded relentlessly with his finger as he scrunched up his face to readjust the eyeglasses on his nose.

We had headed out for a drive that morning with no particular destination, and, predictably, twenty minutes later we were in the car, circling about aimlessly. "So what do you want to do?" I asked.

"Whatever you want to do."

I restrained myself from saying that I wanted to go back to my apartment and put on the TV. I reminded myself that it was good that he felt free to express what he wanted. I pouted as we kept circling around our town's windy, empty roads.

"How about the aquarium downtown?" I offered.

He looked up, a pained expression behind his crooked glasses. He had just gotten them a few months before and they seemed to be constantly on his mind. I had felt a stab in my stomach when Joan told me that the doctor said he needed them. It was the first thing about him that wasn't perfect, the first intimation that, despite all my most deeply held beliefs, he would be subject to illness, frailty, and limitation.

"What's wrong with the aquarium?" I asked.

He shrugged. It should have been obvious what was wrong, I suppose. I remembered our last visit there, not very long ago, on another weekend afternoon when we were at our wits' end to find a single place in the major cultural and educational center in which we lived that could occupy our attention for four hours. We had walked around the giant fish tank, watching the enormous, sodden fish, bleary-eyed in the cloudy water, bump their scales against their glass enclosure. "They apparently like to be inside there," I said, reading from the signs that were posted on the walls and obscured by the heads of dozens of other irritated Saturday fathers and their listless children. I looked down at Sam. "If they were out in the real world, they'd be in a cave and that would be small too."

Sam seemed unmoved by this information.

"You don't have to feel sorry for them," I assured him, assuming without evidence that he did.

"I don't," he answered. "Someone feeds them every day."

Taken aback, and inexplicably guilty, I said, "But someone feeds you every day too."

"You don't feel sorry for me either," he said.

I stopped to consider his logic. It was beyond me and I responded, as I often did, by offering to buy him something. "You want to go to the gift shop?" I said as we headed toward the door.

"Nope, too crowded."

I looked at the shop, which was indeed crowded, mostly with kids screaming to lure their parents in or to prevent them from forcing an exit. Sam appeared to be the only child in America who didn't want a gift. I looked down at him with a mixture of pride and mystification. And he looked back at me as if he was completely puzzled that I didn't take him for granted.

And now a month later we were back in the car still trying to figure each other out. This had become increasingly our pattern in the last year or so. It had been three years since the divorce. For the first year, maybe even longer, we still treated each other like we were breakable. He never cried or complained when we were together; I would suggest something—anything—and he would agree enthusiastically. Joan told me, tiredly, that he was a terror at home with her, and I said almost proudly, thinking maybe I was actually doing something right, that he never was with me. "He's afraid of losing you," she said, and just the thought of that made me so sad that I redoubled my efforts to pamper and reassure him.

And then, just after he started second grade, he changed. Maybe he had finally figured out that lots of kids had divorced parents and his situation was no more precarious than the others'. Maybe he was tired of tormenting his mother, who reported, with relief, that he was really a model child at home. Or maybe he was finally comfortable enough with me to try being a normal, rotten kid without fear of my packing my bags for the west.

He had no reason to fear that I would leave. If anything, in the years after the divorce, he had become even more the center of my life. Work occupied almost all of my non-Sam hours, but not much else of me. The company that years before had acquired my little start-up company had itself gotten acquired. A new set of executives from an even bigger headquarters with even bigger egos came through once again and spun even bigger plans. And once again, I got in good with the new guys. While many of the old management team departed, I got promoted.

I was now the senior vice president in charge of strategic planning. Basically I was in the business of looking for other start-ups to acquire. Whereas ten years ago I had been part of a company that was trying to make something, now I was trying to buy companies that were making something. I had more reports, my staff was bigger and smarter, my paycheck larger—beyond all expectation. By any conventional measure, other perhaps than satisfaction, I was a success.

Of course I had to work constantly, but when I wasn't with Sam, there was no reason not to. My number of old friendships had dwindled, in that way that happens when everyone gets older and busy with parenthood and career. I still dated, of course, or at least tried to. But the women I met through work were either superiors, subordinates, or competitors, and dating any of them was either unwise or illegal. And I had stopped meeting women outside work, because there was no outside work. Occasionally I'd meet women who were attractive at conventions or trade shows, but then we'd do something like exchange business cards and suddenly any chance of romance was asphyxiated. Dave kept suggesting I take out an ad or join a dating service, but I couldn't make myself do it. I think I wanted falling in love to happen the way it had with Joan—sudden, unexpected, out of the blue. But it doesn't happen that way for people who scheduled their lives in half-hour parcels.

And then, every once in a while, when I actually met someone I liked, and we got our schedules to mesh, and we worked our way through the first awkward dates, we would get to the point where you might actually start thinking about the future. But the only future I could imagine was the one I had already had and lost—living in my dream house with Joan and Sam. I couldn't bear trying for that again. And I couldn't bear, I suppose, admitting that I would never get it back.

So it came down to Sam and me. Each week, I marked off the days until our next weekend together, and the minute that weekend was over, I started planning the next one. And, sure enough, the more I cared and the harder I tried, the worse it got. Sam started turning into this kid I couldn't please and couldn't understand and at times couldn't even recognize. And so we wound up in the car on a Sunday afternoon in January, trying to figure out what to do with ourselves.

"I guess that's a no on the aquarium?" I asked.

He went back to the video game. He appeared to be killing lots of bad guys because he was grunting in satisfaction.

"I could buy myself one of those games and we could sit together on a park bench and play all day."

He looked up at me and smiled. He liked the fact that I might do exactly that and he'd have to be the one to say that it wasn't a normal thing for an adult to do. We smiled at each other and the car drove us through a moment of nothing but love. Then he remembered that he had attitude, and went back to his video game. I turned back to the windshield and tried to figure out where we were going.

"How about the ice show?" he asked, a faint note of hope hiding under the affected unconcern.

"The same one we went to last week?" I said; a slightly pained edge may have crept into my voice.

He fell silent; his finger started pounding the game buttons again. I saw his nose scrunch up and feared for a moment it was tears—a reaction I had grown increasingly frightened of as it became rarer.

"If you want to go to the ice show again, that's fine," I said repentantly. "I think we could still get tickets." I checked my watch. "We'd have to hurry because—"

"Forget it. It's stupid."

"No, it's fine."

"Nope. Stupid."

I sighed. "We could go ice-skating ourselves."

He made a movement like someone shivering. "How about a mall?" he countered.

"How about a movie?"

We both sighed. We pulled over and examined the movie ads, finding nothing that sat on the perfect equipoise between silliness and an R-rating. We sighed again.

And so we wound up doing what it seemed we did best—driving around. He put his hands up in the air and we jointly steered into a turn. I made a minute adjustment to the rearview mirror; he did the same to the air in front of him. He called out directions, I did the steering; the goal was to get thoroughly lost in the hope of finding an undiscovered spot that would provide us with whatever we needed.

We got off the highway at a random exit halfway to Boston. We wandered through unfamiliar-looking streets. And then, as we turned a corner, I recognized a couple of buildings and said, "This is Somerville. This is the town where I grew up."

Sam had put aside his video game by then and was reading a comic book that I wondered if I was supposed to permit him to have. "Look," I said again, louder this time. "This is right near where I used to live when I was your age. Up until I was ten. Before we moved."

We were twisting our way through narrow, up-and-down streets lined by triple-deckers tucked one next to the other behind a thin sprinkling of trees. We passed my old grade school, the classic red-brick, caged-window building, looming behind a chain-link fence and a moat of cement playground. I passed a corner storefront, the candy store where I used to buy licorice and baseball cards, now a business that charged poor people exorbitant fees to cash checks and wire money to even poorer relatives overseas.

"This neighborhood has changed," I murmured as I tried to remember exactly how to get to the street where my old house was. Suddenly I pulled over and stopped. "So what do you think?" I said proudly. "Quite a castle, huh?"

The house had only gotten shabbier since the day when my father, flush with his promotion to supervisor at the plant where he worked, had packed us up and moved us out to the suburbs where there were parks bigger than a single basketball court and kids in them whom I would never have to fear in a fight. It was a six-room house, one bathroom on the second floor, surrounded by a chain-link fence, sided with asbestos shingles and roofed with tar paper. Sam looked at it for a moment, then went back to his comic book.

"That's it?" I asked. I tapped his leg. "Come on. Let's check it out."

"It's cold and it's going to rain."

"It is not." I stepped out into the cold air. The sky was the gray of a winter suit. I felt a raindrop whip against my cheek.

I walked tentatively to the house, listening for the sound of my own voice from the backyard. The grass in the tiny backyard that my father had religiously mowed every Saturday was gone, covered with concrete by someone who no doubt took little pride in grooming an uneven, light-starved patch of dandelions. In my mind, I saw my father heave out the mower and heard the sound of the motor turning, smelled the tang of gasoline. I stood in the corner of the yard, hitting a plastic shuttlecock into the air with a slightly unstrung racket that my mother had given to me one birthday in the nervous hope that if we played lawn sports, our little patch of earth would become a lawn. I kept myself out of my father's way, afraid of the growl or worse that I'd get if I came too close to the mower, more afraid of that, of course, than of any possible injury from the blade. The raindrops splashed onto my face; I wondered if that was the only water on my cheeks.

I was quiet when I got back into the car. Sam was still absorbed in his comic book. I fought the urge to yank it out of his hands. He was only a kid. He had no obligation to comfort me.

"Can you imagine coming back to your house in twenty years, how funny that would be?" I asked, sounding plaintive even to my own ears.

He looked up to think about it. "No," he concluded. It was the simple truth. There would be no way he could imagine it and, if he could, he'd be an odd kind of being who in twenty years would experience memory in a way very unlike my own.

I turned the key in the engine and pulled away from the curb. We went up the street that I had looked back on so regretfully from the rear of our station wagon as my parents and I drove off, starting our journey up the ladder of success. It occurred to me that after we moved, we never returned for a visit.

"You know what that is?" I asked as we got to the top of the hill. Without waiting for the silence to become noticeable, I went on. "It's a fort. This is Prospect Hill and this is a fort from the Revolutionary War. It's where the Americans fought off the British." I vaguely recalled a class trip when we were shepherded by some long-suffering teacher who was overburdened by boys and girls more intent on their own struggle for liberty than on their nation's. "Or maybe it was where the British retreated."

I looked down at Sam, who stared up at me with blank eyes.

"You've heard of the Americans and the British, right?" I asked. "Do you happen to know who won?"

He smiled at that. He liked it when I got exasperated. Sarcasm didn't work because he didn't believe that I could actually intend to wound him.

"I ran away from home once and hid out here," I said.

"Seriously?"

I was amazed that I had caught his interest. "Well, yeah. I was nine. Just a year older than you." We had stopped in front of the dilapidated old fort that appeared to be an orphan of historic preservation. There was a plaque, unveiled by self-aggrandizing Depression-era politicians whom subsequent generations of kids had passed judgment on with cans of spray paint. The fort was deserted, much as I remembered it on the day I had come running up here because a fort was the closest thing I could find to a sanctuary, which was what I really needed. "I was in big trouble," I said, smiling.

Sam seemed intrigued. His life was not much cribbed by restriction, so the concept of being in trouble was novel to him.

"I had stolen a bicycle."

He squinted. "Like, for real?"

"Well, I borrowed it, really. From a kid down the street. My dad had taken my own bike away because I kept on leaving it in the driveway. And then I smashed up the kid's bicycle and I knew I was going to get caught and get killed so I ran away from home. This is where I came."

I stepped outside, feeling the wind whip around me. There was barely any light out now. Sam was still sitting in the car, but he had put aside his comic book and had rolled down the window just a crack, unwilling to embrace the outside but still wanting a point of contact.

"Did they find you?" he called out.

"Eventually."

I looked at him for a second. He was half wondering, half skepti-
cal. He had already figured out I wasn't the idol he might once have
imagined, but he still wasn't quite sure why. Finally, he asked, "After
how long?"

I paused again, wondering how much to tell, how much to make
up. "A couple of days."

"You're kidding?"

I smiled. I had finally impressed him. "In those days we were
tougher than you kids, man."

He sank back in his seat and appeared to think.

"I'm going inside the fort," I said. I waited a moment for him to
follow me and then headed off, my pride hurt and not wanting to
show it. I poked at the door that I remembered leading up to the
stairs, but it was barred. I walked around the circular perimeter of the
fort, which was really more of a powder house and had probably had
a very undistinguished military career in actual fact. I kicked at the
frozen dirt and then, clapping my arms around my chest, I turned to
look out over the horizon. I could see my old city stretch before me,
in all its lopsided, bunched-together glory, a vista of flat roofs, squat
buildings, and occasional church steeples. I took a few steps down the
grassy side of the hill; I could hear the ground crunch beneath my
feet. We had come here as little kids, mainly to spy on the older kids
who used the spot to smoke cigarettes and court one another, occu-
pations we professed to despise and yet wanted to study at great
length. I slid a little on my way down and remembered, or thought I
did, crawling along here on my belly, fighting some elaborate game of
combat or chase. The gray cloud that had followed me since I was at
my old house now was chased off by the cold wind; looking down
from my vantage point, I felt like someone who had grown up as he
was meant to, who had traveled and was entitled to come back with
a small, secret sense of heroism. Then I remembered how late it was
and turned back, slipping and sliding as I scrambled up the hill. I
was sweating under my heavy coat when I got back to the car. It was
empty.

I called Sam's name. I looked around. I called his name again. I ran down one street, then another. No one was outside. I thought of strangers who would lure him into their car and I raced back to my car, hot to drive off in pursuit. Then I thought of Sam wandering off and coming back to find me gone and I resolved to wait. Then I pictured the abductor again and wanted to call the police. My head was cleared of every thought, every recollection but a desperate desire to find Sam.

Standing beside my car, I started pounding my head against the thin metal of the roof. How could I have left him alone? How could I have been mean to him about the ice show? How could I have failed him in all the ways that I must have?

I called and called his name. Nothing on the street moved—not a window opened, not a person appeared. I would have to go to the police and hope they could help save me from my failure as a parent. I'd have to tell Joan. I'd have to let the world see just how poor a father I'd been. Slowly, reluctantly, I got back in my car. My jaw shaking, I put the key in the ignition, pushed the transmission into drive, and then, just as I was about to pull away, I saw it. A tiny bush at the edge of the fort, which had been standing when I pulled up, was now bent over. I got out of the car and walked over to it.

Sure enough, just at ground level, hidden by the bush, was an opening in the fort wall. It was covered by planks but when I pushed them, they moved away from a window, held on loosely by a nail on top. I stuck my head into the dank interior of the fort and called Sam's name. There was silence. I pulled my head out, then started to climb, one leg first, through the window. I heard the fabric of my pants tear as I shimmied myself inside. I got my leg through and, straddling the windowsill, I swung the rest of me in and fell four feet to the ground.

There was barely enough light to make my way to the stairs. It was a rickety metal staircase that was much as I remembered. It circled around and around the interior of the fort, passing little slits through which muskets might once have been thrust. The stairs shook beneath me as I got to the top landing and entered a little room under the crown of the fort. Sam was sitting in the middle of the floor, letting me see every gap in his smile.

I don't even remember what I shouted at him. When he saw how angry I was, his smile crumpled quickly and without a trace. I kept my distance from him for fear of what I would do if he were in arm's length. My mind still racing with fear and relief, I turned as if to leave, then turned back, and then away and then back again, jerking about like a figure in a silent movie and shouting the entire time. When I wore myself out, I just leaned back against the wall and stared at him. "And you have nothing to say?" I asked.

He shook his head, dazed.

I threw up my hands. "All right, let's go." He got up, moving carefully as he passed me. We were halfway down the stairs when he stopped and looked up, his head lifted in as defiant a way as his small size and fearful state would let him. "You did it."

"Did what?" I stared at his little chin, trembling as he stuck it out in the air. I opened my mouth and shut it. "You mean, that story I told you?" I squatted down so my face was level with his. "Sammy, that was just a story."

"It wasn't true?"

"Well, no, it was true. But that doesn't mean you could just run off like that and terrify me."

"But you did."

"But you're little. You could have killed yourself."

"I didn't."

"But you could have frozen to death."

And suddenly he smiled. "These days we're tougher than you kids were."

I bit my lip so I wouldn't smile. He stood and waited for the stern look to pass from my face. I felt myself hold my brows in a furrow, my lips pinched together. He kept smiling and then, when he saw nothing was coming, he took a step up the stairs and, without warning, kissed me on the cheek.

I sat back on a step, my mouth open, and watched him march down the stairs, his narrow shoulders straight and his head held up to claim victory.

12

The afternoon after I saw Dr. Sprague, I was sitting at the computer in my office, pounding out imperative E-mails to my staff, when my secretary, Carol, walked in. "There's a lawyer out here to see you."

I didn't even stop pounding. "If it's a lawyer, send him to legal. God, the last thing I want to waste time with is a lawyer."

Carol didn't budge. She had been my secretary for years now. She was a smart woman, in her mid-forties, the sole support of a teenaged boy. She was one of the last smokers in the entire office and I'd often see her on my way into the building in the morning, huddled in a corner, no matter how rainy or cold, savoring that last minute's smoke before she had to go inside. She often seemed tired, and every once in a while I caught a look that told me she was feeling none too patient with my demands, but she worked hard and well. Each year, when I fought to get her the highest raise possible, she acknowledged it with the truly sincere gratitude that is reserved for large sums of money.

I kept on E-mailing for a moment, then looked up irritably, as if I was about to ask why she was still there. Her voice was small but firm. "He says he's *your* lawyer."

I was prepared to rebuke Barry for dropping by unannounced, but, when I saw the expression on his face as he stepped into my office, I somehow knew better than to open my mouth. He walked in confidently, dropped his beat-up briefcase on one of the two angular, chrome-and-leather chairs that sat facing my desk, then parked himself in the other. He didn't say anything, but instead unabashedly examined his surroundings—the large desk, the long conference table, the view over downtown Boston with the airplanes lifting off from Logan Airport and the boats drifting about the harbor. He raised his eyebrows just a bit and said, "Impressive." My office was about twice the size of his, but still I knew better than to say anything.

He tried to sink back in the chair, which was the type of office furniture designed to make the user more alert than comfortable. I told Carol not to interrupt us with calls. Then I waited.

"I got a call from your ex-wife's lawyer today. What's her name— Marjorie? She was calling to convey something of a bombshell."

I still waited, although no longer with any optimism.

"Seems that Mrs. Morrison told her that you aren't the boy's biological father. She says that you already know this fact. That you took a blood test to find it out and told Mrs. Morrison about it yourself."

"And?" I asked, my face expressionless.

"So this isn't a big surprise?"

"Obviously not."

"Were you going to tell me?"

"No."

He sighed and dropped his head back to stare at the ceiling. "Well, you know," he said finally, addressing the fluorescent light overhead instead of me, "this does change everything."

"Why?"

"Because our theory was that you're asserting your rights as the boy's father to see him. But now you're not the father. So I'm wondering what we're asserting."

"I have rights under the divorce agreement, don't I?"

"I suppose so. But the judge is going to make her decision based on the best interests of the child today, not based on what you and Mrs. Morrison agreed to eight years ago. And this new information might make her view that question differently." Barry paused. "According to Marjorie, Mrs. Morrison says that the boy doesn't want to see you now. He's apparently 'devastated,' to use her word."

I sank back in my chair. I stared blankly at my computer screen, watching the faint flicker of the cursor where my last E-mail had stopped in mid-command. I turned slightly and looked out my window, watching a plane's slow ascent from the runway. "So Sam knows?"

"Apparently. You didn't tell him yourself?"

"No. Joan must have." I swung around and pounded my hand on the desk. "Why did she do that?"

I looked at Barry as if he might know the answer. His high brow furrowed appraisingly, as if he were trying to get me straight. Then he asked, "Were you planning on ever telling the boy?"

I shook my head. "No. Why would I do that?"

"Then why did you take the blood test?"

Once more, I shook my head. I just no longer knew why I had done what I had done, what I had once thought or planned or imagined. "I needed to know," I said, my voice sounding like that of someone who had just awakened from a deep sleep. "I had no idea what I would do once I found out. But I just needed to know."

"And now that you know, does it make a difference?"

I looked at him quizzically.

He repeated his question. "Does it make a difference? In how you feel about Sam?"

"No." I stopped. "It makes me afraid I'll lose him. That's all. And I don't want to lose him."

Barry shifted in his chair. "I called the clerk and canceled the hearing that was set for this Friday."

"Why?" I shouted.

"Because if we go into court now, we'll be killed. The court psychologist's report is in our favor, but the psychologist didn't know about this information when she wrote it, so her recommendation is as good as irrelevant. And if the boy is really saying he doesn't want to see you, if he really is devastated by the news and the mother believes that seeing you would only make it worse—*and* there still are the allegations about you assaulting Mrs. Morrison—then given all ⟨ ⟩ why would the judge go out on a limb and rule in your favor? From her point of view, you created this mess."

"So how do I get Sam back?"

"At this point, Mrs. Morrison gets to say when you get Sam back. And I don't see her leaning your way anytime soon."

I nodded, thought for a moment, then stood up. "Barry, I'll call you. I need to think about this."

He got up reluctantly, picked up his briefcase, dusted it off with a few quick swipes as if it had been resting on the ground. He looked around the office once more, taking it all in. "Nice digs." He smiled. "You're obviously a smart guy, Pete. Take my advice and think carefully before you do another dumb thing."

A minute after Barry left, I called Joan up and told her I was coming over. She tried to protest, but I begged her and she said all right. I walked out of work and drove straight to her home; I was there within an hour.

Joan was waiting on the steps to the front porch when my car pulled up. It was a sunny day. I headed up the front walk, my arms at my sides, my steps slow, trying to look calm and reasonable.

"Nice day, isn't it?" I said as pleasantly as I could.

"I still have a restraining order, you know. I could call the police on you for coming here."

"But that's not fair."

She shrugged. "You're suddenly concerned about what's fair?" She was wearing shorts and a T-shirt; she had a glass of iced tea on the step next to her. She picked it up and took a sip, not taking her eyes off me for a moment.

I lifted my head to peer through a window into the house. It was dark inside.

"Sam's at school," Joan said. "And I've arranged for someone to pick him up afterward, so he won't be coming back here today. So don't think you're waiting around to see him."

"Joan, please . . . "

She reached behind her and picked up a portable phone. "Nine, one, one. That's all it takes to get rid of you, Pete."

"The cops didn't believe you once, why would they believe you this time?"

"Because this time I have a witness." She leaned over so she could see past me, and pointed at the Steiners' house just down the street. "I told Julie to keep an eye out. That's her right there." I swung around and saw Julie standing inside the Steiners' picture window. Then I turned back to Joan.

"Joan, have a heart. Just let me see him."

"He doesn't want to see you."

I hadn't really believed that until this moment. Ever since I had gotten the results of the blood test, in the midst of the panic and confusion, I had felt nothing stronger than the urge just to hold on to him, to hold on at least to what we had. I still wanted him, even if he wasn't mine. I was only now realizing that he might not want me, because I wasn't his.

I looked at Joan's face and saw a kind of satisfaction. He was still hers, and she didn't have to share him.

"I told him," she said.

My voice was so low and blurry I could barely hear it myself. "I know. Why did you do that?"

She shook her head angrily, her blond hair slipping out from behind her ears and falling around her shoulders. I thought of our first night together, as she backed toward her bed, her eyes never moving from mine; then the light went out on that image and I felt the hot sun beating down on us.

"Did you think he would never find out?" she asked in a contemptuous voice.

I said nothing.

"Answer me." Her voice was rising. I had never seen her this furious before. It made my legs tremble. "Did you think he would never find out?" she repeated.

"I was trying to figure out what to say to him," I said feebly.

"When?" She waited a minute. "How? What were you going to say? How did you think he would react?" It was as if, with each question, she was slapping my face. Her face flushed with excitement, she said, "You didn't think about anything but yourself. So I had to tell him." She stopped short, as if she was remembering that moment. "I finally realized that I couldn't keep it a secret forever. And I wasn't going to let you tell him. I wasn't going to let you paint me out to be—" She stopped again; I could see her swallow, as if she could taste her own guilt. "I knew it would hurt him, but at least if I told him, I thought I could make it a little better." Then she looked up at me with hard eyes. "And I wanted him to know that you had brought all this down on us by taking that blood test. I saw him sitting in that psychologist's office like some innocent lamb, pleading to see you and not understanding why I didn't want him to. I couldn't bear it. I couldn't bear what you had done to him."

I tried to picture her telling him, imagining where they sat, how they looked. My mind couldn't hold the picture steady. Trying simply to breathe, I asked, "How'd he take it?"

"He cried."

"And then?"

"He fell asleep." Something in her face seemed to catch. "He cried a long time and then he fell asleep."

We were both silent for a while, wrapped in the quiet of a weekday afternoon on a suburban street, the low hum of cars driving in the distance, the faint sound of a lawn mower half a mile away. I could feel my hands clench and unclench, the palms damp with sweat. When I was finally able to speak, I asked, "What did you say to him?"

"I just told him the truth."

"You remembered how?"

She expelled a breath that was like an explosion. "*You're* the liar." She leaned forward, holding the phone in front of her like a gun.

"You lied in court. You stood there in court and lied and said you had never come here. You stood in front of that judge and called me a liar."

"You *were* a liar. You wrote in the affidavit that I choked you. That I assaulted you. God, Joan, I didn't do that." I threw my hands up in the air. "Joan, why in God's name did you go to court in the first place? We could have worked it out between us."

"After you took Sam even though I told you not to?"

"But you had no right to keep him—"

"I'm his mother, Pete. I had every right."

"Well, I'm his—" I caught myself. I couldn't even look at her. I turned away and saw Julie Steiner still at the window; she probably wished she had binoculars.

I took another deep breath and started talking in my calmest, flattest voice. "I'm sorry I came to the house that day and scared you. I don't know what got into me. I never expected you to keep him from me."

"I wasn't going to. Not forever. I was still in shock from when you told me about the blood test. I didn't know what I was going to do. I hadn't even had the courage to call the doctor's office yet. I just wanted a couple of days to figure it out."

Suddenly I was on my knees in front of her. I put out my hands and placed them on her bare thighs. The smooth skin was warm from the sun; she didn't flinch. "Let's just go back to the way things were, okay?" I pleaded. "We can forget about this whole thing."

"We can't now. He knows you're not his father." She put her hands on mine and, grabbing them tightly, pulled them off her legs and dropped them. "Besides, it's just as well. We couldn't go on living that way, with you suspecting and him not knowing and me—" She caught herself, shook her head. "Me hoping, hoping that what's happened would never happen. I suppose, bad as this is, we're better off getting it all out in the open." She stood up, brushing her shorts with one hand.

"Joan, I need to see him. Don't do this to me."

She shook her head. "You should have thought about that before you took the blood test."

I slammed my hand on the step. "Don't blame me for getting that blood test. I knew something was wrong. And I was right. He isn't my kid. Don't pretend it's the same. Don't tell me I should feel the same."

"I'm sorry for you—"

I was standing up now. "You're *sorry* for me. Listen, I've done nothing wrong here. I was faithful, I supported you, I gave you this fucking house—"

"You *gave* me? You gave me nothing, mister. Everything you ever put out had a string attached. You thought you owned me. And now you're just about to find out differently." She turned toward the front door. When she got it half open, she swung around toward me again and stuck the phone right in my chest. "And I swear to God, if you come near this house or near my son again, I'll have your ass arrested, and don't you think for a second I won't."

The door slammed in my face. When I turned, Julie Steiner was still standing at the picture window, her arms folded across her chest, shaking her head back and forth.

———

The next day I sat in my car outside Sam's school as they let the classes out. I tried to sit still when I saw the doors open and the first scraggly group of kids emerge. They came out in threes and fours, usually hunch-shouldered and weary-looking, dragging their feet down the stone steps. I kept my hands clenched to the steering wheel; the window was rolled up, so I wouldn't blow it by sticking my head out and shouting. It seemed like all the tension in my body was funneled down to my left leg, which kept pumping up and down frantically. I had no plan, really, I had thought out no dialogue, and I had deliberately blocked from my mind any thought of consequences. I just knew that I wanted to see him again and it seemed impossible that this might not happen.

He came out with four other boys. They were all dressed alike, baggy jeans, oversize jackets with the insignia of one of the city's sports teams on their backs, baseball caps pushed forward on their heads so that you couldn't see a patch of hair on any of them. They all had indistinguishable, tiny faces peeking out from a mound of synthetic fiber sportswear, like a knight in armor looking out through a visor.

The five boys stopped just outside the entrance gate and hung there, not talking or moving. Several groups of girls walked by, but there was no interaction; one girl turned to say something, but the boys, in unison, looked down and failed to respond. Then four of the boys started to peel off; they seemed to be encouraging Sam to join them, but he shook his head no. There was some back and forth; one of them actually took Sam's arm and tried to pull him, but Sam shrugged him off. And throughout this entire interaction not one of them looked another in the eyes.

Then, amazingly, when the parting seemed inevitable, they began to shake hands, only the handshakes were not quick-pump business formalities; they entwined their thumbs, pressed their palms together, and then slid them apart, executing all these movements with the deliberateness of a Japanese tea ceremony. And then Sam headed down the road to his house on his own.

I started my engine and followed him, going a few miles an hour and hugging the side of the road as much as I could. A car pulled out of the school lot and came up behind me; the driver, a middle-aged woman, obviously a teacher, who wanted nothing more than to put this locale behind her, pounded her horn angrily at my slowness. Sam turned, saw my car, and turned away. He didn't speed up or stop. I had no idea if he had even realized who I was.

But then, when he had turned the corner and walked a hundred or so yards farther, out of sight of the school building, he stopped and stood still. I pulled up beside the curb and sat there. For a few moments neither of us moved. Then I pressed the button to lower the window and leaned my head out into the sticky June weather.

"Hey, guy, need a lift?"

"Not really."

"Well, come on in anyway. It's hot out there."

"I'm fine."

"Please come in, Sam. I want to talk with you."

He kept standing there, his arms folded over his chest.

"Aren't you hot in that jacket?" I asked, trying to sound pleasant. "It's practically summer."

He said nothing.

"You must be doing exams now, right? Isn't school almost over?"

He shrugged.

"You want to go somewhere? We could take in a movie."

No response.

"How about the mall?"

He sighed. "Someone could see us together."

"So what?"

He looked at me, more pitying than resentful, like I was still trying to sell him on Santa Claus or the stork. "I know about the court order."

"Okay," I said, turning off the engine. I opened the car door and stepped outside; when he saw me get out, he made a sudden movement, like he would bolt, and I froze. We stood there, looking at each other across the roof of the car. "I guess your mother told you?" I said.

He looked down at the ground, kicking some invisible stone off the curb. He didn't react, didn't look up or even acknowledge my presence. His face was blank—neither angry, nor sad, nor any of the things that I would have imagined him to be. He was a mystery to me, more than he had ever been.

"I wanted to tell you that day, when we went to get clams—"

"But you didn't." He kept looking down while he spoke; I could barely hear his voice.

"I choked." I felt so helpless I thought I would start crying and fought it, trying to stiffen my trembling jaw; then I thought, What the hell, let him see it. But it was too late. I had frozen. When I spoke, my voice was dry and cracked. "I have no idea what to say to you about this, Sam. I mean, there's nothing that can prepare you for this. I can't even think about it, really." I looked over at him. He still wasn't facing me, but he had slipped his backpack off his shoulders and dangled it in front of him, his eyes fixed on it as it swung slowly back and forth. "I mean, do you even understand it?" I asked. "Do you get what happened?"

He shrugged. "Mom said you got a test to find out you're not my father." Finally he looked at me. I could see he had stiffened his jaw too. Why would he do this just as I did if he hadn't been born with it? He was looking at me and waiting; I said nothing. "So, is it true?" he asked.

I shrugged. "I guess so. I mean, yes. It is true. That's what the doctor said."

He looked away. "Mom said I have another father."

I made no sound, not wanting to react. Then I said, "Did she say anything else?"

"No, she started to cry. She said we couldn't talk about that now, that we just had to get used to being a family, the two of us. She said we would be fine."

"Without me?"

He nodded. His eyes were squinting as he stared into the sun that hung over my head, scorching the back of my neck.

"Did she tell you that you shouldn't be seeing me anymore?"

He shrugged. "She said it would confuse me."

"That's not what I want."

"Then why did you get the blood test?" His voice broke and, hearing it, he flushed with shame.

I started trying to form words. I kept nodding and not coming up with an answer. And then I was just shaking my head. "I don't know."

He heaved the backpack back onto one shoulder. "You must have thought I wasn't yours?"

I nodded again.

" 'Cause you thought I wasn't as good as you?"

"No, no, that wasn't it." I moved toward him, my hand stretched out, and he stepped back. He was huddled inside his massive jacket. His skinny, knobby fingers, the skin broken into half a dozen scrapes and bruises, clung to the strap of his backpack. I saw the pink flesh where he had gnawed at the corners of his fingernails and wondered if this was something new or if he had always done this and I had just never noticed.

"Come on, Sam. At least look at me."

He shook his head. I moved closer and tried to touch his shoulder; as if by reflex, his arm swung out and hit mine. We both jumped back, frightened, and stood there, staring into the empty space between us where a moment before he had struck me.

"I shouldn't be seeing you anymore," he said. "There's a court order. We could get in trouble. Mom told me."

"But I can change that."

He shook his head violently, fighting back tears. "No, you can't. You can't do anything anymore. You're not my father."

"You're just saying that because your mother told you to. She's wrong, she's the cause of all this—"

"At least she's *my* mother."

We were on a quiet street lined with maples; in front of each house was a row of bushes, all in full bloom, pink and white, azaleas and rhododendrons. The grass was its newest green. This was the week when everything looked perfect; people worked all year to make it look this way.

My mouth was dry; I tried to swallow and couldn't. I was afraid to move. I wanted to pull him in the car and drive off, and I knew there was no chance we could even touch. He spent a few minutes staring at the ground and then lifted his head. He was looking at me as if I was just some man who had let him down. "Listen, Dad," he said, then stopped. "I mean, Pete." He waited; I said nothing. "I won't tell anyone that you came by today, okay?"

I nodded my head. "Thanks."

He headed off, then stopped, as if he had remembered something. He turned back to me and reached out his hand. I thought of the boys outside the school, shaking hands, with their thumbs up and their heads down. My eyes blurred and I stood there, my hands pressed down on my thighs. Then I took his hand and held it for a second in the air between us. "You take care, okay?" I said. He nodded, straightened up, and turned to walk back toward his home.

13

I was sitting in Barry's office the day after I saw Sam. I had walked in, my head down, and announced that I had gotten nowhere with Joan and needed help. I looked up and saw Barry's face displaying a struggle between frustration and relief. Frustration because his whole legal strategy had collapsed. Relief for some reason I could not imagine, perhaps only because I was now so completely dependent on him.

I hadn't been at work since I had seen Sam. I sat in my house, going over and over in my head how I could get out of this, how I could get Sam back. Since the blood test, the whole world was different; the only thing that had stayed the same was that the minute I stopped seeing Sam, I wanted to see him again.

I didn't say any of this to Barry, of course. Instead, I talked about how I had visited Joan and tried to patch things up. I brushed away his rebukes about disobeying the restraining order, and just kept talking in a flat, expressionless voice. As I spoke, his mind appeared to be working, his eyes fixed on me. I wondered if he always anticipated this moment whenever a new client walked into his office. Perhaps he had looked at me that first day when I came in, with my tie tied straight and my mind made up, and he had known that it would only be a matter of time before I was floundering about, grasping at straws that had already blown away.

And when I finished, we sat in silence, him watching me and waiting for me to keep talking, me indulging myself in the only bit of control I had, which was to sulk and say nothing and make him respond. If he had had nothing else to do that day, I would have sat there for hours, the time ticking away against the retainer I had given him. He waited for a while and then began to speak in a take-charge way.

"All right. Let's review the bidding. Mrs. Morrison doesn't want you to see the child for whatever reason. Maybe she's angry with you for getting the test. Maybe she sincerely believes it would hurt the child to see you. Maybe she is afraid that you will try to turn the child against her, by getting him to think about how it came to be that you weren't his father. Maybe it's all of those things. Now, if she was starting from scratch, she might have a very hard time getting a judge to take away your visitation rights. But as it is, the restraining order is in place. It's our burden to try to get it lifted."

"And how do we do that?" I asked.

"There'd be a hearing on whether Mrs. Morrison was telling the truth when she said that you came to her house and assaulted her. And you would testify that you didn't. Correct?" He eyed me carefully. I looked away. The fight was gone from me. He sighed. "If we don't contest Mrs. Morrison's version of events, then your visitation rights would be restored only if the judge found that to be in the child's best interests. It would be a very difficult sell, especially since the boy says he doesn't want to see you."

I shook my head, feeling defeated. "Let's just forget it all," I said bitterly, swiping my hand in the air.

Barry got a little smile on his face. "Unfortunately, we can't do that. If we just 'forget it,' as you suggest, then the restraining order stays in place indefinitely. So you don't get to see the boy. And you continue to pay alimony and child support."

"And what if I just stopped paying?"

"Then Mrs. Morrison could have you held in contempt of court.

And your salary would be garnished. And, if you ever had to go back to court for anything, you'd be in very bad shape."

"So you're telling me there's nothing I can do?" I could hear the soprano whine of victimization in my voice, rising through the bass and the gravel. I felt as if I was being fired. I knew he had all the answers and there wasn't a single one of them I wanted to hear. But I thought somehow that if I just stayed there long enough he would figure out a way to save me.

It was as if he was reading my mind. "Let's try it this way," he said. "You tell me what you want."

"I want to see Sam."

Barry sighed. "Pete, I know this is difficult for you to grasp right now. But if what you tell me is true, if you're not the biological father, then you don't necessarily have the right to see him."

"That's ridiculous. Doesn't a father have any rights?"

He gave a little gray smile that I probably wasn't even meant to see. "Oh, the father has rights. Whoever he is. Of course, if he tries to assert them, then he's going to have to pay support. But that doesn't help you, exactly."

"But what if Sam had been Joan's kid, and then she and I got married, and we lived together? Are you telling me that then I wouldn't have any rights?"

"As a stepfather? No, you wouldn't have any rights. That's exactly what I'm telling you. If you and Mrs. Morrison got divorced, you'd have no right to see the child unless she let you."

"What if I had adopted him?"

"But you didn't."

"But I didn't have to. We were married. I thought he was mine."

"What you thought then doesn't matter now, in light of this"—he waved his hand—"this biological evidence."

"So let me adopt him now."

He shook his head again. "You can't adopt him without Mrs. Morrison's consent. And I doubt very much that she'd give it to you now."

"Why would I need her consent?"

"Because he's her child," he said impatiently. "A court isn't going to force her to let you adopt him. The fact of the matter is, when it comes to Sam and who sees him, her word is pretty much final. She's the parent. At this point, she's the only parent."

I shook my head, not willing to believe that I could be so boxed in. "You told me when I came in here the first time that there were always options. Tell me what they are."

He thought for a few moments. Then, folding his hands on his desk, he said, "Well, first thing, we can try to get rid of your obligation to continue paying child support."

"On what grounds?"

"Pete." He visibly reminded himself to be patient. "Because of the lack of paternity. No child, no child support. I think a judge might accept that."

"But I agreed to pay child support when we got divorced."

"You didn't agree. You were legally obligated to, because a father is legally obligated to support his child. But you're not the father. Or so it appears. So maybe you're not legally obligated to support him anymore."

I leaned back in my chair. "I don't care about the money. I'll pay double the child support. I'll pay her anything she wants if she lets me see Sam again."

"Of course, we could offer her that. But you've said in the past that she has enough money now. Maybe she wouldn't be very tempted by more money, especially if she's angry or frightened enough. But she might be very concerned about losing the money she has. She doesn't work, does she?"

"No. We agreed she would stay home and raise Sam and paint, and I would provide the money."

"So she's dependent on your income. Does she have family money?"

I was starting to see where Barry was going. I considered his question, then shook my head. "Her father was a big-shot lawyer, but he retired fifteen years ago, and her parents have been living it up since then. I'm sure they have some money they could give her. But not enough to float that house, that whole way of living. No. And she'd be too ashamed to ask."

"And do you think she would like to scale back her lifestyle?"

I smiled bitterly. "Joan? No. I think she likes where she lives just fine. She bitched so much about leaving the city when we bought the house, but she loved it when she got there. The house, the garden, the pool club. Joan grew up in that kind of suburb. I don't think she can imagine any other way of living." I paused. "Besides, she couldn't earn very much at all. She might be able to scale back her expenses a little—but to the point where she could make ends meet on her own?" I shook my head. "She couldn't do it."

"What about the biological father? He would have to support her, if she pursued him."

I thought for a second. "But what if he didn't have money?"

"He's going to have some money."

"Not as much as me."

Barry chuckled. He liked that. It was a sign that I was coming back to life. But then he got serious again. "Is that likely, Pete? I mean, I assume that this man was someone in your social circle."

I shook my head. "I don't think so. It could have been one of our friends, I suppose. But I really don't think it was any of those men. I've wracked my brain and I can't think of anyone."

"Since the divorce has she been involved with anyone?"

"No. Not to my knowledge. Certainly nothing serious. She always said one marriage was enough for her." I smiled ruefully. "I guess that wasn't a compliment. But you know, I think she liked her independence. No. There wasn't anybody else at the time of the divorce and there hasn't been anyone else serious since then. I'm sure of it."

"So it's likely been a long while since she's seen Sam's father. She may not even know where this man, whoever he is, now lives. Or what he does. She'd have to track him down."

"But she might not want to do that. Right?" My mind was working quickly now. "I mean, it would be a fight for her, wouldn't it? And in the meantime, there'd be no money coming in. She wouldn't like that. She might prefer to keep my money after all."

"But, given the circumstances, she might not be in a very good position to force you to keep paying. Unless you wanted to."

I sat up straighter. Barry was holding out hope, he was suggesting a way to make a deal. I saw myself back on the street, facing Sam, the sun beating down on my head. He was saying, "You can't do anything anymore. You're not my father." Only this time I had an answer. "I can do something," I was telling him. "I can win you back." I just needed time and opportunity. And Barry was showing me a way to get them both.

"So what you're saying is, you call Joan's lawyer and tell her that it's either Sam or the money. Right?"

Barry took off his eyeglasses, folded them up, and started tapping them lightly against his chin. "Well, it's not quite that easy. The judge would have to relieve you of your obligation to pay child support. The judge might not. She'd have to think about the child and she might not want to leave the child without support. I said that we could *ask* to get the support obligation lifted in light of this new information. But it might not work."

"But there's a chance it would. So there's a risk. And Joan won't want to take that risk, will she?"

"You know her better than I do, Pete."

"I do. And she'll be scared. She'll start thinking of what she'll have to do if she loses. She won't like that. And she's not so sure of herself right now, anyway. A part of her must know it's wrong to keep me from Sam, no matter how angry she is. Listen, I know her. She'll give in. Just call her lawyer. You'll see."

I stood up and started looking for the jacket that I had flung to the side when I sat down in his office. I was putting it on when Barry finally spoke. "Pete, there's one other thing you're not thinking about. The boy."

"What do you mean?"

"The boy says he doesn't want to see you."

I shook my head. "She put him up to that. She made him blame me for all this. But I can work on him. Leave that to me."

He watched me for a moment. "And you? Are you certain this is what you want?"

I stopped buttoning my jacket. "What are you asking?"

"There is another way. You could try to cut off your child support obligation altogether and just walk away."

"From Sam?"

"Who is not your son, after all. Maybe it's not in either of your interests to continue this relationship. Is that something you've considered?"

I shook my head. "No. Not at all." I turned around and headed to the door. He called my name, but I didn't stop. "Leave Sam to me," I said over my shoulder. "You take care of Joan."

He was still calling my name when I closed the door behind me.

14

When Marcia opened the door to her house, the first thing she did was reach out and touch my arm. For a second, I thought an insect was crawling on it.

"Peter, please come in," she said. She laid emphasis on the word "please," as if I might refuse despite the fact that I had driven across town expressly to have dinner with her and Dave. I stuck out the bottle of wine that I had found buried at the back of my kitchen cabinet. "This is so sweet," she said, taking it. "Please come in."

Marcia motioned for me to sit in the living room. Before she and Dave had gotten married, she had run a social services agency. She stopped working when her first child was born, and since then she had been in the process of taking over every parents' committee in every school or program that either of her daughters attended. She was forceful and competent and always in search of a project. I feared that I had become the next one.

As I stepped into the living room, Dave came out from the kitchen. He and Marcia stood side by side, facing me, leaning together with sad faces. They were like an American Gothic with compassion.

I collapsed on the couch and looked around, hoping for something to drink. Dave and Marcia pulled two chairs forward and sat next to each other. They both had their hands folded on their laps. They wanted me to tell them everything.

But just at that moment, their older daughter, Daphne, ran up the stairs from the family room. She and her younger sister, Ariel, were having a dispute over access to the television and Daphne, who believed herself to be the aggrieved party, required mediation. Dave and Marcia looked at each other accusingly, as if each expected the other to shirk the obligation. Then Dave sighed and got up, following Daphne downstairs.

That left Marcia and me sitting alone. "So, Peter," she said, "how are you doing?"

I shrugged. "Okay, I guess. I'm busy at work."

She ignored my answer. Her hands were still folded on her lap. "Dave told me everything. So you don't have to go through it all unless you want to."

"I'm not sure that Dave knows everything."

"How are you sleeping?"

"Alone." She blushed and I laughed nervously. "I'm sleeping okay. I have trouble getting out of bed in the morning sometimes."

"Depression is like that."

"I don't know that I am depressed."

The door to the family room downstairs banged open. We could hear the sound of the TV and of Daphne's and Ariel's voices both speaking at the same time. Dave was shouting, "That's final. And I don't want to hear another word about it." Then we heard him stomp up the stairs; when he walked into the living room, his face was flushed. "All set," he said to Marcia. Then he turned to me, stopped, and got that sad look on his face again. He sat down beside Marcia and they leaned toward each other again.

"Peter was just telling me how he's doing."

He nodded. "So you're hanging in there, Pete?"

"How are you eating?"

But before I could reassure them about my diet, the door downstairs banged open. Daphne called up, "Mom, when's dinner?" Then we heard the channel on the TV change, from the screeching of an electric guitar to the canned laughter of a sitcom. Daphne screamed. The door slammed shut again.

Marcia narrowed her eyes and looked at Dave. "All set?" she said through her teeth. Then she got up. "Peter, will you excuse me a moment?" She backed away, holding the compassionate expression until she got to the top of the stairs; then her look changed to one of determination and she headed down.

Dave watched her, and when she had disappeared, he rolled his eyes a little and turned back to me. "So, Pete, how's that lawyer I recommended?"

I shrugged. "He seems to know his stuff."

"Yeah, he's the man, from what I hear. What's he telling you?"

I smiled. "Well, we have a plan. I can get back my visitation rights, if I agree to keep giving Joan money."

"Money?" Dave shouted. "What the hell are you giving money to her for?"

The door downstairs slammed open again. The guitar was back on the TV set. Marcia's steps, brisker and quicker than Dave's, bounced up the stairs. She stopped at the top, brushed the wrinkles out of her pants, and then turned to us, her hands again folded in front of her.

"So, Peter, let me get you a soda."

"I'll get him a Scotch," Dave said, standing up.

"Dave, he's driving."

"He needs a Scotch. Marcia, you talk to him. He thinks he should keep giving Joan more money."

She sat down again in her chair and looked at me inquiringly. "And what do you hope to accomplish with that, Peter?"

I shrugged. "I just want to get things back the way they were. I think we're going to be able to work it out."

Dave walked back in, handing me a Scotch with one hand and holding his own with the other. He had brought nothing for Marcia. "What the fuck are you talking about, Pete?"

"I'm not sure I'm really following your thinking here, Peter. And, Dave, will you please watch your language."

"Well, it's something I've been discussing with that lawyer Dave recommended."

"You recommended a lawyer?"

Dave waved his hand in the air and leaned over toward me. "Why are you *paying* Joan money? You should be trying to get money back, for Christ's sake."

"I figure if I keep on supporting them, she'll let me keep seeing Sam."

"Peter, that's very nice of you, I'm sure, but do you really think that's realistic? And where did you get the name of a lawyer, Dave?"

"That bitch has no business getting her hands on any more of your money after what she did to you."

"*Language!* And what do you think she *did* to him, exactly?"

Dave started ticking off on his fingers. "She got the house, she got half his retirement, most of his savings."

"But she was entitled to that. You said at the time it was a fair settlement."

"You said it was fair. I thought it was crazy."

"You are being very hostile to Joan. Not that she and I were ever close." Marcia turned to me. "I'm sorry, Peter. But, I'm just a little concerned about what you're trying to do here. Do you really think you're going to be able to go back to the way things were?"

"Yeah, Pete, wake up, for God's sake. You think you're just going to pick up with Sam where things left off, like nothing happened? You think it's going to just go on like you're his father?"

"Why not? I've been his father for thirteen years. I'm the only father he knows."

"But now he knows different. And you know different. You think you're going to feel the same?"

For a second, the door to that part of myself where I kept my deepest fears creaked open and I said, "He's not my son. Not my biological son. And that does mean something to me. Maybe it shouldn't. But it does. It's like all these expectations, all these beliefs I've had for years have been snatched away from me." I tried to slow myself down. "But I can get past that. I have to. I can't just let him go. He's all I have."

Marcia sighed; she was being patient with me because I was a man and therefore disabled where emotions were concerned. "It's not about what you have or what you want to have, Peter. It's about what you can give him."

"Give him? I've given him everything. A house, an education, all the goddamn toys and games and activities he wants—"

She sighed. "I wasn't talking about those things. I was talking about what you'd be able to give him emotionally. You have to make your child number one in your life. Are you able to do that, knowing he's not your biological son?"

"That's it exactly, Pete," Dave said, shouting excitedly. "You think you're going to be able to look at him and not always be wondering who his father is, whether he's acting like him or looking like him?"

"Peter, I hate to say this. But Dave does have a point. Although he's not expressing it very well." She shot a look at her husband, then turned back to me. "After all, this news has to make some kind of difference to Sam. For one thing, he's going to want to have a relationship with his father. His own father. His other father. You know what I mean. What if he wants to do that? Are you really going to be able to accept that?"

"If he was adopted, I would."

"For God's sake, Pete. Adoption is something you do when you have no other choices."

Marcia rolled her eyes. "Dave, I don't know where you get these ideas of yours. That is simply not true."

"Oh, cut the crap. Pete is still a young man. He can get married again, have another kid. And how do you think you're going to feel if that happens, Pete? How do you think your new wife is going to feel about you paying half your income to some woman who's raising some other guy's child? And how do you think your real kid is going to feel?"

"Sam is a real kid," I said.

Dave sank back in his chair and closed his eyes. "Come on, Pete, you know what I mean. Sam is a great kid. I love Sam. But you can't just ignore the facts."

Marcia glared at him, then turned back to me, leaning forward anxiously, her hands still folded on her lap. "You know, Peter, I think it's very commendable of you to want to maintain your relationship with Sam. And of course you're going to continue to have feelings about him. But I wonder if it's the best thing—for him, I mean—if you continue clinging—" She stopped herself. "Well, maybe that's not the right word. If you continue *investing* in a father-son relationship when you're not sure if you're going to be able to"—she paused again, then took a breath—"maintain that kind of commitment over the long term."

"Maintain a commitment?" Dave exploded. "For God's sake, he's committed to supporting that bitch for the rest of his fucking life unless he does something about it."

"She was his wife, Dave. And she gave him eight years of her life."

Dave laughed an ugly laugh. "Obviously she was giving some of it to someone else. So why should Pete have to pay the full price?"

Marcia stood up. "Dave, that is an absolutely disgusting thing to say. I certainly hope that you don't think—"

The door downstairs shot open. It was Daphne. "Mom, Ariel's changing the channel again."

Dave jumped up and started shouting, "If you two don't stop it, so help me I'm going to go down there and—"

Marcia was on her feet too. "Don't you dare threaten them. Pay no attention to Daddy, dear."

The TV changed channels. There was a bang, then a squawk. "Ariel, you butthead."

"Daphne, where did you learn that word—"

"Dad, Daphne won't give me the remote—"

"Daphne, quit screaming like that—"

"Dave, you're the one who's shouting—"

"Mom, I am starving—"

Dave and Marcia were both leaning over the banister shouting down the stairs at their daughters. Their backs were toward me. My glass of Scotch was empty. I got up and backed out of the living room, afraid they would hear me. I didn't have to worry.

I made my way upstairs and found my coat lying in one of the bedrooms. I put it on and looked at myself in the mirror. There was a family picture, framed in brass, sitting on top of their bureau. It was the picture they had sent out on their cards last Christmas. The four of them were posed around a pile of autumn leaves, all wearing new sweaters and big smiles. I picked it up and looked at it, ignoring the noise downstairs, the shouting and the TV, the footsteps on the stairs, the doors slamming; I ran my finger over the glass and looked at the faces underneath. Daphne had Dave's coloring; Ariel had Marcia's eyebrows. Ariel would be tall and thin like her father. Daphne would have to battle her weight like Marcia did. I put the picture down and walked out.

When I got downstairs, Dave was in the kitchen banging dishes. I didn't go in to say good-bye. From below, in the basement, I heard Ariel crying and Marcia trying to comfort her.

I pushed open the front door and almost tripped over Daphne, who was sitting at the top of the steps, hugging her scraped knees up to her chest.

"Oh hi, sweetie," I said. "Listen, will you just tell your parents I wasn't feeling well and had to go home?"

"Lucky you. Will you take me too?"

I patted her head. "You be good, Daphne. And listen, why don't you let Ariel watch the TV sometimes, okay?"

She laughed. "All right."

I was halfway down the walk when she called my name. I turned around and faced her across the dark lawn.

"How's Sam doing?"

"He's doing good, Daphne."

"We're in different schools this year and I never see him."

"I'll tell him you said hi, Daphne."

"Will you bring him around next time you come?"

"Sure, I will."

I kissed the palm of my hand and blew it across to her. She grinned, then remembered to catch the kiss and put it on her cheek. I turned and headed back to my empty, darkened car.

15

When Sam turned ten, three years before the blood test, his mother decided to throw him a large birthday party. I kept offering to help, but she resisted. This was something she wanted to do herself, she said, trying to be kind but also trying not to cave in as she usually did when I came on strong. The deal was that I was supposed to come to the party and meet them there.

But, on the morning of the party, Joan called me to say that Sam wanted to come over and see me. It was Sunday, on a weekend that was not my regular weekend with him, and I was still wandering around my apartment unshaven and in my pajamas even though it was almost ten-thirty. This was what I had hoped for, without any real hope; surprised and afraid of disappointment, I answered warily when she asked if they could stop by. She asked sharply if I didn't want to see them; I denied that so emphatically that I sounded desperate. "You know, it's his idea," she said finally.

I was clean and shaven and dressed when they arrived. Sam came running in, a football under his arm, and immediately crash-dived on my living room couch so he could check out the wide-screen television that I had just acquired the day before. In the previous year or so,

I had found myself purchasing more and more objects like this—new sound system, ski equipment, car stereo, cell phones, watches, briefcases—all state of the art, all selected from high-end catalogues or fancy boutiques where the salespeople discreetly plied you with heavily marked-up merchandise. I wasn't even sure why I was suddenly so interested in acquiring so many small things. But I think, looking back, that my life had just hit a plateau: It was a big, wide, empty space and I was trying to spruce it up here and there with a few little trees. I was making a lot of money, but no longer doing the job I had once imagined doing; I had a comfortable town house in a new complex, but it wasn't the house I had once dreamed of owning; I had a son I loved and doted on, but not the family I had always planned on. I had gone far, but not in the direction I had expected, and I wasn't moving anymore. I knew better than to complain. I knew I had it better than most people; in many ways, I considered myself lucky. And I didn't want to waste energy feeling depressed. So, when time was hanging a little heavy on my hands, I found myself buying things that looked new and shiny and perfect and that, for at least a short while, promised to make my life feel a tiny bit different.

I plopped on the couch next to Sam, showing him all the tricks I could do with my new remote. Joan stood nearby, watching us indulgently.

"Pete," she said, "I need you to get him to the party by two P.M. Sharp. Do you understand me?"

"Look at this, Dad," Sam said. He wanted to do disgusting double-jointed tricks that a friend of his had taught him at school. "Can you do this one?" he asked, crooking his finger from the top joint.

"Do I look like a freak of nature?"

"Pete, I was talking to you."

"Did you hear your mother, Sam? Two o'clock sharp." I looked up at her. "Should we synchronize our watches? Maybe I could program my PC to beep." I was being resentful about the party. When she had first suggested it, I had started brimming over with ideas—how about taking a group of kids to Fenway? How about a clambake at the beach? But she had decided to take everybody to Creepy Place, a haunted-house restaurant by the highway that provided entertainment. My job was to write the check.

"This party is costing a lot of money," Joan said.

"Tell me about it."

"Don't ruin this for me Pete. I've put a lot of work into this." She sighed as she walked to the door. "Julie Steiner's been warning me all month that this place is going to be too gory for ten-year-olds. Do you think it will be?"

"They're probably sharpening their hatchets this moment," I said. Sam fell to the floor, clutching his neck. "And then, after they chop the kids' heads off," I said, "they hang them by their feet and drain out all the blood. Like turkeys at Thanksgiving." I pulled up his feet and stood him on his head. "Look at all that good white meat," I said, slapping his butt. He gobbled.

"Be on time, please," Joan said, slamming the door behind her.

The purpose of Sam's visit was to show me how he had finally learned to kick a football. This was not the first time I had seen him attempt to perform this feat. In fact, each week for the previous two months I had been promised a definitive demonstration, but each week when he had tried, there was some technical difficulty that involved him slipping or missing the ball or chickening out at the last minute. But this time he was ready. He was by the front door of my apartment, jumping up and down, while I was still on the couch. "Hurry, Dad, hurry. We don't have too much time." He refused to wear the jacket that his mother had forced me to promise I would make him wear. He opened the door and ran out; grabbing my jacket from the front hall, I ran out behind him.

We set up the game on the big lawn outside my building. I held the ball; he geared up. The first attempt was a washout and he wound up skidding along the still-wet grass to the ball. He jumped up without me having to urge him on, and tried again. And this time, amazingly, the ball sailed off. "No way," I said, genuinely surprised.

"I told you."

We fought over who would chase the ball, an argument he knew he would lose. We did it five more times, with almost uniform success. By the third time, I was more excited than he was. I had visions of college scholarships dancing in my head, then pictured his scrawny body wrapped up in the jersey and armor, with his tiny, still-freckled, messy-haired face poking out at the top. "You are terrific," I said.

"You do it."

"No. Too old. Too sore."

"Do it, Dad. I'll hold it."

I needed embarrassingly little persuasion. I crouched down as I eyed the ball, already hearing the hushed stadium break into cheers and seeing myself with my arms raised, triumphant, to the crowds. I poised myself for one heart-stopping moment, then exploded into a run, heading straight for the ball, aiming my foot, and then kicking with all my might into thin air.

He had pulled the ball away at the last minute. I flew up, spun like a diver doing a flip, and landed with a sickening thud on my back.

For a moment I couldn't move. Then I twisted my head slightly to my side and saw Sam, frozen, with the ball still in his hands and a look of terror on his face. "Now you're dead," I said.

He screamed and I was chasing him. He weaved and dodged. Maybe if I hadn't been so sore it would have been less of a race, but it took a while before I was able to dive at him, bringing him to the ground with a satisfying pair of shouts. We rolled over each other and wound up, me on my back, him on my stomach, still locked in my arms.

"I'm sorry," he said in a little voice.

"Are you nuts?" I shouted. "What got into your head?"

"I saw it in a cartoon. I didn't think it would work."

He tried to get up. "No way," I said. "You're stuck here until we find some punishment to fit the crime." He struggled some more; I rolled over, pinning him under me, tickling his sides until, laughing and crying, he begged for mercy. Then I rolled off him and lay on my back, basking in the bright fall sun and the smell of the wet grass.

He was sitting next to me, looking grave. "Are you going to hit me?" he said.

I sat up. "Oh, Sam, don't be silly. Have I ever hit you?"

"Would you ever hit me?"

"Sam, people don't hit kids anymore."

"Justin, he's this kid in my class, he gets hit. He told me."

"Well, that's too bad for him. But I'm not going to hit you."

"What if I did something really bad?"

"You couldn't."

"What if I"—his eyes looked around to see if he could see something really terrible somewhere—"what if I robbed a bank?"

I lay down again, with my hands behind my head. "Would you split the proceeds?"

"Dad. Seriously. What would you do if I robbed a bank?"

"Oh, I don't know, Sammy. I'd ground you."

"For how long?"

"Fifteen to twenty years."

He sighed. "Dad. Can you be serious, please? What would you do if I robbed a bank?"

"What would *you* do if I robbed a bank?"

"Would you?" He sounded eager.

"No. I wouldn't."

"Ever?"

"Come on, Sam. I wouldn't even go into a bank. You know how I hate lines."

He threw up his hands in disgust. "Stop kidding around," he said, emphasizing each word. Then he stopped to think. As he pondered, he put his finger to his mouth, as if he was trying to silence a baby. I had never seen anyone but him do such a thing before. I thought to myself, It's amazing how they're yours and they're so completely different.

"How about this?" he said finally. "What if you really, really needed money? Would you rob a bank then?"

"If I really, really needed money, I'd go to work."

"No. Say you lost your job and we were really poor and you really needed money because"—again the thinking, again the little finger at his lips doing its mysterious work—"because I was really sick and would die if I didn't get an operation. Would you rob a bank then?"

I thought for a second, actually trying to puzzle it out. There were so many questions to answer: What's true, what do I want him to think is true, what should I tell him instead of the truth? Finally I just gave up and said, "If you were really sick and would die, I would rob a bank."

"You would?" This opened up whole new vistas for exploration. He kept thinking. "How about if Mom was sick and needed an operation?"

"Sam. Enough."

"No. How about it?"

"I'd rob a bank for your mother too."

"How about Uncle Dave?"

"Dave? Oh God, if he needed money, I'd see if I could get his Porsche from him cheap." I jumped up. "And that's it." I lifted him off the ground and held him under my arm like a satchel as we headed back to my town house. When he squirmed too much, I swung him by his arms and let him land on his feet. We walked, him pressed against me, my arm on his shoulders, until we got to my front door and I realized I had left my keys behind when I hurried off to catch Sam.

"Sam, now see what you made me do."

"Dad, I'm cold. I don't have my jacket."

I kept pounding my back pocket to see if my wallet was there. I pictured it, worn at the corners where it rubbed each day inside my pants pocket, stuffed full of money and credit cards. My keys would be sitting right beside it, on the hallway table just inside the door.

"Sam, what time do we have to get you to Creepy Place?"

"Soon, I think."

He looked at me for a solution, already a little reproachful that I didn't have one. This is your fault, I wanted to say. But it didn't matter. I was the adult; I had to fix it.

I looked over my shoulder at the street that ran past my town house development. I had paid extra money to get a place that wasn't on a main road. No buses ran along here. And I didn't have change either. I thought of calling a cab, then thought of my cell phone locked inside my car trunk, parked inside the garage that I needed the coded card in my wallet to enter. I looked at Sam, then back at the road, and, dazed, started walking.

"Where are you going, Dad?" He caught up to me, hunching his skinny shoulders and half running, half skipping so he could keep up and talk at the same time. "Do you have a plan?"

I stood at the side of the street, watching cars whiz by. I thought of his mother at the restaurant. I felt again for my wallet and after I touched my empty back pocket, I stuck my thumb out into the road.

"Dad, what are you doing?" Sam shrieked as a beat-up American four-door rumbled by and came to a stop three feet ahead of us. I walked up to the passenger side, Sam running just behind me. "Dad, do you know this is illegal?"

"Sam, remember what I said about not hitting you. I'm reconsidering."

"Not in this car you're not," the driver said. I looked across the passenger seat at her. She was no more than twenty, with a pale face, thick eyebrows, gold earrings like a pirate's, and a mass of black hair falling over her face.

"I'm going to Creepy Place."

She smiled, and when she opened her lips, I could see chewing gum on her wet tongue. "At least you're dressed for it."

"I'm late for my birthday party," Sam told her. "My mom's waiting for me."

"Then you better get in," she said, opening the rear door. He got in and then, meticulously, tried to buckle up. "That doesn't work," she volunteered.

I settled in beside her on the front seat. She had the stereo on loud. She lit a cigarette.

"How close can you take us?" I said.

"I'll take you right there. It's on my way home." She pulled out in front of an oncoming car that honked hysterically. "I just got off work."

"Cool," Sam said.

I looked sideways at her. I could see underneath her open coat that she was wearing a waitress's uniform; it was too small and the buttons below her neck strained.

"Where do you work?" I asked.

"The Valley Glen mall."

"That's redundant, you know."

She looked at me like I was someone who needed to be dropped at the police station for observation.

" 'Valley.' 'Glen.' Same meaning," I said, sounding less and less debonair with each word.

She looked at me and snapped her gum. "As long as they write my check. You know what I mean?"

We drove in silence. Sam was looking around at the junk on the backseat of her car, picking up some cassettes, a coffee mug labeled WORLD'S BEST KISSER, and an open package of dark, sheer stockings. I introduced myself and she said her name was Vicki.

"You look like a man in a hurry," she said.

"My son's late for a party. His mother's going to kill me."

"Ex?" she said, looking pointedly at my left hand.

I slipped my hand under my leg and said, "Don't you know it's dangerous to pick up hitchhikers?"

She shrugged. "Man with a kid? You looked safe."

I shook my head. "That's crazy. He could have been my cover. Like we were a team."

She looked at me sideways, then rolled her eyes around their orbit of eyeliner.

"No, really," I continued. "I'm sure there are psychopaths who use children as cover. There must be cases."

"You have a safe-looking face."

"You're kidding."

She nodded. "Typical suburban dad." She pulled on her cigarette.

"Divorced. Living in an apartment complex. You get him every Saturday. Hey, this is Sunday. What's wrong?"

"He gets every other weekend," Sam piped up from the back.

The girl looked up into the rearview mirror and smiled at Sam's reflection. "My father got me every Saturday." She looked at me. "He lasted about a year before he stopped showing."

"Well, we've been doing it for nearly six years now," I said proudly.

"Just under five," Sam corrected.

"And we're not going to stop."

The girl flicked her cigarette in the direction of the ashtray; the ashes landed on my left knee. "Whatever." After a moment of silence, she looked at me. "So why'd you and your wife split up?"

"That's personal."

"Hey, this is my car."

I laughed. She turned and opened her mouth again; the gum was on the center of her tongue, right where it crested in the back of her mouth. I looked down. Her dress had hitched up, revealing a thigh so smooth it made you want to run your hand all the way down to her ankle. "You twenty-one yet?" I asked.

"In your dreams." She looked up at the rearview mirror again. "So do they split you over the holidays? Thanksgiving her, Christmas him?"

Sam shrugged. "Sort of."

"Sometimes we spend them together," I said defensively.

She looked at me. "Did you walk or did she throw you out?"

"She threw him out," Sam said helpfully.

I shot around in my seat. "Sam, that's not what we told you. We explained that we made a mutual decision."

"Yeah, I know."

"Remember, we told you—" I paused, trying to remember myself what we had told him.

"Did they do the one about how they were growing apart but they still loved you?" Vicki asked the rearview mirror.

"My mom did that. He did the one about 'we need time to figure some things out, but that won't affect my relationship with you.' "

"I never said that," I protested. "Besides, I would never have said 'relationship.' Sam, you were too young to know what the word meant."

"What word did you use?" Vicki asked.

I sighed and leaned back in the seat. "I said— Well it doesn't matter what I said then. The truth is—" Vicki and Sam looked at me; Vicki put her cigarette in her lips for a last drag; I could hear the paper burning at the edge of the filter. "Well, the truth was, we didn't have that much in common anymore. All we had in common was you, Sam. And I guess that wasn't enough." I looked at Vicki. "You're so smart, you tell him."

"My parents couldn't stand each other. Can't blame either one of them, actually."

Sam laughed, displaying his cheery line of crooked, shiny teeth. "Hey," Vicki said to the mirror. "You're cute."

He dropped his eyes and sank back in his seat. I waited, but he never looked at me for help.

"He must take after his mother," Vicki said to me. "She's good-looking, right?"

I shrugged. She flicked her cigarette out the window and pulled in front of Creepy Place. It was painted black and had a metal ghost crouched beside the entrance. "Here we are," Vicki announced. "Door-to-door service."

"You want to come in?" Sam asked impetuously as he got out the door. I tried to protest, but before I could think of a tactful way to disinvite her, she said, "Sure," and turned off the car.

She shook her hair at the rearview mirror and dropped her coat from her shoulders. When she saw me looking, she unbuttoned the top button of her blouse and then stared at me staring at her.

I dropped my eyes and said, "Could you please hurry? I'm going to be in a lot of trouble."

Vicki pulled out her lipstick, which was bright orange, and applied it slowly and noisily. When she finished, she screwed the lipstick back down and smacked her lips, then looked at me appraisingly. "Nah, you'll be fine." She reached out and pulled one end of my collar out of my sweatshirt, then ran her hand over my hair.

"There, now you really look like a mess. She'll feel too sorry for you to get mad."

Sam had run ahead of us. Vicki and I walked into the dark interior; a teenage boy stepped out of the shadows and raised a claw at us in greeting. Sam had already disappeared into the crowd of his friends, who were scattered around us. They were either lining up for a walk through the chamber of horrors or were fighting over who got the next ride on a virtual reality broomstick.

Joan stormed up. "Are you crazy? I said two. It's nearly three." She turned to Vicki. "Who's this?"

Vicki shrugged off her coat and tossed it at the man with the claw. "I'm the baby-sitter." She walked off into the darkness, looking over her shoulder at me as she went. "She *is* good-looking," she said.

"Pete, who *was* that?"

I tried to wave it away.

"Pete, are you bringing your girlfriends around with you when you see Sam, because we absolutely agreed we wouldn't do that. Besides, how old is she? If you wind up in the state penitentiary, don't expect us to come visit you."

"I have no girlfriends. She thinks I'm dogmeat." I smiled at Joan. "I think it's Sam she's after."

"God help us." Joan looked at me, trying not to smile. "Was he interested?"

"Some potential."

She shook her head. "You haven't been doing the birds and the bees talk again?"

"Again?" I bristled. "How do you know we ever did it?"

Joan rolled her eyes. "Oh, Pete, really, I'm his mother. He tells me everything."

"I don't know about that."

A man with a hockey mask and buzz saw came up to ask about cutting the cake. Joan gave directions, then leaned over and waved at Julie Steiner, who was staggering out of the chamber of horrors with her hand over her mouth. Bethany was behind her, a scrawny girl with wild, frizzy hair; she was crying because she wanted to go back in. Joan looked back at me, as if she was still waiting for an explanation. I had forgotten what I needed to talk my way out of.

"Actually," I said, "if you must know everything, Sam was asking about why we got divorced."

"Oh, that again." She ran a hand through her thick blond hair. "So did you tell him?"

"I said we didn't have much in common anymore."

She looked away. "That sounds okay, I guess."

I turned to her and said, "What would you have told him? Why don't you explain it to me?"

She turned to me wearily, started to speak, then stopped. She looked over her shoulder. Julie had collapsed onto a chair below a dangling spider. She waved at me, then looked at Joan, lifting her eyebrows inquiringly.

"Oh, Pete. I've tried to explain. I don't know that I can do any better than I did." She shook her head. "I was just so tired. You wanted so much from me. You had such an image of what it should all be like. And I just didn't fit in the picture. You did. You were the perfect husband. We had the perfect house. I felt like I was spoiling the scene. And it gets tiring to feel like that after a while."

"But we had Sam," I said, my voice straining to get out. "Wasn't that enough?"

"Almost. I thought it would be. I prayed it would be." She looked up at me and tried to smile. "So it wasn't such a great marriage, but at least you got Sam. I did that for you."

I squinted my eyes. "I wouldn't put it that way, exactly. I thought it was something we did together."

She turned and looked away. "Yes," she said. "Of course."

Suddenly I wanted to get away, to leave her and the party. I looked around, trying to find Sam. Vicki was on the broomstick now, riding it like a bronco, surrounded by a gang of boys, including Sam, who looked over at me and waved. When I turned back to Joan, the corners of my eyes burned. "I have to get out of here," I said.

She reached out and grabbed my shoulder. "Oh, Pete, just enjoy what you have. Can't you?"

I shook free. "Have a fun party. Don't drink any blood."

She kept hold of me. "You know, if you're lonely, you should think about getting married again."

"No one's interested. I look too safe."

"What?" She had cut me off before I could explain. "Pete, listen to me. Someone will be interested. God, just because it didn't work with me, don't give up. I'm a hard case."

"And what about you? You getting married again?"

"No." She shook her head, then looked at me; she looked more sad than anything else, and then all of a sudden she smiled. "You were it for me. I've had my fill."

When Sam came running up, holding a skull he had just won, he found Joan and me still standing side by side, holding hands. He almost turned around, thought twice, then walked over to his mother, who pulled his head to her waist and cradled it with her free arm. Julie ran up with a camera and waved. "Isn't that nice? All three of you together. Now everybody smile."

16

Barry called me at work the next day, a Friday. I was sitting at the head of the long conference table in my office; its polished cherry surface was covered with piles of papers—charts, marketing reports, and consumer surveys. Two of my assistants sat on either side of me, beefy young guys fresh out of business school with slicked-back hair and crisp suits that strained at their broad shoulders. We were evaluating a possible acquisition; I was barking out questions and they were nodding anxiously, pounding on their calculators or rummaging through the papers, desperately trying to find the answer before I jumped to the next question. At the other end of the table was Carol, my secretary. She had left as many empty seats as possible between herself and the rest of us, as if that might protect her. Her role was to dash down notes that we would later turn into memos filled with punch lists to inflict on all the others in the department.

"So what happened?" I asked Barry eagerly, forgetting the mess that lay around me.

"I talked to Joan's lawyer," he said. "You know, Pete, she's not exactly the sharpest tack in the box. When I first threatened to cut off the support, she tried to say we didn't have any grounds, but she didn't sound very convinced. My bet is she and Joan have already discussed this possibility. So I laid out what you had in mind. She said she'd talk to Joan and get back to me. I heard from her within the hour."

"Good," I said. We had her on the ropes. I slapped the table enthusiastically. "So everything's on for this weekend, just like always?"

"Hey, not so fast, cowboy. There's the small detail of the restraining order to worry about."

"Forget about it. It's just a piece of paper."

"No, Pete, you can't forget about it. We have to go to court and get it lifted before you go over there. I can get it done early next week. You can see Sam the weekend after next."

"And miss this weekend? No way. Besides, she's not going to have me arrested." The minute I let that out, I looked up, embarrassed. My assistants were oblivious, immersed in their papers, grateful for this momentary breather so they could catch up with me. But Carol had put down her pen and was staring at me, her chin resting on her hands. Our eyes met and, for a moment, hers didn't waver. Then she looked down and pretended to be reading the scrawled notes lying in front of her.

Barry was lecturing me. "Pete, I'm telling you not to go over there until next week. I'll take care of it then. You can wait a few days longer."

"Don't worry. I know what I'm doing, partner." I hung up the phone. My assistants looked up dutifully; they were waiting for me to quarterback the next play. But my heart was racing and I couldn't concentrate. I excused myself and stepped outside my office. When I was in the hall, I just stood there for a moment, feeling the pounding in my chest; I heard a little noise behind me and started. It was Carol; she was standing timidly in the doorway. "Are you okay?" she asked.

I flushed. Even though I had worked with Carol for years, we weren't friends; I knew little about her, except that she had been married, then divorced. I imagine that she didn't know much more than that about me. And there she was, staring at me as if she could see right through my crisp, expensive clothes; I felt like a weakling and it scared me. Before I could stop myself, I snapped, "There's nothing wrong with me. Is something wrong with you?"

I saw her flinch, then stiffen. She was a tall woman, and when she straightened up, she was almost my height. It flashed in my mind for a moment that she would quit and really throw my life into chaos. I started to babble an apology, but she held up a hand and cut me off. "If you say there's nothing wrong," she said, "then nothing's wrong." She stopped, and for a moment I almost thought I saw a smile. "After all, you're the boss, aren't you?"

———

I called Joan that night. She didn't sound surprised to hear from me. I suggested that I come over to see Sam on Saturday, just for a while, not the whole weekend, just an afternoon to start. I was calm and respectful; she didn't resist and when she spoke at all, it was in tired-sounding monosyllables.

"Is that okay?" I asked when I had laid out my plan.

"Do I have a choice?" she asked. I said nothing.

———

The next day, I got to the house fifteen minutes early. I parked my car in front and sat there, trying to calm myself down, to steady my breathing and keep my leg from jiggling.

It was a hot day. The high late June sun baked the front lawn; there were patches of brown and crabgrass everywhere. The house looked blank and empty. The curtains in the living room were drawn. The flower beds, which I had so lovingly laid out and turned over during our first summer in the house, were bare. There was a pile of mail lying on the front step that Joan hadn't picked up yet.

I tried to remember what I had felt when I had driven home each night while we all still lived here together. Truthfully, I probably was never paying attention. I'd be shouting into the car phone or punching in different stations on the radio or worrying about what I still had to do at work. My route from the train station passed the modern town hall, then the shiny new police station, and finally the old

Congregational church with its square-topped steeple, the town's only unpretentious landmark, erected by its first residents who must have been more modest than the present ones, or perhaps more certain of glory in another life. I would travel down our street and when I saw our house I would feel a pang of hope that they'd be waiting outside for me. Maybe Joan would be watching Sam take his unsteady steps across the lawn or launch his fire engine down the flagstone walkway. Maybe she would wave and he would rush toward me in his lopsided way, his hands stretched out, while she yelled at him to be careful and wait until Daddy parked in the garage. Perhaps it had never really happened that way. Perhaps the picture in my mind was only what I had always hoped for and never gotten.

When Joan answered the door, she whispered, "Come into the living room. I need to talk to you." She didn't look at me as I followed her into the airless room. She sat in the easy chair in the corner; I perched on the couch and waited, trying to look easy to deal with.

"I've been having a problem with him all day," she said.

"Is he sick?"

She shook her head. "Listen, Pete, he doesn't want to go out with you."

"Joan, I thought we had resolved this. The lawyers agreed—"

"The lawyers don't run everything, you know." She waved her hand at me when I tried to speak. "Or your lawyer, I should say."

"Joan—"

"All right. I resolved that I wasn't going to fight with you. Listen, Pete, believe me. This isn't coming from me. I resolved to make this work. I had my misgivings, but—"

My never generous supply of patience was dissipating. "Joan, will you quit stalling—"

"What do you expect me to say? That I like the idea? Your lawyer calls up and says you're going to cut Sam and me off without a dime unless we go along with this?"

"Did you tell Sam that?"

"Of course I didn't. I said we were going to—" She stopped; her hand went up to her mouth. She was looking over my shoulder toward the stairway. "Oh, here he is. Honey, come on in. Your father— Everyone is all here."

"No."

"Sam, please—"

"I told you I don't feel good."

I turned and looked at him. He was halfway down the stairs, clinging to the railing, standing on one foot like a wading bird. He seemed as if he had grown. He had on a pair of gym shorts that hung to his knees and an oversize T-shirt with a picture of a bright red-and-black motorcyclist who appeared to be bursting into flames. His face looked as if he had been sleeping or crying.

"You okay, buddy?" I asked.

He turned away and walked off to the kitchen. I looked at Joan. "You see?" she mouthed. She forced herself to stand up.

As she walked by me, I whispered, "Should I go?"

She stopped and flashed her eyes at me. "How do I know what you should do?" she asked, not whispering. "Do you think he comes with instructions?"

I followed her into the kitchen. Sam had pulled out bread and cold cuts and three jars of condiments, spread them out over the counter, and then left them. He was sitting on a chair, staring out the window into the backyard. He looked up when his mother walked in. "You see," he said, "it's a crummy day out."

"Oh, Sam, it is not," she said impatiently. "It's beautiful."

"I don't feel good."

She held up both hands as if she was grabbing at something in the air. Then she waved her hands at both of us. "Listen, I don't care what you do, but I'm getting ready to do some shopping. You two figure this out."

"Mom, don't leave."

"Joan, don't leave."

She turned to me. "You wanted him. There he is. He's all yours."

We heard her footsteps thump up the stairs and into her bedroom; the door slammed shut.

I put my hands in my pockets and leaned against the wall. "So what do you say to a movie?"

He didn't turn his head. He was looking intently out the window. There was a big tree there, from which I had hung a bird feeder years ago. When he was three, we'd put him in his high chair by the window and he'd get so excited whenever a bird came that he'd throw his toys at the window and scare the bird into squawking flight. I walked over. When I got beside him, he walked off, leaving me there, staring out the window. The rope I'd hung from the tree had frayed; the feeder had fallen to the ground and a squirrel was rooting through the seed that had spilled over the patio.

I could hear Sam head up the stairs and down to his mother's bedroom. He pounded on the door. She didn't answer. He kept pounding and shouting, "Mom, let me in." Finally she opened the door. They started to quarrel.

"Listen, I told you," she said. "This is between you two. I am not going to get involved."

"You said I shouldn't see him."

"That was before. Now I think you should."

"But you said I didn't have to see him because he took that blood test."

"Well, now you have to."

"But when you told me about the blood test, you said what he did was wrong. You said he didn't deserve to be my father—"

The next thing I heard was the sound of my heavy feet running across the dining room floor. When I got to the top of the stairs, I caught myself.

Joan and Sam were standing inside her bedroom door to the hallway. She had her lipstick in her hand and half of her mouth was colored red. "Pete, wait for us downstairs."

I suppose if I had just gone downstairs like she told me to then, none of what happened afterward would have occurred. I still don't know why I did it. I was just standing there, with an ache in my side and blood pounding in my ears. All I could see was that she was there, with a house and a child who wanted her and the power to say, "You stay, you go," and I had none of it. And what's more, it seemed that whatever she had, she had taken from me. I took a step forward.

"Pete, I'm warning you." She pointed to the stairs. "Go down and wait. I'll take care of this."

I saw Sam inching around his mother, trying to get behind her. She tried to close the bedroom door, leaving me outside. I kicked it so hard it swung inside and crashed against the bedroom wall. I stepped inside her room, and caught a glimpse of the unmade bed, caught the fragrance of her perfume and the potpourri she kept on her bureau top. She was steps away from me, Sam hiding behind her.

"You can't take care of anything," I shouted. "You did this to all of us. You were supposed to have my kid and instead you had him with some stranger."

Suddenly she wasn't scared. She took a step forward. She wasn't a large woman or a strong one, but I had never seen her more intent. She put her finger in my face, right between my eyes. "You are not going to talk to me like that in front of my son."

I reached over and grabbed Sam by his arm. He felt no heavier than the clothes on his back. I pulled him toward me, then held him by both his shoulders and swung him around so he was facing her. I heard him say, "Dad."

"You are right in front of your son now," I shouted at Joan. "You tell him. You tell him what you did. Go ahead." I pushed him toward her. "Tell him who his father is. Tell him."

She grabbed Sam's left arm and yanked it. For a full, awful moment, we stood there, each of us pulling one of his arms, while he dangled between us, slipping off his feet. Then I let him go. At the same moment she dropped his arm and he fell to the ground.

"Fine," I said. "Fine." I turned around and faced the wall. I was crying. "Neither of you wants me here." I kicked the wall; I heard a crack and the sound of plaster falling.

She was shouting, "This is my house and I want you to get out."

And then it all felt clear to me. It was as if I had been drowning

underneath a waterfall, tumbling about in a stew of water and foam
and rock, and suddenly I had fought my way to the air. I shook my
head. "It's not your house."

She didn't know what I was saying. She was shouting, "Get out,"
and pounding on my shoulders, trying to push me. I started to back
off and I saw Sam still lying on the ground where he had fallen. "Listen, Sam," I said. My voice was so quiet they had to strain to hear it.
"I wanted to be your father. There's nothing I wanted more. Whatever happened, she did it to us. You just remember that."

Joan screamed something I couldn't understand. She looked
around and then grabbed a picture frame off the top of her bureau.
She threw it at me. It hit my face. When I put my fingers up to my
cheek, I felt the first warm seep of blood. I took a step and heard glass
crunch beneath my feet. I looked down. It was a picture of Sam, in
front of the Magic Kingdom, wearing mouse ears and a big smile.

17

The Monday after my visit to Joan's house, Dave drove me to Barry's office. I had called Dave the night after my visit to Joan's house, as I had on an almost daily basis since the blood test. I would hang on the line while he shuffled to the phone, Marcia ineffectively covering the receiver so she could whisper dolefully, "It's Peter again." And then he would announce, very gravely, that he was taking it in the study—a small room, somewhat overdignified by its name, that contained a cast-off computer and a wobbly bookshelf loaded with college textbooks and no-longer-read guides to having and raising an infant. He would close the door and sink down into the room's one easy chair and ask, "So what now?"

By then, it felt as if he was the only person I had to talk to. Ever since the blood test, I could barely get through the nights alone in my apartment. I could hear the phone not ring each minute that I was home. Instead of reading, I'd switch the TV on and off. Instead of working, I'd sit at my computer, pumping one finger up and down on the mouse as I dealt and redealt solitaire, telling myself that if I eventually won just one game I would get up and do something productive. I wouldn't cook; I'd just sit there and feel hunger root through my stomach, up into my chest and head and mouth, leaving everything weak, cloudy, and sour. I'd want to call someone and would instead start thinking about how my parents were dead, how I had no brothers or sisters, how I had lost touch with all my school friends—facts that had, in the past, made me sad in a philosophic, almost indifferent way, the way you feel about not being able to do the same number of chin-ups or about having to wait longer for a follow-up erection. So I would call Dave.

When I told him about the disaster at Joan's house, I could practically hear him shaking his head. He wanted to say, "I told you so," but I guess by this point he had gotten used to being sensitive. Unfortunately there was nothing else to say. My plan to reunite my former family had just been a way of deluding myself.

I raged about Joan, about how she had turned Sam against me. Of course she had, Dave said.

And I raged that she was living a lie, that she had for years. She must have known—how could she not have known—that I wasn't Sam's father. Of course she knew, Dave agreed.

And I raged that she was able to hide from all the consequences of her actions. That she, who had poisoned our family, got everything that was left of it. Dave stopped me right there. I couldn't get Sam back. He wasn't mine to get. But Joan was a different story. I didn't have to let her beat me. I could reclaim what was mine—and that was the house and the money.

"I can't put them on the street," I kept saying. "I can't just cut off all their money."

"Hey, buddy," Dave said, "you got a legitimate beef and a tough lawyer. There's only one way to go."

———

Barry leaned back so far in his beige reclining chair that I thought he might fall on his head. Unlike Dave, he hadn't been very shy about saying I told you so. And he had even more bad news. Joan's lawyer had called first thing in the morning to report that Mrs. Morrison would no longer agree to drop the restraining order.

"What does that mean?" I asked, disheartened. I felt like a man thrown overboard, floating in the sea and watching from a distance as his boat sinks.

"I repeated that we would attempt to cut off support, but Joan's lawyer wouldn't back down. Either Joan thinks you won't make good on the threat or she doesn't care."

I didn't have much to say. It seemed to me that I was defeated—I had lost Sam and there was nothing I could do about it. Dave was not so resigned, however. He kept demanding from Barry how it was that Joan could keep the house and all the money, even though Sam was not mine. I listened, as if from a distance, again feeling like a drowning man, now clinging to a log and floating about, wondering if help would ever arrive.

Barry responded carefully. "At this point, Mrs. Morrison is in the driver's seat. The restraining order is still in place." He paused and looked at me sternly. "If you had listened to me and waited until I went to court to drop it, things might be different. But you didn't."

I slumped farther into my chair. "Why can't you get the order dropped now?"

"Because Mrs. Morrison will no longer agree. And, her lawyer says that if we go to court to seek to lift it, Mrs. Morrison will file another affidavit about how you behaved when you went to her house on Saturday. According to her, you were"—he paused to adjust his half-moon glasses on his nose, so he could glance down at the notes in front of him—"you were 'abusive' and 'destructive.' " He peered at me over the tops of the glasses. "Sound familiar?"

I sighed and stared at the ceiling, feeling like a recalcitrant child in a principal's office. "Why are we always talking about what I did?" I whined. "No one ever talks about what Joan did."

Dave burst in. "That's it exactly," he insisted, talking to Barry and punctuating his words with jabs of his fist in the air. "How is it that Joan gets everything—she gets Sam and all the bucks and the house as well. Pete paid for that house, bottom up. She wasn't working, all she ever did in that marriage was hang out in the attic and paint pictures that no one ever bought."

Barry had taken off his glasses and was meditatively tapping them against his hairless chin, seeming to reflect on Dave's blustering words. "The house *was* joint property," he said mildly.

"Oh get real. Pete never would have agreed to give her that house if he thought that Sam wasn't his. I mean, for Christ's sake, he could have divorced her for adultery."

Barry's eyeglasses kept up their light patter on his chin. "He could have. Or he could have gotten a no-fault divorce, as he did. The rules aren't so strict anymore."

"You're telling me a woman makes out the same when it's her fault?"

"Depends. On the judge. On the circumstances." Barry smiled. "On the fault."

"But they weren't even married that long. What was it, Pete? Four, five years."

"Eight years, four months."

Barry tried to smile at me, but Dave kept talking. "And believe me, when she met Pete, she saw a good thing coming from a mile away. Christ, Pete here gave away the store at the divorce. It was a great deal for her even if she had been faithful."

"You know, gentlemen, you're asking to undo a divorce agreement that was entered years ago. A divorce court is going to be very unwilling to do that." Dave started to explode, but Barry held up his hand. When Dave stopped, Barry leaned back in his chair and started hitting his stomach, one hand at a time; he had a little rhythm going while he thought. Then he nodded his head a few times to get our attention. "In divorce court, the judge's sole consideration is the best interests of the child. And they're notoriously sympathetic to mothers. Frankly, if we go back to that court and tell the judge about the blood test and ask for relief from the child support order or some revision of the divorce agreement, I don't think you stand a shot. And Joan's lawyer is counting on that. And so she's calling your bluff by not letting you see Sam."

"So you're saying there's nothing Pete can do?" Dave said angrily.

Barry shook his head slightly. "Oh no. That's not what I said." He leaned forward in his chair and waited. He had us on the line; now he was going to reel us in slowly. "You know, gentlemen, Pete's situation is a very novel one. Historically, one of the law's most sacred assumptions is that a married man is presumed to be the father of his wife's child. In the olden days—well, not even so long ago, back when I started practice—it was essentially incontestable. It dated back to the days when illegitimacy was such a social stigma that to 'bastardize' a child—you'll pardon the expression, but that's the word they use—was to make him an outcast. So, in order to destroy the presumption of legitimacy, when a child was born in marriage, you had to prove that parentage by the husband was impossible. The burden of proof was higher than in any other civil matter. And, even if there had been lack of access, as it was called, to the wife, or some medical problem that made it impossible for the husband to father a child, neither spouse was allowed to testify about it. So it was essentially impossible to prove. Unless the husband was away at sea for a year before the birth."

"Maybe women were more reliable in those days," Dave said.

Barry smiled. "I would doubt it. You know, a child is considered a Jew only if the mother is Jewish. The rabbis knew that you can never be certain who the father is. And that's wisdom as old as the Talmud."

I stirred in my seat. "Point?" I asked. And when I did, I could almost hear Sam, deflating one of my canned lectures about honesty or hard work or some other civic virtue.

Barry carefully placed his eyeglasses down on his desk and looked straight at me. "The point, of course, was to ensure that a husband supported the children of his marriage. It was an unquestioned duty. Now, of course, we have the luxury of scientific evidence—of DNA matching, as you found out. So, despite all the anachronistic rules of proof—which are still on the books—we can use scientific evidence to prove that the child is not the husband's. But the law hasn't quite caught up with the implication of that science. Does a man have a duty to support another man's child? Certainly not. But, if that man is married to the child's mother, must he support the child even if he knows at the time of the birth that the child isn't his? Unlikely. If he filed for divorce at the time of the birth, he would probably not be ordered to pay child support. So does that mean that, if he found out the truth only years after the birth, he could recover all the money that he did pay during the years of the marriage to support a child that wasn't his? Not so clear." He smiled at our eager faces. "But it might be worth a try."

"But the judge would never agree to that," I said.

Barry's smile got a little wider. "In divorce court, perhaps. But maybe we could get to a different judge in a different court. I'm not talking about us filing to revise a divorce agreement or to change custody arrangements. I'm talking about us bringing a lawsuit against Mrs. Morrison premised on the claim that she induced you to support her by fraud. And that's a claim we can bring in the superior court, which handles all non-family civil matters. A court that has broader powers to give us equitable remedies, to essentially undo the past. And I don't think the judges there would necessarily be biased in Mrs. Morrison's favor."

"So you think Pete could sue Joan and recover everything he's given her from the time of their divorce?" Dave asked.

Barry shrugged. "As I said, it might be worth a try."

I looked at Barry. "But I agreed to pay her that money."

"An agreement induced by fraud."

"Fraud?" I said. "Oh, I don't know about that."

Barry folded his hands in front of him; he was trying to look very sage and professorial. "Let me ask you this, Pete. Would you have agreed to support Sam if you had known at the time he was born he wasn't your child?"

I paused. I had never considered this. I thought back to that moment in the hospital when, cowering at the foot of Joan's bed, I had first seen the crown of his head. I recalled the rush of triumph and joy I experienced then, but it was a feeling recalled from a million miles away. I knew the answer to Barry's question. "No. If I had known Joan was carrying some other man's child, I would have divorced her and had nothing to do with her. Or the kid. I would never have stayed in a situation like that. Why would I?"

Barry nodded. "So you stayed in the situation because you were deceived?"

"I suppose so. Yes. I did."

"Now let me ask you this. If you found out at the time of your divorce that Sam wasn't yours, would you have agreed to support him then?"

I paused. This was harder, of course. By the time of the divorce, I knew him. I loved him. I wanted to give him everything I had. But I had wanted to give him all I had because he was all I had, he was everything in the world that was mine. And now I found out he wasn't mine, not in the way I had thought. I shook my head, less certainly this time. "Maybe not. I can't say." I stopped to think. "Maybe I would have agreed to support him, but only because I had believed for the years before then that he was mine."

Barry nodded eagerly. I was getting it right. "You would never have formed the attachment to him were it not for Mrs. Morrison's deception. And Mrs. Morrison profited from that deception, because the money you were paying for Sam, of course, went to her."

I heard her standing in her bedroom, shouting at me to get out of her house. Her house, the one I had found and chosen and paid for.

Dave slapped my shoulder hard, shaking me in my seat. "Stop grinding your gears, Pete. I see where he's going with this." He nodded his head at Barry, who was smiling proudly. "He wants to up the ante on Joan. You file the suit, Joan'll be afraid that you'll get all the money back. She has no money now to cover that kind of hit, and if she lost she'd be working the rest of her life to pay you off. She'll be so scared she'll be dying to settle."

Barry nodded agreement. "I think that's a fair assessment." He leaned forward, targeting his little bullet eyes right on me. "And the point is, Peter, you don't have a choice. You threatened to cut off the child support if she didn't let you see Sam. And now she won't let you see Sam. Once you've pointed the gun, you have to shoot or else you've lost. You'll have no leverage, you'll be at her mercy. And right now, she seems singularly deficient in mercy. Unless you do this, you have no chance of getting anything from her—either Sam or the money. If you file the lawsuit, at least you have a chance."

I was having trouble thinking clearly. I could only think of how Joan had betrayed me, how she had run to court to get the restraining order, how she had manipulated Sam to turn against me. I knew I had myself to blame for much of what had gone wrong, but I couldn't accept that my mistakes outweighed her years of deception, the sheer enormity of the fact that she had had another man's son and for years had tried to convince me that he was mine. The angry noise in my head drowned out any sounds of understanding or acceptance. In my mind, it just seemed to be about right and wrong, winning and losing, and she was on the other side.

Meanwhile, Dave was talking excitedly about what a great idea this was. "What's the downside? If he wins, he's free and clear of Joan, and she's out of the house. And if he loses, he's not in any worse shape than he is now."

Barry nodded. "There is another scenario, of course." He waited until we both were hanging on his next word. "The real father. He owes the money that Pete's spent to support his child for the past thirteen years. And maybe he has it—in which case, Joan's off the hook, but you still get the money."

"Or maybe he doesn't," Dave said. "In which case, they're both on the hook."

"And, in any event, Joan would have to tell me who he is," I said. "Right? She couldn't keep that a secret."

"We could put her on the stand and ask her in open court."

I hated this man whom I didn't know, whom I couldn't even begin to imagine. For weeks now, I had sat up at night wondering who he was. I had considered every male acquaintance we had—starting, I am embarrassed to say, with Dave, who might have been a prime suspect if he weren't so pumped on this idea of retaliation. And I wanted to make Joan reveal the father. I wanted to because I wanted to know. But more, I wanted to because I could tell it was something she wanted desperately to keep a secret.

"And what about Sam?" I asked finally. "What happens to him?"

Barry shrugged. "He's in Mrs. Morrison's control now. She has to worry about him."

"But can't I see him again?" I insisted.

He shook his head. "Not now. I've explained this to you. She gets to decide whether you see him. And at the moment, she's not inclined your way."

"And," Dave added, "with things the way they are, she has no incentive to change. She has you by the short hairs right now, and why should she let go?"

"But if we sued her," I said, speaking slowly, as if I was repeating something I had memorized, "if we did what you're talking about, she might be scared. She might back down. She might let me see Sam again."

Barry nodded. "If it looked like we might win, if she was really about to lose all her money, she might not have any other option."

"Pete, the point is," Dave said, "you don't really have a choice. If you don't do this, she's never going to budge."

For over a month, since the blood test, I had been swallowing a diet of disappointment and regret and humiliation, and now Barry was offering me a taste of hope. I wanted Sam back and this seemed like my last and only chance. I wanted revenge on Joan. I wanted not to be at her mercy, to turn the court system against her the way she had turned it against me, to make her face what she had done to me instead of always turning it into a case of what I had done to her.

I looked at Barry and Dave smiling at me and urging me on. I should have run for the door, but the only thing I felt was grateful. I was still drowning, but now they had tossed me a lifeboat, and I didn't want to see that it, as well, might have sprung a leak. I was glad they believed there was something that I could do. I was glad they thought I was the one who had been wronged. I looked at them, nodding at me expectantly, and I thought, At least I have someone on my side.

18

My first warning of what I had put in motion came one morning a few days later, as I was sitting at my kitchen table over an already cold cup of coffee, preparing to leave for work. It was a call from Jim Atkinson.

"Pete, what's going on there?" he demanded without any introduction. He obviously believed that, if it was important enough to make him call me, it was important enough to be on the top of my mind when he called. But his call caught me by surprise; when he asked what was going on, I looked around my apartment as if he might be interested in the relentless drip of the kitchen faucet or the pile of unread newspapers in the living room.

He had received a request from my lawyer's office for the records of the blood test; they were going to be produced in court when I filed suit. "You know Sam and Joan have been my patients as well," he said severely. He obviously meant to call me back to my senses, but it had the opposite effect. He didn't realize that I had become someone who could feel threatened by having to share my family doctor with what had once been my family. My lawyer was just trying to establish the facts, I explained.

"To what end?" he asked in a dry voice.

"Listen, if you're upset about having to take the time to do this, you can send me a bill," I said, thinking it was the rudest thing I could say. The minute the words were out, I felt frightened, like you do when you throw a ball at a glass window and stand, powerless, for that moment before the sound of shattering glass.

"That won't be necessary, Pete," he said. "I've already completed the work." He waited a second; when he spoke again, I could tell his voice was shaking. "But I think in the future you should find yourself another physician."

I sat in the silence after we hung up, thinking that now, with the heart cut out of me and all my other organs turned to stone, I was unlikely to need much health care. I felt the familiar surge of self-pity that seemed to come up from my stomach and then stall somewhere just inside my eyes. Then I picked up the phone and threw it across the room, listening to it bound along the surface of the kitchen counter and land in the sink.

Two days later I got home and saw a giant envelope from Barry's office stuck inside my mail slot. It was a copy of the complaint that had been filed in court that morning. Within a minute of opening it, I was on the phone. Barry wasn't available, his secretary explained patiently. But I didn't want to listen to that. I was too busy yelling at her. "It says here 'Peter Morrison v. Joan and Sam Morrison.' Why is that? Why is it 'versus Sam Morrison'?"

The secretary was uninterested in my dilemma. "It has to say 'versus' somebody," she explained as if speaking to a child. "If you didn't want to sue somebody, why did you go to a lawyer in the first place?"

And then the next morning I walked out of my apartment, still cloudy-eyed from sleep, and when I picked up the newspaper, I saw my name on the front page.

For a while I became dizzy. I found myself still holding the newspaper, sitting in a chair in my living room, my eyes out of focus and my ears ringing. It took me a moment to realize that I had left the front door open.

In a minute, I was on the phone again and this time I got Barry on his way out of the office.

"Yeah, not bad," he said in that modest voice I had come to hate.

"Barry, why the hell did you tell the newspapers about this? I didn't want any publicity."

"Me? I didn't tell anybody. Court documents are public. I guess some reporter was checking the new cases and thought this one looked interesting." He sounded unconvincing, but at that point I could only sputter. He tried to reassure me. "Listen, don't worry. It's only going to help us. Put more pressure on her."

The headline read, "Man Seeks Divorce from Son." Barry was quoted: "A man's not required to support someone else's child. Even when it's his own wife's." There was no comment from Joan.

I called in sick that day and never left the apartment. I spent all morning trying to reach Dave at work. When I finally got him, on his way to a lunch meeting, he let out a low whistle. "Could have blown me over when I picked up the paper. You never said you were going to do any publicity on this, Pete."

I was frantic by now; I had been fending off accusations and attacks all day long in my brain so that, the first time I heard one actually spoken out loud, I burst out with a million excuses at once. Dave cut me off as soon as I opened my mouth. He was soothing me: It was going to be okay, it wasn't my fault. "Listen, you know these things blow over in a day. Tomorrow somebody'll shoot out a fast-food restaurant and you'll be old news." He chuckled. "You should have heard Marcia though. If I'm lucky, she'll never talk to me again."

The phone at Joan's house was busy all day. I called at half-hour intervals to check. She had call waiting and an answering machine; I had never gotten a busy before. I thought of driving by the house, but couldn't imagine stepping outside my apartment.

Barry called me again at the end of the day. He had already heard from three news magazines and the *New York Times*. "I told you, it's a very hot legal issue," he said. "We could be making some real law here."

I had stopped yelling by now. For an hour or so, I had just sat in my chair, the same one I had fallen into that morning. The panicked, frantic thoughts had stopped. My mind was empty. I felt as if there was something growing inside me that would eventually kill me and all I could do was wait for the first twinge of pain. When I heard Barry talking, it was as if I was underwater. He was suggesting that I talk to somebody at a PR firm—just for pointers. He had already been contacted by some group for divorced fathers that was trying to reform the alimony laws. They were wondering if I would speak to them. Barry thought this would be big.

That night, as I was getting ready to go to sleep, I got a call from the producer of a New York talk show. It was a young man. He talked fast, in a high-pitched voice. I pictured him with thick, round glasses and wild eyes. "You know, I really think you've tapped into a lot of rage out there. There are a lot of people who want to hear what you have to say." He was still talking when I hung up.

The next morning, I spent an hour fighting with the phone company to get my number unlisted immediately. "You know," the woman at the other end said tiredly, "you're still going to be in all the phone books and we don't get new ones printed for another six months. Once you're out there, you can't just pop back in." Defeated, I agreed to get a new phone number; my old number was to be answered with a recording that said the line had been disconnected and no further information was available.

There were three cameramen waiting in my apartment's parking garage when I left for work. I stood looking at them, imagining that I was a criminal being led to a public execution. They took my picture and waved microphones and shouted questions, just as I had pictured it would be in the few odd moments of my youth when I thought I might someday be famous.

People tried not to say anything about it at work. An older man, who worked in accounting and always talked about what he was doing with his kid's scout troop, walked away muttering when I went into the coffee room. An executive who was my age ended a long conversation about the problems we were having with one of our subsidiaries' customer service division and, as he left my office, slapped me hard on the arm and said, "Hang in there." I imagined a couple of the secretaries glaring at me.

That evening, as I was standing over my desk, looking dazedly at the disordered piles and wondering what to do next, I heard a light tapping at my door. It was Carol.

Shyly, she walked in to say she was leaving now. This was not part of our usual evening ritual and I peered at her in confusion. She stood there awkwardly, her coat already on, her bag on her arm. I could tell she wanted to say something, but was trying to find the words. I felt panic; I couldn't imagine that whatever she was going to say to me would be something I'd want to hear. I pictured her roosting in the coffee room all day with the other secretaries, condemning my horrid behavior. "I'm kind of busy," I said weakly, although it was obvious from my aimless posture and blank look that this was not true.

She nodded. "I knew something had been bothering you lately," she said.

I shifted on my feet. "Thanks, but there's nothing for you to be concerned about." I could hear the cleaning crews dragging their pails along the slicked tile floors in the hall. I stared distractedly at my desk again, hoping she would slip out. A moment passed and I looked up to find her still standing there.

When I heard myself start talking, I was surprised by how quickly my words came out. "You know, Carol, I'm sure you think I did the wrong thing, but there's a lot about this situation you don't know—"

"I don't think you did the wrong thing," she said.

"You don't?"

She shook her head. "You were lied to. Now you're trying to tell the truth."

Too tired even to think, I sank down into my chair. "You know, Carol, I'm not sure I believe that myself."

She smiled a little. "Funny. You seem like a man who's pretty certain about things." She made a little face. "Like a lot of men. Especially the men around here." She shifted the bag on her shoulder and buttoned the top button on her coat. "If you don't mind my saying so, it may not be the worst thing for you not to be so certain anymore."

I swung around in my chair and looked out the window at my commanding view of the city, the harbor, and the bright summer sky. "Actually, Carol, I don't mind your saying so at all."

"Well, that's a start then," I heard her say. And then the door to my office closed quietly behind her.

———

Every paper in town carried an article on the lawsuit in their Sunday edition. I threw them out without looking at them, then in the middle of the night went through the trash, pulling out the papers stained with bread crumbs congealed in egg yolk, to see what they said. Dave told me there had been a story about the lawsuit on an evening TV magazine show. "The Sunday newspaper even had your wedding picture," he said. "Who could have given them that?"

"You maybe?"

"Why would I keep your picture?"

"Joan's mother sent it to the papers," I said.

"For what?"

"To announce we had gotten married. At the time, we didn't mind the attention."

"Wow, those newspapers must have an incredible filing system," he said. I hung up on him.

Time covered it. *Newsweek* didn't. It was their only difference that week.

At a meeting to negotiate my company's acquisition of a chain of electronics stores, the seller, a bluff, hairy guy with a diamond ring, looked at me and said, "Aren't you the one—" His female assistant, who took care of all the numbers, kicked him under the table. I stopped going to my health club after I was straining forward on the rowing machine and saw my face on the TV screen hanging from the ceiling. One day, I found a handwritten envelope among the bills and junk mail; it was the first letter I had gotten in as long as I could remember and it contained some white supremacist screed about women and lawyers that was apparently offered to me as a token of gratitude. After that, I got lots of letters and threw them all out unopened.

For a few days I kept trying to call Sam at his home. The phone was never answered. And then one day I got a recording telling me that their number, like mine, had been changed at the customer's request and was now unpublished.

I begged Barry to figure out a way for me to see Sam. He reminded me that the restraining order was still in place. "And boy, if she was ever going to get you arrested, she'll do it now."

Desperate, I drove by their home one evening, imagining that somehow I could call up to his window from the backyard. As I turned the corner, I saw a police cruiser swing by and my palms broke out in sweat. The house was dark; there was no car in the driveway, and it occurred to me that Joan had gone into hiding.

I sat at my desk at home composing letters to him and found no words to explain what I had done. I pictured him seeing my handwriting and burning the envelope unopened. There was a pile of crumpled-up papers by my desk before I realized that whatever he must be feeling was so much worse than what I felt that I had no right even to excuse myself. There was nothing I could have said and I came to believe he was better off not hearing from me. I began to believe in Joan's image of me. I pictured Sam in my mind and a steel door closed in front of the picture.

As Dave had promised, the reporters and cameramen disappeared after a couple of days. I made it through my day at work, imagining that each person who didn't return my call was either laughing at me or too disgusted to listen to my voice. When I stopped for traffic lights and the person in the car next to me looked in my direction, I thought that somehow they must know who I was and I waited for them to give me the finger. By the time I got home at night, I was so exhausted by trying to appear invisible that I couldn't bear to go outside again.

So I began living like a mountain man in a snowstorm. I ate through my small supply of canned goods, some tuna, some soups, even a jar of pickled herring that a friend had brought from a vacation in Scandinavia years ago.

But finally I ran out of my limited stock and faced the fact that I had to go shopping. It was dusk, but I kept my sunglasses on as I got out of the car in the store parking lot. I hurried up and down the aisles, madly grabbing anything that I thought I might need. And then when I got to the checkout line, I heard a woman behind me call my name.

I froze. The young guy in front of me in line, with a package of franks and three bags of chips, looked at me curiously, wondering why I didn't turn around.

"Mr. Morrison?" the woman called again.

I made myself turn around. It was Ellen Sprague, the psychologist. I held up my hand and gave a little wave, hoping she would go away.

As she came over, it struck me again how like a bird she was. When I had seen her in her office, she had been perched on her little branch, making quick, darting movements, bobbing back and forth, always with her big, unblinking eyes on me. Now she seemed more like a heron—unusually tall for a woman, thin and leggy, heading toward me without much grace and yet with an odd kind of delicacy. She reached out a small hand that felt cool and surprisingly strong in my grip.

"Mr. Morrison, I've been thinking about you often since I read that story in the newspaper."

The guy in front of me looked up as he was paying for his chips. He was trying to figure out if I was anybody important. The checker, a worn-out teenage girl with a gold stud in her upper lip, had a blank stare, as if she didn't acknowledge being a part of the same world that contained us.

I mumbled something and tried to busy myself by moving my food onto the conveyor. Ellen Sprague watched without comment as I pulled out a stockpile of dried and canned goods; I had shopped like someone fortifying a backyard bunker. When I unintentionally caught her eye, she smiled a little. All she had in her hands were a single chicken breast and a plastic bag containing three apples.

We said nothing as I paid for my order. I hovered over the checker, interfering with her torpid packing of my bags; then, shouting out a cheerfully hollow good-bye to Ellen, I hurried to my car. And when I got there, I found that the headlights were on and the engine was dead.

I sat in the car gripping the steering wheel and telling myself over and over that all I had to do was call Triple A, that the guy who drove the repair truck probably didn't read the papers and wouldn't recognize my name, that there was really no choice and once I started moving, it would inevitably get done. Then I heard a light tapping at my window and turned to see Ellen's face; she was trying to say something through the glass. I shook my head, but she kept tapping, and finally I lowered my window. Half smiling, she wordlessly held up a set of jumper cables.

When my engine started turning again, I almost drove off without saying thanks, but then caught myself. Slowly, I got out of my car and walked over to where Ellen was folding up the jumper cables and putting them in her trunk.

"Listen," I said. "That was very kind of you. And I'm sorry I'm being so—" She looked up, her eyebrows lifted expectantly. But I didn't finish my thought. I didn't know what I was being. I waved my hand into the air impatiently. "Listen, I hope you understand."

She tilted her head sideways, the way she had in her office, thinking over both what I had said and what I actually meant, but this time she gave me a little smile. "Maybe not. But it's okay. Go on home."

I headed to my car, turned on the headlights, and pushed my stick-shift into drive, then I looked back at Ellen. She had put the cables in her trunk and was just standing there, staring off into the night as if she too were telling herself that she only had to keep going in order to get to a place where she was done. I remembered the single chicken breast and that odd way she had kept watching me in her office when I talked about Sam, as if she was trying to reassure herself, to see up close that strange, untouchable surface of another human's heart. So I got out and hurried over and without any introduction offered to buy her a drink. She seemed a little surprised, but she nodded, and then we stood there awkwardly, because it was nine-thirty P.M. in the middle of suburbia, and neither of us was the kind of person who had the faintest idea where a bar might be. So she offered her apartment and I followed her there.

It was a town house apartment, a little more modest than mine, except that its old, comfortable furniture looked like it had had a previous life somewhere other than a showroom floor. There were a few photographs scattered around the living room, mostly of other people's kids, and then some old black-and-whites, probably of grandparents' weddings. On the wall she had a few framed posters with brightly colored abstract designs and announcements of exhibits at various Parisian galleries. I remembered what one of my frat brothers used to say about girls who had just come back from junior year in France and, suddenly lighthearted, I laughed. She caught me and smiled too, although she couldn't have known why. And that made me feel bad, so I got serious again and frowned. This time she tilted her head again, inspecting me with squinted eyes.

She put out some wine and we sat facing each other at the counter in her kitchen. I was tongue-tied, fingering the rim of my glass and tilting it precariously.

"You know," she said, "when I read that story in the paper, it told me a lot." I lifted up my head. For a second I thought she was going to tell me that she had always thought I was an asshole and this had confirmed it. But she was trying to be helpful. "You had seemed so sincere when you talked about Sam. I don't usually see men that good at talking about being fathers. I couldn't imagine why your wife didn't want you to continue seeing him. But I suppose this issue— about the paternity, I mean—must have already come up between you."

I nodded mutely.

"But Sam didn't know at the time I met with him, did he?"

I nodded again. "He knows now. His mother told him," I added bitterly.

"Ah," she said, considering. "So now everything is much more complicated than I had imagined it. But at least I understand your ex-wife's concerns. At the time I thought perhaps she had some reason to keep you away from the boy that I had missed. I thought maybe I had been taken in by you."

"Maybe you were," I said.

"No." She shook her head quickly and, as she did so, a lock of brown hair fell over her eyes and swung back and forth. "I trust my judgment."

"You think I did the wrong thing? By suing?"

She stopped to think about it, letting her eyes drift up to the place where she seemed to keep her store of ideas. But she didn't find what she was looking for. "I'm not sure there was a right answer for you in your situation."

"That's true. But I think I screwed up just the same."

"And you think there was some other thing you could have done that would have solved the problem?"

I gulped down the wine and got up from my stool. I walked away, pacing in the small space beside the counter, knocking against straw baskets from some foreign travels that hung, empty, on the wall. I stretched my arms above my head and felt myself almost exploding through the ceiling. "I could have done better than just being this guy who went after money."

"Oh, but that's not what you're going after. I don't think anyone would believe that."

I smiled at her crookedly. "What then? Revenge?"

She tilted her head again. "Revenge, maybe. That's more likely than money." She smiled a little. "My bet is you're still going after the boy and you think maybe this is the way to do it."

I started nodding my head. "You think that's it?" I paused. "You think it could work out that way?"

She shook her head gently, the smile fading just a little, encouragement shrinking to sympathy. "No. Not in the way you want."

We had a couple more glasses of wine. I sat myself down and asked her some questions about herself, and sure enough heard about the trips to France and even the junior year abroad. I heard about the marriage that broke up. They had wanted different things, she said the first time. And after the third glass of wine, she said that she had wanted children and he had never been ready, and then she realized that she couldn't force someone into having a child he didn't want, and then she realized that she no longer had any reason to be with him.

At one point, I asked her to tell me what Sam had said when she met with him. I knew I shouldn't ask, but I was so anxious to get some crumb of information about him, some confirmation that once he had been on my side and wanted to see me. She started to tell me how he had gotten excited and happy talking about the time he spent with me, how he had argued with his mother when she tried to criticize me. I could see she was telling me this reluctantly; she knew she shouldn't be revealing confidences, and yet she must have seen how much I wanted to hear this. It occurred to me, as I listened to her calm, soothing voice, that she was a kind person, and that I was someone who badly needed kindness. Sitting across from her, I felt more peaceful than I had in weeks, and when she finally caught herself and said she shouldn't say anything more, I didn't want to leave.

She glanced at her watch. I nodded and got up. She followed me to the door and stood there shyly. My hand was on the doorknob when I suddenly felt the idea of her body just a foot or two from me. Without a second of thought or planning, I reached out and embraced her. As our faces moved together, I could see her nodding yes and could feel her hands tremble as she reached up to touch my arms. And then her face twisted to the side and she pushed me away.

I stopped immediately. My hands, clumsy and oversize, dropped to my sides; I pressed them against my jeans as if I was wiping sweat off the palms. "I didn't mean to do that," I said.

She folded her thin arms across her chest—either because she was thinking or because she was trying to put some barrier between us.

Then her little smile started playing at one corner of her mouth. "It seemed sincere enough," she said finally.

"But stupid, right?"

She shrugged. "Sudden."

"Unwelcome?"

The smile spread along her lips; her eyes dropped so that she wasn't looking at me, but then they darted up just to see if I was still there. "You seem like someone who acts too quickly. It's not always such a wise thing as you get older." She raised her eyes now to face me. "And life gets complicated."

I nodded and turned to the door. It opened and I headed out into the muggy night air.

Then I caught myself and turned around. She was still standing where I had left her, her arms still folded, her head tilted in that reflective, unfazed way. "But I could call you, right?" I asked.

She wagged her head back and forth. "You could try and see what happens." Then, smiling so I could actually see the glisten of her teeth, she put her hand on the door and gently closed it in my face.

19

The cameramen and reporters who had eventually deserted my front-door step reappeared at the courthouse on the morning we showed up for a hearing on a motion, filed by Joan's lawyer, to dismiss my lawsuit. Squinting in the bright sun as I got out of the car with Barry, I recognized the shiny forehead and glossy red lips of one of the evening news reporters, the one who always told you about the discovery of mutilated bodies while you wondered if she was doing something different with her hair. Barry headed right toward her.

I tried to go into the courthouse without speaking. There was a small clearing in front of the door, but when I pushed the door, it didn't budge. I tried to get to the door next to it, and a microphone was in my face.

"Is this lawsuit about the disappearance of fathers from family life?"

I kept my eyes down so I wouldn't be drawn into speaking. I felt more than saw their bodies keep springing up around me, like the bad guys in a video game, relentlessly marching in from the sides of the screen. I tried to move forward, as if I would be giving them an advantage just by acknowledging their presence long enough to slow down. But I couldn't move. "Do you see yourself as a spokesman for angry men?"

I bowed my head down again and pushed at the glass door of the courthouse. It popped open; I edged my way around a man with a camera and got in. As the door closed between them and me, I turned around and looked at their faces.

"What is it you're trying to say with this, Mr. Morrison?"

This was a different courthouse than the one we had been in last time. Then, we had been in the divorce court, before the judges who daily preside over the breakups and breakdowns of family life. But, according to Barry, we were moving up in the world. We were look-ing for "equity," he kept saying, which seemed to have some legal sig-nificance that, stripped of all the jargon, meant that we could try to jump from divorce court to superior court. This new courthouse was a few blocks from the one we had been in before; it was a modern building, twenty stories tall, eighteen of them with windows, the top two the jail. When I walked up to the metal detector just inside the entrance, one security guard nudged the other to look at me. I fished into my pocket for my keys and coins, then headed through the detector without setting off the alarm. The older guard slid my belongings down to me, then, looking me in the eye, stuck up his thumb and said, "Go get her."

I skulked into the courtroom and sat at the farthest end of an empty bench, waiting for Barry to come in and shelter me. But he was too busy talking to the reporters downstairs. This time the court-room was nearly empty. A few lawyers stood around the area in front of the bar, talking. The men and women wore dark suits of indistin-guishable cut and all held black bags. From time to time, I could see one of them pointing toward me or taking a furtive glance my way. Then Joan walked in.

She wasn't alone. She had a woman with her, not Marjorie, but a much younger woman, in a bright-red suit with large shoulders and a double row of gold buttons up the front, like a Cossack's uniform.

The woman's face was long, pale, and pointy. She and Joan barely stole a glance in my direction, then marched to the front row. I kept staring at the back of Joan's head, the blond hair falling in a perfectly smooth wave over her neck. But she never turned toward me.

Barry walked in a moment before the court officer said, "All rise." As we were rising, I whispered to Barry that Joan seemed to have a new lawyer. He craned his neck so he could see the pointy-faced woman, and I could hear him mutter under his breath, "Uh-oh."

The judge was an angular, angry-looking man, with a big thatch of white hair and red lines on his cheeks. He seemed impatient from the moment he arrived and I imagined him glaring at me for causing all this stir.

They called our case and Barry rose. He pulled on my arm and got me to stand and follow him to one of the two tables in the front of the courtroom, just under the judge's bench. From the corner of my eye, I saw Joan walking next to her lawyer; her step was firm, her head held high. When she sat down, she crossed her smooth hands, one over the other. I saw that she had rings on her fingers, rings I didn't recognize. I wondered where she had gotten them and then reminded myself that she'd bought them with my money. I felt my heart starting to pound in my chest.

Barry stood up, but before he could get a word out, the judge was barking at him. "This is a family court matter. Why are you here?"

Because the superior court judges were going to be more sympathetic to our arguments, Barry had explained to me; a man couldn't get a fair shake in family court, he had intoned in a knowing way. But it was hard to believe that this new judge would be sympathetic to our arguments, even if he stopped yelling at Barry long enough to hear them.

"This is an equitable action, Your Honor," Barry answered. "We're seeking to recover money that was obtained from Mr. Morrison under fraudulent pretenses."

Joan's lawyer was on her feet. "The family court has equitable powers, Your Honor. If that's their theory, then the complaint has to be dismissed as insufficient."

The judge held up his hand, but Joan's lawyer kept talking. She had a voice like a power drill. She was telling the judge that we were only here as an end run around the family court. She picked up Joan's affidavit about my abuse—the "alleged" abuse, Barry interrupted plaintively—and demanded that the case be sent back to family court immediately.

But Barry seemed to have some grounds and, puffing out his chest, waving his arms, he was standing on them. We were entitled to get back thirteen years of support and the family court couldn't do that for us. That's why we were here and why we would stay here.

The judge turned on Joan's lawyer, whom he seemed to know and addressed as Ms. Kincaid. "Is your client denying that Mr. Morrison isn't the father?"

"Legally, as Your Honor knows, the husband is presumed to be the father—"

"That wasn't my question, Counselor."

"Two weeks ago, he was demanding visitation rights. Now he's abandoning his child."

"Not his child," Barry interrupted.

The judge banged his fist on the bench in front of him and everyone stopped talking. I turned to Joan and, for just a second, she turned to me. Why are we here? I thought, and I guessed that she was thinking the same thing. Then she turned from me and looked up at Ms. Kincaid.

"I asked you a question, Ms. Kincaid," the judge said. "Is Mr. Morrison the father?"

"All we have are his allegations about a single blood test."

"Do you need further testing? If so, I'll order it and you'll report back in a week."

Ms. Kincaid swallowed. "Of course we'd submit to any testing the court orders."

The judge motioned to the clerk, who handed him a pen and a piece of paper. But before he could start writing, Ms. Kincaid launched into her speech again. It didn't matter what the testing said, she was saying. For thirteen years, I had enjoyed the benefits of paternity and I wasn't entitled now to undo those thirteen years at the expense of the child.

"What benefits?" the judge asked, his narrow gray lips lengthening into what may have been his version of a smile.

"Everything that fatherhood is."

"Except for fatherhood itself?"

"For those thirteen years there wasn't another father."

"That we know about."

Ms. Kincaid took a deep breath and started again with her argument that questions of child support should be resolved in divorce court. The judge put down his pen and cut her off with a question. "Are you saying, Ms. Kincaid, that it is completely irrelevant whether or not Mr. Morrison is, in fact, the biological father?"

"At the time of the divorce, Mr. Morrison agreed to pay support—"

"At the time of the divorce, Mr. Morrison believed that he was the father. Are you saying he would have been obliged to support the child if he had known otherwise?"

Ms. Kincaid shifted on her feet. "Of course he could have gotten a blood test at the time of the divorce, and then he wouldn't be in the position of trying to bankrupt Mrs. Morrison by asking for the return of thirteen years of back support."

"So you're saying that, if it turns out that Mrs. Morrison deceived him at the time of the divorce, she would be in a better position today than she would have been if she had told him the truth at the time of the child's birth?"

"I'm not saying that, Your Honor."

The judge's lips parted to reveal a row of even, graying dentures. "I'm glad to hear that, Ms. Kincaid, because it did sound for a moment like you were." He put down his pen and looked around the lawyer at Joan. I saw her slide down a notch in her chair. "Let me ask you again, Ms. Kincaid. Who is the father of this child?"

"My client was married to Mr. Morrison and was having regular marital relations with him when the child was conceived. She believed that Mr. Morrison was the father."

"Although she might have had some reason for doubt?" the judge asked mildly.

Ms. Kincaid didn't answer.

The judge's lips tightened and he picked up his pen again. "Well, it occurs to me that there isn't anyone in this courtroom who's in a better position to know than Mrs. Morrison." He wrote for a second and then looked at Barry. "If the blood test I'm ordering confirms your allegations, what would you be requesting?"

"An order relieving my client of all child support obligations immediately, pending the final resolution of this case."

"The child will have nothing to live on," Ms. Kincaid said.

"Are you representing the child or the mother, Ms. Kincaid?" the judge asked.

"Both, Your Honor. Their interests are the same."

"I wonder." He looked down at the paper in his hands. "Mrs. Morrison's motion to dismiss is denied. Mr. Morrison, Mrs. Morrison, and the child will submit to blood testing at the court clinic this week. The clinic will report the results to me upon their completion. If they exclude Mr. Morrison as the father, I'll enter an order directing him to stop paying child support, other than to continue paying the mortgage on the house. Do you need anything else before trial?"

Barry rocked back on his heels, his big hands pressing on his stomach contentedly. "I want to examine Mrs. Morrison under oath."

Joan looked up at her lawyer, then at me. The judge turned to Ms. Kincaid. "Objection?"

"We'll examine Mr. Morrison as well."

"No objection," Barry trumpeted.

The judge finished writing on his paper. Then he rested back in his large chair and looked out over the roomful of us, the king surveying his unworthy subjects. "If the blood tests come back as I suspect everyone believes they will, and Mr. Morrison is officially excluded as the father, can this case be resolved?"

The two lawyers looked at each other, but said nothing. Neither wanted to say they would agree, yet neither wanted to be the one preventing an agreement. The judge looked from one to the other, then stretched his arms out and linked his hands behind his head. "On the one hand, it would seem very unfair for Mr. Morrison to continue paying child support under those facts. Agreed?"

Barry nodded enthusiastically. Ms. Kincaid appeared to be looking for something in the papers that were scattered on the table in front of her.

"But there's a real question about what more we can do." The judge turned to Barry. "You're asking the court to undo the past. Can I?"

"Mr. Morrison's been paying for another man's child," Barry answered. "And he had no obligation to do that."

"Perhaps an obligation couldn't have been imposed if he knew at the time that the child wasn't his. But he didn't know."

"That's our point."

The judge shook his head. "No, that's her point." He nodded at Ms. Kincaid. "During the years that he thought the child was his, I assume he wanted to do what a father does for his own child. Support him?" He paused. Barry nodded. I nodded. "Give him a home?" I nodded again. "Love him?" I looked down at my hands. I listened to the judge's voice from above my head, its dry, caustic tones and flat vowels falling on me like icy rain. "And the child looked to him as a father for all those years. Not to any other man. So for those thirteen years, Mr. Morrison was the father and he acted appropriately."

Barry shook his head. "He didn't get what he was paying for."

The judge leaned forward. "And that is?"

"A child who would be his for the rest of his life."

"A child isn't an investment," Ms. Kincaid protested.

The judge's upper lip lengthened and his gray eyes seemed to twinkle. "At least not a safe one."

"And," she continued, oblivious, "whatever happened in the past, you can't take money from the mother without also taking it from the child. And the child is the innocent party here."

"If that's the line Mrs. Morrison wants to take," the judge said, looking toward the back of the room over Joan's head, "then she has to think carefully about who it is that's wronged him."

Ms. Kincaid was undaunted. "I'd say, Your Honor, the biggest wrong done him is this lawsuit."

The judge shook his head. "Even if I agreed with you, Ms. Kincaid, I don't think you win." He held up his hand. "So you have some time before you come back here. Think about it. There are some grievances that a court can't remedy."

He handed the paper on which he had written his order to the clerk, who began to read from it in a thick, blurry voice. I heard the sound of chairs scraping, felt Barry's hand under my arm, lifting me out of the seat. As I walked out of the room, I turned back toward the judge, who was bent over some other papers. He looked up, saw me standing there, and, very slightly, very slowly, shook his head with an expression that could have been pity or could have been warning; then he looked down again. When I stepped into the hallway, I heard Barry and Ms. Kincaid arguing and saw Joan, seated on a bench in the hallway, pulling nervously on her rings.

20

A year before the blood test, when Sam was twelve, my mother died. My father had died before Sam was born and since Joan's parents lived in Florida, my mother was the grandparent to whom Sam was closest. Every couple of weeks, I would take him to see her in the apartment where she had moved after my father died and she had sold the house where I grew up. She would feed him and fuss over him and marvel at how he had grown. In those moments, I could briefly feel again as if I had created a family.

The night that my mother died in the hospital, hooked up to an octopus coil of tubes, I called Joan because I had no one else I could imagine speaking to at that moment. She broke the news to Sam, and the next day she called me at home to say that he wanted to go to the wake.

I objected—he was too young, it would give him nightmares.

"He's nearly a teenager," Joan kept repeating. "He's old enough to understand dying."

"But I don't want him to remember her like that."

"It's not your job to control his memory," she said.

I came to pick him up on the evening of the wake. He was sitting in the spotless living room, on the couch that Joan had just recently reupholstered. He was uncomfortably buttoned up in the suit that she had made him buy for her parents' fortieth wedding anniversary the year before. The top button of his shirt was undone; he had made his tie into a lariat and was swinging it back and forth over his head. "Look, Dad," he called as he tried to lasso a ceramic bud vase.

"You're not dressed," I accused Joan as we stood in the hallway just outside the living room, trying to keep our voices down so that Sam would not suspect that we ever had differences.

"I didn't say I was going."

"Then why are you making him go?" I demanded.

"He wants to go. She was his grandmother. He cared about her."

I remembered how he would burst in the door of my mother's clean, orderly apartment.

She would run, puffing slightly, to greet us; as she hugged him, she would worry over his clothing and how long his hair had gotten. When he was with Joan's parents, he always seemed stiff and on his best behavior, folding his hands patiently while his grandfather talked about golf pros and his grandmother warned that he couldn't Rollerblade inside their Florida condominium development because the other retirees didn't think it was safe. My mother always had something baking and she would look at me accusingly as he started to wolf down the cookies, despite my assurance that he had just eaten lunch. "You forget what it's like to be a kid," she would say to me.

"I just think he shouldn't go to the wake," I whispered to Joan, still standing hesitantly in the doorway. "It'll depress him."

She shrugged. "You think he's never been depressed before?"

I wondered, as I went into the living room where he was waiting for me. He had the vase caught in the noose of his tie and was swinging it back and forth mournfully. "I don't know how to put this tie on," he announced.

I knelt down in front of him and put the tie around his neck. "Now sit still," I warned.

"Watch what Dad's doing so you can do it yourself," Joan said.

I was baffled by the fact that he was facing me; I crossed the tie wrong and the knot fell apart when I tried to slide it up to his neck. "Do it this way," Sam said, gleefully trying to tie it like a shoelace.

"No." I yanked the tie from him and then, instantly remorseful, hunted in his face to see if I had squashed some tiny spark of spirit. I could hear Joan moving to stand behind me and it made me fumble more. Finally, she crouched down and shoved me aside. I watched her fingers, their nails painted a pale pink, work a knot into Sam's tie.

"How did you learn how to do that?" I asked.

She sighed; then, without answering me, she reached out for Sam's head and pulled it close to hers for a kiss. We all stood and Joan turned to me. "Are you going to be able to bring him back here afterward? I could pick him up."

"Are you sure you don't want to go?"

"Pete, I haven't seen her since we were divorced." We both shot a look down at Sam, who was standing between us; we could see the top of his head, the hair slicked down by Joan for this special occasion. Our eyes met over him. She lowered her voice. "It would just feel too funny. Besides, this is something you two should do together. You don't need me there."

"I'm sure she would have wanted you to come."

"Pete, don't."

"I would like it if you came."

She shook her head. Her lips mouthed the words "We're not married anymore."

I nodded my head and took Sam's hand, leading him to the door. She followed us there, then bent down to check on Sam's outfit. "Don't get messed, okay?" she said.

He cringed as she tugged the lapels of his jacket.

She leaned closer to him. "Now you remember what I said."

He nodded again, his lopsided face set in a grown-up expression.

"What was that?" I asked her.

No one answered. Instead, she stood up and, as if on impulse, reached over and kissed me. I felt my skin tingle at the touch of her lips. As she was drawing away from me, she whispered into my ear, "I'm really sorry she's gone."

As I drove, Sam sat buckled in his seat, wiggling occasionally and eyeing the car radio longingly; he was not putting on his awful music in deference to my feelings. We drove in silence onto the highway, headed to the town, fifteen miles away, closer to Boston, where my parents had lived since I was ten.

"Are we going to see Nana's body?"

I nodded.

"I have a friend, Jason, in school and his grandmother died and they didn't see the body because they were Jewish. Why do we see the body?"

I shrugged. "To say good-bye."

"Do I touch her?"

"No." I shrugged again. "I don't know. If you want. What did your mother say?"

"She said not to feel sad because Nana was in a happier place. Do you believe that?"

"Yeah, sure."

"I don't think Mom believes it either. My friend Jason said his parents just said the thing about how he should do good things that would make his grandmother proud. Do you believe that?"

I smiled. "I'm sure Nana would have been proud of you whatever you did. You were her favorite grandchild." I pulled at his chin.

"I was her *only* grandchild, Dad."

"I didn't say you had to try very hard."

He sighed. "I cried when Mom told me about Nana."

I nodded.

"Did you cry, Dad?"

"A little."

"Mom cried too. I heard. After you called to tell her."

I turned the car off the highway. A half mile down the road, we passed my high school. There was a hand-lettered sign on a bedsheet hanging over the entryway. It said, GO RAIDERS. REGIONAL CHAMPS. A bunch of teenage boys in oversize varsity jackets stood outside a row of parked buses. The night my basketball team drove off to play the championship game, my mother stood across the street from the school, trying to take my picture without being seen so I wouldn't be embarrassed in front of my teammates. As we all crowded toward the bus, one of my friends saw her and called out, "Hey, Mrs. Morrison." She waved before she could think twice and then, catching herself, put her hand in front of her mouth and looked at me, shrugging.

"Did Mom hate Nana?"

"No, I think she liked her."

"Did Nana hate Mom?"

"No, she liked her very much. Nana thought your mother was a very good mother." I felt something like hunger carve a hole in my stomach. "I think Nana was sad when your mom and I split up," I said.

"Then why didn't they see each other again?"

"Because it's weird, Sam. It's hard to explain. It's just, your parents take your side. Not that it's about sides, but you know." Sam looked at me and shook his head with that sad-eyed look of someone who knew he was being lied to. "Well, take Mom's parents. Now, I don't see them, but I still like them. And they like me, right?"

Sam looked away.

"Right?"

"I don't know."

"What do they say?"

"Grandpa says you have a big head."

"That windbag—"

Sam laughed.

"Don't ever tell Mom I said that. You hear me?" He held up his right hand to swear. "And another thing. What was it that Mom told you?"

"What?"

"You know, when we were leaving. She said, 'Don't forget what I told you.' What did she tell you?"

He shook his head.

"Did she say something about Nana?"

He shook his head again, more vigorously.

"Sam, buddy. Please tell me."

"She said to be nice to you."

"Nice to me?"

"You know, because you might get angry."

I pulled up in front of the funeral home. There was a small crowd of people on the steps, white-haired ladies in dark coats, the women from my mother's church who had been raining baskets of flowers and plates of underspiced food on me for two days. "Angry?" I shouted. "Why would I be angry?"

"Mom said you get angry when you're sad."

I sighed. "I'm not sad, really."

"Mom said you don't always know what you feel."

He looked up at me for confirmation. I stared at him. "Why are you looking at me? I don't know what I feel."

He smiled. There was a gap in the front of his mouth that the dentist had already warned would mean real money. "You feel sad."

"I feel happy you're here."

"I know," he said, getting out of the car. "That's why I came."

At my insistence, they had put us in the largest room of the funeral home. The director tried to urge a smaller room, but I bullied him into submission. Most of the chairs in the room were empty.

My parents and I came from a long line of only children. They had known each other since high school and had never seen much need of friends. My father relaxed in his basement workshop. My mother knitted and prayed, often simultaneously. She didn't socialize until she became a widow, and then she only joined a club at her church, where she knitted and prayed in groups.

And they raised me. I was what they had done; I was what they left behind. I hadn't told anyone except Joan about my mother's death. None of my friends since high school had even known her and I had lost touch with my high school friends long ago. I walked into the room and reached down, grabbing for Sam's hand. Amazingly, he reached up and patted me on the small of the back.

My mother was laid out in the coffin I had selected the previous morning, irritably arguing with the funeral director, who kept talking about each model's durability. "And what is it supposed to be enduring for?" I demanded. There were the flowers from the church ladies and a big basket that I had sent myself, signed, "Your son, Peter," as if my mother might read it and need reminding about who I was. And above the flowers was my mother, laid out in the dress I had grabbed from her closet because the funeral director told me that I absolutely had to bring in something unless I wanted her to meet her maker in a hospital johnny. Her closet had always been off limits when I was a child and, opening the door, smelling potpourri and worn shoe leather, I felt a rush of shame, as if I had walked in on her naked.

"Why, Peter, is this your son?"

I nodded, not looking in the direction of the reedy old-lady voice that was addressing me.

My eyes were planted on my mother's face.

"I never would have recognized him. He doesn't look a bit like you. I bet he looks like his mother. Where's your mommy, son?"

"She's at home."

"Oh?"

I stepped forward, toward the coffin, feeling Sam's skinny hand try to squeeze mine. When we got there, I was again stunned, this time by watching Sam kneel down and do an amazing imitation of someone saying a prayer. "Where did you learn that?" I whispered.

He shushed me and for a second he looked exactly like my mother telling me to sit still in church. Then he rolled his eyes. "Mom said that's what you do. Now you do it." He pushed me in the back and I sank down to my knees. I stayed there for a moment; then, feeling my face flush red, I got up and wiped my wet palms on my pants.

A tall, red-faced man with bloodshot eyes walked up to me. "You must be Petey."

I nodded vacantly.

"Boy, I haven't seen you in a dog's age. And who's this slugger?"

"I'm Sam, Petey's son."

The old man feinted a jab; Sam ducked his chin and put up his fists.

"Whoa, look at the hands on this one. You teach him that, Petey?"

He feinted a jab at me. My muscles wouldn't move; the old man's fist landed on my shoulder. "Hey, you better teach your old man a few things, sonny. What did you say your name was?"

The old man's breath smelled of cigarettes and rye. He wheezed when he spoke. Sam held out his hand and introduced himself, speaking in a poised, well-mannered voice I had never imagined existed inside him. I kept looking at him as if he belonged to someone else. Had Joan done all this by herself? I wondered. Could Sam have a whole personality that I had no part of? I wanted to pull him outside and quiz him about it.

The old man introduced himself. His name was Al. He had played ball with my father. According to him, we had apparently gone fishing together when I was just a nipper, an incident I couldn't recall and actually doubted. I had only the vaguest recollection of seeing him at my father's wake years before.

Sam and he talked fishing and I listened, wondering how Sam had learned to make small talk. Sam lied about whether he and I had ever fished; he made up an expedition on the river and when the man asked suspiciously if there were fish in the river, Sam changed it to a lake and kept going. Then he looked up at me and flashed his gap-toothed smile.

"Dad, Al played baseball with Grandpa," he said, as if I had just arrived.

"I bet your grandpa taught you a thing or two about baseball, right, sonny?"

"No, not really."

Al looked at me worriedly.

"My father died before he was born."

"Is that a fact?" Al asked in a thick voice. "Well, come to think of it, it must be that long since Fred passed away. When you get to be my age, time plays tricks on you."

"It *is* hard to believe it's been that long," I said, trying to be decent. I put my hand on Sam's head. "I've tried to teach him what Dad taught me."

"You better, right?" Al said. He winked at Sam. "Keep your head low and your eyes on the ball. Right, sonny?"

Sam took the batter's stance and nodded seriously. The old man stretched back and tossed an invisible ball over the plate. Sam swung. An old lady said, "Now look at that. They shouldn't be playing in here."

Al waved his hand in the lady's direction. "I thought I would stop by," he said to me. "I used to see your mother around town all the time. She always stopped to say hello. She was a lovely lady."

I nodded.

"Your father was a lucky man. He always said that. 'I'm the luckiest man alive.' Did you know that?"

I shook my head. I had never heard my father say such a thing. I doubted he believed in luck, only hard work and paid-up insurance premiums. I looked down at Sam and said, wildly, "You remind me of my father."

"I do?"

"Sure you do," Al said, wheezing up a lungful of phlegm. "You're the next in the line. Fred had a good pair of hands on him, just like you do."

"You have a good head on your shoulders," I said to Sam.

"That's it. Straight. On the level. Never missed a day's work. That was Fred. You'd do a lot worse than to be like him." He looked around. "There are no refreshments here, are there?"

I looked around too, wondering if I was supposed to have arranged that. I tried to find the funeral director, but he was in the hallway attending to a large party of mourners, the women all wearing hats, one of them complaining loudly about being stuck in a room that was too small.

"I don't think so," I said.

Al slapped my shoulder. "What kind of an Irishman are you?"

We were Scotch actually, Scotch and English and maybe a little French. It wasn't something we ever thought much about. I smiled at Al. "Sorry."

"Now don't be sorry. You have nothing to be sorry for. You had a lovely mother and now she's gone to her reward and you keep carrying on. You have a kid and he's the next in the line. That's all you can do. Right, sonny?"

Sam nodded solemnly.

"Petey, you have any other children?"

Sam shook his head for me. I was gnawing the side of my fingernail.

"Well," Al said, winking at me, "you keep working on it. Maybe you'll have a daughter next who'll be as lovely as your mother was. You're a lucky fellow. Just remember that."

I nodded.

The minister from my mother's church came and took my hand in both of his, making me jump when I felt his warm palm on my knuckles. My throat tightened when he started talking about how proud my mother had always been of me. "Why?" I asked. His eyebrows shot up and, hurriedly, I said, "Why do these things happen?" He nodded and said something that sounded like it came from the Bible. The whole time Sam was looking at me through squinted eyes.

After the service, I hurried away from the old ladies who clustered outside the funeral home, telling them I had to get Sam home because he was tired. They clucked and hovered and patted my shoulder and asked if I needed some more spiceless food. "Thank God," I said involuntarily when we got in the car and shut the door behind us.

"You have to lighten up, Dad," Sam said.

I sighed and looked at him. "You know, buddy, you're getting way too smart for me. Maybe I should let you be the dad for a while."

"No, you're doing a good job."

"I am?" I turned to him. "I think my dad did a better job."

He shrugged. "No. You're doing fine. Really. I think so."

I looked forward. The lights in the funeral home were going out. I saw the mourners from the other room stream outside, the men smoking and holding on to the women, who wept and checked out each other's coats. "I don't know, Sam. Now it's just me and you, really. I don't have anyone older than me anymore." I turned to him. "You can't even imagine what that feels like."

Sam nodded seriously. "Sometimes I think what it would be like if Mom died." He looked away. "You know, late at night, I'll think about it. What it would be like."

"Oh, Sammy, don't worry about that. I'd take care of you."

"No," he said, sighing. "I don't mean that. I mean how it would feel not to have a mother."

"You'll always have me," I said, and as I said it, I realized that it wasn't true. I had divorced his mother seven years ago; he had been without his father more than half his life. I drew in a deep breath. "You know, I've been thinking, since this happened with Nana, that maybe you have your parents inside you. Do you know what I mean, Sam?"

He was looking away from me, fingering the latch to my glove compartment.

"So whatever happens, there's a way that you can't lose your parents if you love them and they love you. I think that's true. I think I'm feeling that now. That could be true for you too."

He nodded. "Okay. We can leave now."

"Are you crying?" I asked.

He pulled up the latch and the glove compartment door opened. A pile of maps cascaded to the floor. He nodded his head and put his fists up to his eyes. I reached down, scooped up the maps, and started putting them back in order on my lap. I listened to his sniffles as he sat there, and thought about saying, "It's okay to cry," and then, to my surprise, I started crying myself. I put my hands to my face and the maps fell again. He looked at me and laughed. Through my tears, I smiled at him. "We're a pair, aren't we?"

"Hey," Sam said with a wheeze, "I'm the next in the line."

21

My deposition was held at Ms. Kincaid's office a month after the court hearing. It took place a week before Joan's did. There had been some skirmishing between Barry and Ms. Kincaid over this schedule, and from the amount of verbiage that Barry used to explain the various strategic ramifications, I surmised that he had lost the battle. I took the day off from work, then spent an hour standing at my closet, changing from a business suit to jeans and back again. I finally settled on khakis and a navy blazer. Then I picked out a regimental plaid tie that must have hung in my closet since I'd turned eighteen and that, a dozen times since, I had considered giving to Goodwill. Subconsciously I must have thought that if I dressed like a college kid, the lawyers would go easy on me.

Joan sat at one end of the table, separated from the rest of us by a few empty seats. She had some papers in front of her and she was either looking at them or else glancing at Ms. Kincaid. When I said hello, she nodded wordlessly without looking up.

Barry sat next to me and kept putting his hand on my arm when he could tell that Ms. Kincaid's drill-like voice was working its way through my self-control. She sat sideways at the table, looking at the wall and forcing me to stare at her sharp, expressionless profile. The table shook from the jiggling of my knee beneath it.

Three weeks before this deposition, the results of the new, court-ordered blood test had come back as expected. I was definitively and officially excluded as Sam's father. The judge ordered that my child-support payments stop. The next day, every one of my financial institutions received a subpoena from Ms. Kincaid.

Barry was nonplussed by this development. "She wants to show that you have so much money you barely missed what you were paying."

"But that's not even logical."

"It doesn't have to be logical," he said, shuffling papers on his end of the line. "It just has to convince a judge."

When we got to my deposition, I wanted to talk about how it had felt to learn that Sam wasn't mine. Ms. Kincaid wanted to hear about my stock options. I wanted to tell her how Joan had broken my heart; she wanted to hear about the time I spent a week skiing with two business-school friends in Montana. I wanted to tell her about how, for all the years I supported Joan and Sam, I would give Joan any money she wanted, above and beyond the monthly child support amount, no questions asked; Ms. Kincaid wanted to hear about the one month, four years ago, I had been late in making my payment.

"You're doing great," Barry said during the break, putting his hand over the mouthpiece of the cell phone that he was using to yell at his secretary back at the office. He didn't look at me when he spoke. Joan and Ms. Kincaid sat in the glassed-in conference room. Every time Joan saw me looking in, she would say something and Ms. Kincaid would turn around and glare. I spent the break standing in the men's room, staring at myself in the mirror; I found a tear in the pocket of my blazer.

At the end of the day, Ms. Kincaid finally let me talk about Sam. I poured my heart out, about how I had lived for those Saturdays we spent together, about how I was always ready for more, how I would take him during the week, any night Joan wanted to be free, on a moment's notice, how she never had to spring for a baby-sitter once in the years since we'd separated.

"And you found the time you spent with the child gratifying. Correct?"

"Well, yes. You could use that word."

"You derived benefit from it at the time. Correct?"

"Are you asking me if I enjoyed it?"

"You derived emotional and psychological benefit from the time you spent with the child. Correct?"

"Yes. I derived considerable benefit from the child."

I felt Barry shift in his seat and I looked at him. He was rubbing the end of his nose. I was falling into a trap.

"I derived benefit because I believed he was *my* child."

"And you believed that until you obtained the results of the blood test. Correct?"

I looked over at Joan. "Correct."

"And within two months of learning the results, you stopped paying Mrs. Morrison anything more for the support of the child. Correct?"

Barry was quiet in the elevator going down.

"I don't get it. Did I blow it?" I demanded.

We stepped outside the office building. It was the end of August; the air stuck to our faces, thick with humidity and car exhaust.

"No, you didn't blow it. She just scored some points."

"Was I not supposed to 'derive benefit' from seeing Sam? Christ, it makes it sound like I was going to a chiropractor."

"Their argument is that if you derived benefit, then you got what you paid for and you're not entitled to a refund."

"But I paid for a son. And I don't have that."

"That's *our* argument." He smacked me on the shoulder. "Chin up. We get a shot at her next week."

———

"And what do you think will happen next week?"

Ellen rubbed a towel across her face as she asked the question. We had just finished playing tennis at the court in my condo development and were sitting on a bench nearby.

I had called her after we ran into each other at the supermarket and offered dinner, the theater, a museum, and Fenway, all in rapid succession, all without arousing any interest. Then I remembered seeing a tennis racket lying in her hallway when I was at her apartment.

"You have privileges at a court?" she asked wistfully.

"Oh yes, but I don't have a partner and I've been dying to play."

She agreed. I left work early the next day to buy a racket and take a lesson from a pro.

"I don't know what I expect to happen next week, exactly," I said, still panting from our game. I was spinning the racket on its head, a maneuver she disapproved of because it always ended with the racket crashing at our feet. "I just hope Joan goes through what I went through."

Without making a comment, Ellen got up from the bench. "This has been fun. You weren't bad for a beginner."

I looked up, alarmed. "I'm not a beginner. I'm just rusty."

She smiled and held out her hand for me to stop. "Your dishonesty is flattering, although a little worrisome. If you want, we can play again next week."

I got up and hurried after her, down the hill to the visitors' parking lot. The sun had just started to disappear behind the horizon of town houses, leaving a wake of orange-and-purple wash. The air was still. I could breathe a faint touch of perfume rising from the heat of her skin.

"Are you mad at me for doing this lawsuit?" I said finally.

"It's not my place to judge." She shifted the bag that hung from her shoulder. "Although of course I do."

I nodded. "And what's the verdict?"

"I think you're a person with a lot of anger. And you're trying to figure out what to do with it."

I felt the heat inside my face seem to explode through my skin. "Don't you think I have a lot to be angry about?"

"That's why I'm trying not to judge."

We walked in silence a little longer. I hoisted the tennis racket over my shoulder, carrying it like a soldier carries his rifle. I could hear the tramp of our sneakers on the grass. "I want to know who the real father is."

"And that's a question you need Joan to answer?"

"I don't get you."

She paused to adjust her shoulder bag again. "You want me to carry that for you?" I offered. She shook her head no, then reconsidered and handed it to me. The bag was heavier than I imagined. As I tried to adjust the strap on my shoulder, my tennis racket slipped from under my arm.

"Peter, when you get this question answered, what are you going to do with the information?"

"Barry says we can go after this guy for money. If he has any. I mean, he owes me, right?"

"I suppose. Will Sam start seeing him?"

I dropped my head back and looked up at the cloudless sky. "I guess. I mean, it's only natural."

"And that's what Sam wants?"

"I don't know. We don't talk. I'm under my lawyer's orders to stay away." I stopped, my shoulder aching from the straps of the bags. "Apparently only Joan gets to decide what goes on for Sam. And I don't get to say anything about it." I started walking again and slipped in the grass. Ellen's bag dropped off my shoulder and landed on my foot. "Damn," I said, starting to hop in pain. The strap caught in the tennis racket, which clattered to the ground. "Fuck," I shouted, stamping my foot.

When I looked over, Ellen was smiling. "Maybe you were just carrying too much." She picked up her bag, feeling it gently to see if anything was broken. Then she looked at me. "Do you need a hand?"

I sank down to the grass and sat there; I picked up my racket and started spinning it. Ellen lowered herself gracefully to the ground, kneeling down and resting back on her feet. She took the racket from me and laid it on the ground, just beyond my reach.

"You think I should try to keep seeing him?" I asked.

She shook her head. "No. I think, given your relationship with his mother, that could enflame things."

"You think I should give up this lawsuit?"

"You can't decide that until you've figured out what you want from it."

"You think I'm anyone you'd be interested in seeing again?"

She picked up my racket and started spinning it on its head. "Now, that I don't know the answer to." She looked at me. "It sounds like you would have been in the past. Maybe you're not right now, but maybe you could be again. Hopefully." She let the racket fall on my lap. "The question is how long we give ourselves to figure it out."

"I'm willing to wait," I said.

She patted my knee. When I reached out my hand, she pulled hers away and pushed herself up from the ground. "But in any event, I don't think that's the big question you need answered right now."

The big question got answered three hours into Joan's deposition. She sat in Barry's conference room, answering each question carefully, with a minimum of words. She never raised her voice. Her long fingers pulled and twisted at their rings; when she paused to think, she would lower her head and play with the bracelets around her wrists.

There wasn't much to ask her, really, when it came down to it. Tonelessly, resignedly, she conceded Barry's every point. She nodded at the papers he thrust in front of her, making a perfunctory effort to read them; she hated numbers and she knew what they added up to anyway. I had given her a lot of money for a lot of years and she had spent it all on herself and Sam. She didn't seem to contest that.

"Why aren't you asking her about Sam?" I yelled at Barry during the break.

"What about Sam in particular?" he said irritably. He wanted to rush into his office and shuffle some other client's papers while I entertained myself in the reception room, reading the stack of interior-design magazines on the coffee table.

"Whether I was a good father. Whether I did things for him. Whether he and I got along."

"But that stuff hurts us, Pete. Remember, our claim is that you *didn't* have a father-son relationship."

"Then how about what's going on with Sam now? Ask her how he's doing without me coming by anymore."

"It doesn't matter," he said.

I started to explode and he held up his hand. "You know exactly what I mean, so don't start shouting at me. What goes on with Sam from now on is not our business. Our business is money. And what happened in the past."

What happened in the past was where Barry finally started going, an hour after the break, as Joan's voice was getting flatter and the tugs on her rings more insistent.

"You and Mr. Morrison agreed that you would try to conceive a child, isn't that so, Mrs. Morrison?"

"We had discussed it."

Barry lifted his eyebrows. "You did more than discuss it, didn't you?"

She shrugged. "I suppose."

"You and he tried to conceive a child, didn't you?"

Visibly trying not to remember, she nodded. "Yes, we did."

"And were you having intercourse with anyone besides Mr. Morrison?"

She rubbed her hand on the top of the table, as if there was something to feel there besides the smooth ungiving surface of wood veneer.

"Objection. What time period are you referring to, Counselor?"

"Thank you for clarifying, Ms. Kincaid." The lawyers smiled serpent smiles at each other. "The time period between your marriage to Mr. Morrison and the birth of your son."

Joan pressed harder on the tabletop.

"Could the stenographer read back the question?" Barry said in a voice that pretended to be helpful.

The stenographer robotically pulled up a scroll of paper on which she had been typing shorthand notations and read: " 'And were you having intercourse with anyone besides Mr. Morrison?' 'Objection—' "

"I did."

"You did what, Mrs. Morrison?"

"Have intercourse with someone besides Mr. Morrison."

"On how many occasions did you have intercourse with someone besides Mr. Morrison?"

Joan crossed her hands in front of her. "One time. I did it one time." She looked up and turned to me, deliberately catching my eyes. "One time," she repeated. Then she turned away and faced Barry, awaiting the next question.

"And what was the name of the individual with whom you had intercourse on that occasion?"

"Kip."

Barry sputtered. Even Ms. Kincaid looked surprised.

Joan shrugged. "That was his name. Kip."

"And what was his last name?"

She seemed to have trouble recalling. Finally, she said, "I'm not really sure now. I think it was Pressman."

"Could you spell that?" the stenographer asked.

Joan shrugged again. "I don't know the spelling."

"And was 'Kip' a nickname or was that his given name, Mrs. Morrison?"

"I don't know."

"And where does Mr. Pressman live today?"

"I don't know. I think he's in New York."

"And when was the last time that you spoke with Mr. Pressman?"

She paused to think. "I don't recall. It wasn't long afterward. A few days, maybe a week."

"After what?"

She leaned back in her chair, one hand absently brushing the ends of her hair. I saw a faint trace of a smile on her lips. "After I had intercourse with someone other than Mr. Morrison."

Barry took a deep breath. "And where was it that you had intercourse with Mr. Pressman?"

"Objection. The witness is instructed not to answer."

"And what are your grounds, Ms. Kincaid?"

"Counselor, you know very well—"

The lawyers began to argue. The stenographer kept clacking away at her machine, pleading with them to talk one at a time. Joan picked up her handbag and started looking through it. She pulled out a pocket mirror and opened it, examining something that she seemed to believe had gotten into her eye. When she shut the mirror, she looked down the table, through the quarreling lawyers, and faced me.

Her eyes had gone soft and dark. She had a look both sad and angry, a look of someone who was being wronged but was too tired to fight about it.

The stenographer jumped when my chair screeched along the slick floors of the conference room. I stormed out of the room and slammed the door behind me. As I headed down the hallway, I looked back once, into the glassed-in conference room. The two lawyers were standing now, leaning over the conference table, Barry waving his hands, Ms. Kincaid stuffing papers into her black bag. Joan had spun around in her chair and sat watching me. The sad look was gone from her face; in its place was the look of an enemy.

22

I was waiting outside the front door to his apartment building when he turned the corner and came down the street. He had long hair, down to his shoulders, with some gray in it. He was thin and his jeans, held up by a thick black belt decorated with metal studs, hung off his hips. He barely glanced at me as he hurried by, clutching a satchel under his arm and muttering to himself. I followed him inside and when he pushed open the door, I came up behind him and followed him into the lobby. He turned around, alarmed.

"You're Kip Pressman," I said.

He nodded, inching backward, away from me and toward the stairs.

"I'm Pete Morrison. Joan's husband."

He shrugged without comprehension, and then, an instant later, it dawned on him. "She called me just last week," he said, almost speaking to himself. "Said people might be calling—" He caught himself. "So you're the husband."

I took a step closer and he held up his hand in front of me. He was a skinny guy, but wiry. He seemed like he wasn't looking for trouble, but wasn't a stranger to it either.

"Listen, man," he said as I approached, "I don't know what you want—"

"I want to talk."

He looked around the empty lobby. "I'm really in a hurry."

I took a step closer. I held up my hands to show I had nothing on me.

"All right," he said, "we'll go up to my place." He motioned for me to follow him. The door to one of the apartments off the lobby had opened a crack while we were talking; it slammed shut as we walked by.

He lived on the third floor of a walk-up. It was a narrow building not far from midtown, crammed between a pizzeria and a storefront with blacked-out windows and no signs that was probably a bar. From the stairs, you could smell tomato sauce and hear the thumping of a drum beat.

He opened the door to his apartment with a little shove. We walked into one big room.

The floor was covered with a mess of clothing and magazines and newspapers and plastic food-containers. "I wasn't expecting company," he said over his shoulder. He headed toward the kitchen, kicking aside a pile of books. The kitchen was small and windowless. I sat at a tiny table. He didn't sit down with me, but walked over to the refrigerator, saying, "Sorry, but I'm starving." He stuck his head in the fridge and started pulling out food that he tossed on the table—a tiny chunk of cheese in a mass of plastic wrapping, some dried-out looking cold cuts, a serving of take-out Chinese.

He sat across from me and started eating the cold Chinese straight from the container. He was so absorbed in the rapid movement of his fork from table to mouth that he seemed oblivious to my presence. Then he wiped the back of his hand across his lips and reached into the refrigerator, pulling out two bottles of beer. He slid one over to me, opened his, and downed half of it. Mine sat in front of me, the moisture condensing on the glass.

"Sorry," he said, suppressing a belch. "I've been working for three straight days editing this video. We were up against a deadline. I don't think I've eaten in two days." He smacked the pocket of his shirt, then his pants; then, remembering, he reached down to the leather jacket he had thrown on the floor and pulled out a crumpled pack of cigarettes. He held it out to me, and when I shook my head, he grabbed one himself, lit it, and blew out a cloud of smoke. "Okay. I'm all ears."

I couldn't think of anything to say. I don't know what I had expected to find when I decided to go down to New York and meet him. It hadn't been hard to find him; he was listed in the Manhattan phone book, the only "Kip Pressman" there. Once I knew where he was, I had to see him, but now that I had tracked him down, all I could do was stare at his face. He was probably in his mid-thirties, but lines were forming around his eyes. He had a long neck and long fingers. He smelled as if it had been a couple of days since he'd showered. I was trying to find some sign of Sam in his face. I suppose what I was looking for was something that would make me finally understand that this man, not I, was Sam's father.

He was on his guard, and he wasn't going to say anything until I started. We sat awkwardly at the table, him patiently smoking his cigarette and waiting for my next move.

"You were working on a video?" I said finally. "I thought you were a painter."

"A painter?" He seemed confused, then the light dawned. "Oh, right, I met her in a painting class. She tell you that?"

"She told my lawyer." Despite myself, I felt an embarrassed smile on my face. "There was this deposition." My voice trailed off.

He looked as if he was about to ask me a question, then he thought better of it. Instead, he shrugged and said, "I used to be in art school. But that was years ago. I've been in film since I came to the city thirteen years ago. Listen, film's bad enough, but there is really no money in painting." He coughed, a deep cough straight from the bottom of his chest. He looked around for an ashtray; then, finding none, he rubbed the tip of his cigarette on the top of the Chinese-food container; I could hear the grease sizzle. "Yeah. Your wife was a painter too. Not bad either. She still paint?"

I shrugged. "Yes." I waited a second, then added, "We're divorced."

"So you just finding out about me?"

I nodded.

"But you were divorced anyway, so it's not like it was a big deal. Right?" He looked up hopefully.

"I just found out about the kid too."

"Oh that." He took a final deep drag off his cigarette, stubbed it out in the food container, then tilted back in his seat, resting his head against the wall behind him. "Man, you could have knocked me over when she told me. Just called me out of the blue and laid that on me."

"What did you say?" I asked, my voice sounding small in my throat.

"I said, 'Joan who?' " He laughed a little, then looked at me. "You know, that's the truth. I had no idea who she was at first." He leaned forward on his elbows. "Even now I have a little trouble picturing it all. She was blond, right?"

I nodded.

"Sweet? Kind of quiet and shy?"

"Maybe with you."

"Yeah, well." He pulled out his cigarette pack and looked inside; he had only one left. He hesitated for a second, then said, "What the hell," and lit it. As he sat there a minute, thinking, he put his finger to his mouth as if he was about to tell me to be quiet, and for a moment he looked so much like Sam I almost got up and ran from the room. I felt my hands gripping the edges of my narrow seat to keep myself from moving.

He was shaking his head now as he thought about the whole situation. "So what's going to happen to me now?" he asked.

"You have to start helping Joan support Sam."

He smiled and stretched his hand out over the kitchen, the stained, cracked porcelain of the sink, the refrigerator that hummed too loudly, the linoleum that was peeling in the corner. "She can help herself. Whatever I have is hers." He shook his head. "Man, I can barely support myself. I pick up work when I can, I spend a fortune in rent for this hovel, and there's nothing left. Here." He stuck his finger in the side of his mouth and pulled it back, revealing a gap halfway to his wisdom teeth. "This is killing me, man. I've wanted to get it fixed for five years." He looked at me and shook his head. "Where I live, there are no dental plans."

"Yeah, but he's your kid."

He nodded. "I guess so. That's what she tells me. Joan said something about having to do a blood test." He looked at the veins standing out on his skinny arm, as if he was already imagining the pierce of the needle, the warm gush of blood. "Doesn't seem real somehow." He looked up at me. "What's the kid like?"

"He's a great kid," I said, forcing the words out of my mouth.

"He look like me at all?"

I flinched. "Don't ask me that, please."

Kip nodded. "Yeah. Okay." He shook his head, staring at the dirty tabletop. It had occurred to him that he had to say something kind, and he was looking inside himself for the place where he had last seen his kindness, before it got buried under the pile of hostility and resentment. "So this must be brutal for you. Listen, I'm sorry, man." He rolled his eyes. "You have no idea how sorry." He sighed and stubbed out his cigarette. "It seems like I can never get ahead. Now I'm going to have your ex-wife on my case." He looked up at me. "You know, I already have a kid."

"You're kidding?"

"Yeah." He smiled a little. "Nice kid. Little girl. She's about five. I dated her mother—that was only six months." He laughed ruefully. "But at least I recognized *her* name when she called me. And, man, I got her up my ass every month for a support check and I got the child welfare people trying to garnish any paycheck I manage to get my hands on to pay off the arrears." He shook his head. "You know, I said to your wife when she called, 'I'm sorry, I'll help when I can, but listen, you can't get blood from a stone.'"

I turned away and looked out into the living room. "I'm not going to let you get away with that," I said. "I can sue you too, you know. You're going to have to come up with something."

He nodded his head. "You could be a real pain in the ass if you wanted to." He jumped up and reached into the refrigerator; I was facing the seat of his jeans, two hand-size patches of worn fabric, one already frayed and revealing brightly colored jockey shorts beneath. He pulled out another beer, twisted it open, and poured it down his throat. He gave a satisfied beer sigh, and wiped his mouth again. "You could make my life miserable if you wanted. Wouldn't get you much money. Probably wouldn't even cover your lawyer's costs." He smiled. "Doesn't look like you need money though." He reached out and touched the lapel of the camel-hair sports jacket I had tossed on that morning, running from my apartment to catch the shuttle to New York. He rubbed it between the tips of his fingers. "But then it isn't really money you're after, is it?"

I pulled myself away from him roughly. He didn't move. He dropped my lapel, but left his hand resting on the corner of my chair, his bony fingers dangling in the space where my shoulder had been. He was nodding to himself, figuring it out, his eyes on my face. "If you really wanted money, you wouldn't be here yourself. You'd send some rottweiler lawyer out, right? So tell me. What do you want?"

I picked up my beer, which was still standing on the table in its little ring of sweat. I opened it and drank it down. The first thing I could think to ask was, "Do you wear glasses?"

He looked at me, puzzled for a moment, then nodded. "Yeah. Contact lenses." We sat for a moment longer, and he asked, "Is that it?"

"No," I said. "I want you to tell me about it. You and Joan."

He nodded. "Yeah. Sure. You'd want to know that." He looked at me. "You don't have any cigarettes, do you?" I shook my head. "Nah, you wouldn't. Not the type. All right. Joan. Like I said, it's still a haze to me. But we met in this art class she was taking. It was a lot of other people like herself, amateurs, mostly women. I was about to graduate and I was assisting the teacher, you know, just to pick up some extra money. I had to go around and look over everyone's shoulders and tell them how well they were doing their shapes and maybe they needed to start working on texture. And it paid dick too." He sighed. "But your wife was decent, better than all the other ladies there. Although she didn't know it. You'd tell her she was doing good and she'd look at you with these big eyes, like, 'Do you really mean it,' and I was, like, 'Yeah, but it's not such a big deal.' But I liked her. And she would hang out after class some afternoons and talk. She seemed like she had a lot of time on her hands. You were working a lot, I bet. Right?" He looked at me for confirmation. I nodded. "And that was basically it. Just talking. Sometimes coffee. She wanted to hear all about my work. She was all excited I was going to New York and trying to do it for real. I guess it was something she always thought about doing." He made a noise that sounded as if he was going to spit. "If only she knew what's waiting for you here. But anyway, I was twenty-one then. It was flattering. She was an older woman—what was she, about thirty, thirty-one then?"

"Twenty-eight."

"Yeah, older woman. Now I can't get a twenty-eight-year-old to look at me once she sees I'm broke. But that's another story. Back to Joan." He looked at me. "You enjoying this?"

"I can't imagine what she ever saw in you."

He seemed to consider it for a minute, as if it was hard for him to imagine also. Then, with a sudden burst, he jumped up from the table and loped into the living room; I could hear him bustling around, moving things about and cursing softly under his breath. Then he said, "Here it is," and he came back with a photograph in his hand. It was a picture of him, lying on the grass by the Charles River, near where they give the outdoor concerts in the summer. He had his shirt off; his hair was as long as it was now, but lighter and curlier. The skin around his eyes was smooth. He had a wicked smile that curled up in one corner. It flashed into my mind that, in ten years, Sam might look a lot like this, and the picture started to blur. I looked up and saw Kip standing there, staring down with a look of shameless pride. "Face of an angel, right?" he said.

I threw the picture on the table. He snatched it out of the puddle

the beer bottle had left. He held it in his hands, unable to stop looking at it. "I'll tell you. Your wife wasn't the only woman who thought
so." He sat down. "So that was why she liked me. Plus she was getting
an art rush because of my so-called talent. Plus I asked her a little
about herself. She was one of those who won't say a thing and then
suddenly it's like you push a button and you can't keep it from coming out. It was kind of cute, really."

"She talk about me?"

He shrugged. "Her husband didn't understand her, right?" I
twisted in my seat; I thought I might hit him and he possibly thought
so too, because he wiped the smile off his face and held out his hand
toward me, trying to calm me down. "Listen, she didn't really talk
about you at all. Not that I can remember. I think she— You know, at
first she didn't like admitting that she was married." He stopped and
thought for a second. "She mainly talked about painting. She had
wanted to be a serious painter before she got married, and she felt she
was slipping away from that. I think she thought she was becoming
boring. Crazy to look back on it now—a twenty-eight-year-old
afraid of getting older. But I think that was it. She was primed for a
fling." He thought a moment longer. "She said something about how
she was afraid that someday she'd have a kid and then there'd be
nothing left of her to put on canvas." He laughed nervously. "Kind of
ironic, huh?"

I jumped up and stalked into the living room, just to get away from
him. My hands were clenched behind my back.

He kept talking from where he sat in the kitchen. "You know,
man, it just wasn't that big a thing. I mean, we knew each other for a
short while. We were friends. One night I was working late at school
to set up some exhibit at the gallery. Again scrounging up some
dough. And she offered to help and then drove me home, so I asked
her upstairs and we had some wine." I turned around and looked at
him. He was lost in thought, trying to revive the memory in his
mind. His mouth twisted in a smile. "She didn't have birth control, I
remember that. She wasn't planning for this to happen. Can't say I
wasn't warned. But I was pretty persuasive and she said she thought it

was safe." He looked up at me again. "She was someone who had trouble standing up to people. Right?" When he saw the expression on my face, he held out his hands in front of him, palms outward. "This is what happened. This is what you wanted to know."

"It only happened that once?"

He nodded sadly. "Just once." He shook his head. "They always tell you it only takes one time to get caught, but you never really believe it." He saw me stiffen and, again, he held up his hands. "Listen, man, I know it's not a joke. But, look at it from my point of view. It was a long time ago. I'm sorry, but it just wasn't that important in my life."

He had finished talking now. He sat waiting for me to speak. I stood there, looking down at him. I felt bigger and stronger, armored in my sports coat and high-grade suede shoes. I had a ticket to the shuttle tucked against my heart; I could fly out of this crummy apartment and this rotten existence any time I wanted. There was nothing about his life that I wanted in mine, except Sam.

"So," he said finally. "Does that tell you what you wanted to hear?"

I shook my head wordlessly.

He sighed. "But that's all there is to say." He tried what he must have thought was an ingratiating smile. "You going to let me off the hook now?"

"I'll ask my lawyer."

"Well, like I say, you can't get blood from a stone."

I nodded and turned toward the door.

"Listen, man, take care of yourself," he called out to me.

I turned and looked at him, sitting at his tiny food-littered table, fingering an empty bottle of beer, and I nodded. "Yeah. You too. Take care of yourself."

23

I was running a meeting in my office one afternoon in early October when the call came. I was at the head of the long table, staring down at a row of product development and marketing types whom I had been haranguing about commitment and quality assurance. My two recent-MBA jock assistants were there, nodding vigorously and sweating; one of them still wore patterned suspenders and used cologne, facts that I obscurely held against him. There was also a new guy from marketing, a creative type with odd-shaped glasses and an idiosyncratic idea of business casual, who was sitting at the end of the table and watching me wordlessly, with a sour expression on his face, toting up each of my demands on some mental list as if he anticipated a revolution and was already preparing for the summary trial that would precede my execution.

And then Carol walked in with a funny look on her face and announced that I had a call.

"I thought I said I didn't want to be interrupted," I snapped, not looking up.

"I think you'll want to take this call," she said firmly, and when I looked up to bark her into submission, I saw the look on her face and thought better of it.

Everyone at the table looked at their hands as I stretched over to yank my phone off its multibuttoned handset. The voice on the other end was soft and drawling, and spoke so slowly that after a minute I wanted to jump into the telephone wire to start pulling the words out. The voice was calling from Filene's, the downtown department store.

"Why are you calling me?" I asked impatiently. "I don't even have an account there."

Well, the voice wanted to know, without much interest and certainly no urgency, did I know a young boy, answered to Sam.

I looked down the table, then up at Carol. She was watching me thoughtfully as I swallowed and answered the caller, "I do."

"Wouldn't happen to be his father, would you?"

I would have sworn Carol could hear the whole conversation. She looked steadily at me as I listened to my voice croak, "Yes."

"Well, we have him waiting here. One of our guards picked him up for shoplifting and we're not going to let him go till we get one of his parents down here to sign for him."

"You're holding him?" I asked, and as I spoke I felt my face get hot. I felt the phone pressed against my ear and looked out at the long table helplessly. Everyone was watching me now, waiting for my next move, and I felt as if I was dangling from a string. Suddenly, unaccountably, in a voice that betrayed just the slightest amount of trepidation, Carol said, "Don't you think you ought to break now?"

One of my assistants swung around in his chair and for a moment I thought he would bite off her head for this presumption. But before he could say anything, I nodded and said, "Yeah. Right. We've done enough today. Let's break and team back tomorrow."

My assistant turned back to me as if I had lost my mind. But everybody else in the room relaxed in their chairs. They liked to break and team back; it meant at least relief and the hope of salvation from whatever problem was haunting them. My team broke up into little rivulets of banter and backstabbing. I looked past them at Carol and mouthed the words "Thank you" as the voice on the phone drawled directions to the security office.

I hadn't been in Filene's downtown store since I was a grad student. I walked along the seedy pedestrian mall of the downtown crossing, past stands with vendors hawking useless merchandise for teenagers and tourists. Autumn had just arrived, bringing with it a wicked, biting wind that blew down the street; I wrapped my topcoat closer around me, burrowing inside it as if it was a blanket and I was huddled on my bed.

The security office was on the top floor of the store, down a hallway that was neither carpeted nor very well lit. I smelled mildew and wet cardboard and kept my arms close to my body for fear of scraping my coat against the filthy walls.

The drawling voice on the phone belonged to a man in a uniform who was about six feet five and as narrow as a rail. He was folded, it seemed, into three sections behind a fake wood-and-metal desk that was covered with forms and half-full Styrofoam cups. He nodded indifferently as I walked in, following my movements with large watery eyes that were colored yellow around the edges.

"So you're this boy's father?" he asked, bothering neither to stand nor to direct me to a chair.

I stood stiffly at his desk. When I nodded, he shifted around a little in his seat, adjusting his long limbs and drumming his fingers on a pile of paperwork. "He says he don't have a father. What do you say about that?"

I felt my mind working through the possibilities. I looked around the room. There was a door in the back, black metal with a tiny window that was covered by a grate. I wondered if that's where they were holding Sam.

"What did he tell you?" I asked.

"Told me a few times to fuck myself. That's about it."

I fought back a smile. Good for you, Sam, I thought. Then I collected my thoughts and asked, "So how'd you get my name if he didn't give it to you?" The moment I started talking I had to check

my voice to find that pitch that I used on police officers and bureaucrats, giving them just enough deference to let them know that I
wouldn't challenge their authority as long as they didn't try to exercise it in any way that I'd find inconvenient. It was a pitch you could
find when you were a middle-aged guy in a suit, and occasionally it
compensated for the high blood pressure and lower life expectancy.

He thought about my question a bit, sticking up his chin so he
could stroke the stubbly skin of his throat. Then, without saying anything, he reached across his desk, picked something up, and pushed it
across at me. It was one of my business cards, spindled and wrinkled.
I looked at him quizzically.

"That yours?" he asked.

I nodded.

"Found it in his wallet." He pulled open a desk drawer and took
out the tiny wallet I had bought Sam for his last birthday, eight
months ago, three months before the blood test. Together we had
explored all the secret pockets for important papers and cards that a
thirteen-year-old hasn't begun to accumulate. So, just to get him
started, I gave him one of my cards, saying, "You ever need something, give me a call." I rubbed the card back and forth between my
fingers, as if I could feel Sam there. I wondered if he had forgotten
about it, leaving it tucked away in its secret pocket. Or maybe he had
almost thrown it away, but thought twice. I looked at the man in the
uniform, who was still stroking his neck and watching me.

"So what do you want from me?" I asked, automatically reaching
into my back pocket for my wallet. "What did he take?"

The man dropped one of his long arms over the back of his swivel
chair; it reemerged holding two sneakers, black, with thick, complicated soles and a pattern of lightning rods sewed up the sides. "How
much?" I said.

"Two hundred."

"For sneakers?"

The man smiled. His teeth were large and yellowish.

"Fine," I said, pulling out two bills and handing them to him.

He didn't move. "You want to buy some merchandise, you go down to the sales counters. That's how it works."

"Then what do you want?"

He handed me a form to sign. One paragraph warned that if the "subject" ever set foot in the store again, a prosecution for trespass would result. The other released the store from all manner of liability resulting from the subject's "detention."

"And if I don't sign?"

"You can take it up with the police."

"Oh come on. He's only thirteen. You don't think the police have anything better to do?"

He shrugged; then, amazingly, he lifted one long leg from behind the desk and stretched it out in front of him like a cancan dancer. Methodically, he pulled his pants up from his shin, revealing an undistinguished-looking nylon sock and a patch of stubby-haired flesh with a big gash across it. "You see that?" He rolled his yellowing eyes over at me. "Your boy did that."

"Maybe you scared him," I suggested.

He looked up at the ceiling and let out a low whistle. "I could have scared him good after he done that. Cost me my job, but it'd be worth it."

"Listen," I said, reaching again for my wallet, but he held up a big palm and shook his head. My hand stopped, pressed against the bulky form in my back pocket. "All right," I said, "I'm sorry. He's going through a lot right now. His mother and I—" My eyes darted around the room for a story. "We're getting divorced and it's been hard on him."

"Oh yeah," he said wearily. "I heard that one before."

I leaned over his desk and hurriedly signed the form; when I was done, I handed it back to him.

"What you going to do to him?" he asked without much interest.

I shrugged. "Oh, don't worry, I'll talk to him. I'll let him know he can't do this kind of thing. . . ."

My voice trailed off as the big, yellowing eyes leveled on me. He shook his head and gave me half a smile. "Man, I know what my daddy would have done to me. Would have beat me within an *inch* of my life."

"I can't do that," I said.

The man snorted, then pressed his big hands flat on his knees and seemed to push his scarecrow frame from behind the desk. Tugging on a circle of keys that hung from his belt, he pulled one free and opened the grated metal door. With a little bow, he spread out his hand to wave me in. "All yours. I don't envy you."

I walked through the door, the guard following me. We stepped into a hallway even narrower and dirtier and more poorly lit than the one I had already walked down. I moved slowly, listening to the creak of our shoes, feeling my way by running my hand along the rough, grimy surface of the wall. At the end was a small room. I opened the door and saw Sam inside, lying on his back on a bench, staring up at the single lightbulb that hung from the ceiling. I hadn't seen him since the disastrous Saturday I went to his house, over three months ago.

"Hi," I said.

He glanced at me, then back up at the lightbulb, not betraying even a flash of surprise or relief. He's getting good, I thought, and the thought made me sadder than anything that had happened so far that day.

I felt the guard's breath on me; it smelled of coffee and hunger. I stepped away, sliding inside the room and leaning against the filthy wall. "They found that card in your wallet and called me."

Sam shrugged.

"I think I straightened everything out. We can leave now."

He rolled over on his side so he was facing the wall.

"If you want, I can call your mother and she can get you instead."

From the dark against the wall, his voice emerged. "No."

I looked over my shoulder. The guard was watching me, chewing slowly on a piece of gum. I smiled nervously, then turned back to Sam. "Listen, buddy, why don't you just leave with me? I'll take you back. Drop you off wherever you want." He didn't budge. "You don't have to talk to me or anything."

"Why'd you bother coming?"

I shrugged. Then I felt the guard push me aside and step into the middle of the room. His long shadow wrapped over the bare wall and fell across Sam's back. His voice boomed, "Now listen, you little piece of shit, I am *not* your father and I do not have to take your garbage, so you get your ass up and out of here before I even think to count to three."

Sam stood up. His head was hanging, but I could see a little smile on his face. He walked through the guard's shadow and then, just as he was passing him, he stopped and looked up. "Give me back my belt."

"You took his belt?" I asked incredulously.

"I'll give you your belt across your back if you don't get out of here," the guard promised.

Sam hitched up the pair of jeans that was falling off his hips and moved forward.

We didn't talk as we collected Sam's belt and wallet and walked out of the store. I thought the salesladies were looking at us as we made our exit, a shamefaced man in an expensive coat and a sulking adolescent with a baseball cap pulled over his face, and hands sunk deep into the pockets of his pants. We marched, a yard between us, down Washington Street; the wind whipped the trash around our legs. A yard apart, we entered the garage where I had left my car and climbed the urine-smelling stairs. My car alarm met us with its friendly three-note greeting. It was the only sound we made until we were out of the garage, past the city limits, and on the highway headed back to his house.

"You want to talk about it?" I asked finally.

"About what?" His voice had a ragged edge, as if it had been scraped on rock. He kept looking out the window, slumped down in his seat, his arms folded in front of him, his seat belt defiantly unbuckled.

"Why you stole the sneakers, for starters."

"What do you care?"

I rubbed my hand along the leather-cushioned steering wheel. "I do care, Sam. Of course I care."

I heard him stir. "You going to tell Mom?" He had rolled the car window down and stuck his arm outside, letting the cold wind beat against his hand.

"No, I won't tell her. We're not talking, exactly."

"No kidding."

"You going to tell her?"

"Yeah, right. As if."

"Why didn't you give the store her name so they could call her?" I asked.

"She has things to do."

"Oh, Sam, she doesn't have anything that's more important than you."

He turned to me, his skinny face pale. "Quit dreaming, okay. She has a job now."

I stopped short. "You're kidding? Where?"

He looked away again. "Macy's."

"What's she doing there?"

In the reflection on the windshield, I saw his face break into a small, rueful smile. "She's selling sneakers."

"What'd she get a job for?" I asked.

He turned slowly and looked at me, until my face flushed and I turned away. We were in his neighborhood now. At any minute, we could pass someone who would recognize us. I didn't want this moment to end, awful though it was, so I yanked the wheel to the left, and, the tires screeching, we headed back to the highway.

"Where you going?"

"Let's drive. We can talk."

"Let me out."

"Listen, Sam, I want us to talk. I want you to understand what's going on here."

"I understand." His ragged little voice warned me to stop, but when I glanced over, I saw he was still looking at me, waiting.

I took a deep breath. "The thing about us—about us not being related. I can't change that. None of us can. And I wish it hadn't happened."

"Then why'd you go looking for it in the first place?"

"I can't explain, Sam. I can't explain, but I had to know."

"Fine, now you know. So let me go."

"Listen to me. I had to know. I had to know because—because it makes a difference. I mean, it just does. It's a fact. We both needed to know the truth. And now that we know, we have to figure out what to do about it. At first, I tried to keep things the same, but that was stupid. I should have known that once you knew, you wouldn't want me around in the same way. And your mother wouldn't. But I still care about you and I want you to know that—"

"I don't care about you," he said.

"I don't believe that."

"You think I care about you? You're not so great. I'm glad I don't have to spend every goddamn Saturday with you anymore. You think I miss that, driving around trying to think of things for you to do so you don't feel bad about getting divorced? I have friends, you know. I have things I want to do. So don't feel sorry for me. And Mom's doing fine too." He turned back to the window again. "And I want you to let me out."

"Fine then. Have it your way." I pulled the car off the highway again so I could make a turn. We were in a town that I had never seen before. The houses were all double-deckers with asphalt shingling. The only businesses we passed that weren't boarded up sold auto parts. I slowed down because the roads were narrow; groups of men, who were hanging out on the street leaning against parked cars, turned to look over their shoulders at us. I was on a one-way street that took me a quarter of a mile in the wrong direction before I could turn, and then led me to another one-way street that took me even farther from the highway. I started jerking the steering wheel, leading us down one narrow street after another, getting more and more tangled. I could feel my heart pounding and my eyes starting to cloud at the edges.

"You can't even drive right," Sam muttered.

"I've been driving you around for thirteen years, you little—" I hunted for a word and then looked at him. His head was turned away from me. I could see the soft line of flesh at the back of his neck. I inhaled and could smell the faint, sour odor of sweat on his skin.

I had to keep my eyes on the road to avoid a collision, and the whole time I kept trying to turn my head, hoping to see some response from him. "Look at me," I said.

"Let me out."

"Why are you treating me like this?"

"You're kidding, right?"

"No. No, I'm not." I pulled the car over, jerking the wheel so hard that my tire pounded against the curb. We felt the car shake, then sat in silence. I put my hands up to my head as if I was going to start tearing out my hair. "I'm not kidding. I don't understand why you turned on me. Why wouldn't you go out with me that day I came over? Why were you ganging up with your mother—"

"Why are you still going on with this?"

"With this? This is us. I've loved you all your life."

"That's because you thought I was your son."

"No. That's not it."

He turned and looked at me with eyes of such scorn it made me lose my breath. "It's not?"

I stopped, trying to slow down my thoughts because I knew that what I said now was important and had to be true. "Yes, yes, of course I loved you because I thought you were my son. That was a part of everything. Of our whole life. I can't separate what I felt from that. But that doesn't mean that now we can't have a relationship. So maybe it won't be the same. Maybe legally it's different. Maybe you feel different. But I want you to be in my life. I want to be in your life." I stopped talking. I couldn't think straight. I couldn't even stand to look at him.

"You want to be friends?" he said.

Helplessly, I nodded.

"Fuck you."

"Hey, don't talk to me like that."

"That's how I talk to my friends." He started to cry. "It's not fair." I reached out my hand to him, but he pushed me away. "Take me home."

"No. Wait."

He twisted around in his seat, opened the car door, and jumped out. He started walking down the street, his hands shoved inside his pockets. I sat in my car, staring forward blindly. For a moment, I almost thought of driving off; I could picture my hands turning the key in the ignition, steering me back onto the highway, back to my quiet, empty apartment. Then I took a deep breath and headed out to the noisy streets.

I found him a block away. He had gotten as far as the first major intersection and had stopped amid the chaos of backed-up cars, honking horns, and people shoving past him on their way in and out of a discount music store that blared with the sound of drums and electric bass.

He turned when he heard me come up; he seemed about to run, then stopped. When he looked up, his eyes were still wet and wide with fright. I put my arm on his shoulder and we stood there for a moment. "Come back to the car," I pleaded. He nodded. We headed back to the car in silence, once again a yard apart, our minds buried inside ourselves.

It was getting dark by the time we got back to his neighborhood. Leaves were starting to blow off the trees and dance down the quiet streets. I could smell wood smoke. I pulled over a few blocks from the house.

"I better let you off here."

He nodded.

"Listen," I said, "we can't figure everything out today. But please let's get together again. We can forget about the stupid court order. We can just get together and—"

He shook his head. "Don't bother." He looked at me. "You don't have to."

"I want to."

He shook his head again. "I don't want to."

I heard him pull the handle of the door; the lock popped open, but he didn't move.

I tried again. "I know you're angry with me. You have every right to be."

"You don't know anything about me."

"Sam, I've known you all your life."

"I'm not your little son. I'm not you. Don't think I am."

The car door swung open behind him; the cold air blasted into the space between us.

"Listen, Sam," I said. "I don't want you to be stealing things."

He shrugged.

"I mean, if you need something, you can just tell me. Christ, it was only a pair of sneakers." I turned to him, my hand already tugging on my wallet. "Here, take this. Buy yourself a pair." I pulled out a handful of bills and pushed them at him. Wordlessly, he took them in his hand and looked at them, as if he thought they might move. Then, looking straight into my eyes, he took the bills and tossed them out the door into the whipping wind. I caught my breath and, before I could think, I smacked him in the face.

He paused only a second, just long enough for the red mark to come up on his cheek; then he jumped out of the car and started to run. I turned to my door and pushed it open, felt the seat belt tug me back, and then struggled to get free. I ran, skidding, around the car, but he was gone. I stared at the empty streets, almost hearing the dark, complacent quiet of the suburban night settle on them. I looked down. Caught below my foot was a fifty-dollar bill.

24

In the weeks after our tennis date, Ellen had started making me dinner on a regular basis. I can't remember how, exactly, we fell into that pattern, but we were at the point where we needed some kind of routine. Without it, I kept calling her up, and hemming and hawing for a while as if we didn't both know why I was calling, and then when she finally started to sound like she needed to get off the phone, I'd suggest something completely improbable, like miniature golf or the ballet. "The season hasn't started yet," she said, laughing.

I sighed. "Really? Well, I just want to see you and hang out."

"Then that's what you should have suggested."

So I started coming over carrying a bottle of wine that the guy at the snobby wine store in Cambridge picked for me, which at first she would examine and comment on until she realized that the oenophilia was solely for her benefit. "Would you prefer beer?" she asked.

I nodded. And so we had a pattern. She made these meals, nothing very complicated, just chicken breasts or lamb chops. After my months of hermitlike isolation, after my years of single existence where the best meals I got were takeout at my desk, they were like manna. I wolfed them down, barely stopping to drink some beer, and I would look up and see her watching me. "It's flattering," she said when I caught her staring. "I never thought of myself as someone who nourished." She got bolder, adding a sauce or a chutney or some odd, unpronounceable grain that they sold in bins in the overpriced yuppie health food store. Talking about my mother, I once mentioned how she always made pot roast on Sunday and the next night I was over, Ellen produced a pot roast. "Does it taste like your mother's?" she asked fearfully.

"No, thank God. My mother was a terrible cook."

After dinner, we would take our coffee into the living room and sit there. She would put some soft music on in the background and we would settle into the big, Laura Ashley–like couch that, after a while, seemed to surrender its fussiness and become comfortable, and would talk or flip through magazines or sometimes just simply sit there, her shoulder resting against my side, listening to each other breathe and sigh.

It seemed as if somehow, magically, we had sailed right through the shoals of dating that had snared all the relationships I had pursued since my divorce. We didn't spend a lot of time trying to get to know each other. It just seemed to happen. And, amazingly, she seemed to accept me. She would smile at me, shyly, her head tilting nervously to the side and her hair falling over her eyes, and for a moment I would feel again like someone a woman might want to be around; I stopped being either the jerk whose ex-wife had cheated on him or the jerk who was suing his ex-wife. At a time when I barely understood or forgave myself, she did both. I could calm myself by looking in her eyes. She was the first woman who ever made me feel as if I wanted to put my head on her shoulder. It was like the moments after sex, when you just lie there; I started thinking that those moments were the best after all, and I wondered if, for us, sex was just not necessary, a phase that we had skipped on our way to this comfortable spot where we sat, curled next to each other on the couch, perfectly at ease.

But the night after I picked up Sam at Filene's, when I went over to Ellen's as we had planned earlier in the week, I couldn't let things be easy. At dinner, I had trouble sitting still.

She set down this big bowl of thick, creamy, orange soup, and I sat there, my spoon stuck upright in my fist, not moving, like the balky kid in the TV commercial who won't eat his cereal.

"It's squash," she said hesitantly. "Maybe you don't like it."

"It smells good."

"I wasn't sure if you'd like it. It has ginger—"

I dropped the spoon with a clatter on the shiny wood table. "I said it was fine."

She folded her thin arms in front of her and leaned back in her chair. I could feel her watching me, trying to figure me out, and I couldn't imagine whether she was feeling fear or anger. I pushed my chair away from the table and stood up. "Listen, I'm sorry, I just can't do this tonight." I swiped my hand in the air as if I was trying to brush something away. "I just can't do anything, it feels like."

"What happened?" It was her shrink voice, patient, wary, resigned. I turned my back to her and looked out to the living room. I saw the soft, frilly pillows of the couch and thought to myself, If you go on like this, you'll never sit there again. But something in me was gnawing like a rodent on the bars of a cage, blind, implacable, and bent only on getting out.

"Don't you ever wonder why you bother with this?" I asked in an ugly-sounding voice. "I mean, what's in it for you?"

From over my shoulder, I could hear her slender body shift in her chair. "No. That hadn't occurred to me before." She paused. I wondered what warning was going off in her own mind, and what restless, defeatist urge was whispering to her even now to ignore that warning, to test how weak the foundation of our small contentment was. "Do *you* wonder?" she asked.

"Yes. I do." I straightened up when I said it.

"And what have you concluded?"

I shook my head. My back still to her, I said in a level voice, "I think you must just be this naive, well-meaning person who feels sorry for me and thinks you can help me or reform me or something. And you don't know how bad—" My voice broke.

"How bad you are?"

I thought to myself, I should turn around. I need to see her face. But, instead, without turning, I said, "Or maybe you're just so lonely you don't care."

Then I heard the scrape of her chair. I stood there waiting for her to come and hand me my coat. I had jumped off the cliff and my heart hadn't stopped. It wasn't even pounding. It just kept its steady, quiet rhythm, like the ticking of the bedside clock when you lie awake at two in the morning, not hearing the sound of anyone's breath beside you.

I turned around. She had left the dining room. I forced myself to move, although there were weights of hopelessness around my ankles. The kitchen was empty; the big pot of soup bubbled imperturbably on the stove. I inched my way through her apartment as if I was blind and feeling my way by hand. I came to the door of her bedroom. It was shut; I had never been inside it before. I pushed it open and found her sitting on the edge of her bed, her legs gathered up in front of her, her chin on her knees.

She didn't look up when I plopped down on the bed beside her. "I told you I was bad."

"Peter, if you want to stop coming here, it would be better if you just said so and didn't say cruel things."

"You think that's what I want?" I reached out my hand and she turned away, her body straining to escape my touch. I tried to move closer and she put her head down on the top of her knees so I couldn't see her face. I tried to turn her around to face me, and she said, "Please let me go." Then I got my hand under her chin and lifted her face and saw the red around her eyes.

"Why would you cry over me?" I asked.

"Oh, please, get out of here." She jerked her head away. If she had only acted as angry as she had a right to be, that would have been the end of it. But she didn't. She just sat still and didn't say any of the things she should have. That wasn't the miracle; that I might have predicted. The miracle was that I realized, right then, how lucky I was, and felt grateful.

"The soup looked good." It was the best I could do at the

moment. I thought for a second. "Coming here is the best thing in my life. It's so good it makes me scared. It's like this fragile thing and I'm so scared of breaking it that I just want to throw it down and get it done with. I'm afraid if I open my mouth, you'll suddenly wake up and realize what a jerk I am."

She lifted her head just a bit and stole a look at me. She was trying not to smile. "What makes you think I haven't realized that already?"

"I hit my kid today."

"Sam? You're not supposed to be seeing him."

"Well, I did. I got a call from Filene's. He'd been shoplifting. He's going crazy because of all these terrible things I've done to him, and then I didn't know what to do and I got so frustrated I hit him."

She shrugged and lifted her head, sitting up straight at the edge of the bed. "You sound like the parent of a teenager."

"Except I'm not." I felt that rodent start gnawing again. "I couldn't understand him and I just let him down."

"Sounds like a lot of parents."

I put my head back and screamed. It was more of a bellow, really; it started just above my diaphragm, and scraped and vibrated as it made its way up through my throat. It hurt, but it was better than throwing something, and when it was over and I looked down, she had turned around so she could face me, her eyes wide, smiling. "You like this?" I asked.

She shrugged. "It's revealing."

"You like men who hit their kids?"

"Is that who you are?"

I shook my head. "No. Actually, it wasn't even that bad. The slapping, I mean. You know, offering him money was a lot worse." I looked down at my big hands, the pale spatulate nails, the little fur of blond hair above each knuckle. "And even that wasn't so bad. And the fact of the matter is, given my situation, there wasn't anything I could do that's right. Right?" I looked at her imploringly.

She shrugged again, her mouth folded up in a sad curve that promised no words.

"And I can't undo the fact that I took that damn blood test. And what's more, even if I hadn't taken it, I probably would have found out in some other way. I felt like I wasn't his parent because, as a matter of fact, I wasn't. If I had ignored it, it would have gotten worse. And I couldn't hold on to something that wasn't mine. Right?"

She leaned over and kissed me on the cheek. It was a light kiss, more a consolation than anything else, but the minute I felt her close to me, I realized that we hadn't skipped a phase at all. We just hadn't, until that moment, arrived.

I put one arm around the back of her waist, and it was the thinnest, most delicate waist I could ever remember touching. I rubbed my hand up her side and pressed my face into her shoulder. I heard her body release a long sigh; I felt it pass beneath her ribs and then escape from her; it seemed to take all her strength, and when I placed my hands on her face and brought it toward mine, there was no resistance. Our sides were pressed against the mattress. Our faces moved apart; our eyes caught each other's. "Are we scared?" I asked. She shook her head.

And the next movement was a welter of arms getting free of sleeves and hands pulling at buttons. I closed my eyes and heard the amazing sound of laughter and, as we rolled around, it wouldn't even have mattered whose it was.

25

I was waiting in my car for Sam when he got out of school the next day. He headed down the stairs alone, a backpack slung over his shoulder. Eyes down, he walked by without seeing me. I honked my horn lightly. A couple of girls who were standing near him turned and looked at me, then at him. He looked around and, just for a second, I saw his face open up and something like a smile break through. Then he shut down and nodded his head, signaling me to drive down the block. I stepped on the gas and, when I got to the corner, I waited, my eyes shut, until I heard him bang on the passenger-side window.

I opened the door, but he didn't get in. He just stood there, looking down at me.

"I'm sorry, Sam. I fucked up."

He nodded.

"I mean, I really fucked up. Okay? I started this whole stupid thing and I shouldn't have. And then I did everything wrong and I screwed you up." I heard my voice break. "And when I gave you that money yesterday, I was out of my mind. It was the only thing I could think of that I had that you might want."

There was a long silence. I kept my hand clenched around the steering wheel because, if I let it go, I would want so badly to touch him and I knew that I couldn't. I just waited while our hearts beat. I had put him to a test and I couldn't do anything to help him through, except wait and hope that somehow, sometime, I had given him enough sense or attention or love to do the right thing.

Then I heard his voice, croaky with adolescence and embarrassment, say, "It's okay."

"Please get in the car."

He got in the car. He started to put on the seat belt; then, remembering that I could no longer make him, he let it snap back. "We better get away from here," he said.

It was a gray day. The trees were already shedding and piles of leaves lay in the gutters, matted from the early-morning rain. I headed down the familiar streets, deliberately stifling the impulse to come up with an idea. I was just going to drive until we got where we had to be.

"Mom wouldn't like it if you were seeing me," he said after a while.

I shrugged. "You're not going to tell her, are you?" I asked.

"Nah." He sighed. "She has enough on her mind."

"It's not hurting anybody for us to see each other. Just because we're not blood relatives doesn't mean we're not family."

"I thought that was the idea."

I shook my head. "It was a stupid idea."

"So what do you want to do?"

I tried a smile. "I don't know, Angie, what do you want to do?"

He looked at me like I was crazy. "What?"

I wanted to reach out and pull his cap over his eyes. I kept clenching the steering wheel. "Forget it," I said. "You're too young to understand."

He looked away. "You're weird."

I thought, Do you like me after all? but knew I couldn't say it. I would never say that to a friend. Not to Dave, not to one of my frat brothers or racquetball partners. Not to any of the male friends I had made over the years, friendships that were based on bonds of familiarity passing as indifference and a pledge not to say anything too personal. That was how I had to treat him. That was where we had arrived.

"We could go shoot some baskets," I offered.

"Nah, let's drive."

"Anywhere you want."

"Just drive." He rolled down the window and stuck his head out, like a dog, almost panting in the wind. Doesn't he drive anywhere with his mother? I wondered. But I knew that Joan got in a car strictly to get from one place to another, and I suspected that lately they hadn't been going that many places.

So we drove in silence, in and around the neighborhood, past the park where I'd taught him to throw a ball, the school where I had taken him on his first day of kindergarten because Joan was afraid that he would cry if she went, the grocery store where I used to put him in the seat of the shopping cart and push him over parking lot speed bumps while his mother screamed that I was going to kill him.

"So how's school?" I asked.

"School sucks."

"Besides that?"

"That's it."

I started whistling under my breath, some tune that sounded a little like the one that goes "Hallelujah, come on get happy," but never seemed to get past the first couple of bars. I saw him sneaking looks at me and trying not to smile.

"Don't you ever have to work anymore?" he asked irritably.

"I took the day off." I smiled at him. "Besides, work sucks."

"I'm going to get a job."

"You're kidding. Doing what?"

He shrugged. "I don't know. Maybe bagging down at the supermarket."

"Oh." A light drizzle started to fall. For a moment, we were lulled by the rhythmic back-and-forth of the windshield wipers; then the blades screeched angrily across dry glass. I turned the wipers off and the drizzle splattered on the windshield. "You know," I said, "maybe I could help you get a job. Some friend of mine might need someone in their office. You know, like in the mail room or something."

"Get real."

"Why not? It'd be good pay."

"Right, so all your friends could look at the freak kid with no father."

I turned the wipers back on. "No one would think that. No one would even know."

"It was in the *newspaper*."

My jaw began to quiver. I closed my eyes for a moment, and the next sound I heard was the blast of a car horn from beside me and Sam shouting, "Watch out." I slammed on the brakes and I heard the screech of tires behind me. I looked in the rearview mirror and saw the driver mouthing obscenities through her windshield.

In a weak voice, I said, "Sorry."

"Christ, do you want to get us killed?"

I shook my head.

We were on a quiet strip of road, passing by a boarded-up house-wares store that stood in the middle of a big parking lot. I pulled into the lot and stopped. The rain had let up. Sam twisted around in his seat and looked at me. I took the keys out of the ignition and handed them to him. "I give up. You take over."

"What are you talking about?"

"All yours. Take us for a spin."

His forehead crinkled. "You kidding?"

"You always wanted to drive. This is your chance." I pushed the car door open and got out, motioning for him to crawl into the driver's seat. "Hey, you're going to start robbing stores, you better be able to drive the getaway car."

He smiled, that beautiful gap-toothed smile that made my heart pump a little burst of joy into my blood. "What if I kill us both?" he asked.

"The rate we're both going, it'd probably be an improvement."

He slid around the stick shift and settled behind the steering wheel as I got in on the other side. He was moving around every which way at once, pulling every lever and turning each knob simultaneously. "Keys," I said. Automatically, he obeyed. The keys turned, the motor kicked. Then he looked at me. "Gears." He pushed the stick forward; I could hear the scream of stripped gears, and the car sputtered to a stop. "Press the clutch." He slid down in his seat. It took four tries for the car to jump forward, jerking out of neutral and into first, then second, as we lurched across the parking lot.

As I pointed, he steered us in circles around the deserted shop, touring the vast expanse of cracked concrete. Each time we spun past the curb cut, I felt my fists clench, wondering if he'd careen out to the highway and take us to certain deaths; each time, without pause, he kept turning us around our circle. He was staring through the windshield intently, holding the wheel so tightly his knuckles practically popped through their skin; I could almost hear his brain reciting the litany of "clutch, stick, gas" as he shifted in and out of second gear. By the sixth time around, I settled back in my seat, felt my neck relax, and realized I was not able to do a thing to protect us except to trust him.

He skidded to a stop in the same spot where we had started. He pulled out the keys and handed them to me.

"You done?" I said.

He nodded.

"Wanna go for a beer?"

He smiled. Then he pushed open the door and stood there, his too-long curls flopping around in the wind. I watched him walk around the front of the car and, when he got to the passenger side, he opened the door and said, "Move." He didn't talk much as we headed back down the road, but at least he was sitting forward and his seat belt was on.

"You playing basketball this year?" I asked finally.

"Nope."

"How come?"

He didn't stir. "Sports are for losers," he said.

I felt a shout rising from my chest, then caught it. I could see him watching me from the corner of his eye as I forced myself to sit back and concentrate on the road. A minute passed.

"So what are you doing with all your free time, other than committing larceny?"

"Not much. Hanging out."

We could both hear my pants scrape across the car seat. I held the steering wheel like it was a life raft. After a moment, he seemed to take pity on me. "I joined stage crew. You know, we set up for plays and everything."

"You interested in that?" I looked into the rearview mirror, hoping to see a guardian angel following me down the road. "You know, plays and stuff?"

"Sure. I like that stuff." He looked away. "You know my father is an artist."

"Yeah, I know."

I felt his body jerk around on the car seat. "You met him?"

I nodded, still keeping my eyes on that empty rearview mirror.

"What's he like?"

I paused for a second, then said, "Nice, Sam. Very nice."

He moved again. "Mom said we can get in touch with him. Not right now. But someday maybe."

"That sounds good."

He nodded.

We had gotten to his neighborhood. In another minute, I could turn down the corner to his house and drop him off as I had on a thousand Sunday nights. I pulled over to the curb.

He looked at me, waiting. I cleared my throat. "Listen, Sam, I have something to say. It's maybe the hardest thing I ever had to say."

He started to laugh. "This is going to hurt you more than it hurts me."

"I— What do you mean? I never said that to you."

"You're right. You didn't." He smiled. "So what is it?"

"It's about us. You know—this thing, this lawsuit, between your mother and me—I know you're taking her side. And I guess I should expect that." I looked out onto the street. "I guess I admire it, really.

From your point of view, I did the wrong thing. Maybe I shouldn't have started it all. I thought I had reasons, but they just weren't good enough to cause all this trouble for you."

He shrugged. "Lots of kids' parents sue each other. You're just finally acting like normal divorced people."

"But in our case it's not that simple. There are these circumstances—"

"You going to kick Mom and me out of the house?"

"No, of course not—" I stopped myself. Of course that's what I had planned to do. It suddenly seemed the most ridiculous idea in the world. "No, I'm going to work that out. You'll be okay. Don't worry—"

He shrugged again. "I'm not worried, really. I wouldn't mind moving. Most of my friends have moved." He smiled. "Mom always complained about the house anyway. I don't know why she suddenly cares so much."

"Sam, you know I tried to be a good father—"

"You were fine. You don't have to keep apologizing." He wiped his palms on his pants legs, just as he had seen me do a million times when I didn't know what else to say. "Why do you have to talk about things all the time?"

I sighed. "I want us to keep seeing each other, like today."

"But it's not allowed."

"Don't tell anyone."

"You want me to lie to Mom?"

"You tell her everything now?"

He liked that. I got his great grin as my reward. I could feel my eyes filling with tears and, when he saw it, he blushed and looked away. He was ashamed that I couldn't get a grip. I had to wait until he was ready to look back again.

"How can we see each other if we're not related?" he asked.

I shrugged. "We could be related in a different way. By choice."

"Why?"

"Well, we know each other pretty well. And we have some stuff in common."

"Like what?"

I thought for a second. "I don't know. You're the only person I know who'll see slasher movies with me."

"I only went because you liked them."

"All right. We both like bowling."

"We haven't bowled in years and you always get angry because you get splits."

"Sam, I miss you so much, I can't stand it. You couldn't begin to know."

He nodded. "All right. I'm getting out now."

I stopped. My teeth bit down so hard on the inside of my cheeks that I thought I might start bleeding.

He opened the door, then turned around. "This Saturday, okay?"

I nodded.

"Meet me outside the Burger King at the mall. Just pull up. At eleven. Okay? Don't come by the house."

"We can do whatever you want."

He smiled. "I thought we were doing this for you."

"Okay. We'll do whatever I want."

"Great. A slasher movie and then a lecture about how important math is."

"Don't tell me you want to quit math too?"

He gave me another smile. I wondered when the last time I had kissed him was, and realized that, whenever it was, it might have been the last time ever. "Pete, you have got to get a life," he said. Then he got out of the car, grabbed his backpack, and walked away.

26

That night, I felt like a kid kicking a can down the road. I kept smiling at strangers on the street; they looked at me suspiciously, probably wondering if I was going to ask them for money. I sang out, "Have a nice day," to the tired-looking man who pumped my gas and, when he shockingly smiled back, I wondered if this was what life was like for nice people. I rolled down the car windows on the way to Ellen's house and just breathed in air; even the fumes on Route 2 felt like a cool breeze.

I headed over to Ellen's uninvited, not even thinking for a minute I would be unwelcome. In my mind, she was responsible for my success with Sam, for what seemed like my turning a corner in this long struggle. As I walked to her door, I was swinging a bouquet and envisioning a time when I'd be carrying an engagement ring, wondering only if I still had to officially say "I love you," as if the many times the night before, muffled in sheets or flesh or, in the end, near sleep, might not have counted. I slapped my open hand on the door and put the flowers forward as soon as it opened a crack. It took me a second to realize she wasn't taking them from me.

She had obviously been crying. She was dressed in sweatpants and a sweatshirt and her hair was mussed. She stood in the doorway without moving, looking at me as if she was trying to remember who I might be.

"What did I do?" was the first thing I said.

She was pretty nice about it. She let me come in, although she never took the flowers and I wound up laying them sideways on some little table by her door. She handed me a piece of paper and it took me a few moments to realize that she wanted me to read it. It was a notice from some government agency, a licensing board. She was being summoned to some kind of inquiry about "possible violations of regulations governing professional conduct."

"What is this crap?"

"Us. It's about us."

I looked down at it again. The "Re" line had her name, with a number just below it. The fact that she had already been assigned a number seemed the most ominous part of all.

"Did we do something wrong?"

"I did. I saw you socially."

I laughed. "Well, that may have shown poor judgment, but it can't be illegal."

She looked up, pushing some hair away from her eyes. "I was assigned by the court to give a recommendation in your case. That's my job. That's what I depend on for my living." She caught herself and forced her voice under control. "It looks like I was—influenced. Or biased. It's unprofessional conduct."

"Oh come on."

She took the paper back from me and held it in front of her for a moment as if she was checking it one more time to make sure it wouldn't disappear. Then she folded it up neatly and put it down.

"Oh, Ellen, this can't be serious. I mean, can't you just talk to them and explain? You didn't even see me 'socially' until after you gave the stupid report."

She shrugged. "I suppose. My lawyer said not to worry. The worst they'll do is give me a reprimand."

"Your lawyer? What do you need a lawyer for?"

She shot me a look. "You think you're the only person who needs a lawyer?" I stood there watching as she walked away from me to the couch. I thought, superstitiously, that if she sat down, I could sit beside her and this whole thing would be over. But she walked by the couch and headed to the window. She fingered the cord of the venetian blinds, opening the dusty slats to let in little bars of twilight. "I should have known better."

"But it's ridiculous. You have the right to see who you want."

She shook her head, still not facing me. "No. I knew I shouldn't. It's just that I wanted to so much—" She caught herself. Beneath the bulky sweatshirt, her shoulder blades flinched, then froze, with the struggle to hold back tears. When I took a step forward, she stiffened and the venetian blinds shut with a clatter. She squared her shoulders and crossed her arms in front of her. "I've decided we shouldn't see each other." She held up her hand when I started to protest. "I'm not going to fight with you about this, Peter. This isn't what I want to do. But it's what's best for me and you're going to respect that."

I felt myself squinting to see her better. I could smell the sickly odor of the flowers that still lay, in their green wrapping, on her hallway table. I kept shaking my head and opening my mouth, and she didn't move. She didn't give an inch. So I nodded and headed to the door.

When I got there, I turned back. She was still standing by the window; she hadn't relaxed a muscle, even around her eyes, which I could tell were filling with tears. So, in the end, she won with her weakness; I knew I had to go without even trying to stay. I nodded my head and then, as an afterthought, when the front door was open in front of me, I stopped to ask, "How did they find out? The licensing people. They weren't following you, were they?"

She tilted her head, as if I already knew, or at least should have. "Joan, don't you think? Joan must have told them."

When I saw Joan, she was kneeling in the center of Macy's shoe department, her head piled over a disorganized heap of open boxes. Seeing her there, I stopped short. The store was in the mall near Joan's house; I had left work early the day after I saw Ellen, hoping to catch Joan at work. Stomping from my car to the store, I had worked myself into a fury, going over and over in my head all the things I would say to her.

But then, seeing her there, some protective instinct from our past kicked in. I wanted to deliver her from this, just as, when we had first started dating, I wanted to rescue her from her ratty apartment in the South End. I watched her face as she frowned, trying to match the shoes that lay around her, turning them up and down, back and forth, unable to find whatever it was she was looking for, and I saw, for the first time, how the skin around her eyes had started to age. Her hair was pulled back and, when she lowered her head, you could only see brown roots. No one walking up to her to try on some sneakers would think that this was the beautiful woman I had once rejoiced at winning.

She looked up and saw me. My face must have shown something of what was going on inside me, because her flash of anger passed instantly and was replaced with resignation. She looked over her shoulder, then back at me, waiting for me to come forward.

I walked up, my hands buried in my pockets. She didn't move. I was standing there in front of her and she was on her knees; it looked as if she was about to propose. And before either one of us could speak, a teenage girl with a rat's-tail braid and a fake tattoo on her doughy arm came up and held out a pair of sneakers. "How much are these again?" she whined.

I assumed Joan would snap at her. Instead, she stood up and smoothed her dress, taking the sneakers and examining them carefully. "These are the ones on sale. Are you interested in these?"

"I think they're too tight." We looked to our other side, where the voice came from. An older woman, obviously the girl's mother, was standing there, wiping her forehead with the back of her wrist; her doughy arms were decorated with shopping bags, satchels, and a purse. She pointed to another pair. "You said *they* were on sale."

Joan checked the other pair. "I don't think so. But they're both the same size."

"I *told* you," the girl said, leaning across the space between Joan and me so she could aim her condescension directly at her parent. "They are *exactly* the same size."

"I know what I saw, Jennifer, and these pinch."

"I know what I feel."

"I'm the one who has to pay the doctor's bills."

"We don't pay the doctor's bills. We have insurance."

"I have to work to get the insurance."

Jennifer sighed and clasped the sneakers to her uncomfortably noticeable breasts. "Fine. I'll go barefoot."

The woman looked at me for support. "Did I say that?" she demanded. "Just because I don't want her to be crippled."

"Why don't you try on this pair and I'll check the fit," Joan offered in a patient voice. I kept waiting for her to tell these people to get lost, and she didn't. I realized that being nice to these customers was Joan's job and I felt a sharp jab of guilt.

Jennifer huffed past her mother and plopped down on one of the seats. We could hear them murmuring heatedly to each other.

Joan turned to me. "I assume you don't want sneakers."

I shook my head.

"How did you know I worked here?"

I started to answer and caught myself. I couldn't let her know I had spoken to Sam. I stood there like a fish, with my mouth open for a minute, and then managed to get out, "Barry told me. He found it out in when he and your lawyer were exchanging information about our finances."

She eyed me warily, then let it go. She looked around her little territory. Jennifer was cramming her foot into a sneaker; her toenails were painted black. Joan said, "So are you satisfied? I'm achieving financial independence."

"Do you like the work?"

"Pete, I don't want to be angry with you, mainly because I have things to do. Did you come here to gloat?"

"No. What do you think I am?"

"Excuse me, miss." We both turned. Jennifer had planted herself beside us, her arms folded across her stomach—either to indicate ferocity or to prop up her breasts, it was not clear which. "They fit fine. Look."

Joan dropped to her knee and started feeling Jennifer's feet. The mother came over, still laden with bags. "Do you see what I mean? Look how that toe sticks out."

"They're supposed to be snug," Joan said from the floor.

Jennifer nodded agreement. "I do *not* have to buy everything ten sizes too big just so I'll grow into them."

"Did I say that?" Jennifer's mother demanded from me.

I shook my head imperceptibly. Jennifer turned to examine me, as if I was a specimen in biology lab. I was slowly registering on her screen—male, too old to date, not worth further notice. She turned, down to Joan. "I know my own size."

"Well," Joan said, leaning back on her feet. "This style runs a little small. We could go to a bigger size." She shot a shrewd look at Jennifer. "I might have them in red in the next-larger size."

"Red?" her mother said. "She can't wear red sneakers."

"Why not?" Jennifer stamped her foot; she just missed Joan's hand. Joan stood up and offered to get the larger size. As she moved off to the rear of the store, I followed. She turned and, in a lowered voice, said, "Make it quick, okay. I'm busy."

I cleared my throat and scraped my foot as I tried to gather my words. "Joan, look, I know we have our differences." I caught the expression on her face and thought she might bite me. "Listen, whatever we do to each other, let's not take it out on innocent people."

"Like Sam?"

I looked away. It occurred to me that Joan had done her part in injuring Sam on several occasions—his conception not the least of them. But I hadn't come here to trade recriminations. I looked back at her. "No, I didn't mean Sam. I meant Ellen."

She wrinkled her face as if she didn't recognize the name.

"Ellen Sprague," I said. "The psychologist who did the evaluation for the court."

Realization dawned on her. Her face cleared, and then, in a

moment, hardened. "You came here to talk to me about your girl-friend?"

"She's not my girlfriend."

"Oh, Pete. Don't lie to me. We know—"

"How do you know?" I demanded.

She paused, as if she hated having to answer my question. Then she said, "A paralegal in my lawyer's office lives next door to your girlfriend. She sees you coming there at nights." She gave me an unpleasant smile. "She recognized you from the TV news. Congratu-lations. You're famous."

We heard a bang. Jennifer had removed her sneakers and thrown them on the floor, upsetting a precarious tower of boxes nearby. She and her mother stood facing each other, oblivious to the chaos of upturned footwear that lay on the ground between them. "Forget it," she said. "I'm not buying anything."

"You can't go to gym class with those old sneakers," her mother shot back. "They have holes in them."

"If we're so poor, why can't I?"

"Jennifer, so help me—"

Joan rushed past me and returned a moment later with three boxes in her hands. As she passed me, she tripped. I jumped forward and caught the boxes. She tried to pull them from me, but I stood there, holding them out to Jennifer, who wouldn't look at me. "Try this one," Joan said, taking a box off the top of the stack I held in my hands.

"I just want to go home." Jennifer fell back on the seat. Without unfolding her arms or raising her head, she lifted up one foot so Joan could kneel down and force on a red sneaker.

"Oh, Jennifer, stop making a scene," her mother said.

"You started it."

The mother turned to me, her old ally, once more. "Do you have children?"

Automatically, I nodded and said, "A boy." Joan stopped working and turned around, on her knees, to look up at me. I stared back at her, refusing to let my eyes drop.

The woman shook her head. "You're lucky. Boys aren't nearly as much trouble."

"How would you know?" Jennifer said. "You don't even know any boys."

The mother stiffened. She was trying not to be provoked. Joan was lacing up the sneakers. "There, that fits perfectly. Move your toes."

Jennifer held up her foot to admire it. "Maybe I want green," she said.

Joan pushed a strand of hair out of her face. The woman looked down at her, shaking her head. "Do you have children?" she asked Joan.

"A son." Joan looked at me again. Again I didn't turn away.

"You're lucky too. You can make his father buy his damn sneakers."

"He doesn't have a father."

"Join the club."

Jennifer stomped her red sneaker on the floor. "I do so have a father. It's just that you keep scaring him away asking him for money."

"Money for you."

"I told you, I'll go barefoot."

Joan stood up and backed off. I moved closer to her. She turned to me and whispered, "Why don't you just go?"

Jennifer and her mother had each grabbed the other red sneaker and were pulling it back and forth between them when I shouted, "Because I have something I want to say to you."

Joan froze. Jennifer and her mother froze. A customer who was rummaging through the display of Italian loafers on a sales rack twenty feet away froze.

"You have no right going after Ellen like that," I said to Joan. "She didn't do you any harm."

"I don't know what you're talking about."

"You do too. Your lawyer is making trouble for her."

"No. She's just protecting me and my interests."

From the corner of my eye, I saw Jennifer drop the red sneaker. Her mother sat down beside her. They were both looking at us. Joan stepped up to me; I could smell an odor of perspiration, masked by a perfume I didn't recognize. She pointed her finger, the long, sharp, pink nail aimed at the spot between my eyes. "Listen. I don't care what you and your little girlfriend do. But I'll be damned if I'm going to let her sit in judgment on me and Sam and tell me I should be letting you see him."

"She wasn't judging anyone. She was trying to figure out what was best for the kid. At least she cared about him."

Joan's eyes widened. "Don't you dare say that to me about my son. I know what's best for him."

"Let me see him then."

"He doesn't want to see you."

"He does so. He said—" I caught myself. It was too late.

"You've been seeing him?"

"You can't stop me if he wants to. What are you going to do—lock him up?"

"I'll get the judge to stop you."

"Oh for Christ's sake, can't you forget all that legal stuff and let us live our lives?"

"Forget the legal stuff? When you're suing me for everything I have?"

"I'll drop the whole thing. Just let me see Sam."

She took a step back. I could hear a box crush beneath her foot. She stood there in silence, her long, manicured fingers pulling at a button on her blouse.

"Miss," Jennifer said, her voice a little shaky, "I think we've decided on the red sneakers."

Joan took the sneakers from her and placed them in a box. Looking away from me as she passed, she headed to the cash register, trailed by Jennifer and her mother; the mother shot me a glance of reproach but Jennifer, to whom I had previously been invisible, slowed down for a long, searching look. I smiled nervously and she rolled her eyes.

I followed them to the cash register, where the mother was fumbling in her purse, juggling the other bags that still hung from her arm and muttering that she was sure she had just seen her credit card. I looked at Joan. "I mean it," I said. "You can keep the house. You can keep all the damn money. Just drop the restraining order. What do you say? Deal?"

Joan looked away from me without speaking. She turned to the woman expectantly.

I moved closer. "It's the best thing for him."

The woman snorted. I could hear her mutter, "Men."

Jennifer stomped her foot. "That's your whole problem. You hate men."

"Just men who know what the best thing is."

"As if any men might care what the best thing for you is."

Her mother slammed her purse down on the counter. A pile of papers and cards fell out, none of them a Visa. "You think those skinny kids with acne who can't even put their baseball caps on the right way care about you?"

"You want me to hide myself in the house like you do?"

"With men like your father out there, you could do a lot worse than hiding."

"Ma'am, do you have your credit card?"

"I'm just looking for it."

"Oh, forget about the sneakers," Jennifer wailed. "Let's just go."

"Jennifer, I am not going to go through this again at another store."

"I'll go shopping with Dad this Saturday."

"If he shows up."

"He would if you didn't act like you were going to arrest him every time he showed his face—"

"Ma'am, the credit card."

"I had it right here a minute ago."

"Oh for Christ's sake." Again all three of them froze when I spoke. In the moment of silence while they all looked at me, I reached into my back pocket and pulled out my bulging wallet. I threw a hundred-dollar bill on the counter in front of Joan. "Just take it, for God's sake, and let them get out of here."

The three of them looked at the bill. Then Jennifer's mother grabbed the bag with the sneakers and stuffed it in her satchel. She started sweeping her cards and papers and mess into her open hand-bag. "Come on, Jennifer. Let's go."

"We can't let him pay for it," she protested.

"It's his money. Let's get out of here." She pushed Jennifer forward. As she passed me, she looked up and made a face. "Thanks a bunch, big shot."

We could hear them quarreling all the way to the exit. Joan kept staring at the hundred-dollar bill. Finally, she picked it up by the tip as if it were covered with worms and held it in front of her.

"Joan, please, what do you say? I'll drop the suit, give you anything you want, just let me keep seeing Sam."

When she spoke, her voice was calm and expressionless. She kept looking at the money, as if she was addressing it. She sounded like someone who was recalling a dream. "All you thought about was yourself. And that's all you're thinking about now. You broke Sam's heart when you got that test, Pete. I'm not going to let you hurt him again." She hit the key of the register. The cash drawer popped open in front of her. She let the bill drop from her fingers and watched it float down. "I've let you pay for me for years and I've done whatever you wanted in exchange." She looked up. "Sorry, big shot, but Sam and I aren't for sale anymore." The drawer slammed shut, the little bell rang; Joan turned and walked away.

27

Barry was unsympathetic when he heard about Ellen's problem. Mainly, he wanted to ask how I could be such an idiot as to start "running around with" the court psychologist. "Come on, Pete, you're a nice-looking guy. Can't you find someone who's not going to get you in trouble?"

"Ellen's the one who's getting in trouble."

"Yeah, well, she's a big girl. She should have known what was going on. But this hurts us too. Bad enough you have a girlfriend, so they can make it look like you just want this money to start with someone else. But the court psychologist. This woman's testimony could have helped us. Now that Joan's lawyer knows about this, I can't use it."

"Barry, listen, I don't want to go on with this."

"All right. Subject is closed. You just stay away from Ellen Sprague and everything will be okay."

"That's not what I mean. I want to drop this whole thing."

"What are you talking about?" Barry asked, his voice betraying that he already knew what I was talking about and was steeling himself to fight it.

"I want to drop the lawsuit."

"Well, you can't. Not now."

"Why not?"

"Look, Pete, I know this is rough. But just hang in there. We have a trial scheduled in a couple of weeks. It always gets dirty right beforehand, but it'll work out."

"No, it won't. The whole thing's a mistake. I just want to forget about it."

"Give in?"

"Sure. Why not?"

"And go back to paying child support like you used to?"

I nodded eagerly. "Exactly. Tell them I'll start paying again. Tell them I'll pay twice what I used to. Anything they want. Just get them to drop the restraining order."

Barry sighed. "Isn't this where we came in?"

"Please do this for me."

Staring down at the papers on his desk, he shook his head. "You know, Peter, it seems to me that you only want to play when you have bad cards, and when you finally get a good hand, you want to fold. I'm beginning to wonder about your business sense."

"Hey, Barry, guess what. These aren't cards."

"And what about Sam?"

"What about him?"

"The kid said he didn't want to see you."

"I changed his mind. He'll see me now."

"You've been seeing him? Despite the court order?"

I leaned back in my chair and folded my arms. Chaotic though this was, it was my life and no one was going to tell me how to run it.

He kept staring at me for a long time. Then he leaned back too. "You think you can undo everything you've done? Go back to being Sam's father and seeing him every Saturday, and you and Joan are just your normal divorced couple with a little more bad blood between you than usual? You feel the same, he feels the same, she doesn't hate you any more than she did before, and everything's okay. All for the price of a support check?"

"You have a moral objection, is that it?"

"I have a reality objection. It's not how people operate."

"Name some people who've tried and failed."

He shook his head. "I can't do this for you. You don't have a leg to stand on. The mother has an absolute right to tell you not to see her kid. As far as that kid is concerned, you are a total stranger. And dropping the lawsuit isn't going to change a single, solitary thing. If she doesn't want you to see the kid, all she has to do is say 'Get lost.' Which it sounds like she's done."

I stood up. "The only way she can keep me away is if the restraining order stays in place. And that means we go forward with the suit. And if she does that, she risks losing the house and every penny she has. She may not want to take the risk. Give her lawyer a call."

"I tried this once before. It didn't work out."

I shook my head impatiently. "First off, that was back when she was still getting my support check. Now it's been three months since the judge cut her off and she may be thinking differently." I paused for a moment, and added, "And before, Sam was on her side. He didn't want to see me. That's changed now."

Barry nodded sagely. "So you think that the fact that you've gone behind her back and seen her son and turned the boy against her is going to make her more likely to forgive you?"

I stood up. "Please try this for me, Barry. Please."

He shook his head in disgust. Ignoring him, I walked to the door of his office; then I turned around. "Listen, I'm sorry about losing my nerve like this. I know you would have done a good job if we had gone forward."

"Hey, listen, you're paying me either way."

"Yeah. But it meant something to you too. But for me, I just don't care anymore if we have a good case. I just want to get it over with and get my life back again."

"You know, Pete, I wouldn't mind so much if I thought that's what you were going to get. But I don't think the life you want is waiting for you anymore. And I don't think you've figured that out yet."

I was sitting on a bench in Copley Square when Dave came up. It was that time of year when the days have shrunk and people step out of work into darkness. They were rushing through the square to the train station, as if they had just realized that there was no more sunshine waiting for them when they got home. A week or two earlier and they might have spared a moment for the scruffy, long-haired violinist, with his empty case soliciting dollar bills, who stretched up on his toes and swayed as if he were becoming the long, lilting strains of his own music. But on that night, I was the only still person in the whole square. The orange of sunset burnt a halo above the dignified, impassive mass of the public library.

"Hey, young fella," Dave said as he strode up to me. "You look like someone who just got off the bus from the boonies. Come to town to find your fortune?"

I smiled and made room for him on the bench. He hesitated, assuming we were in a rush to go somewhere; he looked around as if he was afraid to be spotted sitting down on a public bench with nothing in front of him but an empty space. Then he smiled and sat beside me. He stretched and let out a sigh. "Hey, check out that sky," he said.

"Yeah. Just imagine. It's there every night and all you have to do is look."

He looked at me and then slapped my leg, holding on to my knee and shaking it. "What's with you tonight? You look like you just gave up a weight."

"I did."

"You unload that loser utility stock I've been warning you about?"

I shook my head. "Bigger even than that. I'm letting Joan off the hook."

He drew his hand away from me. "I didn't know you had her on it in the first place."

"I wish I had known that." I leaned forward, my elbows on my knees. I said, "When we got divorced, I knew I had lost her. But I hadn't really. She still needed me, for money, to help with Sam. It was like we were still married, in a way. And I still wanted something from her. Even when I found out about Sam, I still wanted *something*. Maybe I just wanted her to say it wasn't true." I looked at him; he was watching me, his brow creased so he could get this right. "But in any event, it wasn't anything that she could or would give me. And I've been doing a lot of harm. So I told Barry to throw in the towel."

"Completely?"

I leaned back. "Well, of course, it isn't that simple." I grinned at him. "Lie down with lawyers, get up with technicalities. She still has me on the hook with Sam."

"What hook is that?"

"The restraining order. Unless she drops it, legally, I can't see him."

"And you think she'll do that for you?"

I looked away. "She says she won't."

"You've talked to her?"

"I tried to." I sighed, looking at the breeze bounce a few dry leaves up and down the broad steps of the public library. "But I hope when she thinks about it some more, she'll see this makes sense. That it's the best thing for Sam. She has to realize that."

"Because you want it so bad?"

"She needs the money."

Dave shook his head. "You know, deep down, she was never really a money kind of a girl."

"But she's gotten used to it by now, hasn't she?"

He paused to think. "You know, I'm no fan of Joan's. But if she's as shallow as that, you wouldn't have fallen in love with her in the first place."

"But if she doesn't drop the restraining order, what am I going to do?"

He shook his head and didn't say anything. We sat there a while as the square emptied and night fell. Finally, he put his hand on my shoulder and shook me. "Let's grab a bite."

We walked close to each other as we headed down the street. I knew that if we were different men, he would have put his arm on my shoulder and he knew, probably, that I would have liked that. Instead, we bought each other rounds at a noisy bar, and every once in a while, when we looked away from the TV set and caught each other's eyes, we would nod and smile and then look down.

28

Barry called Joan's lawyer to make peace. Joan's lawyer threatened to have me arrested.

In the meantime, I kept calling Ellen, but only got her answering machine. I stopped leaving messages after the second time, but I still called, waiting each time for the click of the machine before I hung up. And then finally she actually picked up.

"You're certainly persistent," she said.

"Is that a virtue?"

"Not in this case."

"I tried to talk to Joan about you."

"Please, Peter, don't do anything that could make it worse."

"I'm trying to drop the case. If I do, you'll be off the hook."

She sighed. "Don't worry about me. I'll be able to work things out."

"If you got things all straightened out, could we see each other again?"

"You know, Peter," she said, and her voice simply sounded tired, "you have a lot of conflict going on around you and I feel like I just want to protect myself. I don't want to be the little boat that gets swamped by your waves."

"If I fix it, though, can we see each other again?"

Her laugh was short and reluctant, but at least it was a laugh. "If you could figure out what fixing it meant."

Barry stopped returning my calls by the end of that week. "Mr. Morrison, he's gotten your messages," his secretary explained patiently. "He will call you when he hears something from Ms. Kincaid."

"But I want to know by Saturday," I kept saying.

Finally, tired of putting me off, she asked, "What's Saturday?"

I hesitated. "I'm meeting with someone who's involved in the case and I'd like to know where things stand before I do."

"Does Barry know about this meeting?" she asked suspiciously.

"It's only my accountant," I said. "Barry wouldn't be interested."

Saturday morning at eleven, I was sitting in my car, parked outside the Burger King. Sam kept me waiting fifteen minutes and when he finally came in sight, he was slouching along, his baseball cap pulled down over his face, as if there was nowhere in the world he ever had to be. I thought for a moment he would keep walking and go by me, but at the last minute he opened the car door and dropped in.

"Where'd you tell your mother you were going?" I asked, trying to sound nonchalant, as I started the car.

He looked at me pityingly. "Mom works on Saturdays. She doesn't check up on me now."

I said, "Oh," and we pulled out of the parking lot.

"Where to?" he asked.

"Let's run away someplace."

"Can't. I have a date tonight."

"You're kidding?"

"Let's go shopping." He smiled. "Don't forget, I still need some sneakers."

He made me take him to a mega-mall on the other side of Boston. I kept suggesting side trips or detours, movies or parks, anything to avoid shopping, but he was insistent. He gave me flawless directions and told me where exactly in the enormous lot to park so we'd be poised for the best strikes on the stores inside. He led me expertly up and down the aisles, seeming to know by intuition how to make his way through the maze of merchandise and Muzak. I dawdled behind him, complaining that I was hungry, but he ignored me. He methodically combed each music store. I waited by the fake waterfall in the mall atrium, or else stared listlessly at stalls selling T-shirts decorated with grainy-looking pictures of grandchildren, or coffee mugs personalized with messages to embarrass an office mate. Sam dragged me from one clothing store to another, where I stood clumsily in between racks, my head thumping from the retail-frenzy-inducing music while he tried on endless indistinguishable pairs of oversize jeans.

"But you don't buy anything," I complained when he finally consented to sit with me while I got a burger and fries.

"Hey, it's about process, not results." He backhanded my arm. My eyes widened as he said, "Take a breath, man. There's no race to win."

At the end of the day, almost as an afterthought, he finally went to a store that pronounced itself as specializing in athletic footwear. He tried on every single brand of footwear, engaging in an amazingly detailed conversation with the sales attendant, an ambling, mumbling, teenage giant wearing sweatpants and an earring, who seemed completely absorbed in determining how Sam's foot landed as he ran. Then, with great deliberation, Sam picked the cheapest pair of sneakers and marched up to the counter. I trailed after him waving my credit card. He ignored me and pulled some bills out of his pocket, a move that necessitated his reaching so deeply into his baggy pants that his hand must have brushed his knee. "What are you doing?" I protested. He shoved the bills at the bored salesman, who likewise ignored me and tried, in a halfhearted way, to strike up a conversation about sweat socks.

"I would have paid for those," I protested on the way back to the car.

"No need."

"But I wanted to."

"Your loss."

I stopped in the middle of the parking lot. "You still angry with me?"

"Well yeah," he said, as in "Well of course, moron." But then he smiled. "But that's not why I won't let you pay."

I considered that one. "New rules?"

He shrugged. "You have a better idea?"

I shrugged too, and then, grinning, slapped the shoe box out from under his arm. When he fumbled to catch it, I snatched it away and held it in the air just above his head. He started jumping; I dodged and swiveled. He held out his hands and checked me. I tried to move, he tackled me, and we wound up almost hugging, the new sneakers sprawled over the oil-streaked parking lot. A tired-looking woman, trailed by three toddlers, walked by shaking her head. "Wait until his mother sees that," she said kindly. "Boy, will you be in trouble."

"Lady," Sam said, "you have no idea."

On the way back, I pulled off the road at a grassy area by the river and he grudgingly followed me out of the car. It was unseasonably warm and for a long time we just sat there silently, watching some seagulls arc and dive over the dirt-specked water. I could almost hear, in my imagination, the sound of a stone skipping across the river's surface, the quick, light steps of things tossed away.

Sam stretched and emitted a prodigious yawn. I looked at him and lifted my eyebrows. "So what's new with you, big guy?" I asked.

He shrugged as if he was too burdened with new things to be able to pick any one in particular. "They're having a drug scare in school," he offered casually.

"You're kidding," I said.

He rolled his eyes. "Nothing much. Just weed and some pills. A couple of kids got expelled."

"In junior high school?"

"Oh, get a life, please."

I shut my eyes and lay down on the grass. I felt his foot kick mine. "Hey, Pete, you ever do drugs when you were a kid?"

I shrugged. "Just weed and some pills."

"For real?"

"Well, weed. Or pot, as we Stone Agers called it."

"You inhale?"

"Oh, get a life, please."

He lay down next to me on his stomach, his face hovering over mine. My eyes closed; I could smell his breath, still little-boy sweet.

"I asked you two years ago and you said you never had," he pointed out. "What's making you so honest now? You think I've grown up or something?"

"Nope, that's not it."

"Then what?"

"I don't have to be the father anymore."

He thought about that. "So you don't have to lie?"

I thought about that. "Don't know. We'll have to see."

When we got back to his neighborhood, he thanked me very carefully, and, without waiting to be asked, told me he would be free the following Saturday. "But only late. I have something to do in the morning."

"What?"

He shrugged. "My personal business." Then I watched him check my expression. "Okay?"

"I'll be there," I said. "Waiting outside our favorite Burger King."

I was still smiling when I walked into my apartment and saw the message light flashing on my answering machine. It was Barry. I caught him at home just as he was walking out the door and he didn't sound all that happy to be interrupted.

"Listen, Pete, I'm in a hurry. But I've got news."

I waited for him to say something more. After a moment, I knew what it would be.

"She won't let me see the kid."

"Not only that, but according to Kincaid, they're going to have the entire police force armed with those restraining orders and ready to pounce if you so much as try. They are really dug in about this."

"Even if I start paying the support again? Even if I drop the lawsuit?"

"You know, I actually heard Kincaid say, 'We don't care about the money.' I mean, I heard it with my own ears and I couldn't believe it. It was a milestone in my career." He attempted a laugh. "This ex-wife of yours has really gotten stuck."

"So what can I do?"

"Nothing."

"Can't you move to drop the restraining order?"

"I told you we don't have grounds. He's not your kid. We already submitted the blood test results to the court. Remember?"

"I can drop the suit."

"And the restraining order stays in place and she keeps the house."

"Or I could keep the suit going."

"And maybe win the house. But not the kid."

"Why?"

He was speaking patiently, because he knew that I already knew the answers. "Because the suit is about getting the judge to say that you're not the kid's father and don't owe the kid anything. That's what you're trying to prove."

I thought for a second. "So they're trying to prove the opposite?"

"I guess you could say that."

I took a deep breath. "I have to think about this, Barry."

"All right." I could hear him breathing against the phone. I knew he wanted to get on with whatever personal pleasure he had lined up for his Saturday night. He was doing me a favor that I didn't deserve, because I had never done him one. "You want my advice?" he asked.

"Isn't that what I pay you for?"

"Not my legal advice. My personal advice. Just this: Let the kid go. I know it's hard. I can see it's hard. But you don't have a choice. And if you keep fighting Joan on this, you'll never win and you'll make it hard on yourself and hard on that lady friend of yours. And hard on the kid too in the end. Let him get on with his life too."

"What life would that be, exactly?"

"You think he can't live without being your son? In a way, that's how he's lived his whole life. Now at least he can face up to it. And by clinging to him, you're just making it harder for him. And yourself. And that's my advice. No fee."

"Thanks."

"So what's the verdict? We drop the suit?"

"No. Fuck her. She won't give me Sam, I won't give her the house."

"Thatta boy." He waited a moment before speaking. "And you'll stay away from the kid?"

I moved the phone away from my ear. I could hear him calling my name. I stood, staring at the wall of my apartment, watching the second hand of my kitchen clock lurch forward. I put the phone back to my ear. "Sure. Whatever you say."

"You know, Pete—" He caught himself. "You do know, right?"

I kept holding the phone after he hung up, listening to the words he had left unsaid.

29

The next day, I went to Ellen's apartment and got as far as her front door. Then, my hand raised to knock, it occurred to me that she could get in trouble for seeing me and someone could be watching. I hesitated, turned away, then turned back. If I dropped this thing, even if it meant giving up Sam, Ellen and I could see each other without worrying about any consequences; we would be just an ordinary couple, with some bad past and no particular reason not to be happy in the future. If I didn't give up, then she would be hurt and I couldn't look her in the face again. I knocked and, hearing the sound of my hand on the door, I almost turned to flee.

Nothing happened. I listened to the sound of the empty town house. I rested the side of my head against the door, feeling that our very brief relationship, our few months of kindness and quick moments of hope, lay inside if only I could make my way to it. I closed my eyes, as if I was resting on a pillow. "You jerk," I said aloud to myself. "You fucked everything up." I heard the sound of the door shaking on its hinges and felt a small circle of heat growing on the spot where my forehead hit the wood.

"No, you didn't."

I turned around and she was standing behind me, her keys in one hand, a shopping bag in the other. "You didn't fuck everything up."

"I didn't?"

"Well, not all by yourself. You had help. Your ex-wife, for one." She shook the keys on her chain as she stepped beside my large, useless body. She turned the lock, pushed the door open with her shoulder, and stood by tolerantly as I stumbled into her foyer. "And your lawyer. And your best friend."

"It's not over yet."

"I didn't think it was."

She set about the business of unpacking, straightening up, bustling about with quick, determined movements while I stood in the foyer, lonely and awaiting attention. She came out of the kitchen with a watering can and headed for the plants that climbed and trailed around her windows. "I told you not to come here and I meant it," she said evenly. "I'm angry that you didn't respect that. I'm not going to throw you out, but I'm going to tell you not to come again. And I'm going out with some friends soon, so if you have something to say you should make it quick."

"I'm thinking about dropping the suit."

"If that's what you want, then go ahead."

"It would be good for us. No reason for Joan to keep pursuing her complaint against you. No more pressure."

She kept pouring the water in a thin, disapproving stream over the vigorous top of a rubber plant; I could hear the water sizzle as it got sucked into the dry soil below. Her lips were pressed together, and her eyes resolutely avoided my face.

I went on talking. "The catch is that I can't see Sam again."

She looked up, the watering can still tilted. She stood there, staring at me, not hearing the splash of water on the carpet. Moments passed; then she said, "Damn," and looked at the puddle beside her.

I walked over to where she was standing, took the can out of her hands, and put it down on a table. "Tell me what I should do."

"Don't ask me that."

I took her hands. She started to pull away, then stopped. "Joan is his mother," she said. "She has the right to say who he sees. And she probably thinks this is in his best interest."

"Which it's not."

"Are you so sure?"

"Yes," I said, my voice rising, "I'm sure."

She stood there for a second, her hands still resting in mine, her thin body poised to move, her face turned away. Then a great breath of anger blew through her. She grabbed her hands back so hard I almost lost my balance and I thought for a second she would slap me. "What do you want me to say?" she shouted. I stepped back and she grabbed me by my shirt and shook me. "You want me to tell you what to do? You know what I want. I want to be able to see you without worrying about how it can hurt me. I want you not to be caught up in this battle you're fighting with some other woman you can't let go of." She pushed me away and then her hands flew up to her mouth. She turned away from me and looked out the window. "Why did you make me say that?"

I reached around her, feeling how big my arms were as they pressed against her thin shoulders. It was as if I swamped her, my chin touching the top of her head. "Okay, it's okay," I kept saying until she stopped crying and shaking and caught her breath in a dry sputter of hiccups.

She inhaled once deeply and then asked, in a little voice, "So are you going to do what I want?"

I pressed my cheek against the back of her head. "I guess I could start over again," I said, more to myself than her. I kissed her hair. "We could have a baby."

She shook her head; it scraped against my lips. Her whole body was saying no. She just stepped out of my embrace and before I could move, she was across the room from me, her arms folded in front of her. "You don't want that?" I asked miserably.

Her face struggled with a laugh and a sob. "Oh yes," she said, shaking her head no. "I want that." When I stepped toward her, she held up her hand. She said, "I want that too much to get it this way."

We both stood in the middle of her overcrowded living room. I knew that I had to wait for her to move. She was the better one of us and she had to decide how this worked out. I felt the wonderful relief of turning your future over to someone else, even if it was simply to have that future taken away. And then, while I waited for a portentous move, she said, "We need something hot to drink."

I started to laugh and nodded my head. Smiling, she went into the kitchen. I heard the clanking of a pot and cups and waited until she came out. She handed me a steaming cup of tea and then we sat down at the table.

"This is it, Peter," she said finally. "I don't want you to have to give up Sam for me. I don't want you to start all over again. I don't think people can. If I get you, I'll have to take you with everything you've done and earned and lost up to this point. If we can't take each other that way, then it won't work."

"You think I can keep him?"

"I think that's for you and him to decide. Maybe just you." She sipped the tea. "Maybe Joan. Maybe the judge. Not me, in any event." She sipped again.

"If I go to trial, you could get hurt."

She set down the cup. "If you go to trial, if Joan presses this complaint against me, I could be censured. Maybe even suspended. It would be horribly humiliating and I would hate it. Then it would be over." She picked up the cup. "If you let Sam go because of me, just because you wanted to spare me, then we'd have that loss forever. You wouldn't be the man that you were when you first came into my office. And I don't want to be responsible for that." She took a deep drink from the cup. "So make up your mind without thinking about me. I'll love you with him or without him. Either way I'll take that as part of you."

I nodded, and took her hand, warm and moist from being pressed against the cup, and held it for a moment. Then I smiled. "But I still want you to make up my mind for me."

She pulled my hand up, pressed it against her lips, and smiled too. "Peter, you were the one who wanted to take the test. Now let's see if you pass it."

———

When I pulled up in my car, Dave was on his front lawn, hunched over a motionless rake with a pile of leaves at his feet. He seemed to be surveying the futility of it, of buying a piece of the outdoors and then spending the rest of your life trying to keep it as neat as your parlor.

"Hey, farmer," I shouted, "you look ready for a beer."

"Hey." He waved. "You bet I'm ready."

Just then, the door to the house opened and Marcia stepped outside. She was bundled up in a bulky sweater and was wearing her reading glasses, which meant that we had disturbed her while she was doing something more important than listening to us exchange pleasantries. "Dave, you know you still have to go to the hardware store. And Ariel is finished with soccer practice at three and I need you to pick her up." She pretended just to have noticed me. "Oh, Peter, you're here. This is kind of a busy time."

Dave smiled at me weakly, a little smile of regret that told me he would have liked to shield me from this rudeness if he could. I got out of the car and walked over, kicking a spray of leaves in front of me.

"I have to make a decision. About my court case."

Marcia released a loud sigh. "Peter, we didn't agree with your decision to start that case in the first place, and we really can't get involved—"

"Marcia," Dave interrupted pleadingly.

I held up my hand. "No, she's right. It was a bad idea. Now I have to figure out how to get out of it."

Marcia shook her head. "I would think you could just drop it."

"It's not that easy."

She turned around to go back inside the house. "Dave, please don't forget about Ariel's soccer practice—"

"Joan wants me to give up seeing Sam." Marcia stopped and turned to look at me. "Forever," I added.

I heard Dave's rake drop and the whoosh of leaves lifting up into the breeze.

For the second time that day, I got offered tea. Marcia screamed at Daphne to get out of the living room, where she lay transfixed by a music video of young blond men on motorcycles circling around a woman in leather and chains. Dave trailed leaves across the living room carpet and Marcia visibly stopped herself from shaking him.

They were both very concerned. Dave wanted to blame Joan, who was a bitch and only cared about money. Marcia wanted to defend Joan, who was probably acting in Sam's best interest, as she understood it. Dave insisted that if Joan was taking that position, I should hold out for the house. Marcia told him not to be crass because obviously I was in pain. Dave looked chastened and asked if I was in pain. Marcia made an exasperated sound in the back of her throat and asked him if it wasn't obvious. I drank tea and thought about the night I had come here four months before, laying plans to buy Sam back and imagining how in a short while I could bring him over to play with Daphne and Ariel as if nothing had ever changed. It occurred to me that, if Sam really wanted to play with them, Joan could bring him, and that anyway, he probably wouldn't want to because the kids were too old to play and certainly too old to play together. It had been foolish to make plans; even if I had been his father, it would have been foolish.

Dave put his hand on my arm. "I don't know how you get past a thing like this."

"You think that's even a possibility?" I asked.

He grimaced. "Not really. But I don't see what your choices are."

"I could fight for him."

"Be realistic. How can you win?"

I looked down, into my tea. "You think I can just accept this?"

"She's the kid's mother. She gets to say."

"But what about Sam? Nobody's asking him."

"Look, Pete, this sounds brutal, but it happens all the time in different ways. Kids get attached to their stepfathers or to their mother's boyfriends. Then the couple breaks up and the man is out of the kid's life, just like that. It happened to this friend of mine from work. He has these two ex-stepkids he helped raise from the time they were two and three and now he never even sees them. Ex-stepkids. Hell, there isn't even a real word for it."

"And this is supposed to console me?"

"No." He removed his hand from my arm. "Consoling is not a job I'd take on. Not today. But you know, in a bit, it'll get easier. Listen, you'll be free. You can start over. Buy yourself a new house. Find yourself a new wife. Start a family. What are you—forty, forty-one? How old is that?"

"You know, they could move out of town," I said. "I wouldn't even know where they are."

He shrugged and made a face of cold comfort. "Yup, when it's over, it'll be over. That's true. You'll have to get used to that idea. Christ, Pete, people lose their goddamn arm and they still live."

"And you think that's worse?"

Dave looked at Marcia. "Help me here."

I looked at her too. "Help us both."

Her face was clouded with thought. She looked from one to the other of us, and then, after a long pause, she asked simply, "How would you fight for him?"

I shrugged my shoulders.

"Well, you better find out, Peter."

"Marcia, are you crazy? You're telling him to prolong this agony—"

She leaned forward so her face was near mine, blocking out Dave's. "Listen to me, Peter. If you can fight for him, do it. He deserves that."

"And if I lose?"

She sighed. "Men." Then she leaned back in her chair. "If you lose, Sam loses. And that's why you should fight."

The tea at the bottom of my cup was cold. They didn't offer me any more. Marcia held out her hand for my cup and I gave it to her. I was holding my arm up and looked at it. "Not bad for an amputee, right?"

They walked with me to the door and opened it. The sky had clouded and, although it was still the middle of the afternoon, it had already gotten dark. The wind was raw and I clenched my hands against the cold. I felt a hand on my back; whose it was, I couldn't tell. I turned around and saw them both behind me, side by side, framed in their door, the heat of their home behind them, watching me as I headed down the path to the street.

30

The next day was Monday. I tried to get out of work early, but the vice president of marketing from our western region was in town and wanted to strategize. He rested his fashionably unshiny rubber-soled shoes on the conference room table while he talked about ways to cut off our competitors' legs, and I kept pretending to stretch so I could reach my arm out and check my watch. With every new idea, he'd start pounding on the speaker phone that rested beside him, summoning in some new component of our team to provide input. Carol was dragged in toward the end of the day to take notes; she watched me thoughtfully as my mind drifted off to the conversation with Sam that I needed to have that day, before I lost my nerve.

She was standing in the hall as I raced out, minutes after my tormentor from the west had headed to his hotel's health club so he could "work his way through" some of the concepts he had been inflicting on the rest of us. "Big date?" she asked.

"No, not really."

"Tough to have a life," she said.

"When you work here or in general?"

She smiled. "You doing any better, Pete?"

I almost asked why she would care and then it occurred to me that she actually did. And I thought that, as I seemed about to lose the most important relationship of my life, I shouldn't be so wasteful of the small mercies that were left behind.

"You know, Carol, I think I'm doing a whole lot worse, actually."

She nodded. "That doesn't surprise me."

I creased my brow. "It doesn't surprise you because I'm such an asshole?"

She smiled. "No, because you were and now you're not anymore. It's not a transition that goes very smoothly in this world."

———

I called Sam from my car phone, praying with all my might that Joan wouldn't answer. When I heard his voice, I almost shouted with relief until I remembered what I had to say.

"Listen, buddy, what are you doing?"

"Mom's working. I'm just hanging out."

I sighed. "Can you meet me? It's important."

"I have homework."

"Please do this. I have to see you now."

He let the silence sink in for a few moments, then told me where to pick him up.

He was waiting when I drove up, hands buried in his pockets, ball cap pulled forward, hunched over to shield his face from the wind. "What's up?" he said the minute he got in the car.

"Let's get out of this neighborhood quick." I was worried about the police that Ms. Kincaid had threatened to set on me. I actually told him to duck down in the car as we drove off. When we had gotten a mile or so from the house, I asked, "You eaten yet?"

He shrugged. "I told you. Mom's working late tonight."

"So who feeds you?"

He smiled. "I'm a latchkey kid now. I reheat."

"Well, we can do better than that at least."

We went to a diner by the side of the highway; it was brightly lit, enormous, and nearly empty, with only a scattering of truckers and sleepy-looking, not very well-dressed businessmen spread out among the tables, drinking coffee and staring blankly at sports pages. Our waitress was short, broad, and soft, with a sweet face and a big bosom. "So how are you boys doing tonight?" she greeted us, and I wanted to bury my face in her breasts and cry.

Sam fussed with the menu and asked a million questions before ordering, then called her back to change his mind. I kept trying to get his attention and he kept wondering if he should have ordered the tomato soup. I began by saying that I had been talking to my lawyer and he said he had to go to the bathroom. When he came back, he launched into a long story about how some kid at school had gotten bitten by a dog and his leg had swelled up and they thought maybe it was rabies but then the teacher had said that it couldn't be because then he would be frothing at the mouth.

"Sam, listen, I have to tell you something important."

He put his hands on the table and folded them.

The waitress arrived with our food. "Now, which of you gets the tuna? And was that a diet you ordered?"

Sam was disappointed that he didn't get coleslaw on the side. A discussion ensued between him and the waitress about accompaniments. The menu reappeared. I looked at her impatiently and she gave me that kindly, red-faced smile. "It's a pleasure feeding them when they're this age, isn't it?" She took his renewed order and told him just to give a wave if he wanted anything else. "He has your smile," she said to me as she turned to walk away.

Sam produced the smile for me. I wanted to reach out and grab his hand, and had to fight myself to keep my own hands on my lap, my back straight against the back of my seat. I started speaking, going slowly, forcing myself to look him in the eyes even though it was so painful to see how small and young his face was. "You know, Sam," I said, fumbling, "I just want you to know. Whatever's going on with your mother and me—" I took a breath and started again. "You know I want to be in your life. You know that. Right?"

He rolled his eyes and looked up at the ceiling. "I thought we had this conversation when you got divorced."

I sighed and started again. "Your mother doesn't want us to see each other anymore."

He pushed his tuna sandwich into his mouth and took an enormous bite. "So what?" he said through the bread.

"No, I mean for real. She doesn't want me to ever see you again."

He swallowed and looked out the window at the parking lot where trucks pulled in and out of the dark. "She's a slag," he said finally.

"Hey, don't talk about your mother that way."

He looked at me as if I had two heads. "*Hello.* You're the one who's suing her. Remember?"

I nodded. "That's the point, Sam. I want to end this whole lawsuit thing. It's killing us."

"So end it." He picked up the sandwich again and took another bite. I watched him chew and swallow and then carefully reach for his soda. He took a sip and looked out the window again. When he turned back, he seemed surprised that I was still there. "So end it, okay? You need my permission?"

"I need her permission. I mean, I need her agreement."

"And?"

I swallowed too, my mouth empty, my throat dry. "And she says— her lawyer says—that I can't see you."

"So don't tell her. You're seeing me now, right?"

"I shouldn't be. I could get arrested."

He rolled his eyes, as in, Hasn't everybody been arrested?

"The thing is," I continued, "it's not just that. Although it is that. It's more than that. I mean, the way things stand it's illegal for us to get together. And we can't keep doing it on the sly. She'll find out. And you'd be lying to her and I can't have you doing that, not forever. I mean, you're probably lying to her now, right?"

He dropped his eyes. "She's been asking me if I've heard from you. Did you say something to her?"

I shook my head. "Maybe I let something slip. I went to her work to see her and I— Oh, Sam, I screwed up, but you know it was inevitable that she'd find out."

"She told me I shouldn't be seeing you, that it would only confuse me."

"And does it?"

He smiled a little. "No more than usual."

I reached out for his hand, but it slipped back on his lap just as I was about to touch his knobby, gnawed fingers. "It confuses me sometimes," I said. I took a deep breath. "I don't want to give you up. But I may not have a choice. I don't have any legal rights if your mother won't let me see you."

"Is this about money? Is Mom trying to take you to the cleaners?"

"No, Sam, that's not what it's about."

"Ethan from school's father's always complaining that his mother took him to the cleaners. She said she was doing it for Ethan's sake. But I think she just wanted to screw him. Mom probably wants to screw you too."

"Well, I guess she'd have some reason." I caught myself. "Listen, your mother's not like that. I mean, she may not be the greatest—" I caught myself again. "But it's not about money or screwing me. It's about you. She really believes you're better off without me. Because I took that test and hurt you and she just doesn't think I can ever make it better." He kept looking at me. I didn't stop talking. "But she's wrong. I know she's wrong. The problem is, it's not in my control."

"And what about me? Don't I get to make a decision?"

I leaned back. "You want it straight, Sam? You don't have the right."

"Ethan got to say to the judge that he wanted his father to have joint custody."

I shook my head. "It's not like that for us. Legally, I'm not your father. I don't have any right to custody, and even if you say so, you can't give it to me."

"What if I tell Mom I want to see you?"

"It'll only make it worse if you tell her you've been seeing me. It'll just mean you're more confused."

"But how can she stop you?" he said, his voice rising.

I shook my head. "It's incredible. I know. She just got this order and I—"

I stopped, unable to explain anymore. I looked across at him. His face had gone slack, except for his lower lip. I could see his jaw move as he clenched his teeth together. Sitting there, across from me, he had just gotten too old to cry.

We waited awhile. He was looking down at his sandwich, half-consumed in two mouthfuls, now abandoned on his plate. He pushed it around with his fingers, then knocked the plate violently.

"Could I see you ever?" He shrugged, like maybe this wasn't such a big thing to ask. "You know, not now, but, like, when I'm twenty-one or something?"

I put my hands over my face, then forced myself to move them away. I tried to smile. "Yeah, when you're twenty-one. That'll be okay."

"And not before?"

"I can't say. It's not up to me. It's up to your mother."

The waitress was swinging by as I spoke, and stopped, clucking her tongue. "Oh, that's right. Blame it on the mother." She gave us a big smile. "That what my boys' father always did."

"I need another soda," Sam blurted out.

She was taken aback. I nodded my head at her and she bustled off. I looked at Sam. "Maybe she's right."

"The waitress?" He made a face.

"No, your mother. Maybe she's right."

He waved his hand. "You never thought she was right about anything before."

I fought a smile. "I guess. But now I can't do anything about it."

"Can't you, like, sue her?"

"I already am."

"So maybe you'll win."

I shifted in my seat. "The problem is, if I win, I lose."

He shook his head. I had lost him. I took a breath and tried to explain, thinking that these were not the facts of life I had once imagined telling him. "You've got to understand. I brought this on myself. On both of us. I was so angry that time I wanted to see you and you wouldn't, and I blamed your mom and I just couldn't see straight. So I sued. And we proved I'm not your father. So there's no going back from that."

He was still looking at me, expressionless, waiting. He wanted neither an apology nor an excuse; by this point he was so accustomed to being betrayed that both had lost their novelty and neither helped. All he wanted was a solution, and he was still young enough and still—despite everything Joan and I had done to him in the last six months—sheltered enough to believe he would get one simply because he deserved it.

I shook my head. "The lawsuit isn't about us. It's about money. If I win, maybe I'd get back the house or some money, but I wouldn't have a right to see you again. Because the judge would have decided that I wasn't the father and didn't have to take care of you or your mom."

"So, what if you lose?"

"If I lose, it means that the judge decided that I did have to take care of you. Or at least I had to in the past. It would be like him deciding that I had been the father."

"Couldn't he decide that you still were?"

I shrugged. "But I'm not. There's the blood test." Sam's shoulders sagged. He was ready to give up. But I was still thinking. "But I suppose if I lost big, the judge *could* decide that I still had the obligation to support you. I mean, that's what your mother's going to claim. That I believed you were my son and treated you like my son and so I had to pay for you. And I suppose," I said, saying this all out loud for the first time, "if the judge decided *that,* it would be pretty close to deciding that the blood test didn't matter. And if it didn't matter—"

Sam was looking at me, bewildered. "I don't know what you're talking about."

"Good. I don't want you ever to have to think like this."

The waitress was standing beside us shaking her head. "You didn't even touch your burger," she reproached me. She made tutting noises as she picked up the plates. "You want me to wrap this up? How about dessert? We have some delicious pie." She clattered and chattered and smiled at each of us in turn. "How about you, sonny? You look like a man with a sweet tooth." Sam shook his head violently. "Oh, sweetheart," she said, "nothing's so bad that some ice cream wouldn't make it a little better."

"Have some ice cream, Sam."

He shook his head. "Nah. Get the check."

The waitress looked at me and shrugged. "When my boys were that age, I couldn't keep them in sweets. But they're a mystery. You just wonder where they come from sometimes, don't you."

We headed to the car in silence. On the drive back, I caught every green light; five miles and I didn't touch the brake once. I pulled up a few blocks from his house and got myself ready to say good-bye. I turned to him but he wouldn't look up.

"So will I see you again?" he asked.

"We probably shouldn't before the trial. If we got caught, it could turn the judge's mind against me."

"And when's the trial?"

"Next week."

"And after that?"

I put my hand on his shoulder and he let it stay there. Neither of us moved for a long while. Then, carefully, I turned him toward me and, holding him by his shoulders, I looked straight at him. "I got to tell you, Sam. I could lose. Or win. Or whatever. I could end up not being able to see you. And I don't know what I can do then."

"I could run away and come live with you."

I shook my head. "You have to live with your mother. She loves you." I sighed. "I don't agree with her, but she's doing this because she thinks it's best for you. I guess, if it happens that way, we just have to say that maybe it is best for you. And maybe someday she'll change her mind."

He pulled away from me and turned to the car door.

"Whatever happens, I'll always love you," I said to his back.

He nodded and touched the handle of the car door.

"I'm sorry," I said. "I'm sorry I ever started this."

"Yeah, well, you were crazy. It happens."

"I want you to be my son."

He nodded again and pushed the door open. "Good luck," he said without turning around. I reached my hand out to touch him but he stepped quickly onto the sidewalk and closed the car door on me.

I sat there in the silent car, holding the steering wheel, staring into the dark of the street. Nothing was moving. A few lights flickered from behind living room curtains. A dog, stuck in its backyard, yapped to be taken back in. I heard the car door click open. I turned and, in a moment, he was in my arms.

31

It was all familiar when I showed up at the courthouse on the morning of the trial: the featureless gray building looming over the sidewalk; the crowd of photographers and reporters and TV cameramen who bustled at the glass doors, screaming things in my ear that I didn't even hear; the embarrassing shuffle at the metal detector; the gawkers in the lobby; the hush when I entered the courtroom and all the spectators turned to figure out if I was the one.

Barry was oozing testosterone. He stood behind the table where we were going to sit. He had an enormous, coffinlike bag from which he kept pulling papers that he arrayed in front of us like the sandbags on the rim of a trench. On the other side of the room, Ms. Kincaid was looking calm, pretending to be absorbed in a piece of paper that she tilted up just enough so nobody walking by could see what it was. Joan was hiding somewhere, and she didn't enter the courtroom until the minute before the court officer, a big-bellied man in a blue suit that probably hadn't fit him for ten years, came out and said, "All rise."

It was the same judge we had had before. He stormed onto the bench, apparently already angry that we were here, even though this date had been set for months. When he sat, we sat; the minute we sat, he started barking and the lawyers jumped up again. There was a flurry of arguments I barely followed, about this point in evidence or that document that should be excluded. The lawyers pulled out papers and rattled off case names and accused each other of being "disingenuous" or "dilatory," insults that they slipped smoothly into their sentences like razor blades tucked into Halloween candy. The judge egged them on for a while and then blew up, shouting that it was time to get on with it. And so we did.

There was no jury, just the judge. He would decide everything, maybe that day when the evidence closed, maybe later. Barry had explained that we had no right to a jury, for some reason that had to do with the status quo of something or other before the American Revolution and made my eyes glaze over. The bottom line was that we were probably better off with the judge; a jury would feel sorry for the mother.

Our case, as Barry had explained it to me, was, in the end, straightforward. He had laid out his whole strategy to me, laboriously and with great pride, in the few meetings we had had to prepare in the last week or so. This was our case "in a nutshell" he enjoyed saying before a particularly long-winded exposition. But after a few minutes, even I could put it in a nutshell: I was not the father. I had thought I was. I had spent a lot of money because I thought I was and Joan had been the beneficiary of that money. Now she had to give it back.

Her case was the opposite, except she couldn't deny that I was not the biological father. So she had to prove that I had an obligation to support Sam because, for years, when I didn't know the truth, I had assumed I was his father and enjoyed being his father. Her case was trickier than mine; she had to convince the judge that I had a moral obligation that arose from her own immorality.

Barry went first. He began with the medical evidence establishing that I wasn't the father. Some doctor droned on about genotypes and chromosomes, and when he was done, Ms. Kincaid had nothing to ask him. We knew now what we had known for months: There was no genetic way I could be Sam's father.

The only new development was that the lab had conducted a new blood test on Kip Pressman, who had submitted under court order. The results had been positive. There was a match, the doctor intoned, with a 99 percent degree of certainty.

Then, with a little smile, Barry called Joan to the stand. This was supposed to be a surprise to the other side and it prompted the expected outburst from Ms. Kincaid, who broadened the vocabulary of velvet-edged spikes to include "unseemly" and "manipulative." The judge yelled at each of them for a while and there were muffled conferences at the side of the judge's bench, from which they emerged with Barry smirking and Ms. Kincaid red in the face. Joan went to the stand.

There wasn't much that she could deny. In the world created by Barry for the purposes of this case, our entire marriage boiled down to the one seamy moment when Joan had intercourse with someone other than me.

She was dressed plainly, in a brown suit that I guessed cost a lot of money in an effort to look otherwise. She wasn't wearing lipstick. Her hair was shorter than when I had seen her last. There were bags under her eyes and I thought she had lost weight. But she sat straight in her chair, her hands folded on her lap, her legs uncrossed, her head held up so we wouldn't miss a thing she said. She listened carefully and spoke slowly, and it wasn't until you looked at the expression in her eyes that you could see she was willing herself to be anywhere but where she really was; it was, I realized, an expression I had seen often in the last months of our marriage.

"And Mr. Pressman, with whom you had intercourse—how long had you known him at that time, Mrs. Morrison?"

She shifted in her chair. "Several months, I believe."

"Can you be more specific?"

"Maybe six months."

"Do you remember giving a deposition in this case, Mrs. Morrison, at which I asked you questions and you answered under oath?"

"I do."

"And do you remember that at that deposition, I asked you how long you had known Mr. Pressman and you said a month, maybe two?"

She shifted again. Helpfully, Barry produced a transcript of the deposition and placed it in front of her face. She ignored it, and looking at the rear of the courtroom, she nodded. "Perhaps it wasn't as long as six months."

He removed the transcript from in front of her and stepped back two paces. He stood there, the transcript rolled up in his hand as if she were a dog and he was training her to sit.

"And when I asked you his name at the deposition, you couldn't recall his last name. Isn't that correct, Mrs. Morrison?"

"If that's what you tell me."

He opened the transcript and started turning the pages. Before he could finish, she nodded. "I couldn't recall his last name."

"And you never told Mr. Morrison about this"—he was searching with his tongue for one of those sweet-tasting razor blades—"this encounter?"

"No, I didn't."

"Not at the time? Not at any time afterward?"

She shook her head.

"You have to give a response, Mrs. Morrison. For the record."

"No. Never."

"And you never discussed with Mr. Morrison the possibility that the child you bore was not his child?"

"No."

"Although you realized at the time that there was such a possibility?"

She started to protest. He moved toward her, the transcript in hand.

"When I got pregnant," she said, "I believed that Mr. Morrison was the father."

Barry stopped, lifting his eyebrows as if he had been struck by a remarkable occurrence. "And yet you didn't use birth control during your encounter with Mr. Pressman?"

She shook her head; her tongue slipped out for a moment and wet her lips.

"And you realized you were pregnant within a month after your encounter with Mr. Pressman?"

She nodded her head.

"And yet it never occurred to you that Mr. Pressman could be the father?"

"It was only one time."

"And you were under the impression that it took more than one time to conceive a child?"

She flushed as the audience laughed at her. Ms. Kincaid grew more absorbed in the document she was reading. The judge's lips narrowed.

Our divorce agreement was produced and recognized by Joan. She was required to read the terms. She nodded agreement to the detailed provisions obliging me to provide child support throughout any number of inconceivable contingencies. She acknowledged that after the divorce she had kept the house. She acknowledged that she had paid for her food, for her car, for her clothes, and for her vacations, all with money that she had received from me. She was reminded that she had never worked a day after Sam's birth.

"And Mr. Morrison agreed to that, didn't he?"

"He did."

"And he did that because he believed that it would be beneficial for the child to have a mother who stayed at home, didn't he?"

"I wouldn't know."

"He said that to you, didn't he?"

She shrugged. Helpfully, Barry reminded her that she had to answer for the record. "Yes," she said hoarsely. "That's what he said."

"And that's what you wanted as well, wasn't it?"

"He never wanted me to work. He liked having me at home."

Barry's eyebrows lifted. Joan's hands, still folded, tightened their grip. "Do you mean that he liked having you keep house?" Barry asked.

She nodded. "That's what I meant."

"He liked having you prepare meals and arrange things and do errands?"

"Exactly."

"And he liked having you do that, even after he left the house?"

She stopped nodding.

"We need an answer for the record, Mrs. Morrison."

"Yes. Even after he left the house."

"So he liked you doing these things, even though you weren't doing them for him personally?"

"Yes."

"Because you were doing them for the child whom he believed to be his son."

She said nothing. Barry paused. "Yes, Mrs. Morrison?" he prompted, apparently sympathetic with her inability to grope for an answer.

"I suppose."

Barry nodded, impressed by the significance of this supposition. He turned, then stopped as an idea struck him; he swung back toward her, tapping the transcript against his leg. "And, Mrs. Morrison, isn't it true that you were the one who initiated the divorce?"

She nodded, and then before he could correct her, she lifted her head so her neck was stretched out, and said, "Yes. It was my idea to get divorced."

"And despite that, Mr. Morrison agreed to support you so that you would not have to go to work?"

"Yes."

Barry was dumbstruck. "And, while you were reaching these agreements, under which you would continue to be supported after the divorce, without any diminution in your lifestyle, you never mentioned to Mr. Morrison the possibility that he was not the father of the child?"

"No."

"It never occurred to you even then?"

"No."

Barry nodded, satisfied. It all made sense to him now. He was done.

———

Mercifully, the judge allowed a break. When I saw the expression on Barry's face as he stood by the urinal, I wondered if his penis had grown so big he couldn't get his hands around it. Things had gone very well, he modestly noted.

When we got back to the courtroom, Ms. Kincaid had some work to do. Delicately, sensitively, as if it would be painful to recall, she led Joan to remember how Mr. Morrison had always insisted on joint custody of Sam, how he had wanted and received liberal visitation rights, how Joan had given up her own time with Sam to let the boy be with Mr. Morrison.

"Mr. Morrison had the child for Christmas every year?" Ms. Kincaid asked, her drill-like voice catching with surprise.

Wearily, Joan nodded agreement. "Christmas. Thanksgiving. Whatever he wanted, I let him have."

"So you gave up your own time with your child in order to permit him to be with Mr. Morrison?" Ms. Kincaid said.

"Yes," Joan said, nodding her head vigorously. She was having an easier time, now, remembering to answer for the record.

"Even when it inconvenienced you? Even when it was not on a regularly scheduled visitation day?"

Yes, there had been many occasions when she had been inconvenienced to accommodate Mr. Morrison's demands to see the child. Last-minute schedule changes necessitated by Mr. Morrison's work obligations. Vacations rearranged. Yes, it was Mr. Morrison, not she, who had taken Sam each year to the Christmas village downtown, who had taken him to his first circus. "I knew that he enjoyed seeing Sam and I felt he was entitled to it," Joan recalled. "I thought Sam should spend as much time with his father as possible."

Ms. Kincaid looked at me sadly. Had I not realized this? Was I only now seeing the level of Mrs. Morrison's sacrifice?

They turned to the question of why Joan had not worked. Ms. Kincaid was stunned to learn that Joan had offered to get a job many times, but Mr. Morrison had always insisted that she stay home to care for Sam full-time. Joan, it turned out, had always been anxious to resume a career, but again she had given in, to please Mr. Morrison and to put Sam's interests first.

Our divorce was revisited. Ms. Kincaid uncovered the fact that it was Mr. Morrison, not Joan, who had proposed the terms of our divorce agreement.

"You didn't ask for more money than he offered?" she asked.

"No. I wanted to be fair. I just wanted enough to take care of Sam." In fact, Joan would have been willing to live on less. It was Mr. Morrison who insisted that they remain in the large house, keep up their membership in the pool club; he wanted these things for Sam, and Joan had gone along because she wanted the best for her son as well.

"And after the divorce, did Mr. Morrison seem to have insufficient money for himself?"

Joan ventured a small smile. "No. He had plenty of money."

Ms. Kincaid hated to do it, but she was forced to recall the ski trip that Mr. Morrison had taken with his friends. "And Sam didn't go on that?" she asked, sounding puzzled.

Joan shook her head. "No. It was a little getaway for Mr. Morrison."

"Now, during all those years, did you ever take a vacation by yourself without Sam, Mrs. Morrison?"

Again Joan shook her head. She hadn't.

Ms. Kincaid returned to the house. "It wasn't you who suggested purchasing the home that you lived in, was it, Mrs. Morrison?"

"No. It was Mr. Morrison's idea. He wanted to live there. He thought it was the right community."

"And what do you mean by that, Mrs. Morrison?"

"The right people. The right schools. I think some of the other vice presidents from his company lived there."

Joan, of course, would have been content to stay behind in the city. But she went along, for the sake of Sam, and trusting me. And she had agreed to stay on in the suburbs after the divorce, despite the isolation, despite the difficulty of being a young, single woman in a community full of couples. She did this for Sam because she believed that she should raise Mr. Morrison's son in the way that Mr. Morrison wanted.

"And Sam is happy there in his home, isn't he?"

"Yes," Joan said, apparently thinking a thought that brought tears to her eyes.

We heard about Sam's schooling. We heard about his roots. We heard about this, as Barry fumed, through Joan's mouth, because the "parties" had agreed—at my insistence, with Joan's eager agreement—that Sam would not be called as a witness. Barry had shrugged. "He can't help either of you. He makes her look like trash and you like Simon Legree." So, in Sam's absence, Joan got to be his spokesperson and, it seemed, Sam wanted to keep the status quo.

Barry was jumping out of his seat before Ms. Kincaid had barely finished her last, mournful question about how much poor Sam had at stake.

"You've already told the child that Mr. Morrison is not his father, haven't you, Mrs. Morrison?"

"Mr. Morrison took him for the blood test—"

"That wasn't my question. You told him that Mr. Morrison is not his father, isn't that correct? Yes or no?"

"Yes."

"Mr. Morrison didn't tell him that, did he?"

"I felt—"

"That was your choice, wasn't it?"

"Yes, but I had to. Sam didn't understand what was going on between Mr. Morrison and I—"

"He didn't understand because he had been led for years to believe in a fact that wasn't true, isn't that correct?"

"Yes."

"And who led him to believe in that fact, Mrs. Morrison?"

I saw the judge lift his head, stretching, like a reptile lying in the sun, momentarily intrigued by the sight of an insect flying just above him. He opened his mouth, closed it, and then shut his eyes, just in time to hear Joan, her voice shaking, say, "I did."

———

That afternoon, as everybody's lunch settled leadenly in their stomachs, Barry called my accountant to the stand. The accountant smiled at me cheerily as he stepped in, bouncing a little in his steps, and I feared for a minute that he was going to stop by my table and schmooze. It occurred to me that he was not someone who was often invited to talk about his work.

He had brought charts and slides to help us. The judge seemed to be flipping through some papers on his bench. The clerk, who sat at a smaller table below him, talked in hushed tones on a telephone. The reporters sneaked out of the courtroom, and from the hallway came the sound of laughter and a faint wisp of cigarette smoke until the pot-bellied court officer bustled outside and roared at the smoker to put it out.

For a while, I tried to keep my mind on the numbers that were displayed on an overhead projector, but even I drifted off eventually. It depressed me to see the balance sheets of our life together, the steadily increasing earnings that I had proudly showered on Joan and Sam, the measure of my success and worth, the one thing that I knew I could deliver, now toted up, crunched, and projected on a tiny screen that stood awkwardly in the middle of the courtroom floor.

And then, just as I felt the buzz of sleep around my ears, I heard Barry call my name. My head snapped up. The witness stand was empty. The judge was bent forward impatiently. I pushed my chair from the table and forced my legs to lift me up and walk what could have been a mile across the cavernous room to the dais and chair where I had to sit to tell my story.

Barry was preening by now. Everything was going his way. He had worked with me well to get ready for this and he knew I had the story down. "Lay it on thick, Pete," he had counseled me. "They won't be able to lay a glove on you."

"But what will she ask me?" I had asked repeatedly as we prepared for my cross-examination.

"What can she ask you? That you don't care if he's your biological son? Of course you care. That the blood test didn't matter to you? You wouldn't have taken it in the first place if it didn't matter. That all those years of sacrifice, and child support, and money—for Christ's sake, especially the money—were worth it, even though Sam wasn't really your kid? Get real. How's she ever going to get you to say that? She has to argue that you were his father, and you weren't. Just tell the truth."

So I did.

Barry led me a little in the beginning, when my voice was still too low and I was talking into the knot of my tie. The judge snapped, "Speak up," and Barry held a finger to his ear, as, hoarsely, I explained how Joan and I had talked about having a child, how I had agreed, how excited I had been when she told me she was pregnant. I described buying the house when he was born, papering the nursery and coming home laden with stuffed animals and toys that Sam had already outgrown by the time I bought them.

As I talked, I slowly straightened up in my chair and looked out over the room in front of me. The reporters were crammed into the front row, clutching thin notepads. In the row behind them, I saw Dave and Marcia; Dave winked and held up his thumb, Marcia shook her head and looked like she might cry. I raised my eyes a little over their heads and, for a moment, dizzy with nervousness and fear, I wondered if I would see my mother, and then I wondered if I would see Sam. My voice sounded like it did when I was dreaming; I heard it emerge from a distant place, saying things that seemed to come from someone else's brain.

"So, Mr. Morrison, did there come a time when you began to have doubts that Sam was really your biological son?"

I nodded. "Yes." I swallowed. "I don't know that I would have put it that way, but yes, I started to have doubts. He didn't look like me. That was always true. He didn't really act like me. He didn't enjoy many of the things that I did. He could spend hours sitting by himself without any entertainment." My voice caught. "My mother always said she wished I had been like that. But I wasn't."

"Was Sam like his mother, in your mind?"

"No, not really. He didn't look like either of us. He had these big ears—" I felt myself smile, but it seemed to come from outside me, as if I were a canvas and someone were drawing a smile on me. "We used to call him Mickey Mouse when he was in his high chair. And my mother used to always say it must come from Joan's family. And then Joan's mother said it must come from my family. And I thought it was odd."

"So you had these doubts when he was very young?"

I shook my head. "Very young? No. I thought he was mine. I mean, I had seen him be born. I had held him when he came out—"

Barry paused, lifting his head up just a bit, as if he was embarrassed to watch while I composed myself. I fumbled for a glass of water.

"I didn't doubt it. But it was there. It was in my mind. And it started getting bigger. When he started school, you know, I saw more differences between us. I thought it was because—because I wasn't living at home by then. But it was more than that. I couldn't understand it. And it kept preying on my mind."

"Did you ever mention these concerns to your ex-wife?"

"I said things like it was strange. But she always said it was my imagination. And I thought—" I drank some water. "And then one day I realized that I was trying to convince myself, that I no longer believed it. And so I decided that whatever happened, I just had to know."

I talked about the blood test. Barry led me up to the day when I told Joan the results, and then he sat down. I was now Ms. Kincaid's witness.

She seemed at first to have a hard time approaching me, as if she was not going to be able to restrain herself if she got too close.

"You testified that you agreed to the idea of having a child, didn't you?" she began.

"Yes."

"And you were excited when Sam was born?"

"Yes."

"No doubts then? Correct?"

"No. Never crossed my mind."

"Despite the big ears?"

"Nope. I thought they were cute."

She nodded, pondering. "And, when you got the divorce, you requested joint custody and generous visitation rights, correct?"

"I did."

"And you got them?"

"Yes."

"Everything you asked for, you got?"

"Objection," Barry shouted.

Before the judge could speak, I answered, "I did. Everything I asked for, I got."

Barry's face fell. I turned to Ms. Kincaid. She was watching me thoughtfully. I watched her think, as I had watched people across the table in countless negotiations, wondering if they should ask for just that one more thing. I tried to keep my head from nodding, from letting her know she could take the next step.

"And those things you testified about—his not looking like you, his not being good at sports—they didn't prevent you from wanting to spend time with him, did they?"

"No. They didn't matter. I loved him despite them."

She turned away for a moment. I kept my eyes from looking at Barry. Her back to me, Ms. Kincaid asked, "So these doubts of yours didn't stop you—at that time—from feeling like you were his father?"

"They never stopped me from feeling like I was his father."

Her head lifted. Although I couldn't see her face, I knew exactly what was in her eyes, the glow of determination as you're about to take the biggest leap you can.

"Even now, Mr. Morrison?"

"Even now I feel like his father."

Barry asked for a recess. Smiling cruelly, the judge refused. Barry never got another chance. Before he had sat down, his mouth still hanging open, Ms. Kincaid asked her next question.

"It was your idea, Mr. Morrison, to let Sam and his mother stay in the house after the divorce, wasn't it?"

"I bought the house for Sam to live in. I want him to live in it. It's no use to me without him."

"And you agreed to pay the child support—"

"I wanted to pay so that he could live in the place I chose for him. It had good schools, it had parks. I liked to visit him there. I looked forward to it each week. Our time together was the highlight of my life."

"And, despite these child support payments, you were able to afford a place to live for yourself?"

I shrugged. "I could afford everything I wanted. It didn't matter. The only thing I wanted was to spend more time with Sam."

I heard Barry slam a pile of papers on his table. I heard the creak of the judge's chair as he swung around to face me. Ms. Kincaid had stepped back to the table where she had been sitting. I saw her look down at Joan, a question in her eyes. Joan shrugged and shook her head.

Ms. Kincaid held her chin in her hand for a moment; she started to speak, then stopped; she thought a moment longer. "And you felt that way even as Sam got older and you started having these doubts?"

"I feel that way today."

She shook her head, as if she was checking to see that she was still conscious. "Mr. Morrison, isn't it true that you tried to see Sam on at least one occasion after you learned the results of the blood test?"

"I've seen him on many occasions after I learned the results of the blood test."

She sank down on the edge of the desk. "How recently?"

"Last week."

Again she shot a look at Joan. But Joan wasn't watching her anymore. She was leaning forward, her head on her hands, staring at me.

"And why," Ms. Kincaid asked, "did you do that?" It seemed as if this was the first time in the entire trial that someone asked a question because they wanted to know the answer.

"Because I love him and want to see him, and because I think he should continue to see me."

Ms. Kincaid thought for a moment, then turned to Barry. "Your witness, Counselor."

32

Barry called me with the news a week later. The judge had ruled in our favor. I got the house and all the money. Joan kept Sam.

"You're not happy," he said when he finished reading the decision to me. It wasn't even a question. His voice sounded tired.

"Is there any appeal?" I asked.

"Not by you. You won."

"I guess."

"You know, Pete, it really couldn't have turned out any differently. About Sam, I mean. You couldn't hold on to him."

"It's okay, Barry. Listen, thanks for everything you've done."

"Pete, if there's anything I can say—"

I set the phone down, gently, before he had finished speaking.

The judge's written decision arrived in the mail the next day from Barry's office. Barry had clipped a short handwritten note to it that said, "Case closed. Best wishes for a new start." His final bill arrived a few days later.

The judge had found me to be a "credible, indeed a convincing"

witness. "The plaintiff's stated desire to continue in a paternal relationship with the child despite the lack of a biological relationship
is," the judge concluded, "a commendable sentiment and is, if anything, evidence of the strength of the plaintiff's desire to have and
raise a child. In this case, however, it is without legal significance.
Because there is no biological relationship, there is no relationship
that the law will recognize."

The night after the trial, I had called Ellen. I got her answering
machine and just started repeating, "Please pick up." By the second
time, she did.

"I heard about it on the radio," she said.

"Did I pass the test?"

I waited, trying to picture her thin face struggle to find words. "I'm
making dinner," she said. "Come over and we'll talk about it."

The day I got the judge's decision, I drove by her place and put a
copy in the mailbox. I went for a drive and when I got home a few
hours later, she was waiting by my front door. She took my hand and
led me back into my house. We spent the rest of the evening sitting
on my couch. We didn't say a word about it and she didn't once let go
of my hand.

I tried to get through to Joan the day after I got the decision. I
reached her at work. She lowered her voice and said she didn't want
to talk. I started to plead and, sounding desperate, she told me to meet
her that night. She gave me the address of some spot in a suburb
north of the city.

It turned out to be a cocktail lounge, with a big, circular bar and a
mob of noisy minglers.

I fought my way through the crowd and saw Joan sitting at the
bar, talking with another woman, a young-looking brunette. Joan's
back was to me and I stood there for a moment, getting jostled and
elbowed by the guys behind me who were hurrying over to a

crowd of women waiting for drinks. Joan's companion was talking in an animated way, waving a long, thin cigarette about, when she caught me staring. Looking intrigued, she slowed her story down and lifted her eyebrow inquiringly. I shook my head. Before the brunette could say anything more, Joan looked over her shoulder in my direction. When she saw it was me, she turned back to her friend and said something. The brunette picked up her cigarette, blew a cloud of smoke in my direction, then got up and waved me to her bar stool.

"So this is where you hang out these days?" I said to Joan when the other woman had drifted off, shooting one last, appraising glance, and I had sat down.

Joan reached into her purse for a pack of cigarettes. She ignored the expression on my face, smiled at me, and said, "I'm waiting for you to say something I need to hear."

"I came to talk about Ellen."

"The girlfriend?"

I nodded. She pulled out a lighter and flicked it. I saw the flame connect with the tip of her cigarette and felt a blast of smoke in my face. "So tell me," she said.

"I want you to drop that complaint or whatever it's called that you have against her. That licensing board is going to have a hearing if you don't, and there's no reason to get her in trouble. She didn't do anything to you."

"Your lawyer picked her for Sam and me to see. You were dating her."

I shook my head. "No. It wasn't like that. We didn't start dating until weeks afterward. It was a coincidence."

"Her report said you should have visitation rights. Even though I said you shouldn't—"

"That's what she thought." My voice broke. "That's what I thought. But it didn't happen anyway, so what do you care?"

She pushed some hair out of her eyes and swung around on the bar stool. "You don't like this place, do you, Pete?"

I shook my head. "Do you?"

She shrugged. "It's my night out." She was surveying the room in front of her as if she was in a museum and the noisy crowd was some new kind of sculpture garden. "I work most evenings now. I never had to fill a night off before. I don't know where to go yet."

"And what do you do with Sam?"

She made a rueful face. "Sam can't wait for me to get out and leave him alone."

She leaned back against the bar and put her elbows up. I was looking at her profile. I could practically feel how smooth her cheeks were; I could almost taste the glisten of moisture on her lips. I was hunched over, still wanting a million things from her, and it occurred to me that there was no longer anything she wanted in return.

"How's Sam?" I asked.

"Good. We're both good."

"You look good, Joan."

She thanked me. She turned to put the cigarette out and signaled for the bartender to bring her the tab. "I am good," she said as she pulled money from her purse. "I think I am finally starting to be good."

"Look, Joan, about the house. I'm willing to give that up. If you want to stay on, don't worry about the court thing."

She shook her head. "No. I've told my lawyer to forget about an appeal. I'm giving up the house. I'm ready to move." She shut her purse and looked at me. "I think it'll be a good thing for me to get out of there."

I took a deep breath. "I don't really want the money—" Before I realized what I was doing, I felt my hand clasping hers; her long fingers froze for a moment and then relaxed in my grip. She turned to me, pressed her other hand on top of mine, and said, "I know you don't, Pete. I always knew that."

"Then why don't you keep the house? I'll start paying you support again. I don't care. You don't have to let me see Sam. I just don't want you two to be without the money—"

She held up a hand and, when I stopped speaking, she rested it

lightly on my lips. "I don't want your money, Pete. That's the point."
The bartender came up and told her what she owed. Automatically, I
reached for my wallet, but she shook her head and pushed some bills
at the bartender, telling him to keep the change. He winked at her
and she blushed a little. Then she turned back to me.

"That's the point, Pete. You know, when this whole thing started,
when you found out about—about Sam, and everything started getting so horrible and you threatened to cut off the support, all I could
think about was how scared I was to lose the money. To not have the
house and not have your check coming every month. I was over forty
and I hadn't worked in thirteen years and I had no idea what I would
do." She laughed. "I kept picturing some—some awful place that Sam
and I would have to live. Some cross between a crack house and the
garret in *La Bohème*. And then, you know what? I got a job."

"Joan, I'm sorry—"

"Don't be sorry. I love it. I work with these great women. I like
being in a store. It turns out I'm much better at selling than at shopping." She arched her eyebrows. "Who knew, right? I'm getting promoted, you know. Assistant buyer. I've broken out of the minimum
wage."

"That's good. I'm proud of you."

She waved her hand at me. "Oh, what do you care? The point is,
I'm proud of myself."

"You find time for your painting?"

"No, thank God. I'm so glad I don't have to go into that awful little room and squeeze out those tubes and put my heart and soul into
producing something that nobody wants to look at, much less pay
for." She grabbed her coat. When I reached out to help, she hopped
off the stool and swung the coat onto her shoulders in one smooth
movement. "I have to go home now, Pete."

I threw some money on the bar for my drink and hurried to follow her through the crowd. Two guys with slicked-back hair and
geometric ties turned and said something to Joan as she edged by
them. She flipped her head up at them, smiled, then kept moving.

One of the guys took a step after her, and I pushed myself in front of him, calling her name as she moved toward the door.

It was a cold night and we stopped for a moment just outside the door, exhaling little clouds of fog. She had her car keys in her hand and headed to the parking lot, me beside her.

"And what does Sam do while you're working?" I asked.

"Sam's my worry now, Pete. You can't ask."

I stopped. She took a step forward, then turned around and came back to me. She put her hands on my shoulders; we were so close we could have been about to kiss. "I know that's a horrible thing to say to you. I really do. I saw you on the witness stand and my heart broke. You know, Pete, if you had never found out about Sam, I would have been happy to go on the rest of our lives with you as his father. I couldn't have imagined a better father. But that's not what happened. And I had to keep reminding myself, even when you were on the stand, that it was your choice, your decision to take that damn blood test and open this all up. And once you did, there was no going back. You couldn't be Sam's father. I could see that in his face when he found out. It was like he thought it was something wrong with him, that he wasn't good enough." She dropped her hands from my shoulders and shook her head. Little tears formed at the edges of her eyes. "I know it was my fault. Because of what I did." She made a little sour face of recollection. "My one little act of rebellion. And I spent years afterward paying for it. It's a funny thing, you know. I felt so much guilt toward you that I started getting angry with you. The guiltier I felt, the angrier I got. I don't know why it works that way."

She stopped talking and looked at me for a reaction. I felt the flesh on my chin harden as I kept my mouth clamped shut. She waited. I think she was hoping I'd ask her a question, find out why she had done what she'd done. But finally, I realized, there was really nothing I wanted to know about her or Kip or our marriage or any of it. When she saw that in my face, she nodded. "I made a mistake, Pete. But it was one little mistake and I spent my life trying to be a good mother after that. And I thought I was doing it. Believe me, Pete, there were a million nights that I prayed you were the father. I didn't know. I wanted it to be you. It should have been you. And when all that time passed, and nothing happened, I almost started to think I had imagined it all, that of course you were the father. I had almost forgotten about it when you stormed in that day and told me about the blood test." She shook her head. "And when it all came out and I saw how it was hurting Sam, it killed me. Because I blamed myself. And then all that anger, all those years of anger, just came out and I blamed you. It was your fault. And then mine. And then yours. And all the lawyers were only making it worse and nobody could figure it out. And then I just realized that Sam had to walk away from this. Sam and I both. Maybe this was bad, but this was his fate. He's not your son. And it's not something you can pretend your way around or ignore. And he's too young to figure it out."

She stopped and took a deep breath. "When I realized that you were seeing him again, it made me furious." Thinking about it, her face flushed and, as if by reflex, she reached out and struck my shoulder. "You are such a jerk. You started this whole thing and then you wouldn't let him go. No, don't say anything. I know now that you were seeing him because you loved him. I know that. But you were wrong. You shouldn't have been. You had chosen to go and you couldn't come back. How could he trust you again? How could he be sure that someday you wouldn't decide all over again that you just couldn't love him because he didn't have your wonderful genes? And I knew Sam was going to get too confused and that I had to make the choice for him." She shoved her hands into her coat pockets. I could see her take a step back from me and straighten up. "Maybe I'm wrong. I think that even now. What right do I have to make this decision? But you know what, Pete? He's a thirteen-year-old boy with only one parent, and that's me. So I have to decide. And that's it. You're a decent person and I forgive you for whatever you've done, but I don't want your money or your house and I don't want you seeing my son. Now, let me go to my car. I'm freezing."

I watched her as she unlocked the car door and slid in. The door still open, the roof light on, she looked up. "I haven't answered you about Ellen, have I?"

I shook my head.

"I was angry about that too when I found out. The nerve of you. There I was fighting for my son's life, I thought, and you're dating the goddamn child psychologist, trying to turn her against me." She almost smiled, looking back on it. "What were we doing there?" She looked up at me. "I hope I never get involved with lawyers again. You start to think like them. The mailman comes up the front walk and you wonder if he's carrying a letter bomb."

"I shouldn't have sued. It was an awful idea."

She shrugged. "Hey, I had it coming. Years of sponging off you under false pretenses, as our friend the judge decided." She shook her head as if she was trying to erase what was inside. "But I don't care. I'm just so happy it's over. Don't worry about Ellen. The whole idea of the complaint was my lawyer's. She thought Ellen would be a witness or something, some complicated plot that made total sense to me at the time and now seems like a bad dream. I already told the lawyer to drop the complaint. Ellen should be finding out any day now."

"Thanks, Joan."

She shrugged. "Don't mention it." She slammed the door shut and put the key into the ignition. I saw her stop for a moment to think and then, moving quickly, as if she was acting against her better judgment, she rolled down the car window and said, "I'm embarrassed to admit it, but I've been trying to remember what this Ellen of yours looks like. I only saw her that once when we went in for the interview. She's kind of skinny, right? Intellectual-looking?"

I nodded.

"Not your usual knockout type, is she?" I didn't say anything, and after a moment, she shrugged. "Well, anyway, I hope it works out for you." The key turned in the ignition; the motor turned over. "You know, Pete, I might as well tell you. There's an opening for an assistant buyer in one of our Florida stores. I'm still kind of new to be looking for a transfer, but I'm going to try anyway." She looked up at me. "My parents are there, you know, and I could use a little family support. And it would be good for Sam. He would have my father to pal around with."

I bit my lip. "You want to get him away from me, don't you?"

She nodded. "Yes. That's it exactly." She reached her hand up through the open window and held it toward me. I dropped down to my knees beside the car; I could feel the grit of the parking lot dig into my flesh. She rested her hand on my cheek and drew it close to her. I felt her lips, then her cheek press the top of my head. For a moment, we just stayed there, our faces against each other's, our eyes wide open, the cold wind slapping us back to our senses. Then she took her hand away and I felt the car move into gear.

"We're not staying in the house now," she said. "We're with some friends of mine. And I have someone picking him up after school. I've told the people at school to watch out for you. That order is still in effect, so don't forget it. I don't want you trying to get in touch with him. Do you hear me?"

I nodded mutely. I had already driven by their house and seen it empty, waited outside the school and not seen Sam come out with the other kids. I knew I was defeated.

Seeing that realization in my face, Joan suddenly softened. "You take care, Pete," she said. Then she shut the window and moved her car into reverse.

I nodded and kept nodding, my eyes on the empty parking space, as I listened to her car drive onto the highway.

33

Barry called the next day with news: Joan's lawyer had phoned to say they weren't going to appeal.

"I know," I said.

"You do?" He waited. "Oh, well."

Joan's lawyer offered to turn over the house as soon as possible, if we would agree to a payment plan for the thirteen years of support that Joan now owed me. I told Barry to release Joan from any obligation to pay me money and to put the house up for sale.

For the next two months, I received a sprinkling of legal papers notifying me of the progress of the sale. According to Barry, the real estate market was hot. "The Realtor says you bought well," he offered.

Within a week after the house was listed for sale a buyer was found who offered my asking price. I gave Barry a power of attorney so he could sign all the papers for me. Some nights, after dark, I would drive by, slowing down as I passed the house, never stopping. Joan had already gotten all the furniture out; the windows were dark. One week the FOR SALE sign was up; the next week it was gone. The day after the closing, I went by for one last time. A moving truck was pulled up. There were boxes littered on the front lawn. One of them had spilled over, and a toy truck, made of wood, trailing a string, lay on its side on the grass.

———

I was getting ready to go to Ellen's house one Sunday afternoon about two months later when the doorbell rang. I almost didn't answer, since I didn't think it would be anyone but the Jehovah's Witnesses. When I opened the door, Joan was standing there.

It was a sunny day, possibly the first hint of spring or maybe just a brief break in winter. Joan wasn't wearing a coat or a hat. She looked as if she had run out of her apartment. She had on sunglasses, but, when she stepped inside, she didn't take them off and it occurred to me that she wasn't trying to hide from the sun.

I said nothing and let her walk in. She stood in the foyer, looking around for a moment; then she started to storm through the town house, darting her head back and forth into each room. She was headed up the stairs when I finally said, "What are you doing?"

She stopped, but didn't turn around. "Pete, don't play with me. Tell me where he is."

"Sam?"

"I want him."

"You lost him?"

She turned and stuck her hand out in the air, her finger pointed toward me. "I'm warning you—" Then she looked at my face, saw whatever was there, and stopped.

A few minutes later, she was sitting in the living room, drinking a glass of water I had gotten to help her swallow her tears.

"He's been missing for a day?" I said, standing over her and trying not to sound as furious as I was.

She nodded. "He wasn't in the house when I got home last night. I waited and waited. Then I started looking."

"Why didn't you call me earlier?"

"Why would I call you?"

"Then why did you come here now?"

She sipped some more water, then coughed it up. "Because I thought you had kidnapped him."

"And how do you know I didn't?"

"I know, Peter. I know you didn't."

I sat down next to her on the couch. There were two feet between us. "Did you call all his friends?"

She shook her head.

"Why not?"

She shook her head again and I could see the tears coming back. "Pete, you don't know. It's not like it was when you were—" She took a breath. "When you were around. He doesn't have friends in the neighborhood. I don't even know who his friends are. I get up and leave in the morning. When I come back, he isn't there. I don't know what he does all day."

"Do you ask?"

"Would he answer if I did?"

I shrugged. "He's a teenager. I guess it's normal."

She shook her head. "He's a teenager who lost one father whom he loved and got another one who—" She waved her hand. "Who isn't interested. To put it mildly. And his whole personal life has been in the paper." She bit her lower lip. "And he lost his house and has to leave his school and he has a mother who's moving him to some new state. And he hates me. He hates me and blames me for everything." She started crying in earnest.

"He hasn't called me once," I said limply.

She nodded through her tears. "I figured that. He knows you lost. Maybe he blames you too. But he's given up. I can see it in his face. He's given up on you and he hates me. He walks around like he's asleep. The only sound he makes is a grunt. And that's his life."

I patted her on the shoulder while she leaned over and hit her forehead with her hand. "Don't be so hard on yourself," I said, and I meant it; I could just as easily have been saying it to myself. "It was a hard thing we all went through. You did the best you could."

She shook her head. "It's all my fault."

"No, it's not. I mean—hell, it's all *my* fault. I was the one who took the damn test."

"No, before that. Before everything. Right from the start. It's my fault."

I shrugged and leaned back. "You know, lots of women have babies with the wrong guy. At least you tried to keep it a secret for a while."

She tried to smile. Patting her shoulder, I had slid closer to her and suddenly, we were only inches apart. I could feel her breath on my face and then her fingers on my chest. And I stood up.

"Let's go," I said, grabbing a coat.

———

Joan had already been to all the obvious places, she assured me. But when we started to go over it, we began to realize that we each had different ideas of what was obvious.

"Why would he be hanging around in the schoolyard on a Saturday?" she asked irritably.

"You know, playing ball or something."

"Do you think he's Horatio Alger? He wouldn't be caught dead in a schoolyard."

She was right; the schoolyard was empty. She suggested the movies.

"Do you know how many cineplexes there are around here?" I demanded.

"He doesn't have a car. He couldn't have gone far."

She had brought a picture of him, taken by the class photographer last year. I almost felt sorry for him, having this dorky photograph, with his hair slicked down and wearing an ungainly jacket and tie that Joan must have insisted on, now being shown to every theater manager in the metropolitan area. Fortunately, barely past adolescence themselves, they were either too self-absorbed or too distracted by popcorn retails to pay much attention.

"If he went to one of those theaters, he's dead by now," Joan said as we drove off from the last one.

"You can't die in a theater. It's too climate controlled. Besides, they throw them out after each feature. Listen, let's be scientific about this. He's been gone at least overnight, right?"

"At least. Maybe longer. I haven't seen him since yesterday morning."

"Did he take any money?"

"I don't know."

"What do you mean—" I caught myself. "How about clothing?"

She shrugged. "I don't know, Pete. I don't keep track of what he wears." When I turned to look at her, she made a face. "Given everything that's going on, do you think I should make a fuss over whether his pants are clean?"

I nodded. "You called the police?"

"They took a report and said they'd start looking." She smiled. "It was the same cop. Remember? From when you came by and tried to kill me." I smiled back. It was as if we were reminiscing.

"And what did he say?"

"He said it was probably you."

"Great. I'm surprised I haven't been arrested yet."

She rolled her eyes. "They're probably afraid of your lawyer."

———

Ethan's mother stood at the doorway suspiciously, trying to block her son from the contagion of our distress.

"Why would Ethan know where he is?" she demanded.

I sighed. I could hear Joan behind me, wanting to slip away from this woman's front steps. "Because, Mrs. Bentsen—"

"Ms. Silva. I'm not Bentsen."

"I thought Ethan was—"

"His father's name. Not mine."

I sighed again. "Listen, Ethan is his best friend, I think. He must know."

She shook her head. "They haven't been hanging around together lately. I got the impression that Sam wasn't going to school so much."

I turned back to Joan for confirmation of this news. She shrugged. "The school never called me," she said.

"You can't count on the school to do all your monitoring for you," Ms. Silva said as she was pushing the door closed. Before it shut, I stuck my foot in and she crunched it. I let out a cry and she stood there a moment, frozen. Then she looked at me thoughtfully. "Why are you looking for him, anyway? I thought you had divorced him."

"Look, Ms. Silva, all I want is my son."

She looked over my shoulder at Joan, then back at me. "Well, you should have thought of that when you still had one." And in the moment before I could speak, the door closed.

Joan hurried back to the car without saying anything. I paused for a few minutes, walking away from the Silva-Bentsen's screen door, taking in the anonymous evergreen planting, the picture window and black shutters that marked this house as identical to every other one in the neighborhood. I looked up and spotted Ethan staring out the window of his upstairs room.

He waved at me, then pointed to the side of the house. I walked around, found a door that seemed to lead into the basement, and waited there. In a moment, short of breath and barefoot, Ethan appeared. He looked as if he had been awakened from a deep sleep or profound boredom, and he peered at me to make sure that I was really there.

"You looking for Sam?"

"You know where he is?"

"He split? Cool."

"Are you going to help me, Ethan?"

He shook his head no. It was a simple answer to a simple question. "Why not?" I pleaded.

He shrugged. "Don't know where he is. He didn't tell me."

"Did you talk about this with him?"

"He's been real cold recently. I think this Florida thing has him wigged. I mean, when he told me he was moving, I was like, man, why wouldn't you want out of here?" He turned around to look with scorn at the house, and no doubt at his mother, who was sheltered, oblivious, within. I grabbed Ethan's shirt, whether to shake him into some semblance of intelligence or simply to hold on to any piece of driftwood in this flood, I couldn't have said. But it got his attention and he managed to focus. "So, what are you worried about?" he asked.

"Ethan, for Christ's sake, he could have gone off with someone—"

"You mean, like a guy with candy and a raincoat." He laughed. "Come on. Sam's over the hill for that stuff."

Now I was clutching his shirt to occupy my hand so I wouldn't slap him. "Would he have gone to a friend's house?"

Ethan furrowed his brows to reflect on that one. Then he shook his head. "You know, I don't think so. I mean, like I said, he's been cold. Kind of stuck to himself. I think he's going through some changes," he added judiciously. "My bet is, he's by himself."

I let him go and nodded, turning to walk away.

"Hey, man."

I stopped and looked over my shoulder.

"So you really divorced Sam like they said?"

"Is that what Sam said?"

"No, he wouldn't talk about it. Like he was embarrassed. But I was, like, this is really cool. I wish my old man would divorce me."

"You think?"

He shrugged. "It would be something different at least."

I turned and resumed walking.

"Hey," Ethan called again. He waited for me to turn. "It ever occur to you that he may not want you to find him?"

"No, Ethan. That never occurred to me for a minute."

I drove Joan back to my place, thinking that maybe Sam had shown up there. We sat by the phone and called every single parent or kid we could think of. It was getting late in the afternoon and we were quarreling about whether we should go back to the police. And then I said, "I have an idea."

When we got in the car and started driving, she didn't ask any questions. She watched out my window as we passed the rows of apartment complexes and shopping plazas. She was looking at the neighborhood where I lived as if she had never seen it before.

"Why didn't you move back into the house after you got it from the judge?" she asked finally.

"You're kidding, right? You think I could?"

She shrugged. "You always liked the house. I mean, you already live in the neighborhood—"

"I'm moving from here."

She looked up. "Where are you going?" she asked anxiously.

I smiled. "I'm not following you to Florida, don't worry." When she started to pretend that wasn't what she had been thinking, I interrupted. "Ellen and I are moving in together."

"The shrink? You're kidding?" She looked away again, although I thought that this time she wasn't watching the scenery. "So it's getting serious." She took off her sunglasses and opened her purse and pulled out a compact. She started powdering her cheeks where the tears had run into brown, uneven smears. "That was quick," she said, her lips barely moving apart.

"Circumstances brought us together."

She clicked the compact shut. "You deserve to be married, Pete." When I turned to her, she got a surprised look on her face. "I meant that as a compliment. Really." And we both laughed.

We pulled off the highway and started winding our way through narrow streets crammed with triple-decker houses. "Isn't this where you used to live when you were a kid?" she asked.

"You remember?" I asked, smiling despite myself.

She rolled her eyes. "You took me on the Pete Morrison tour a dozen times when we were dating."

I slowed down to make way for a couple of boys on bicycles; they veered in front of me suddenly and then just as suddenly slowed down, talking to each other over their shoulders and balancing themselves on their bikes, hands in the air, gesturing their way through some silly boys' argument. I was about to put my hand to the horn, then stopped myself and slowed down, tailing them patiently as they lolled their way down the street.

"What's that ugly thing?" Joan said when we started inching to the top of the hill, the car's engine whining as it struggled to climb the almost vertical incline.

"The fort. This was the colonial army's first outpost in Boston." I furrowed my brow. "Or maybe it was the British's last outpost. I forget."

"This isn't much of a history lesson."

I shrugged. "It is if you want. My history." I rolled down the window. "I brought Sam here once," I said. "Years ago. I told him this story about how when I was a kid I stole a bike that belonged to my neighbor and then smashed it and ran away because I thought I'd get in trouble."

"Was the story true?" she asked indifferently.

I had to think for a minute. "Sort of. I was here a few hours and it poured rain and I got soaked. I ran home and threw myself on my parents' mercy." I smiled sheepishly. "The roof hasn't been repaired since the Revolution, I think."

"And was Sam impressed with that story?"

I grimaced, remembering that moment years ago. "I didn't tell him the actual truth. I said I had stuck it out here for a couple of days. I wanted to make it more—" I felt my voice catch. "Heroic. I wanted him to be impressed by me."

She shook her head. "As if you needed to try."

When I stopped in front of the fort, a few teenage boys were sitting outside, not even bothering to pretend that they weren't getting high. They watched suspiciously as I got out of the car and walked over to the fort. I scanned the gray-stoned walls and boarded-up windows. "Is my son up there?" I asked, nodding stiffly at the fort.

The teenagers looked at me mutely. I stared at each one, trying to find the person hidden beneath the acne and hair and defiance. I was older, better dressed, richer, and, at the moment, helpless in front of them. I just waited for them to think it through. The oldest-looking one, the one with the meanest expression and a scar over his eyebrow, finally budged. He nodded a little, then lifted his head toward the fort. I nodded thanks, then turned back to the car.

Joan was still sitting inside, her hands folded on her lap. I tapped lightly against the window. She lowered it. "You go up by yourself," she said.

"No. Both of us."

"He wants you."

"No. Both of us."

She trailed behind me on the rickety iron stairs, holding her breath against the stench of rot and urine. We said nothing to each other. I called out his name and heard no response. I turned around the last curve in the staircase and faced the small room at the top. There was one window inside and the boards had been torn off. The glare of the setting sun caught me in the eyes and I stood there a moment, blinded, swaying on the top step; Joan waited behind me, not knowing what was ahead.

Then I put my hand up to my eyes to shade them and I saw him crouched in the corner of the room, wrapped in a coat, surrounded by some candy wrappers and empty chip bags, his face folded up into a look that had stopped being angry, then stopped being scared, and was only now about to stop being hopeful. Even though he was hunched over, he seemed as if he might be a couple of inches taller than when I had seen him last.

"Why did you come?" he asked without any sign of interest.

I moved into the room and walked up to him. The damp of the floor chilled my seat as I lowered myself to the ground. I picked up the Walkman he was listening to and pressed the stop button. He watched me and then took the headphones off, letting them drop to the ground between us.

We sat there for a moment, saying nothing. My eyes fell on one of the open chip bags and, without thinking, I picked it up and looked inside. It was empty. I put it to my lips, blew it up tight, and then smacked it hard; the air leaked out the top and the bag deflated without a sound. He took it from me, blew it up, and exploded it with a single hard pop. I reached my arm around and pulled him next to me. I could feel him trembling as he buried his face in my side.

"Your mom asked me to come," I said.

"You going to give me back to her?"

"She's here now."

He lifted his head just slightly, like someone being awakened from sleep, and Joan walked into the room. She stopped just at the entrance; the sun was right in her eyes but she didn't take out her glasses. Sam dropped his head back against me.

"Don't blame her for this mess. She didn't want this to happen. Neither did I."

"Well, I sure didn't," he said, his voice muffled by the down of my jacket.

"Okay, we're even. So where do we go from here?"

"Not home."

"Can't stay here."

"I'll run away again."

"You'll get sick of that eventually."

"I'm not going to Florida."

"You don't have to."

He looked up when I said that, first at me, then at his mother. I didn't turn to her, tried not even to hear whether she moved. I kept my eyes on him; it was his job to get her answer. "You don't have to," she said.

He looked back to me. "What business is it of yours?"

"I'll make it my business."

He looked back at his mother. I closed my eyes and kept them closed until I felt his face press to my chest again. To this day I don't know what passed between the two of them, but when I opened my eyes and put my finger under Sam's chin, he was smiling his crooked smile.

We lumbered our way down the stairs and headed to the car, Sam between the two of us, each of us with an arm on his shoulders. As I turned around to look back, the boy with the scar held up his thumb at me, then put a joint to his mouth and inhaled deeply.

EPILOGUE

The Realtor lifted her eyebrows when Joan and I showed up the next week to buy a new house. Reading it all wrong, she tried to find us something in our old neighborhood, but Joan wouldn't even take a look at the listing sheets. We picked a house, in a new town with a new school system, miles from where we used to live. The Realtor got it wrong until the end; when the papers were drawn up, they listed Joan and me as joint buyers and we had to repeat ourselves three times when we told her to take my name off the deed.

The money for the house was the only money Joan ever took from me again. I never figured out the rationale for that and she never offered one. I tried sending her the regular child support check just like I had in the past and she returned it each month, uncashed. For a while I tried to slip Sam some cash each week when I saw him. Once I forced it into his pocket when he was leaving me and the next week he produced a certificate for three ballroom dancing lessons for Ellen and me that he had bought with it. "Just in case there's going to be a wedding, I don't want you to disgrace yourself," he said.

We saw each other pretty much the way we had before. I sold my own town house and bought a new place with Ellen, in the town where Sam and Joan lived. I don't know what he told his old friends who knew what had happened. It occurred to me that Sam was the rare person who got a second chance at life before his first kiss, and I suppose that's not a terrible way of looking at it. I suggested to Joan that he see a psychiatrist and she said that if she had that kind of money, she'd go herself.

I worried at first that he wouldn't want to see me once he knew he could. Then I worried that he wouldn't listen when I fell into my old dad routines. And then I realized that both of these things were sometimes true, and probably would have been true, even if none of this had happened. Maybe the only difference was that now, when I was lecturing him and he was tuning me out, we still, deep down, felt secure, and that's a safety net we never would have had otherwise.

Ellen and I were still thinking about setting a wedding date when she got pregnant. Unlike Sam, we had waited a long time before we got a second chance, and we weren't going to let it go.

I hesitated a little before I told Sam the news and had a whole speech prepared about how the new baby wouldn't change how I felt about him, a speech that went to great grammatical pains to avoid any sentence in which I had to find a word for the relationship that he and I had and treasured and fought for, but never could exactly label. But when he saw me starting to stammer, he shrugged, like "So what took you so long?" and in a minute we were quarreling over whose unbearable music we would listen to that day.

A few days later, while we were going somewhere in the car, he looked at me sideways and asked out of the blue, "So this time are you getting a test up front?"

I shook my head. "Not necessary."

"You sure?"

"They can't test for what I need to know."

"You know, Pete," he said, smiling and looking out the window as we barreled through the town where all four, and soon to be five, of us made our home, "you just may get through this after all."